THEY WERE DREAMERS

BOOKS BY JAMES F. MURPHY, JR.

They Were Dreamers   1983

Nightwatcher   1982

The Mill   1981

Quonsett   1978

JAMES F. MURPHY, JR.

THEY WERE DREAMERS

A SAGA OF THE IRISH IN NORTH AMERICA

ATHENEUM

NEW YORK   1983

Library of Congress Cataloging in Publication Data

Murphy, James F., ———
    They were dreamers.

    I. Title.
PS3563.U737T5 1982   813'.54   81-69138
ISBN 0–689–11250–5   AACR2

Published simultaneously in Canada by McClelland and Stewart Ltd.
Composition by Service Typesetters, Austin, Texas
Manufactured by Fairfield Graphics, Fairfield, Pennsylvania
Designed by Harry Ford
First Edition

For the Canadian-Irish
about whom too little has been written

Special thanks to my typist Terry Ryan, and to my wife Margaret A. Murphy who first introduced me to the beauty and serenity of the island; also a special acknowledgment to Bill Profitt of Summerside, P.E.I., for whom I have great respect and admiration.

CONTENTS

PART ONE

CANADA

1832–1833

CHAPTER I

BRENDAN MCMAHON braced a hand against the small of his back and straightened from his labors. He brushed the beaded sweat from his brow. His upper body was the color of burnished leather and carried no excessive flesh, only the sinewy muscle of the farmer. Firm, long fingers, surprisingly artistic, combed back the thick black hair of a Galway Irishman. The dark good looks suggested a mixture of Spanish blood. And indeed, his mixed blood was pumping with life and excitement. This day the very soil under his boots seemed to throb with new life.

The Canadian sun had been a friend throughout the long summer, visiting the fields and valleys often and then journeying elsewhere for a few days to allow soft rains to salve the baked earth. Sun and rain, sure blessings for an abundant harvest. God had been good.

As Brendan stood in the red dust of his potato fields, his deep blue eyes roamed out to the calm and subtly rolling Northumberland Strait, where tranquillity rode in timeless rhythm along an indigo canvas under the gold of an August sun. Yellow shafts of light cut a sharp swath across the waters like flashing swords.

His heart swelled, and he sighed at the beauty that was so close to him. It was all so grand, this vast and rich country bursting from its seams with vitality and opportunity. And it was their land to work, his and Mary's. He thought fondly of John Wallace and the night the old islander had given him the deed as they sat in the candlelight of a tavern in Saint John, New Brunswick. Captain Robert Fraser had looked on fondly as John pushed the yellowed parchment across the rum-stained table. It all seemed so long ago, and yet it had been just two years before. He wondered where Robert and John were. He squinted at the horizon almost as though he might see the barquentine *Aileen Donan* sailing toward him, his two friends waving from her bow.

Far down the beach, three Micmac Indian children played in the red clay of the shoreline, the warm waters licking at their feet.

Above them, sharp-faced capes projected over the beach, their grassy shoulders as green and lush as his own native Ireland.

Prince Edward Island was so like his own Galway and the verdant, rolling hills of Connemara that at times he had to remind himself he was in Canada, not tilling a field in Spiddal. But it ended there with the geography and the pocket-sized villages and farms. Here in this vast land there was sunshine and hope. In Ireland there were only cruel rains and crueler landlords. Here there was optimism and growth. In Ireland in 1832 there was only pessimism, starvation, and slavery. He reflected on his mother and sisters, safe from slavery at least, on the Aran Islands. His mother's first letter had been blotted with tears of happiness that he was alive and well. It was generally believed he had capsized with Tom Gill in the Irish Sea, and when Tom's body was found, it had been assumed that Brendan had floated farther out and been swept up in the mountainous seas.

He felt an ache at this remembrance of the loyal friend who had taken him by curragh through rough seas to Galway and Mary. But since then a golden world had opened up before him. He had been given a chance to carve out a life for himself. Back in Ireland there had been only misery and starvation. The muddy burial grounds, grim reminders of despair, abounded in the heaped-up graves of those who had died too young. But enough. "Enough," he cursed the past aloud, and drove it from his head. Dwelling on the past and its injustice was the Irish way, and it did nothing but debilitate and paralyze. Brendan McMahon would not be crippled by sentimentality and self-pity. He threw out his broad chest, breathed in the magnificence of the day, and heaved a great sigh of contentment. He had his land and his wife, Mary. He smiled as her face flashed before him. Mary. He put aside his reverie and turned abruptly, looking up to the log house he had built from the ruins of John Wallace's original dwelling.

He cocked his head and leaned forward. Had he heard a sound? His eyes opened wide, and he dropped the short one-handled plow by his feet. "Jesus," he cried, "that was Mary. Jesus." He gasped again and took off at a gallop across the fields and up through the golden straw of the August grass. He hurdled the stone fence, barely losing stride, racing along the narrow path and scattering the hens that flew, clucking, into the shrubs, leaving their frenzied feathers floating behind.

He stopped quickly at the thick wooden door and caught his breath. He must regain his composure. Another shriek split the air inside the cabin. He banged open the latch with his fist and burst into the one room that served as kitchen, bedroom, and living quarters.

On the square oak bed where they had spent so many nights making love under the broad-beamed ceiling, Mary now lay with her raven hair fanned out against the pillow, her face twisted in a tight, distorted mask of pain.

"Mary, is it time?" His voice cracked.

She nodded her assent in rapid movements of her head, breathing deeply and shaking, as she kneaded her back with clenched fists. "Oh, God, it's my back, Brendan. *Brendan*," she shrieked as spasms rolled over the rounded oval of her stomach.

He approached softly as she squirmed and tossed in frenzied movement from one side of the bed to the other and continued digging her hands into her spine.

He was horror-stricken. Perspiration broke out across his high forehead. Iron hands were wrapped around him. He could not move. He could not speak as she continued to writhe in convulsive jolts.

"Brendan," she screamed again. And there was a sudden gush as water broke and flowed from her. Her belly jumped and jerked.

Her screams and grotesque, contorted face wrenched him from his paralysis, and he fell to her side.

"What, what can I do, Mary, my lovely Mary? What can I do?"

Here he was, a farmer who had seen bloodied life torn from the womb of birthing animals, had brought them forth himself into the black midnight of a stall or stable, yet he was helpless at the bedside of his own wife.

"For the love of God, what do you want me to do?"

"Go for Mishaw, the midwife, tell her it is coming early. *Hurry. Oh, Jesus, Mary, and Joseph, hurry.*"

He scrambled to his feet and flew through the door. His heart hammered in his chest as he tore along the path of birch trees that led to the Micmac camp. He raced on blindly, branches stinging and slapping his face, his eyes burning and his legs churning. His energy and stamina had never deserted him in his twenty-one years of life, and he prayed fervently that they would not fail him now.

He called on every reserve of strength he had as trees and shrub and hedgerow flashed by him. His breath was coming in choking sobs, and he felt the panic washing over him. His legs were becoming as heavy as tree trunks from the thick grass, and each step grew more labored than the last. He crashed through the birch forest and out into the clearing below the village. He thought that his lungs would explode, that he would expire on the spot if he continued, but he knew he must. The anger he directed to his own inadequacy further weakened him. Cursing, he gained the hill and screamed out in short, bursts as he stood in the hot square of the village, "*Mis-haw. Mis-haw. Mishaw.*" And then he sank to his knees, gulping for air.

Indians crawled out of the cool shadows of their wigwams and trotted to his aid, to lift him gently. "Mishaw." He gulped. "It has come. The baby. It has come early."

Padenuque, the old chief, stood quietly in the shade of his wigwam, a smile lighting the wrinkled stitches of his leather face. He clapped his hands twice and said softly but firmly, "Mishaw, you have work to do. Take Rozné with you, and the wagon."

"Yes, my husband," she answered, and horse, wagon, and Rozné, their daughter, were off down the path with the dust swirling behind them in red, ghostly wisps.

Brendan looked after them and then at Padenuque, who said, "Rest easy, Irisher. Birth is as natural as the potato in the field. It can harvest itself with no help from the farmer who planted it."

Brendan's breath came more easily now, and his boyish grin was wide and ingenuous. "Aye, Padenuque, aye, but this harvest day I am thankful for any help I can get." He made a gesture of thanks and nodded slightly, twisting his neck and winking in the Galway tradition, turned then, and trotted back to the cabin.

He slowly regained his composure and purposely slowed his trot almost to a walk, knowing that Mishaw and her daughter would have everything under control. After all, he rationalized: I would only be in the way. This is women's work.

Sea birds cawed and squawked in veering, curving flight above the Strait, and the whoosh and resulting thump of wave against sand and rock lulled him through the shadows of the white and black grove of birch. He shook himself free of the panic that had so recently seized him and lifted his nostrils to the fragrance of the wild flowers. But as he did, a cry, foreign and far off, rode the slight breeze and carried across the dingle. He listened, and the cry became an incessant shriek, an irritated and impatient wail. "Mary, my God." He cocked his head again, and a sudden smile broke across his face. A baby. A baby. Tears rolled in salty trails down his cheeks as he galloped up the hill. He approached the cabin, wiping them away with embarrassment, and opened the thick wooden door.

Mary lay back against the muslin pillow, her face bright and glowing, a Madonna fresco of contentment, illuminated with a new kind of radiance he had never seen in her before. He let the door swing open, the morning sun washing and bathing the room in yellow light. Her Galway eyes sparkled as she motioned him forward.

"Come, now. Don't be afraid."

He hesitated at first and then slowly approached the bed.

"Look, Brendan, my husband. Isn't this the most beautiful baby you have ever seen?"

He almost seemed embarrassed by this tangible manifestation of their nights of love, and he reddened as he looked over at Mishaw and Rozné. Mishaw shook her head wisely and laughed with a bit of a cackle. He reddened more under the deep tan.

"Well, Brendan, what do you have to say for yourself?"

He knelt beside the bed and held out a shaking hand to the dark, wet little head that wrinkled up its pinched and pink face beneath the quilt. His fingers moved tentatively and gingerly over the soft skin. "My God, Mary McMahon, what a beautiful little creature. But you don't think he's too small, do you? I mean, glory to God, I never saw such a tiny creature in my entire life. Sure it would make me wonder how he could live."

"Brendan." She spoke softly, with a slight hesitancy. "You would be loving me now, would you not?"

"Well, Mary McMahon, what would make you say such a silly thing? Didn't I cross an ocean to find you?"

"I know. I know. But I must tell you, the baby is not a boy. It's . . . she's a girl. You have a daughter. Would that be disappointing you now? Did you want a son so bad?"

"Disappointing me?" He rose to his full six feet two inches. What do you take me for? You go to death's door, and you bring me back a daughter, and you would be thinking I'd be disappointed. Sure you must think me an awful rogue. And I am, Mary. I never felt such fear in my life. I would sooner fight ten men than go through that again."

"Oh, I love you, Brendan McMahon." Tears filled her eyes, and he felt his own eyes dampen as he knelt down and kissed her softly on the forehead and then gave a softer kiss to the infant, who slept peacefully in the warmth and glow of this new world.

"Look at me. A fine, strong lad *I* am," he said as he wiped his eyes.

"Ah, the deep Irish you are. Hard on the outside, soft as porridge on the inside. I was thinking of a name. Brendan, I would like to name her Gabriella after my own dead sister. Would you be objecting to that?"

"Gabriella, after the angel. I think that would be a lovely name."

He shook himself with a sudden realization. "My God, here I am, a family man. We have been blessed this day, Mary. Our family will grow and prosper in health and happiness in this grand and magnificent country. Mishaw, hand me that jug of poteen resting by the fire. A man needs a drink on a day like this. It isn't every day he's blessed with a daughter. Am I right, Mary?" His smile brightened the entire room.

"Well, I wouldn't be knowing what other men need"—she smiled back—"but I know what an Irishman needs, and indeed, it would be a swallow or two. Indeed."

CHAPTER II

JOHN DOUGLAS watched the dust spiraling from behind the approaching riders. He quickly descended the stone steps that led from the upper chambers of Glenverness, threw open the thick bulk of the door, and ambled into the courtyard. He stood, legs parted, with his hands on his hips, his eyes on the riders. There were two of them, and they were traveling quickly along the stone-glutted path that led into the oval where he stood. The day was dry and unseasonably warm for August. There had been little rain anywhere in County Galway, and the dryness showed in the patches of yellow straw that mingled among the hawthorn trees and humpbacked hills brooding over the Douglas manse.

It had been the home of the Douglas until his death two years before, a large multiroomed house made entirely of stone. The cold, immovable stone was more than accidentally a symbol of its cold-hearted, thick, and unbending inhabitants.

The Douglas had had it built by the starving peasants of Spiddal, who, when not serving him in one task or another, scratched and clawed at the fields on farms owned by him. The Douglas had been an abusive and tyrannical landlord, and now, two years after his death, his son John was showing himself to be every bit the tyrant his father had been.

The riders were on him now and dismounting with an easy fluidity of motion.

The younger one, a lad of twenty, ran toward him with his hand raised high over his head. The hand clutched a letter. The lad's ruddy complexion matched the red in his hair, and his open, boyish face beamed with delight.

"I have it, John. I have it. It came all the way from America."

"Good. Give it here." Douglas snatched the letter and studied the envelope. It was addressed to him, and it came from Channing P. Evans III, Evansborough, Massachusetts.

He tore it open and read it slowly. The hand was small and neat. There were no curls or flourishes, just a simple, concise, and clear script.

Dear John Douglas,

 In response to your query of February 18, 1832, I am happy to recount the following to you.

 The man Brendan McMahon was employed here in Evansborough for a short time, and while here he became involved in a turnout with other Irish laborers. He did not stay here long. He and an Irishwoman, one Mary Roark, took flight with a runaway slave and made for the northern border.

 My men and I tracked them down and engaged them in a skirmish. The black man was killed, but McMahon and this woman escaped. My sources here have traced them to a place in Canada of which I am totally unfamiliar, Prince Edward Island. I do not know where on the island they are since the source, in seeking information from the woman's uncle, Coleman Roark, unfortunately, appeared too inquisitive, thus alerting the uncle and sending him into secrecy.

 I apologize for having no further information, but I do hope this will help in some way and that you will be able to avenge your father's brutal murder at the hands of McMahon. He, too, has done me considerable disservice,

       Sincerely,
       Channing Patch Evans III
       Evansborough, Massachusetts
       The twenty-seventh day of April, 1832

The corners of the Douglas's mouth moved slightly in the suggestion of a grin. He was not given to smiling, and it seemed even now, with this apparent good news, the effort was difficult for him.

"Well, John, what is it? Will we be able to find our father's murderer? Will we?"

The Douglas folded the letter and shoved it inside his leather tunic. "Aye, Roderick, aye, we will indeed. And it's because of your intercepting that letter from Coleman Roark to his brother. So the McMahon has taken the Roark woman for his own. Well, he had best enjoy her for the time because he will not be enjoying her for long.

"Come, we shall eat and drink. You both deserve it. You, too, Donal, come, my mother has set a place for you. But I must advise you. Say nothing of this to her."

"Oh, not a word, John." Roderick's eyes were wide with excitement. "I swear."

"I shall say nothing," added the one named Donal. He was Irish and a peasant, and his loyalty came directly from the rumbling in his belly.

They walked on, into the great large hall of a room, their boots echoing off the stone floor and walls. The mother, a slight, almost wizened woman, sat rigidly straight in her chair, nodding shyly to them.

"We have a guest, Mother, Donal McCann. Sit, Donal. Roderick, pour the mead. We all deserve a drink this night."

The mother's eyes narrowed slightly. "Why, my son? Do we have something to celebrate?"

"Oh, no, Mother. It's simply that we all have worked hard in the fields this day."

They drank and ate with enthusiasm, occasionally exchanging glances and knowing smiles while the mother drifted into tearful monologues on what a good man the senior Douglas had been and how theirs had been a golden marriage.

John Douglas, who had a burning memory for most things, could not help thinking that his mother was entering into premature old age. There had been too many scenes in his life of a red-faced, Scots-tempered father berating her cooking, her dress, and her lowland manners.

They had been married in Dundee, her home, but had moved soon after to the Highlands home of Douglas ancestry. For four years they resided in Inverness until Douglas, a man of some means and considerable influence, was granted vast acres of Irish soil by the king. The adventure of it, as well as the potential to triple his income, had brought them to Spiddal.

Little had the Douglas dreamed that he would be living on this stone-choked land that abutted Galway Bay. It was an area of sea fog and continual mist and rain, with land that seemed to harvest rock instead of potato. But he was a single-minded and proud Scot, and he was determined to make the land work for him. The fact that he was never entirely successful drove him to drink and frenzy. His wife withdrew into a shell of silent acceptance, and his two boys whored and whipped the starving peasants into feudal submission.

The meal finished, the mother excused herself quietly from the table, and an old Irish servingwoman removed the dishes, grumbling and mumbling a conversation to herself in Irish as she did so.

After she had retired from their presence, John Douglas rose and stomped across the floor. He returned to the table with a tall cut-glass decanter from which he poured into their tankards, and his own, rum as black as bile. He hoisted his rum in salute: "*Sláinte.*" They raised their own in return and quaffed the drink in one swallow, Roderick shaking his head and smacking away the biting taste with his lips.

"Now that's a bloody lot better than that poteen you drink in the village, Donal McCann. Am I right?"

"Aye. It's a man's drink all right, John."

Douglas poured three more tankards full and sat back in the heavy oak chair.

Roderick sipped more cautiously of the bile and asked, "When do we go after McMahon, John? When will our father be avenged?"

The Douglas leaned forward. His fierce eyes, a deep, penetrating, and distrustful brown, darted from one to the other. His voice, raspy from the rum, was a conspiratorial undertone.

"Lads, we do not go to McMahon. He comes to us. He will crawl to us on all fours like a filthy dog, and when he does, I will personally put a blade through him the way he stuck one in my father."

"Oh, the filthy bastard. I want him, too. He murdered *my* father also."

"Aye. Be easy, Rod, you will have a slash at him."

Roderick threw caution aside and drained off his rum, and then, as though just realizing the reality of it all, he said excitedly, "But how do we get him to leave Canada? Surely, it's an impossible journey to go there once—but to return? What say you to that, John? Donal?" He touched the Irishman's sleeve. Although one was Irish and the other Scots, they, too, were almost like brothers.

"Aye. It would seem a sensible question." Donal advanced prudently. He was always cautious with John Douglas because the Douglas's moods were mercurial and because he knew, of course, that since he was Irish, his place with the landlord was always tentative.

Douglas studied McCann's round face for a moment and made an attempt at a smile.

"Donal, there is a special quality we Scots possess. It is patience. Am I correct on that account, Roderick?" Roderick grinned broadly, knowing full well what was coming next. His florid face was flushed now by the drink.

"You see, Donal. When we were growing up under this very roof, our father would recount a favorite story to us. He told it so many times that if he altered the original text, we would immediately correct him—that is, if he did not have too much of the drink in him, because on those occasions he would strike us a good one across the face for interrupting him."

"What was this story, John?"

Roderick rose, walked to the stone hearth, and placed more peat on the fire. The August night was turning damp and chilly. The Douglas continued.

"On June twenty-fourth, 1314, Robert the Bruce defeated Edward the Second's attempt to relieve the English garrison at Stirling, and in that famous Battle of Bannockburn Scottish independence was won. But that battle and that victory did not come easily. For one full year before, Robert had lain like a hunted animal in a cave that was dug into the face of a rocky cliff. There was barely a visible path to the cave that looked down into an icy river, and for that reason he was undiscovered. But day after day he dreamed of independence for Scotland, and one day he noticed a spider slowly and patiently weaving a web. The design was intricate and involved, but the spider never tired and never despaired. It was watching that spider that gave Robert the Bruce the patience he needed to plot his victory. We Scots have a sense of history and tradition unlike you Irish, Donal."

Donal observed the flame coming into the Douglas's cheeks and knew the rum was beginning to burn in his stomach.

Anger burned in Donal McCann's stomach. He wanted to shout in the Douglas's face that the Irish, too, might have a sense of history and tradition if English and Scottish landlords would relax their stranglehold of taxation and deprivation and allow them to live and grow as people. But he said nothing. He was no Brendan McMahon who would strike out against a landlord. Donal had a widowed mother and a younger brother and three younger sisters much the same as

Brendan. And he saw what Brendan's blow for independence had wrought. It had scattered his family and sent him out of his native Ireland across the seas to far-off Canada. No, discretion was indeed the better part of valor. He would lick the Douglas's boots if it would gain him a few scraps to feed his family. The anger subsided, soothed by his own practicality. "Not only do we Irish have no sense of history," he said with a laugh, "but we don't even have any sense." He could be self-deprecating if it were likely to prove profitable. A desperate man could show more than one disposition to the world.

The Douglas chuckled from his belly, his large, powerful shoulders shaking.

"Well," Donal asked, smiling, "now that I understand it will take patience, John, how do you plan to get McMahon back to Ireland?"

"I have a plan. It will take time, but it will get the results." He turned in his thronelike chair and gestured to the swords that hung over the hearth. "There, right there, that's where I plan to hang the McMahon's head."

CHAPTER III

THE LINGERING shadows of August now blended into the wheat-gold days of September. The warm blue waters of the Northumberland Strait rippled with the gentle freshness of a summer that seemed wishing never to end.

All along the North Cape, the scattered farms prepared for winter. It would come with a swiftness, like a thief in the night, invading the fields and valleys, attacking the barnyards, blowing nor'east drafts of snow and cold along the corridors that fanned out to Tignish and Nail Pond, where Brendan and Mary prepared for the onslaught by stacking wood and storing hay.

"Do not be fooled," William Profitt, their nearest neighbor, had said. "The sun will warm your back through September and October, but early November will spring on you like a wolf on the lamb. Be ready for it. Brendan, lad, be ready."

And Bill Profitt was right, as though he had written the almanac for 1832. The snow blew in slowly, and at first it was almost too wet and heavy to cling to the ground. But around noon of the third day of November the sky was a gray and leaden sweep that hung low over the island and loomed over the log house.

Inside, Brendan McMahon watched the snow as it whirled in a white blur, drifting across the red clay fields, topping the jagged capes with white plumes. Behind him, lying in the tiny wooden cradle, Gabriella gurgled, and a stew hissed hot and bubbly in the iron kettle that hung from a hook over the open fire.

Mary hummed softly as she knitted a warm vest for Brendan. Her hands were talented, and her ability gave her immense satisfaction.

In fact, there was an almost visible character about the peaceful log dwelling. Outside, the world raged on as bitter winter attacked with battalions of snow. But here in this room, warmed by a heaping wood fire and a reciprocity of love, it could have been the lingering summer.

Bill Profitt, along with the neighboring and friendly Micmacs, had helped Brendan harvest the hay and the potatoes. The Indians were now gone off deeper into the wood to hunt stouter game and to hibernate like bears, not to return to the settlements until late spring.

It was strange how in little more than a year Bill Profitt had become such a friend. His father was a Northumberland Englishman, and his mother from Durham. They had emigrated to the island in 1800, bringing with them only the clothes on their backs.

Bill Profitt's father had built the first stone house on the island. It was a house as strong and as durable as the Profitt men, solid and square, and, like them, stolid enough to stand the abuse of nature.

It was a house where Brendan and Mary had spent many a fine evening in the company of Bill, his wife, Isabella, and their two sturdy boys. But there would be little visiting now when it would mean trudging through the snowfields and back. The McMahons did not have a horse or trap, but those would come in time. After all, look at all they had achieved thus far.

Brendan turned to Mary, his tight, broad chest rising and falling in a deep sigh.

"Well, now, what was that great breathing from the south of Ireland all about?" She dropped her knitting into her lap and looked up at him as he came over to her, bent down, and kissed her forehead.

"I have never been as happy in my entire life, Mary." He knelt by her chair. "Look at what we have. We have potatoes enough for the winter, fish, and hay to feed our great horde of animals." They both chuckled at the image of their scrawny but predictable goat, which lay on a bed of straw in the corner of the cabin.

"Sure the thing isn't going to be with us all winter, is it now, Brendan?"

"When the snow ceases, I'll make a path to the barn, and she'll bed there with the oxen and cattle and horses. God, woman, I'll have to build two more barns to house all this livestock."

"Oh, go on with your blatherin', Brendan McMahon."

He stroked her bird-soft hair with his rough hand. "You are happy here, are you not, Mary?"

"I am that, Brendan. Happy and contented as she is." They smiled softly at the sleeping child.

"We've had our difficulties, and I suspect there will be more," he mused. "But we are here in our own home on our own land. We have more than enough to get through the winter, thanks to the Profitts and the Micmacs. It is a great contentment I feel, Mary."

The snow continued for three full days, and then an amber sun burned through and the island glowed and sparkled in the light of snow and sun. The birches, overburdened by weighted branches, bent low to the fields like white old men.

"Come, Mary. Come to the door. It is the mastery of God Himself. Never have I seen such beauty. Come here and look for yourself."

She wrapped a blanket tightly around Gabriella and joined him at the door. The baby took suck from her breast, and she eased the puckered mouth to the nipple. Before them the world was white and startling. The sun and snow blurred their vision.

And then quite suddenly, as though a hand had snuffed out a candle, a black cloud trailed across the sun and the fields turned gray and dark before them.

Mary shuddered with an intense and unexplainable fear and walked back to the fire.

"What is it, Mary? I can feel something in this room. Are you keeping fit today?"

She held the infant closer. "I do not know. I have a strange feeling, a premonition. Suddenly I have great fear."

"Fear? Of what?"

"I do not know. One moment everything was so beautiful, so peaceful. And the next I felt a stab of fear like a knife ripping through me."

"Now, there you are just like an Irish peasant girl. You listened to too many stories by your father's hearth: ghosts and banshees and the little people. If the Irishman's curse is drink, and well it may be, then the Irishwoman's is pessimism and superstition. Good Lord, woman, what can go wrong for us? We've been truly blessed."

CHAPTER IV

THE HOOKER *St. Patrick* bobbed like a cork in the green estuary of the Aran Islands. The waters were dangerous and difficult to pilot, so the curraghs brought passengers and goods ashore.

Donal McCann, whose people had lived on the largest island, Inishmore, for hundreds of years, was totally familiar with his surroundings, but Roderick Douglas craned his neck in awe at the jagged, Atlantic-beaten rock.

"That bloody island is all rock," he whispered to Donal. "Bloody rough rock. I thought Spiddal was made of stone. How do these people survive out here?" They both were leaning over the railing of the Galway to Aran ferry, waiting for the long black-tarred curragh to come alongside. The curragh, the Aran islander's only means of fishing the violent sea, slithered over the tops of the waves like a long black worm.

"Keep your voice down, Rod. Throw as little suspicion our way as possible. These are island people, and they are suspicious by nature, so the less said, the better. I know these islands well, even though my own mother and father decided to settle for a better life in Galway."

He smiled, wondering if that had been truly the right decision. Here, at least, neighbor protected neighbor from any outsiders, and although it was a hard life on this wind-torn, sea-lashed rock, they nonetheless had fish virtually swimming into their nets off the shoreline. If it had not been for the island fever of confinement, it might not have been such a bad life. At least here one was free of the landlord's taxes and whip. Here a man could stand in the free wind and look out to sea and perhaps dream of someday escaping to America without leaving a family unprovided. Even though Brendan McMahon's flight had been necessary, he'd known his mother and sisters would be safe and protected. And of course, safe they had been, and protected, when the Douglas attempted to find them, more than once. On those occasions when he began questioning the fisherfolk, they shut their mouths and turned their eyes to the open sea. The McMahon women seemed suddenly to have been swallowed up by a giant tidal wave. No, such things could not be handled by the aggressive force of an outsider, as the Douglas discovered quickly enough. No mainland power or threat could strike fear in the men and women of Inishmore. When the gruff questions were asked, the women had simply been transported by curragh to the two other smaller islands, Inisheer or Inishmaan. The Douglas finally, and with reluctance, decided the one way to get to the family was through an Irishman who could be bought. Donal McCann was that Irishman. He worked a small croft on the Douglas's land, was unable to pay his taxes for the privilege of working a Scotsman's farm, and could not hope to feed his mother or brother and sisters. Donal McCann was not caught up in the cries of revolution and Irish independence that men like McMahon and Daniel O'Connell shouted throughout the land. The only cries he heard were from the empty stomachs of those he could not feed.

"Come, Roderick, they are ready for us. Now remember, you're a student from Dublin interested in the history of the island. You paid me to guide you because my ancestors lived here for centuries. Here, grab hold of the rope. You descend first. Off with you now."

Roderick Douglas slid easily down the thickly knotted hemp and slipped effortlessly into the waiting curragh, which rose and fell with the tide. Donal was next, and within minutes they were helping the Aran islander beach the long, slithery craft in the sand.

"You're a Hennesey, I believe," Donal said to the sea-worn face of the oarsman.

"Aye," he answered tersely.

"I'm a McCann. I have cousins here. The Gills. Are they still in the old house on the west face of the island?"

The man was slow to answer. He looked them up and down, and then he muttered, "They might be."

Donal nodded and trudged off up the craggy path to the top of the hill. A sudden wind blew in from the Atlantic, and Roderick thought they would be tossed out to the sea.

"Bend down until we get to the gully and lanes. The stone fence will break the wind's force," Donal shouted to him.

It seemed colder and windier than any August Roderick Douglas had ever known. Yet they were only thirty miles off Galway Bay.

The narrow lanes were enclosed by stone fences that ran in a weaving maze across the rugged landscape. In some places the lanes were so narrow they had to walk in single file.

"Here, stop for a moment, Roderick. I must get my bearings. I believe my cousins live at the end of this lane. Yes. So it is. I am sure now. Let us continue."

The wind screamed overhead like the tantalizing sirens of the deep, but there was no temptation for them to join the women of the sea in their lost chambers below. A steady rain slashed and tore at them, pushing them along until Donal halted at a stone cottage sitting squarely at the end of the lane.

Although summer nights linger long in the light of day, this night, because of mist and rain and wind, was prematurely turning a deep gray.

"Hello. Hello in there? Is anyone to home?"

Two faces barely appeared over the open top of the half door.

"Would you be Gills in there?"

Before the two untidy, dirty-faced children could respond, a coarse-faced woman, seared and scarred by weather, stepped cautiously out of the cottage. She was wearing the traditional black cloth dress and blood red apron of the Aran Island woman, and her voice was harsh and demanding.

"What do you want with us? Why are you here?" She spoke in Irish, and Donal answered her in the same tongue, adding a touch of the Aran patois with which he was familiar.

"I look for lodging. I am Donal McCann. My mother was a Gill. Surely you remember me. You are Maura Gill, are ye not?"

The harsh lines disappeared, and she threw back her head and laughed.

"Well, look at me, being caught by me own cousin and I not even prepared for visitors. Bad cess to me, and may I be washed off this miserable rock in a tornado for not recognizing me own flesh and blood. Come in with ye. Come in this instant, and shake the wet off."

She led them into a sparsely furnished but neat house that smelled of fish and brine. Nets hung from the old beamed ceiling, and a spinning loom dominated the center of the room.

"How is the family? And where is your own Peter? I suppose he's emptying the whole ocean of fish, leaving none for the others."

She turned her back on them and reached for the smoking kettle that hung over the smoldering peat fire.

"Ah, he'll not be dropping his nets this night or any night. He joined the fish three years ago this very month."

Roderick shot a glance at Donal.

"Jesus, Mary, and Joseph bless us." Donal crossed himself twice and kissed his fingers. "Will you forgive my bloody big mouth and my stupidity, Maura?"

She poured the hot water into cracked mugs, then spooned bits of tea leaves across the top and stirred until the water turned brown.

She was a strong-looking woman in her late twenties, buxom, with large, round breasts that immediately caught the eye of Roderick Douglas. Although her face was ruddy from the weather, she had high cheekbones and a classic nose. Had she lived among the wealthy of Dublin or London, she would have been a striking woman. As it was, she was attractive in a fiery, almost provocative way. When she moved, her hips and buttocks swayed slightly, and in pouring the hot water, she bent over in an exaggerated fashion, exposing ample cleavage and the firm roundness of her breasts. Donal sensed in her movements and in her enticements that she was a woman in search of a bed mate. She had been widowed young, and for three years she obviously had not felt a man's body beside her at night. The Arans were strict in their code of morality, and although there were undoubtedly men who would gladly slip between her thighs, none would dare take the chance of discovery or the wrath of the village priest.

Before his first sip of the steaming-hot brown tea, Donal McCann had already decided to be with her this night.

"How is your uncle Thomas keeping fit these days, Maura?"

"Oh, Jesus, do ye hear nothin' in Galway City? Sure and I thought you were all so high and mighty, livin' the city life and knowin' everything."

"What do you mean?" He smiled coyly. He knew it was the same Thomas Gill who had drowned after leaving Brendan McMahon off the shore of Galway Bay. It was common knowledge on the Galway quays.

"Sure Tom Gill joined the thousands of other Aran men who have fished the sea and in turn have fed the fish." Her tone and phrasing were lyrical, lilting, and her inflection had a perfect meter to it. Her speech was an unspoiled poem, basic and full of the sea and the soil.

"You have had your troubles, I see."

"And have ye met any Irish people recently who haven't had their troubles?" She cocked her head, and he had to share her pessimistic wisdom. "What brings you to this pile of rock in the middle of an angry sea?"

"My friend here." And he gestured toward Roderick, whose long red hair was rain-slicked from the sudden squall. Roderick smiled his boyish grin, never taking his eyes off her full bodice. "He's a student at Trinity College, all the way from Dublin to study prehistoric ruins. Bloody waste of time if you ask me, digging in the earth and rocks."

"Well, if it's rock you want, you'll get plenty of it here." She studied the red hair and the firm, sharply pointed chin. There was something more than boyish behind those hot eyes that she could feel boring into her body. Her island sense of people, stranger and friend alike, told her she did not like this scholar.

She shifted back to Donal. He was big and good-looking. He was not tall like the scholar, but he was broad, with strong shoulders and a back that seemed to burst his tunic. She liked strong-backed men; they were good to hold onto.

Her green eyes roamed just a bit in a playful way, and Donal smiled.

"Would you have a drop to warm a weary traveler's insides, Maura?"

"I have more than a drop, Donal. If there is one thing we have more of than rock, it's poteen. My own drowned Peter made it by the jugful." She rummaged behind two sea green lobster traps and brought forth a stone jug. "Here, hold it to your lips and light your fires."

Donal crooked the jug expertly in his hand, tipping it past his ear while holding it securely by the handle. The liquid sent sparks shooting through him.

"God, woman, but that is powerful. He must have made it with thunder and lightning. Here, Roderick, give it a go."

Roderick was not as expert with the jug and at first had difficulty with his grip.

"Your man is not an Irishman, I see," Maura noted, pleased at her earlier judgment of disdain for him.

"Give it to me," Roderick snarled. "I'll drink the whole bloody jug." His face became as red as his hair with the blood of anger that was a Douglas trademark and flaw.

He swallowed three great gulps until it seemed the roof of his mouth was a peat fire.

"Christ, woman, the bastardly whiskey must be made of seaweed and salt water." He sputtered and fumed, taking great rapid breaths.

"It's a *man's* drink," she said simply.

"Oh, is it? Well then, I shall have another go at it." And he quaffed three more swallows that had his throat breathing fire.

"Easy now, Rod, we have a busy day for ourselves tomorrow. Do not be forgetting our search."

Donal took the jug and sipped from it as Maura mixed crisp dried seaweed and faggots among the bits of gray peat in the open hearth. The fire blazed up almost immediately, taking the damp chill from the stone house. Her cheeks glowed crimson as she stood watching the flames lick at the dried wood.

The two dirty-faced children, having fled at the first sight of the strangers, now returned to the doorway.

"Come in with you now, and be havin' a bite. Come in and greet your cousin Donal and his friend, all the way from Galway."

They entered the room shyly and sat at the wooden table while she placed tin plates of potatoes and cabbage before them. They ate hurriedly as Donal sipped from the jug.

"Give it over here again," Roderick commanded. His voice was gruff from the drink, and Donal could see it would be a short night for Roderick Douglas. Already, he was heavy of foot and his speech was faltering.

"Say, Maura, you must be lonely with your man gone." Roderick smiled.

"I get along. Island people are thick with kindness."

"Especially the men, I would judge." He licked his lips.

"The men have been good as well." She knew that he was feeling the effects of the poteen and that his animal instincts would soon surface. He was transparent, a child trying to be a man, so rather than insult him, thus causing a situation, she would answer him directly, without effrontery.

"How good? As good as I could be?" He bellowed a laugh and drank more freely from the jug.

"Are you a good provider?" The temptation to tease was on her, and the deep-rooted tradition of wit had seized her.

"Am I a good provider? Did you hear that, Donal? I've provided half the women in Galway City."

Maura cleaned up the tin plates from the meal and shoved the two boys out the door. "Stay with Mrs. Hennesey, lads. Tell her I'll explain in the morning."

She watched after them as they scampered along the muddy path.

"Here, now let me fix you some bit of food. You must be famished, coming all the way here on the hooker through rough seas."

"I could do with something in my stomach besides poteen," Donal said, sitting at the table.

"And you, young sir? Can I fix you something?" Roderick swayed slightly as he came to the table.

"How about my fixing you?" He put his free arm around her as he drank from the jug. His hand tightened on her shoulder, and he peered down at her round breasts with unmasked pleasure.

"Well," she said, removing herself from his grasp, "we will see what the evening holds for us. Am I correct, Donal?"

"Aye, correct you are. Sit yourself, Roderick?"

"Sit yourself be damned. I'll stand my ground. Who are you to be ordering me around?"

"I'm not ordering you. I am simply suggesting that you would be more comfortable sitting at the table." Donal's voice was even and casual with not a hint of the annoyance he was feeling.

"Don't drink too much of that jug; that is very powerful whiskey, Roderick." He knew full well the admonition would prompt just the opposite result.

"Bloody peasant farmer's now tellin' me not to drink too much. I'll drink all I bloody well please. No bogtrottin' Irish peasant tells me what to do."

"Good for you to be your own man, my young friend." Maura smiled. "Good strapping man like you certainly knows how to swallow from the stone jug."

Donal McCann did not look up but busied himself removing the gray, peat-singed potato jackets with a fisherman's knife.

Maura took another jug from behind the traps. "Here, when you've done with that one, you can start on this."

Roderick's eyes danced in his head, and he steadied himself by holding onto a protruding stone from the hearth. "Now that is true hospitality, my lovely woman." He continued his swallowing while Maura sat across from Donal. A thin smile broke out across her mouth, and Donal returned it ever so slightly.

Roderick Douglas began to stagger away from the fireplace and was about to pitch forward into the table when he managed to catch himself.

"Fine whiskey. Fine." He lifted the jug to his mouth and drained it. Then, looking at the empty vessel, he hurled it across the room where it smashed into six large pieces.

Donal and Maura continued eating, apparently without taking notice.

"How much is in these jugs anyway?" he shouted as he uncorked the second one and swallowed a healthy portion.

He was visibly drunk now, and sat on the stone floor in front of the fire, continuing to drink with abandon.

When the meal, such as it was, was over, and Maura had cleared the dishes away, Roderick Douglas seemed virtually unconscious on the floor.

Donal reached down, picked up the jug, and took a full draft, then passed it smilingly to Maura, who swallowed long and satisfyingly from it.

The fog had brought an early-evening darkness to the cottage and with it an intimacy.

"Why did you send your lads off to another bed, Maura?"

"Oh, I had my reasons. I thought your man here would cause some trouble and it would be best that they be free of that." She sighed heavily, and when she did, her full breasts rose amply under her black dress.

"Now surely you wouldn't be expecting me to believe that? A woman who has all of your excitement and adventure, sure I'd wager there has been many a scene under this thatch in the past."

"Well then, why do you think I sent them off?" She cocked her head coyly.

"Maybe, as the sleeping lad there said, maybe you'd be just a little lonely from time to time."

"And if that be so, what do you think can be done about it?" she responded with a hearty defiance.

He rose from his chair and went to her. Her arms were by her sides, but as he placed his mouth on hers, they came up and tightened around his broad back. They swayed into each other, their bodies throbbing with desire.

"Come," she said. "Leave your drunken friend here and come with me."

He followed her around to the back of the cottage and into the small, snug barn that smelled of straw and rusted sea-worn fishing nets.

He went in behind her and latched the door. Tiny shafts of light crept through openings in the roof. A bloated sow snorted in the shadows.

"Well, Maura, the poteen has been good to us. Just enough to give us the desire, but not enough to hinder the performance."

Her body fitted snugly into his as he rubbed his hands along the tops of her breasts and then palmed them in a slow, rotating motion.

"You know how to please a woman, Donal McCann."

"I know how to please myself, too, Maura."

He unbuttoned the top buttons and pulled her dress down off her bare white shoulders, exposing her oval breasts. His mouth covered hers as he slowly lowered her to the hay. His hands caressed and his mouth and tongue covered her upper torso. She pushed him away and got to her feet. She stood over him and let the dress fall to the straw, and then she mounted his rising, thrusting body. Their humping torsos worked rhythmically, and they grunted their satisfaction until every ounce of strength and inner drive was given, one to the other.

They lay silently in the straw for several moments, and then Maura spoke. "It's not the sin of adultery that brothers me so much as the sin of incest."

"Oh, be gone with you, woman," he said, chuckling. "Sure we're fourth cousins. That's hardly related at all." They laughed in the darkness.

"Why do we not stay *here* this night? It will be good for a lonely, full-blooded woman to have a man visit her in her sleep."

"Aye. I would like that. We will."

He lay in the straw, feeling the deep, sexual satisfaction pour through him, but he thought guiltily of his family back in Spiddal. He had a mission to perform, and he must succeed for his family's sake. The bastard Douglas would throw them all out of their cottage quicker than not if Donal did not fulfill his assignment. Roderick was a boy, certainly no one he could count on. He must not alert her; as full of animal desire as she was, she was still an Aran woman with deep convictions and loyalties.

"What would you say to my coming back and settling here again, Maura?"

She turned her naked body to him, and he traced his hands along her legs and thighs and up to her breasts.

"I would look fine on that, Donal McCann."

"We could get a dispensation. Your priest would be happy to see you marry again, so your children would have a proper father."

Her breasts were hard as rock in his hands; she was a solid and fine specimen of a woman, and marriage to her would not be displeasing.

He ventured cautiously. "But my mother and the brother and sisters, could they make a place for themselves here?"

"And why not?"

"They are Spiddal people, mainlanders. This is a remote and grim island. My family left here once before."

"It would not be the first family to come back. Or . . ." She hesitated, and the Atlantic roared in the distance as it blew and lashed against the island.

"Or what?" he questioned.

"Or to come from Spiddal."

His eyes widened in the dark. He must be ever so cautious. *She* had brought it up, but he must virtually walk on the tips of his toes with his next question.

"Oh, the McMahons? They came here, did they not?"

"You know about them?" She whispered it into his ear.

"Everyone in County Galway knows about them. Surely that's no secret."

"Do I make it seem a secret?"

"Well"—he laughed—"there are only the two of us, and the pig, so why do you whisper it? Anyway, the pig understands only Gaelic."

She giggled into the straw.

"Look, though, what it did to them. The McMahon drowns in the sea, and his family is left with no man to protect them."

"They are surely well protected. There be many Aran men who would seek the hand of the older girl, Cathleen, the beauty that she is. Sure, they heap fish and potato and peat at their doorstep."

"Surely they do not." His derision rose in the dark.

"You call me a liar, Donal McCann?" She clenched her teeth in anger. "I can show you this night how they enjoy all the comforts and protection of those who have men about the hearth."

"Then show me. If I can be sure my family is cared for in the event I drown fishing that bloody angry sea, then I will return with them, and I shall be putting my boots beneath your bed before a fortnight is passed."

"Damn your eyes, Donal McCann, I will show you."

"Hold on a minute, woman. That can wait." The straw rustled under him as he turned over on her and entered with a new hardness that brought a grunt from him.

Maura led him along the smoothly worn stone path that twisted and bent away from her house.

The wind from the storm-pounded seas below drove rainy gusts against them.

"Look there. We cannot go in. We all are sworn to secrecy because the sons of the man Brendan McMahon killed have sworn to avenge their father's death."

"Death?" he countered. "You mean murder, do you not?"

"Murder I do not; the mother swears it was an accident. The landlord fell on his own knife. The mother was in the cottage with the two girls, and she saw it all. She is a good and saintly woman who would not lie."

They walked down the lane. At the bottom the long, narrow stone house sat quietly. Flickering candles and the red glow of a fire gave the cottage a contented warmth.

"You see the pile of peat? That will last three years. Here, pass by the window, but do not be brazen about looking in. Steal a quick glance or two."

He could see the mother sitting at a spinning wheel while two young women busied themselves arranging flax. They passed on quickly. He noticed that the house was directly above the narrow stone corridor that led to the sea.

"Well, what think you now? Do you see how strangers are treated and protected on Inishmore? So if you do ride the rampaging saddles of the sea and get yourself drowned, your family will be well cared for. Does the visit satisfy your curiosity?"

"Aye, it does that. Now let's return to the straw. I feel the urge coming on me again."

The next morning, after fish and bread and tea, they took their leave of Maura.

"We are going to dig among the ruins of Dun Aengus and see what the scholar can unearth from those prehistoric times, Maura. But I do not know how much digging the scholar is capable of after all the poteen he consumed."

Roderick Douglas's usually florid complexion was gray, and his disposition, along with his mouth and stomach, was sour.

"Never mind your small talk, McCann, let us be on our way." He turned to the lane and began climbing through a gray rain.

"It was a good night we had, Maura; we will be having more of them in no time at all. I'll be back soon."

"Aye, and it will be good to see you again, it will. Safe home and Godspeed."

He strutted up the lane and in a few moments was descending the other side of the hill. It was really too bad, he thought; she was one grand woman. There were not many like her in Galway. But who in his right mind would live on a pile of rock in the middle of the Atlantic?

"Well, what is our plan?" Roderick's spirit was low, and he made no pretense about it.

"Rest assured, Roderick, while you were sleeping I was discovering the house of the McMahons. We shall nestle ourselves in the ruins of Dun Aengus, and when night falls, we will steal a curragh and row to the western tip of Inishmore and do our deed. Come."

The day slipped by slowly for Donal. He dozed under cover among the ruins of the old fortress while Roderick squeezed out every pain from his poteen-racked body in the sleep of the dead. At the first curtain of dark Donal woke Roderick, and they proceeded quietly down the rock to the shore below. They slipped along the low, craggy base of Inishmore, inching their way along over rock and sand until they came to the corridor that led up to the McMahons' house. All along the shore sleek black curraghs were beached for the night. They had their pick, and they chose one that was larger than the rest. They secured it at the foot of the stone lane and made their way up to the house. Darkness was settling slowly because the night was clear and the ocean calm. They crept along the path until the house was in front of them and slipped stealthily past the window in the back. Donal pressed his back against the house and shot a glance into the cottage.

The mother and two daughters were tidying up after their evening tea. All about was quiet except for the cry of a baby from somewhere above the lane.

"All right, we must be quick. There are no men about. We should have no trouble. We will go on in through the rear door. Are you ready?"

"Aye, I'm ready. It is my father's ghost that gives me the purpose I need."

They moved quickly by the window and through the unlocked door into the long one-room cottage.

The mother looked up, startled. "What—what is it ye want, bursting in here like this? Leave. Leave at once."

"You mind your tongue," Roderick snarled, "and sit to table, all three of you."

The two girls trembled in terror, unable to speak.

"Do as you are told and no harm will come to you," Donal snapped.

They obeyed and sat dutifully at the table. The younger girl burst into tears, prompting another snarl from Roderick Douglas. "Stop that. Stop that this instant, or I'll rip your bloody tongue out of your mouth." The mother began to rise, and he pushed her back into her chair.

Donal tore a rope from the ceiling, flinging away the clothes that were hanging there to dry. He tied the hands of the mother and younger girl behind their backs and then knotted the rope to their chairs.

"You, come here," he said to the one he knew to be Cathleen. Maura was right. The girl was a beauty.

He tied her hands and grabbed a long cloak from a hook while Roderick stuffed fish and bread and potatoes into his haversack. "All right, come," Donal said to Cathleen.

"But where are you taking her?" The mother sobbed in shock.

"She will help avenge my father's murder," said Roderick. "She will die unless that murdering bastard of a son of yours does not return for his punishment."

"Come, Roderick, enough. We have little time." The girl was resisting, so Donal threw her over his shoulder and raced up the lane and down to the waiting curragh, with Roderick serving as a rear guard and brandishing two pistols.

They reached the black craft and placed the girl in first. She suddenly stood up and screamed into the night until Roderick slapped her with an open hand across the face. She stumbled backward then and almost fell into the sea, but Donal reached out and held her firmly as Roderick pushed the beached craft along the sucking sand until it met the first, second, and finally the third wave. Then he jumped in, and they both rowed madly out to the blackening sea, Galway, and the waiting Douglas.

CHAPTER V

For Brendan McMahon it was as though someone had come back from the other side of the grave. The day had been long and gray. Snow drifted in great heaps along the sharp-edged capes, and the Strait could barely be seen through the blur. The air was as cold as blue steel. Then came the tentative, almost polite knocking at the door.

"Good God, who could that be on such a hellish day as this?" Brendan said, looking up from the fishing net he was mending.

"Must be Bill Profitt or one of his sons. Go see, then. Don't keep the frozen traveler waiting at the door."

Brendan looked sideways at his wife. Her tone was less than lyrical, and her hands worked nervously and almost irritably over her sewing. Cabin fever, he thought. We both have it, cooped up in one room like chickens. It's no wonder we're out of sorts. He thought this, but he did not say it.

"All right, all right, be easy, woman, your voice is as sharp as a blade." He walked to the door and pulled back the iron bolt. The door stuck for a moment with crusted snow, then gave way and blew in on him. He stopped around it, and there, standing before him, was a figure more ice than man.

The traveler's mustache was frozen stiff, and his blustery frost-bitten face was pinched in pain.

"Good God, man, come in and stand by the fire."

The snow-laden apparition stumbled past Brendan, who shouldered the door shut against the biting windblown snow.

The man stood hunched by the fire, biting his icy mittens off finger by finger, and then he slowly turned to face Mary and Brendan. A sudden dawning, an illumination, shot across Brendan McMahon's eyes as the man threw his fur cap down and the snow began to melt from his shoulders and white hair.

"John," he shouted, "John Wallace!" Brendan went to the stooped figure and embraced him with spontaneous affection.

"John, John. Mary, I've told you about John Wallace. This is his land. Oh, John, my God man, sit, you must be frozen to death. Mary some hot stew for my friend. Here, sit, sit here in the rocker by the fire."

Mary put down her sewing and ladled out the steaming stew that had large chunks of mutton and rabbit floating in its thick brown gravy. Her frown described more fully than anything the puzzlement she felt at that moment. John Wallace, she thought. An old man come home to die, to live out his years on *his own* land. It would never be theirs; life was just one struggle and failure after another.

"Mary, bring the stew to my friend, quickly."

John looked up at her out of deep, tired eyes. "So," he said weakly, his tongue still unaccustomed to the warmth, "so this is Mary. Well, lad," he continued in a jerky, almost stuttering voice, "she was worth all the travel."

Mary's eyes softened as she handed him the steaming bowl, but he could not hold it in his frozen fingers. So Brendan spooned the hot stew into him, and the old man's eyes filled with tears of joy and gratitude until, finally the warmth of the room and the stew worked their magic, and the circulation crept slowly back into his body.

He ate every mouthful that Brendan served him, and when Mary gave him another helping, he accepted it hungrily.

Life came back into him, and he took a third bowl and dipped his bread into it, shaking his head with satisfaction.

Mary cleared the things away, and John sat back, contentment lighting his face. He wiped the melting ice from his mustache and sighed.

"What have you done to the old place?" he said at last, and before Mary could answer in defense of what she thought was an improvement, he added, "It's the best-looking home on the island. You see, Brendan, I told you I left it a ruin, but you two have performed a miracle." Mary's gaze softened even more, and she handed him a mug of tea.

Brendan, who had been desperately restrained, now bowled him over with questions. "Where did you come from? Where is Robert Fraser? Is the *Aileen Donan* still the greatest ship under sail? How is the crew? Eamon and the others?"

John chuckled into his chest. "Heavens, Mary, does he go on like this all the time? The lad is a storm of words and questions."

"I'm afraid we have been cooped up so long it's conversation with others he would be wanting, Mr. Wallace."

"Hold up now, Mary. It's John I am to Brendan, and John I will be to you."

He smiled, and his smile was so sincere it was infectious, and in spite of the confinement and the obvious danger of losing the house and land, she smiled back and said, barely forming the word, "John."

His eyes twinkled. "Good, that's much better." His strength was returning as he rocked back and forth. "Now one question at a time. I left a healthy Robert and his crew in Saint John. The ship is as good as ever, I might add. I left in mid-October, but I must not have recollected I've lived sixty-eight winters and am not as quick on land as

I was on the deck of a merchant vessel. I was too far away to turn back when the snow struck, so I took each day as it came. I finally reached the island at Charlottetown, let me see, that was a week past, and then the snows blew me along the icy roads until I arrived at Tignish early evening last. I just didn't have the strength to come in on you in the dead cold of a winter's night, so I decided to finish the journey this day. Can you believe it took me most of the day to walk from Tignish to Nail Pond? Oh, the old body is wearing down like an overworked plow horse."

"But you are here, and that is the main thing."

"Oh, Brendan, my lad. I almost forgot." John began slapping his upper and lower chest until the crackling sound of paper was heard. "Here it is, practically next to my skin, eh? A letter the post dispatcher gave me. Said it must have been coming for months. Here, lad. He asked me if I knew tell of the old Wallace place. Frenchman, he was. 'Old Wallace place,' I said, 'there's no such farm anymore. That's the McMahon place now.'" He chuckled again, and Mary's frown disappeared completely.

Brendan took the letter and grinned at her in return. "Damn, but it's good to have a friend to visit, John; you help thaw out the place."

The old widower was not inexperienced in domestic affairs. "You're still just children, you will have your ups and downs, but these tired old eyes tell me you will have more ups than downs."

Brendan, wishing to be polite, put the letter into his pocket. "So, now, John, can we get you anything else? Are you warm now?"

"You could do us all a favor and read your letter; don't stand on ceremony with me."

"Aye. I will." Brendan nodded. "It's from the village priest, Father Nelligan." His hands trembled slightly as anyone's would when receiving news from home. A letter, to him, always meant death or sickness. It was as though an Irish letter could be only the script of tears and sorrow and despair. There were dark moments in the dead of night when he cursed his ancestral melancholy.

He began reading quietly to himself, his lips moving quickly at first and then slowing until he dropped his hand, the letter dangling by his side. A reddish purple flushed his face, and he summoned a great heaving breath from his lower stomach, exhaling it and repeating the process again more quickly.

"What is it, lad? Is it bad news? Brendan, you're in a daze."

He could not answer John Wallace. Mary snatched the letter from his hand, and he walked to the fireplace.

Mary read the letter aloud:

Dear Brendan McMahon,

    It grieves me deeply to relate a tragic event that has occurred concerning your sister Cathleen. She has been kidnapped from her home on the Arans by The Douglas. Islanders and villagers alike have been brazenly told of this as though there were no law. And indeed, no law is there, except the Douglas. He has shouted it through valley and hillside that he wants the McMahon to return and stand trial for the murder of Douglas's father. He rages in drunken fits that all he wants is justice.

Brendan, my son, it pains me to send this news to you. I spent many long hours at prayer asking the Almighty Father for guidance, and finally, I decided that you should know. I know you and Mary have been blessed with a child, and it would be a difficult journey for you to return if you so decide.

But God in all His Mercy will protect you, and justice will be served. We all know it was an accident, and we in the village will rally around you. I just felt you should know since your dear mother is seriously ill from all this.

I leave it to your own conscience what to do.

God bless you,
Father Nelligan

The words hung in the air like icicles until John Wallace said gently, "I did not know you had a child, I am happy for you. A girl or a boy?"

"A girl," Mary said, crumpling up the letter and throwing it into the fire.

The three of them watched the flames feed on the paper, scorching it brown and then gray as it curled into ash.

"May I see the child?" John asked.

"Surely, John," Brendan answered almost in a whisper, and he went to the other end of the room, where a blanket hung from a line of rope, separating the sleeping quarters from the rest of the house.

He brought back the bundled-up round pink-cheeked baby, whose black satin hair seemed to shine.

John put out his hands and held the baby tenderly; the little face peeked out from the blanket, and Gabriella's blue eyes sparkled.

"She has her mother's lovely eyes and features, thank God."

The attempt at humor did not lighten their hearts any, but his intention was appreciated in the slight smiles from both of them.

John rocked slowly, and the baby fell off to sleep, her pink velvety eyelids closing gradually.

"Well, Brendan, we must face it. What are you going to do?"

"Jesus, woman, I do not know." He sat on a barrel and clutched his head in his hands as though to keep it from exploding.

"Father Nelligan is a good and fine man, but he must have the mind of an innocent lamb if he thinks he and the rest of the villagers could protect you in a country that is ruled by English and Scottish landlords. They want you back as an example, my husband. The only justice you will find will be at the end of a rope. Your death will show the other poor wretches that there is no escape for them, at least not in this miserable life." She spit the words out in anger and frustration.

"Do they bloody well think I am going to walk up to him and say, 'Hello, John Douglas, remember me? I am Brendan McMahon. I'm the one who killed your father when he ordered me never to attend a rally for the great Daniel O'Connell'? Is that what they expect? Is it? What am I to do, John? What would you do?" The usually strong voice was almost pleading.

"Brendan, my lad, I know this is tearing you apart, as it would tear me apart if I were in your place, but, lad, you are a husband and a father. Only you"—he paused and looked over at Mary, who continued to study the bits of gray ash—"and your lovely wife can make this decision." He rose with more strength than he had shown on his arrival. "I will go now."

"Go? Go where? There is a driving storm all about us. You will stay."

"Brendan, you have words to share over this. It is not for me to be present. I saw the old barn as I passed through the field. You have repaired it well. It appears warm and secure. I can build a little fire. I shall be quite comfortable there. I hoped that I could stay the winter and help out. There are things I can show you about surviving on this lovely gem of earth. Would you be in accord with that? And when the weather turns soft and friendly, I thought I could build a little place down in the hollow by the creek. I would not be in your way," he added shyly.

"In our way?" Mary turned from the hearth and came to him to place her warm hands over his. "It is a blessing from heaven that you came to us on this, the darkest day of our lives. We need you, John. We need your counsel and your wisdom."

"Thank you, my dear Mary, let me think on this while you discuss it together. Talking will lighten your burden." He pulled his heavy jacket tightly up to his jaw, squared his fur cap on his white head, and pulled on his mittens. "I will be in the barn if you need me. Talk your hearts out. It will be good for you, believe me."

He opened the door and pushed his way through the blinding snow to the tight, secure little building that sat like a white hill near the drifting powder of the potato fields. He was home, and when the weather cleared, he would visit the grave of Eva, his bride, seven years gone this coming spring. Yes, he would be content here. After all, he had come back to the island, to his home, to die.

CHAPTER VI

THE NIGHT BLEW and howled sharply against the cabin as Brendan and Mary lay in each other's arms, her naked breasts hard and firm against his chest.

"You know that I have to go back. You know that in your heart, Mary, do you not?"

She sighed deeply. "Aye, I do. But you will not walk up to them and surrender yourself. That would be suicide."

"I'm not that crazy. I will seek help. There are people. There is Daniel O'Connell; he will tell me what to do. I swear I will get Cathleen back even if I have to kill another Douglas."

"Oh, Brendan, are we to be forever denied a happy life? Does God have something against the Irish that He has cursed us so?"

"Hush, Mary, that's blasphemous talk. We will survive, and someday, because of people like Daniel O'Connell, Irish people will live freely and hold their heads high."

"Oh, I pray that to be true."

"But I worry about you and the child. I could be gone for months. How will you survive? There is Bill Profitt, to be sure, and his sons, but you are only a woman."

She tensed and drew back her body from him. "Only a woman? You cannot be meaning that?"

"But I am meaning it. This is rugged country, and farming is exhausting work."

She bolted up in the bed, flushed.

"Look, you, I left Ireland and crossed an ocean without your help, and I was only eighteen years old. I secured a position for myself in the Evansborough Mills, and I did that on my own. I gave birth to your daughter with no help from you, and I did it in this room with no doctor. Two days later I was up getting your bloody breakfast, so don't tell me I can't survive. I love you, Brendan, but I am no Dublin fancy lady sitting in a Georgian parlor. I'm a farm girl, and I know what farm work is just as much as you. I am a twenty-year-old woman, wife, and mother. I can take care of myself. It is you we must worry about. Can you survive?"

Her body was rigid beside him.

"Damn it, Mary, I did not mean to offend you. Jesus, but you have a hellish temper when you have a mind."

"You're bloody well right I have, and I can use it to my advantage. Now, let us get some sleep; Gabriella will be waking soon for her suck. I hope I have enough left after you. Good night."

But she did not fall off to sleep so easily. Troubled, she lay on her side, the hot flush of temper subsiding now into a cold fear that danced a feathery dance around her heart. All that fine, independent spirit was so much bravado. And her temper—good God, she thought, will I ever be able to control it? Hellish, Brendan had called it. And hellish it was, even to her. Brendan, lying so close to her in the square framed bed that he had fashioned himself.

She remembered the night he completed it and the boyish way he had reddened when he said, "Well, I think it is sturdy enough to withstand the wear and tear. Well, what I mean is the two bodies." He blushed a deeper purple when he stammered that. And Mary had thrown back her head and laughed that throaty warble, and then he, too, had grinned and scratched his spiky black hair in embarrassment.

A boy, she thought tenderly, in many ways he was just a boy. Oh, surely he had the strength of two men, but his thoughtfulness and sensitive nature were of a poet, a child poet. He was, as she had said many times before, the deep Irish. She saw him working the fields hour after hour in the rain and snow and heat and then heading off to the shore to dig mussels and oysters, bringing them home in a large sack, his grin of pleasure lighting up the cottage like a flaming hearth. And the way he held Gabriella, as though she were some china doll whose very body might break. Gabriella, fat and pink-cheeked, snuggled into that warmest spot for babies, between the face and the groove of a father's shoulder.

Brendan, humming the Irish and soothing the baby into the soft pink world of sleep. All these images flashed before Mary. Tears burned her eyes, partly out of guilt for her impetuous outburst and partly out of fear and loneliness at the thought of his leaving. Good God, it wasn't as though he were going to Malpeque overnight. He would be sailing across the sea, not sure of how long he would be gone or, God forbid, if he would ever return.

She turned toward him. His long body lay motionless as the light from the moon framed his sharply defined face. Such a sensitive face, she thought, as she bent over and kissed him softly on the cheek. "I love you, Brendan McMahon, forgive the wild banshee in me."

The next morning Brendan posted a letter to Father Nelligan asking the priest to tell the Douglas he'd return as soon as the weather would permit.

John Wallace was a solid presence to them both. He guided

Brendan to the frozen ponds and instructed him in the art of ice fishing, showing him how to drop lines so they fell far enough below the
black holes that puckered the pond, but not too far, reminding him
that the fish swam closer to the surface during winter.

He took him below the snowy capes to cull the Irish moss that
swept in all along the shoreline, a substance the texture of which was
akin to seaweed but which was medicinal as well as edible and burn-
able.

John Wallace made the North Cape an outside schoolroom that
yielded both knowledge and sustenance. But as each day passed,
Brendan's heart ached at the realization that the first break in winter
would herald his immediate departure.

That day inevitably and irrevocably arrived, and he knew it only
too well one April dawn as he gathered driftwood on the quiet beach.
He bent to pick up the wood and suddenly felt a shift in the wind
that blew against his face. It was balmy and carried with it the scent
of earth and sea. It was the wind of spring, and he could feel new life
straining and tingling about him.

The sun was warm on his face, and as he looked toward the capes
he saw shoots of green grass pushing through the melting snows.

He climbed a rounded bluff and surveyed the fields. The glinting
snow sparkled, mixed with the blood red clay that was so magically
and mysteriously the color of the soil. He felt a tug at his heart,
secured the wood in his arms, and set out for home.

When he arrived at the house, he looked down at his boots. They
were muddied from the overnight thaw, and he wiped them clean
with a piece of burlap.

"Spring is in the air. The wind has lost its bite, eh?"

He continued wiping the boots clean, and he did not answer
John Wallace's observation.

The old man walked past and knocked on the door.

Mary opened it, and as she did so, her gaze continued past to the
dripping fields and then down at Brendan, who leaned over, busying
himself with his boots.

"I didn't want to track mud into the house," was all he said,
looking up at her.

They ate breakfast in silence, and when he was finished, he went
behind the curtain of their sleeping quarters and packed a few things
into his haversack. It was the same haversack he had packed when
they left Evansborough, and the grim reminder of Channing Evans
and his party in pursuit of them brought this most recent pursuit into
bold relief.

Night after night the three of them had plotted his route. He
would cross the Strait with Totem Paul, who ran a ferry service. From
there he would travel to Saint John and look for Robert Fraser and
the *Aileen Donan*. If Robert were not in port, he would simply wait
until he arrived. John estimated that the ship would be in port, sailing from either Glasgow or Liverpool, in April or May. He would sail
with her back to Ireland, where he would steal into Galway and try

to muster men and arms to fight the Douglas. It all sounded so easy.

But now the time had come, and the heaviness around his heart was like a stone. He picked up his sack and strode purposefully to the table.

"The less said, the better, Mary. I love you with all my heart and the breath that is in me." He leaned over and kissed her softly on the mouth, her tears and his spilling down their cheeks.

Gabriella slept in her wooden cradle, fashioned out of birch by John. He knelt beside her and kissed her gently and then rose.

"I know Mary's an independent and strong woman, but take care of her anyway, John." He squeezed the old farmer's hand, and in seconds he was gone across the muddied fields and up the hill where the land dipped down into the valley.

CHAPTER VII

I<small>T WAS NOT</small> until late afternoon of the third day that a weary Brendan McMahon came upon the log shack partially hidden in a grove of birch trees. He approached along the sandy shore of an inlet cut into the edge of land that bordered the Northumberland Strait. He halted and wiped his brow with the back of his hand. Sun streaked through the curled branches, casting a twilight glow on the chapel quiet of the grove.

The extreme quiet and peace prompted a crafty and stealthy advance. He called out in a whisper, "Is there anyone about?" His voice was barely audible above the tide that rippled musically behind him.

As though he had been waiting for any change in the tone or feel of the day, Totem Paul burst from the shack, ducking his head to clear the doorframe.

The man rose in front of Brendan, who stepped back to take in his great size and bulk, his bullet head and thick black hair. "Jesus," was all he could say.

"Who are you? And what is it you want from Totem Paul?" the voice thundered. The accent was French.

Brendan forced a smile. "Well, one thing is certain, Totem Paul, I wouldn't be looking for any trouble."

The big man roared his approval and thrust out his hambone hand. Brendan shook it, feeling the vise tighten as though his knuckles would break.

"Brendan McMahon from Tignish. I would be needin' the ferry service to New Brunswick. I must get to Saint John."

"Too late. Dark come soon. The Strait still recovers from winter. She turns wild in dark, like a good woman, huh? But I take you in morning. Eh? I take you then. What you say to that?"

"How much is the fare, Totem Paul?"

"How much do you have?"

Brendan fingered the shilling pieces in his tunic pocket. "Fifteen shillings?"

"Fifteen then," Paul responded. "Fifteen I did not have a few minutes ago. I cook some stew, share a plate with me. You sleep there under the stars." And the paw of a hand gestured toward a lean-to, the sturdy branches of which supported a canopy of dead leaves. "You crawl in there and sleep the sleep of the kings, with God's own sky as your roof. You are tired. Go now, throw your blankets on the soft leaves, eh? I heat the stew. Do you like rabbit?"

"I do, Totem Paul. I do indeed."

"Well, it is not just rabbit. This winter was hard. But, Brendan McMahon, whatever I throw in, you will like." He roared off into the shack.

The wind began to pick up, and the Strait churned the blue water into a milky froth. The big man knew what he was talking about, that was for sure, Brendan thought, as he peered far out at the changing sea.

"Come and sit for your stew. It will be hot in a minute."

Brendan entered the tiny shack. It was impossible to think this big bear of a man could live comfortably under its low roof.

"You see why I do not offer you night's comfort behind my log walls. We be in each other's arms, God Almighty! I know I am a big man, tall as a Totem, Micmacs say, but you are—how you say?—no dwarf yourself, McMahon. You have good shoulders. I'll bet you run from no man."

"Well"—Brendan spoke between mouthfuls of tender meat—"almost anyone, Paul." And they shared chuckles between bites of stew.

"This is the best rabbit I have ever had, Paul. It is so tender; sure you're a better cook than my own wife. What is your secret?"

"Oh, no secret. I mix in a little this, a little that."

"Would you care to tell me what this and that might be?"

"Only if you keep secret. There is rabbit, possum, squirrel, and snake."

"Snake? Did you say snake, Paul?" Brendan pushed away from the table and rushed for the door. The big man kept on spooning in the stew, taking little notice of his dinner companion's quick departure.

It was several minutes before a white-faced Brendan dragged himself back through the door.

"Something bother you? You never have snake before? God Almighty, but I think it good."

Brendan slumped into the hard wooden chair. "To be sure, I have not. There are no snakes from where I come from. Saint Patrick sent them slithering out of Ireland years ago."

"Oh, Ireland your home? I heard it said to be one wild country. I knew Irishmen when I shipped under merchant sail out of Quebec. They were fighters and singers." He laughed.

"Well, Tignish is my home now." And Brendan went on to tell his story, hesitating for a moment on his mission to Ireland and then crashing recklessly ahead as though he had sensed a friendly ear.

"You would place yourself in danger to rescue your sister? You are a good lad. But a foolish one. If is true, what you say, you walking into death trap. You no wiser than the possum, or the squirrel, or the rabbit. This Douglas have men and arms, eh? How do you fight him alone?"

"I am not sure. I know a man. He is the greatest thing that has happened to Ireland since the patriots of ninety-eight. I know he will help me. If I can find him before it's too late."

"What's his name?" Paul leaned his mountainous shoulders over the table.

"Daniel O'Connell, the noblest statesman in the world, and he will free my people from the English and Scottish landlords."

"Hmmm, I see by your eyes you have much belief in this man. That is a good thing, eh? To believe in someone."

Indeed, Brendan's eyes burned and became large when he spoke of O'Connell. "Ireland is a beautiful country, and it is being ravished by absentee landlords who are like vultures picking it clean. The people are taxed to death farming land that isn't even their own. But Daniel O'Connell will change all that, mark me."

"That is good, you have him. If only my people had this kind of man."

"Your people?" Brendan was puzzled.

The big man sat heavily on the edge of the wooden bed. It gave slightly under his mammoth bulk.

"You see, Brendan, you Irish are not the only ones who have suffered under the English landlords. I am Acadian, and my people lived and worked the fields of Grand Pré for over one hundred years, eh? Then the English come and send my people away. *Ma mère, mon père* were born in bayou country of Louisiana in the south of the American states. They spend their lives coming back here to Canada, to Nova Scotia, where our beautiful Acadia was. Their family land was owned by English, just like that. No papers. No proof. Just because the English government say that it is so. My brothers and sisters die in early year, but I a big, ornery bastard, I too strong. *Ma mère* and *mon père* rest in the village churchyard. They finally have their own land in Grand Pré." He shook his head philosophically. "So, Brendan McMahon, my Irish friend, do not tell Totem Paul about the English. I know them bastards good." He picked up a thick birch branch and broke it in half, dropping both pieces to the dirt floor. "I know them good." He spit out for emphasis. "Now we sleep. Dawn come fast."

Brendan lay among the warm, dry leaves, looking up at the clear sky. It was early spring, and the sharp points of stars that speared the winter heavens were softer now and glittering. Night sounds bumped and rustled around him. Totem Paul's hand-carved birch boat caught the lapping of the choppy water, and fox and rabbit pursued their ritual chase somewhere in the woods behind him.

He felt the ache of loneliness in his heart and silently cursed the duty that had befallen him. In the intimacy of his own thoughts, he wished Father Nelligan had never written to him. It was a terrible and shameful thought to have, but have it he did. Then he saw his dear sister, in the hands of the Douglas, and his breath came quicker. Troubled as he was, he finally fell off to sleep under the great starlit sweep of the Canadian sky.

Just before dawn, when objects and figures are not quite distinguishable, Brendan woke with a start. A noise from below the shack near the water's edge stirred him. He sat up and listened to the night. It came again, and this time it sounded like the undercurrent of guttural voices. He moved forward out of the lean-to. Squinting into the haze, he now saw four figures, who were untying the heavy ropes of Paul's boat.

"Bastards," he said, "the bastards are stealing the boat." He bounded out of his blanket and raced for the shoreline, shouting as he did so, "Paul. Awake. Awake. The bloody bastards are stealing the boat."

Brendan raced headlong into their midst, shouldering one into the curling tide. He flailed away with right- and left-handed punches at the other three. A flashing fist caught him square in the face, and his vision blurred for a moment as he tumbled backward into the water. When he attempted to rise, the first man, just getting his footing, waded up behind him, and crooked his right arm around Brendan's throat, slowing choking him to death. Summoning one final effort from some deep reservoir inside, Brendan rose from the water and managed to slip his right arm over the man's head. Then, in one quick movement, he clutched the man's hair and flipped him over in front of him. The fallen figure attempted to get up, but Brendan smashed a fist against his cheekbone, and the man fell back into the water.

Shaking the blur from his eyes, he saw the other three approaching. They stalked him slowly, and he waited for them to come into the water. They never had the chance. A rolling mountain of flesh, a human avalanche, descended on them from nowhere as Totem Paul grabbed two of them by the shoulders and began smashing their skulls together as though they were miniature coconuts. When their bodies went limp to his grip, he dropped them into the water and approached the third. "You want him, Irishman?"

"Whatever pleases you, Paul."

"I think he be mine, too."

The man, in terror now, made an attempt to run past the giant form. However, Paul was not only large and strong but quick, and he faked a move to the right as the man, thinking he was faster, came back to Paul's left. Totem Paul was waiting for him and shot a thunderbolt blow into the man's chest. Brendan winced as he heard the rib cage crunch. The man slumped into the water.

Brendan waded to the sand, and Paul's bearlike paw tousled his wet hair. "You good with your fists, Brendan McMahon. I like a man know what to do with his hands."

The four groaning figures sputtered and spit out water and crawled to the sandy beach.

"Now you go, or Paul break you like sticks." His voice bellowed along the beach and through the pines that were gaining definition with the arrival of early morning.

They rose drunkenly to their feet and scrambled into the thicket.

"And if you come back, I kill you," he shouted after them. "Come, Brendan, we have breakfast. I am hungry."

The boat was square and open, its scooped-out spine made from oak. It was durable and strong and rough. The design was simple, much like the man who had built it from the forest and honed it down with an ax.

The seas were calm in the early-morning quiet. The sun kissed the tips of the waves and turned them amber.

"I like out here," Paul said from amidships, where he effortlessly parted the churning water with his mighty oar. "It is peaceful. And I a peaceful man."

"Yes. I saw that," Brendan agreed with amusement.

Paul's smile filled the boat. "I am no bully. I am no one to look to hurt the other man. But"—he shook his head and clamped down on his jaw—"I do not let the other man hurt me. Or the people who are my friends."

"That is a good way to look at life. I, too, do not run the countryside in search of trouble, but when it comes my way, I back down from no man."

"I see that in you, Irishman. That is why I like you. That is why I wish to help you. Tell Paul something, Brendan. Do not lie. I will know if you lie. Tell Paul. If he come with you to Ireland, could Paul help?"

"What? What are you saying?" Brendan almost stood up, and the boat tilted nervously for a moment. Paul simply gestured him back down with his raised palm.

"What I am saying, I have said," he answered tersely. "I say no more. I am a man who says the words that are in his head."

"Could you help? You bloody well *could* help, my friend. You're a bloody army by yourself. But I couldn't—"

"You do not have to. I already say I would."

"But—but what about the boat? The ferry service?"

"I sell the boat. I make money. It is of no importance. I can someday make another with these hands."

Brendan shook his head in wonder. The hesitancy he felt, the inadequacy of one man against many, the nagging doubt about his being able to rescue his sister—all had vanished in the brightness of the Frenchman's smile.

"I tell you. I do not forget what the bastard English do to the people of Acadia. Now, enough of talk. We must make time. Look, the sail she fills out. Full sail and strong oar. We have no trouble now."

The journey would take two full days, but the wind and weather were good. Occasionally an ice floe, having broken off from the northern currents, floated past, an ironic harbinger of the oncoming warmth of spring and summer. The first night they would settle in at Miscouche on Bedeque Bay, and the next morning they would cross over to Cap Pelé, New Brunswick. There they would sell the boat and proceed on foot to Saint John. Brendan felt a light feeling around his heart when he thought of seeing Robert Fraser and the rest of the crew of the *Aileen Donan*. It is good to have friends in this world, he mused. They help ease the pain of loneliness that a man feels for a wife and daughter.

CHAPTER VIII

THE RAIN SLANTED and blew in off the Atlantic, punishing the clusters of thatched houses that huddled in the yellow furze and heather of the hills. At Ceann Léime, in the extreme west of Ireland, a great chain of ragged rock stretching to the open sea caught the rain's wrath and was hidden momentarily under a watery tumult of wave and spray.

Daniel O'Connell gazed out at the boiling surf as it broke across the rocks in a violent outrage of storm. The sides of the carriage in which he was a passenger were open to the weather and the rain pelted against him. The chestnut horse kicked up huge divots of mud that flew up in its wake and splattered against driver and passenger.

O'Connell, full-bodied, with brown, curly hair and the round cheeks of a cherub, wiped the wet from his face. "You know, Patrick, that scene is so similar to Ireland's plight. We are the rock, the foundation, and we take a terrible thrashing from our enemies." Patrick Leary, tall, lean, with a sharply defined nose and a grim mouth, held the reins firmly, staring straight ahead. "There's no holding nature back when nature has a mind," O'Connell added.

"Does it follow then," Leary offered logically, "that if the rocks are Ireland and the sea is the English, there is no holding back the English if they have a mind?"

O'Connell smiled thinly. He was suffering great fatigue. He had been on the road for a fortnight, speaking in field and church and barnyard, speaking wherever he could assemble Irishmen and women.

"There you are again with that bloody logic you learned from those French Jesuits." He breathed deeply as the battered chaise rounded a bend, leaving the frantic battle of sea and land behind them. "There is a time for logic, and there is a time for poetry. I choose at this time in this bitterest of Aprils to be poetic."

Leary's eyes twinkled, and his mouth cracked in a slight smile. The two men were comfortable together. Leary, like O'Connell, had been educated in the outlawed hedge schools sequestered in the

Kerry hills and, like O'Connell, had gone on to the Continent for further study. Both were barristers, but O'Connell was ten years the senior.

"But God, this Connemara countryside can be cruel, especially in weather like this. I miss Kerry. Do you not miss it also, Patrick?"

"Aye. It is the greenest, softest haven on this earth."

"Oh, now who is turning to poetry?" O'Connell laughed.

A flock of golden plovers, their smooth backs soaked through, seemed to blow with the wind, allowing it to take them above the grand sweep of moors that now appeared before them.

"You'll not find birds the like of them in Kerry, Patrick."

"We are a tamer county in every way, Daniel, but you're a loyal rogue, you are."

Their easy banter was suddenly disturbed by the approach of five riders. The one in the lead rode furiously, his horse seeming to fly out of the gorse. The sudden appearance of horse and rider threw the chestnut into fright, and the chaise lurched to one side, struck the muddy embankment, and slid into the muck of a peat bog.

"Why, you arrogant bastard!" O'Connell cried out in rage at the rider as the other four flew by in furious pursuit.

Patrick jumped from the listing carriage to inspect the damage. "You'll have to get out, Daniel. I can't upend it with your burly bulk inside."

O'Connell climbed down just as the rider turned his horse and trotted back. He halted a few feet from where they both stood in the muddy trench and peered at them over the horse's head. "What did you call me?" His face was red and bloated from drink.

"I called you an arrogant bastard," O'Connell roared up at the horseman.

The four other riders now drew alongside the one who was obviously in command.

"You will never say that to me again," the rider snarled, and pulled his whip out of its leather pocket below the saddle.

"Don't, John. I warn you, do not strike this man."

John Douglas turned to the voice. "God damn your eyes. Who told you to be giving the orders?"

"The man is Daniel O'Connell. Strike him, and thousands will hunt us down." Donal McCann wanted to say "hunt *you* down," but that kind of proper distinction would be foolhardy.

"Oh, I see, I see." Douglas's tone softened. "Thank you for telling me this, Donal." He smiled sarcastically down at O'Connell.

"So you are the great man who is going to lead Ireland out of its misery and poverty."

"That is exactly what I intend to do," O'Connell snapped up at him."

"And what do you think we landlords are going to do, sit back and allow it to happen?"

"You may not sit back, *foreigner*, but it will happen. It will happen." He pointed a finger for emphasis.

Patrick took one step forward and stood ramrod-straight, acting as a shield for O'Connell.

John Douglas, his jaws clamped tight in loathing, his eyes burning into O'Connell, rasped back in a voice trembling with emotion.

"You peasant Irish scum. Without us you could not survive." He snapped his reins, heeled the flanks of his mount, and said to the others, "Come, these peasants have work to do."

O'Connell watched them round the bend from which he and Patrick had just come.

"Who was that bastard, Patrick?"

"I do not know. I have not seen him skulking around at rallies like the other bloodsuckers. But I will be on the lookout for him. He appears to be a mean one."

"And wasn't that an Irishman riding with him?"

"Aye, he had Galway speech. Traitorous wretch!" Patrick answered.

"Traitor to what? To whom? If Ireland does not fight for its own independence, there is nothing to be loyal to except myth and legend. There are many wretches out there who do not know in which direction to turn."

"Daniel, sometimes your rhetoric borders on the righteous rather than the right."

"You're younger than I, my friend. The world is not all black and white. There is much gray about us, and the wise man must recognize it. Well, enough speechmaking. Let's put our shoulders to this bloody carriage and be on our way. I want to be in Clifden before tea."

Clifden, or as the Irish-speaking inhabitants called it, Clochán, overlooked the stormy Atlantic on the west and bowed under the mountainous shadows of the Twelve Bens on the east. It was the capital of Connemara, Ireland's rugged, melancholic West. Its hills were spotted with whitewashed cottages, crowned with sodden thatch and trailing gray curls of peat smoke.

Daniel and Patrick came to a halt in front of a large, sprawling stone house that sat in a cluster of hazel, birch, and hawthorn, a clandestine retreat for animal as well as man.

As they descended the carriage, the great wooden door at the entrance flew open and a red-bearded, enormous bulk of a man filled the doorway.

"Daniel O'Connell." His voice was deep but had a lyric ring as it rose out of his chest. "As I live and as I breathe, it is a blessed honor to have you at my table this bitter and savage night. Come in, my friends, and warm yourselves by the fire."

As they entered the house, tables scraped along the worn stone floor and men jumped up from their places. A spontaneous round of applause brought a flush of happy embarrassment to the Kerryman and Patrick. O'Connell acknowledged them with a wave of his hand, and when the dozen or so hard-bitten, leather-faced farmers ceased their clapping, he smiled and said, "The cheers should be for you as well. You are fighting the good fight." More cheering filled the room as the travelers shivered off their cold in front of the fire. The big man with the red beard approached them, holding two steaming pewter mugs.

"Here you be. King of the Beggars," he said affectionately. "To O'Connell's service to the poor, hot rum. It will chase the devil rain away."

"God bless your kindness on this bitter night, Padraic O'Murcada. May I introduce my friend and fellow Kerryman Patrick Leary. Patrick, the O'Murcada is the finest *seanchai* in Ireland. Will you be telling us some stories tonight, my friend?"

Padraic and Patrick shook hands, and the great red beard bristled. "Aye, I would be feeling a warm glow of honor and pride to be able to entertain Daniel O'Connell this night. But first, over here. Sit for your meal. Eat up and give the house a good name."

The meal was roughly served, but it was filling. There was an ample helping of lamb and fresh trout from the nearby lakes. The potato crop had been good from the last harvest, and although the potatoes were by this time a bit old, there was still a succulence when the hot, creamy butter flowed liberally over them.

Scones, piping hot from the hearth fire, and barley cakes with hot tea and a good dollop of poteen pushed the full stomach of O'Connell through his woolen vest.

"My gracious, but your wife is a marvel with food, Padriac. That meal was fit for a king."

"Aye, Daniel, and a king it was who partook of it. The King of the Beggars. Right, lads?" Padraic shook his red fist in the air, and the cheers resounded again.

"Are you planning on speaking to us, Daniel?" the rough voice of a farmer shouted from across the room.

"We need your message," another said.

"And your leadership," added another.

The rum and poteen and the full meal had brought on a drowsiness, but when O'Connell saw the gleam and spark of excitement and hope in their eyes, he pushed away from the table and rose to speak.

Chairs scraped again as they turned to face him, and they leaned forward in silent anticipation. He opened his vest and patted his full belly. "It's difficult for a man to speak of poverty and deprivation after a meal like that." He paused, allowing their wry smiles to fade.

"There are many Irishmen and women who do not know and have never known the immense satisfaction of a full stomach. God bless them. But for our satisfaction we thank the O'Murcada, our host and fabled storyteller." O'Connell bowed gracefully in the direction of the red-bearded giant.

"I plan on speaking to every Irishman and Irishwoman in every valley, field and village, from every hill, mountain, or donkey cart. I will speak in the fluid lyric of the Gael or the harsh cold tongue of the English. But speak I will, and heard I will be." They cheered his golden tongue, and his face, tired and drawn before, now flowed with new blood. His blue eyes flashed.

"We all know what oppression is. Did I not hear from my dear father's lips that smugglers' boats sailed up the river Kenmare in my own beloved Kerry to transport Irish lads to France and Spain in order to study in the Catholic seminaries of Europe? Catholic lads who had the sacred call to the priesthood, and they had to be smuggled out of their own Catholic Ireland. Did not many of us hide in the hedges with our outlawed books? And our schoolmaster on too many occasions flogged by English whips for imparting to us the history and poetry of Ireland? Was it not in these shrubbed and isolated retreats that we whispered the names of Patrick, Apostle of Ireland, Brian Boru, Ireland's high king, and James the Second, who, if he had kept the throne, would have seen that Irish lads had no need to leave their own beloved shores to answer the call of Almighty God. Do we not harbor silently and deep in our hearts black, venomous hatred for that devil out of hell Cromwell? Will we ever forget the slaughter of every man, woman, and child in the little village of Drogheda?"

His words echoed and rang against the stone. His listeners were mute and grim, paralyzed by his golden litany.

"And myself, even after I, with your help, won the battle for emancipation by gaining a seat in the House of Commons from County Clare, was I not denied the right to that seat because of my Catholicism? But I will not be kept down and you will not be kept down. We will succeed.

"My friends, we are gaining strength every day. Our plan for every Irishman and woman to place one penny in the weekly church collection is turning the tide. Just two weeks ago I fought the courts and magistrates in Cork City who sentenced four Irish lads to a public whipping and deportation to Australia because they had in their possession books—books of Irish history."

His voice was beginning to strain with exhaustion. "I will say no more this night, my friends. It is honored I am to speak with you, thank you."

He sat down, and their cheers and shouts washed over him. Patrick Leary nodded over at him with deep respect because he saw the lines of fatigue beneath O'Connell's eyes.

The O'Murcada came forward with a stone jug of poteen, which he passed around to the outstretched grasping hands. Then he placed a thronelike chair in the middle of the square room, sat, and faced them. He lighted his clay pipe, took a great mouthful of whiskey, reminded his listeners in the pure Gaelic, "*Is túisce deoch na scéal*"— ["The drink precedes the tale"], and began a story of ancient kings and powerful kingdoms.

And for Daniel O'Connell, sleep would come gratefully and peacefully in the low-beamed loft on this fierce night. In the weeks ahead the King of the Beggars had much to do throughout Connemara, and he could not accomplish his mission without rest.

CHAPTER IX

NOT FAR FROM where Daniel O'Connell slept, halfway between Clifden and Cloch Na Rón, one mile from the mainland, the tiny island of Inishbofin lay exposed to the continuous onslaught of the Atlantic's spring caprice.

From the stone battlements of a battered Norman castle, John Douglas studied the turbulence as he peered through the vertical slits in the west wall of the banquet room.

"This O'Connell," he said to the raging weather, "this O'Connell, he must be stopped."

A dozen men, some slumped in their heavy oak chairs, others hunched over goblets of wine and rum and mead, listened quietly.

"We have owned this island and this fort since it was granted to my father by the king, and a bloody, fat-bellied Irish peasant is not going to take it away. I am *the Douglas* now, and if I have to declare war on this politician, then I will do it." He turned slowly toward them. They all were landlords, and their combined holdings embraced most of Connemara. They listened because they knew that O'Connell was gaining strength and that the idle rabble was now being aroused by his rhetoric.

"These meetings he holds. What does he accomplish at these open rallies?"

A pink-faced man named Kirk, with little pig eyes and a broad nose, stood at the end of the table. "He talks to them, John." The man was older than John Douglas, as most of the others were, but he had respect in his voice as he quietly gave his answer. They all knew the moods that came quickly and unpredictably over the Douglas, and none wanted to ignite his fiery temper by offending him.

"He talks to them. He *talks* to them," he repeated sourly as though he had tasted something foul. "Is that all these filthy Irish do? Do they never act? Well, I tell you, my friends, if that is all they ever do, we will have no reason to worry. These peasants live in the past. They live on myth and legend."

Kirk placed his goblet on the rough-hewn table and suggested delicately, "Of course, you are correct, John, but I might add that as of late the crowds are becoming larger and the shouts for home rule are stronger. The government is referring to them as monster rallies, and I have friends in high places in London who have told me that Sir Robert Peel himself is beginning to weaken in his policy toward Ireland."

"Peel! What does he know of Ireland? Does he know what it is like to live among these swine in the wet, soggy bogs in the middle of nowhere? Well, Peel and London can have any policy they want; but we are the landlords, and if peasants cannot pay their rents or work our farms, then we will bloody well drive them into the sea."

"Aye."

"Aye, John."

"Um, of course."

"Yes, yes, of course, John," they mumbled in concert, and swallowed mightily from their mugs. John Douglas left them in the tapestried hall that boasted the coat of arms of the Douglas clan and the swords and battleaxes that had been used by ancestors at Culloden and the Battle of the Boyne.

He took the smooth stone steps three at a time in his usual show of impatience. The fort was cold and damp, and it had the brackish smell of the surrounding sea.

At the keep he heard the snarling of voices and the scuffling of heavy boots over stone. Turning into the lower corridor, he faced Roderick and Donal, who were slamming each other into the walls. The stronger Donal had good advantage as he crashed his bulk into Roderick Douglas. "I say, you can keep your filthy hands off her. She's not one of your whores." He shot a right hand out and knocked the younger Douglas to the floor. "Scottish bas—" He did not complete the curse as he saw the hovering figure of John Douglas filling the low archway, his coarse red face looking violent under the flambeaux that flickered beside him.

"Scottish what, Donal?" His voice was blade-sharp.

"Er, nothing, John. Nothing."

"Scottish bastard, was it?"

"I l-lost my head," McCann stammered. "My temper got the best of me."

"Oh, it did? Well, listen to me, you Irish scum, you had best keep your temper to yourself and your mouth shut along with it. We allow you in our company because you *are* Irish, but only because we can use you in dealing with your savage countrymen. If I tire of you or you displease me, I'll send you back to the stinking bog. You'll be worse off with your own, who will know you for what you are, a traitor."

Donal McCann stepped back, looked down at his cocked fists, and slowly loosened his knuckles. He said nothing, but anger and shame raged behind the wall of his chest.

"Now, what were you two fighting over?"

Donal remained mute. Had he spoken at that moment, the anger would have cracked his voice.

"He accused me of touching the girl. He said I was treating her like some London whore." Roderick rose from the damp grime of the floor. Blood flowed from his right nostril, and he pressed it back with his left fist. The knuckles of the fist were bloodied, and the skin was torn off.

"You are a sorry sight. You, a Douglas, and a common Irish bog-trotter brings the Douglas blood pouring out of you. Did you put your animal hands on the girl?" John Douglas moved to within inches of his younger brother. "Well, answer me, did you?" He grabbed Roderick by the tunic and repeated the question. "I said, did you?"

"Ye-yes, but he stopped me before I did anything."

"You're like a horse in heat," John Douglas shouted with vehemence into Roderick's face, and his right hand, palm open, smashed across the cheekbone, bringing more blood from the nose.

"Now listen, the two of you. I do not care if you wish to take turns with her. Her chastity is of no interest to me. But I do not want her to cause a problem with my band. If the others upstairs thought you were putting your swords into her, I would have a mutiny. So keep your blades in their sheaths until we get the McMahon, and then you can do what you like to her"—a thin smile traced his lips—"and I might just join you. Now shake hands. I'll not have my followers fighting with each other."

Each extended a hand reluctantly and nodded silently. The Douglas dismissed them with a jerk of his head and continued down the dripping passageway until he stopped in front of an oak door that was bolted from the outside. He threw the bolt, and the door swung open. He reached for the torch above the doorway, proceeded into the darkened room, and shut the door behind him.

Cathleen McMahon lay stretched out on a straw cot. He approached her rigid form.

"Well, how are we tonight, my lovely Cathleen?"

She did not answer but stared at him with narrowed eyes.

His hand reached out and glided over her breasts. He stuck the torch into its iron holder over the bed and felt her now with both hands.

"You are a fine, healthy Irishwoman, Cathleen McMahon, and I burn with desire for you."

She looked down at his exploring hands and kissed them softly.

"Now, now that is more to my pleasure."

She opened her mouth and suddenly clamped down hard with her teeth.

Pain shot through him, a stinging, searing pain that brought blood from his hand. He screamed as she bit sharply, digging her teeth into him. He finally wrenched free, striking her with his free hand as he did so.

He staggered back, squeezing the bloodied hand, tears burning his eyes.

She did not move from the cot as he held the trembling hand up. "You will pay for that. You will pay for that with your body, you unholy bitch out of hell. Do you hear me, bitch? Do you?" His voice caromed off the wet walls and along the passageways. Footsteps echoed over the stone floor and stopped at the door.

Roderick and Donal stood in the open doorway, breathing heavily.

"What? What is the matter, John?" his brother asked. "Why were you shouting?"

John Douglas swung around in a blind and furious rage.

They saw the bloodied hand and looked at each other as the Douglas swept by them.

"Lock that bloody door," he screamed as he shuffled headlong down the passageway. "Keep that bitch out of hell away from me, or I'll kill her before the McMahon comes for her."

CHAPTER X

Saint John, New Brunswick, was a teeming, swaggering port city the crooked cobblestoned streets of which housed shops jutting out of alleys and walkways, claiming to sell everything and anything.

The crowded main street spilled over with loggers who smelled of sweet spruce, Micmac and Malecite Indians bearing black shiny furs over their backs, fishermen and trappers and hunters whose wagons listed like sailing ships under an abundance of moose, rabbit, deer, fish, and pelts.

The city had a strange mixture of scents. Salt water, fish, game, and wood—all came rising up at them as Brendan and Totem Paul made their way through the jostling, pushing, brawling, shouting waves of humanity.

"I think it be better in my own deep woods of Acady than this place. Too much noise." Paul placed his two meaty paws over his ears and rolled his round brown eyes.

Brendan threw back his black, curly head and laughed, his laughter lost in the noisy bartering of pelt for fish and fish for fur.

Here it was as always, the sea and land at odds, one continuously giving in to the other. "Come, we will go to the docks to see if Robert Fraser and the *Aileen Donan* are anyplace to be found."

Along the long wooden wharves brigantine, schooner, and barque lay at anchor, hovering over and crowding the smaller shallops and sloops. The colors of foreign flags flapped in the April afternoon, while the puffed-out sheets of square sail billowed and whipped from brig and barquentine alike.

The sea air was crisp, and it pulsed new life in them. Their journey had been exhausting. Overland it had taken a little more than a week, but they had slept out in the open and lived on what fish they caught or squirrel they trapped.

Scanning the harbor, Brendan saw no sign of the *Aileen Donan*, but he motioned Paul to follow as he explored the forest of tall masts that split the sky.

"Not here," he said dejectedly. "He's not here."

"Cheer up, Irishman, we go to wet our lips, and make us feel good inside, n'est-ce pas?"

Brendan looked at the hundreds of idling vessels and then back at Paul's artless, beaming smile. "I agree. I have a hellish thirst, and I know a public house that serves good liquor."

They threaded their way through the docks and climbed the hill to the center of town. It was market day, so the bustling town was even more frolicksome and full of vitality than usual.

The Royal Scotsman bulged with seafaring humanity. Shiny black-skinned mariners from the Caribbean sporting gleaming gold earrings, firm-jawed Scandinavians with hair the color of wheat, sanguine-faced Scots, and lithe English—all jostled and bellied up to the crudely fashioned bar.

Four Yanks out of Nantucket chorused sea chanties, while various groups joined in raucous games of darts, ring toss, or arm wrestling.

"I learned a valuable lesson in this pub doing just that," Brendan said to Paul as he nodded in the direction of two salty titans locked in each other's grips like horned combatants in a primeval jungle struggle.

This was a world of flesh and muscle and sweat, of men who made their money by the strength of their arms and backs. A grimy, rollicking world of sea yarns, briney exaggerations of foreign ports and dark, midnight women, all told in the patois of the sailing man.

Paul moved toward the bar, reached for two tankards of ale with one hand, and grabbed off a bottle of rum with the other. Brendan waited at a corner table, studying the scene around him. The drinkers at the bar murmured at Paul's giant size and then returned to their grog.

"What lesson did you learn at the arm wrestling, Irishman?"

Brendan drank from the bottle, swallowing rum that was as black as tar and then drowning the flames with a chaser of ale.

"Good God"—he smacked the fire away with his lips—"that's damn healthy grog. What lesson?" he asked. "I learned not to jump, not to be impetuous. I lost the match, but I won an education. I learned to size up my opponent." He smiled in reflection, and then suddenly the smile died on his lips as a forearm as big as a tree stump was wrapped around his neck from behind.

He felt powerless, and Paul, in the middle of quaffing his rum, spit it out in a black spray as he kicked back his chair and lunged for Brendan's attacker. His right hand shot out, catching the man flush on the chin and toppling him to the floor like a fallen oak. Brendan turned quickly to the figure who was dragging himself slowly to his feet as Paul was about to reach down and smash the man's head over his bent knee.

"No. No," Brendan shouted. "Jesus, man. He is my friend, Paul. Let him be."

By now the room had closed in on the trio. "He has strange way of showing he is your friend," Paul roared.

Brendan reached down and grabbed the man's outstretched hand. "Eamon, Eamon, old friend."

"Old friend indeed! Where the hell did you get him?" He gestured at Paul, gingerly rubbing the point of his chin. "He's as big as a building, McMahon."

The crowd broke up and returned in disappointment to the bar.

"Aye, he is that. Come. Sit."

Eamon forced a smile. "Do I dare to sit at the same table with the bloke?"

"Paul, this is Eamon. We sailed on the *Aileen Donan* together. He's Robert Fraser's first mate."

Eamon Fitzgerald pulled a barrel head up to the table, sat, and swallowed thirstily from the bottle of rum.

"I'm not sure that I'm happy to meet you like this, Paul. Maybe you and I will have a go another time. But McMahon is my friend, and we must not let anything spoil that." He shook Paul's hand with a powerful grip that brought a respectful smile to the Acadian's mouth. "*Oui*, another time. *Très bien*. Be good. Be good, eh?"

Brendan quickly jumped in. "Eamon, where is Robert? I looked all along the quays, but the ship was nowhere to be found."

"Well, lad, number one, I am no longer the first mate, and number two, I expect them in port tonight or tomorrow at the latest. They made a short haul of lumber to Boston."

"What do you mean, you are no longer mate? You were the most trusted man Robert Fraser had except for John Wallace."

"Aye, lad, do not trumpet it in my ear. I am embarrassed enough about it. The night before we were to sail for Edinburgh I met a delicious little Indian girl. We drank our way up and down Saint John, and I found myself nursing a bloody skull the next afternoon. It wasn't until I was fully sober that I remembered the ship was sailing with the tide. Needless to say, by the time I reached her mooring there was nothing left but a snaky pile of rope. Oh, Brendan, lad, I was sicker then than I had ever been from a night of drink. I waited every day on those wharves until she came to port a month later."

"Well, what did Robert say?" Brendan almost stammered in his excitement.

"He told me he expected loyalty from his shipmates. When a man is to sail, there is no excuse except death—his own—for not being aboard."

"This Fraser, he is one hard man, eh?"

Eamon narrowed his eyes in Paul's direction. "Robert Fraser is the best blasted captain on the open sea. The man was right. I let him down, and now I'm paying for it."

Paul nodded, appreciating the code of loyalty that one man showed another.

"But tell me about yourself, Brendan. What brings you back? What happened in the States?"

Brendan told him about finding Mary in the Evansborough Mills and the strikes and incurring Channing Evans's wrath and their eventual escape along the canals and up to New Hampshire and the flight to Canada. And then this rescue attempt.

"And you say that old John Wallace is back at the homestead?"

"Aye. It was a tonic to see his white head again."

"He's quite a man, he is. But to get back to this mad plan of yours, do you really think you have a chance at rescuing your sister? I hate to say this, lad, but she could be dead by now."

Brendan rubbed a farmer's hand through his black, curly hair. "I've thought of that, Eamon, but I do not think so. This Douglas wants me, and he knows if he harmed her to the point of death, the word might out and I would not come to rescue a dead sister. Of course, he would be wrong because if that ever did happen, I would hunt him until I had his red skull in my hands." He clenched his large hands into fists.

"All right, lad. All right, relax. I'm sure you and this great broth of a man know what you are about. Come, let's go find you a place to stay for the night."

They slept long and well under the broad beams of a brothel that hung out over the green waters of the harbor. The fresh air of the ocean blew in on them and coaxed them awake.

"Come, Paul, we must find Eamon and be off."

Brendan tapped on several doors until the bearded Eamon stumbled to the door and opened it. Brendan caught sight of the naked body of a sultry and bronzed Indian girl squirming around on the bed. "Come back to bed, Eamon. Come and say good morning to me."

Eamon smiled sheepishly. "Wait a moment, lad. I'll just be putting my pants on." And he closed the door softly.

They waited for him on the cobblestone sidewalk. In the sky a legion of screeching hungry gulls dived and plunged toward the aquamarine bay in search of food.

"Come along, lads, we're off."

The harbor was alive with color and activity.

"There, there she is, sitting as pretty as a picture. You see her, Brendan?"

Brendan's heart raced, and the blood came to his cheeks. "Aye, I see her."

The *Aileen Donan*, free of her cargo, rose up in the water, a proud, buxom, undulating woman of the sea, bowing to no man or ship, her white skin like a cold, textured ivory, haughty and aloof. Her lines curved gracefully from prow to stern. They approached slowly.

Brendan saw Robert Fraser on the bow, resting his elbows on the taut ropes and peering out at the wharf rats below pulling line and hoisting cargo.

For a moment Fraser seemed to freeze, and then slowly his face brightened and broke into an enormous smile. "Brendan," he shouted, "Brendan, what a sight! God, lad," he kept shouting as he trotted down the gangway, "what a sight for these sea-weary eyes." The two embraced like wrestlers.

"Let me look at you, lad. I think you've put on a few stone, and you've been doing some outside work. You have the soil back in your face. Good lad. Welcome. Come, your mates will want to see you. And your friend, too. Paul, you say. God, man, you're as big as a ship. Come."

They followed, and Brendan turned slowly around to see Eamon hanging onto the tow line of a Caribbean barque. Robert Fraser walked briskly along, and as he ascended the wooden gangway, he shouted over his shoulder, "Tell my first mate to stop loitering and shake himself awake. There's work to be done aboard."

Eamon straightened out of his dejection, a smile breaking across his face, and bounded after them.

"Aye, Captain. Aye, sir."

After the reunion, over a mug of hot coffee, Brendan explained his mission to Robert Fraser, who leaned forward and patted him on the knee. "Our destination is Belfast, north of where you are going, but rest assured we will have you back in Ireland in a fortnight."

Two days later, as a lashing rain ripped along the shoreline, whipping the waves into a frothy, boiling foam, the *Aileen Donan* plowed out of Saint John, her lithe body mounting wave after wave, taking all the sea had to offer and still thrusting her prow forward for more.

Brendan stood with Paul on the rain-tattooed deck, watching tree and soil and rock and bird slowly fade into the wet mist. His heart was as heavy as stone. Somewhere back there, beyond the valleys and farms, Mary Roark McMahon dug in the wet red clay, scratching and clawing new life into the spring soil.

"I know you are sad, *mon ami*, I can feel it like a thing to be touched. But no mind, you will see them again. Trust the Frenchman, eh?"

"Aye, I will trust the Frenchman," Brendan murmured to the wind. "Aye, I will that."

CHAPTER XI

Spring roamed the shimmering Northumberland Strait, and with its arrival, cabin doors opened on a fresh golden world. All along the Tignish coast men and women bent over their fields, bodies pulsating with the joy of spring. The long dark days and nights with people locked inside gloomy cabins were over. Another winter had passed, and the glaring, sunburst world lay stretched before farmer and Indian like a green and delicious delicacy to be savored and enjoyed.

For Mary, of course, there was the vast loneliness and emptiness. True, spring had arrived and touched even her waning spirits. But was this what she had left Ireland for, a rutted clay-packed farm on the tip of an island that fell off into the sea? Had not her goal been the city? Fancy clothes, a bonnet tied coquettishly beneath her proud chin? And hadn't she attained her goal when she successfully gained employment in the Evansborough Mills? Her ambivalent feelings for the young and arrogant millowner stabbed at her as she recalled their bittersweet romance. God, had she made the right choice? Surely she loved Brendan. But Brendan was a farmer. Had he tricked her in bringing her to this wretched outpost? Back in her village in Galway she had long decided to break from this bondage to the earth. What had an Irish farm ever offered her or her family? They could not even own their land. Ownership. The thought of owning their patch here on the island, that thought alone helped ease the depression that clutched fiercely at her heart and soul.

Good God, with Brendan gone, the farm was her responsibility. Physically she was as sturdy and as strong as any woman, and many a man for that matter. But her loneliness, her complete and desperate plight, depressed her so fully that it sapped her strength.

In the nights after Brendan left, she lay listening to the water lapping against the cape, idly dreaming of the girls she had met in the mills. They were independent Yankee girls who were eager to learn, to grow, to join a world that was changing. Florilla Russell, for example, just a little older than she, but so much wiser and educated

to the ways of an industrialized society. It was Florilla who had called
for the strike that turned the tide and brought the raises and the better
hours and improved working conditions. It had been exciting, and she
had felt her bosom swelling with pride, her face flush with excitement
when she decided she, too, Mary Roark, of Oranmore, County Galway,
Ireland, could be a force in a world that had always been ruled by
men.

She shifted her head into the wind, and the breeze tossed her
raven hair casually in little webs against her face. That excitement
was gone from her life. She was back to the earth. It was as though
her stars had planned it that way. Give the upstart country-fresh farm
girl a taste of modern living, and just when she has swallowed long
and deep from the glass, uproot her, send her packing north to a
windy hill and a barren field.

The wind carried the sound of her name, and with it came the
smell of burning wood. She waved limply in the direction of John
Wallace, whose wide face smiled at her as he waved back.

John had already cleared much of the birch-lined back pasture,
and now he was burning the slash that glutted the fields. Soon, as the
stumps rotted and were pulled out and burned, the land would be
plowed and the potatoes would be planted. And the hope of a good
harvest would carry John and the rest of the islanders through the
backbreaking days that lay ahead.

At least she had John, she thought. She had his strength and
wisdom, and for that she was thankful. Yet with her gratitude was
mixed a subtle resentment of which she was ashamed. For it was his
generosity to Brendan, his bequest of land, that had brought them
here in the first place.

Bill Profitt and his boys also dug out stumps and burned them,
and the smoke trailed in a tranquil curl out to the dunes beyond the
tall, long-rooted marram grass. The smoke passed leisurely over the
deep bays and tidal inlets, eventually disappearing down east of the
promontory on which she stood. Micmac canoes lay beached in the
sun. The Micmacs had come back, as though answering some deep,
instinctive call, and now they worked their own tribal patches alongside Scot and Irish and Frenchman.

But with all this seasonal rejuvenation came the thaw, turning the
earth to red mud that sucked obscenely underfoot and spotted and
streaked the wide flooring of the cabin and the hanging-out-to-dry
blankets and sheets that puffed and clapped in the breeze. It was as
though some ugly devil hand had smeared all in sight with its bloodied
talons.

On this balmy, wind-washed morning, drier than the previous
misty days that were so reminiscent of Ireland, Mary kicked at the
muddy patches, loosening the soil with the toe of her boot. Up the
road, Gabriella lay asleep in the quiet, noiseless shadows of the cabin.

Behind John Wallace, in the hollow next to a fresh-water brook,
his two-room dwelling was showing signs of completion. He had

worked on it not with the quick hands of youth, but with the steady, measured care of age. He was pleased with the location. Perched on a grassy knoll with a rolling dingle of thick grass below, the house had an uninterrupted view of the water. He would be able, in time, to sit in his chair by the window and watch the seasonal caprice of the waves moodily turning from vibrant, tossing green to pacific blue and somber gray. The Strait would sparkle and roll and jump before him, and he would teach Gabriella, as she sat in his lap, its subtle nuances so that she would know it and respect it as one should respect a formidable adversary. The Strait could turn its icy back on the huddled cabins in winter or topple the unwise sailor from his birch craft with one powerful swing of its watery fist in stormy spring. It would be good to teach the growing child.

His short-handled ax cut crisply through the white wood, and his heart held an inner contentment that was almost complete. The one black, nagging thought was of Brendan. John was not a prayerful man. His Scots ancestry was fundamentalist Presbyterian, and there were occasions when he did not understand the fetishes, as he called them, of the Catholic French and Irish.

There was the strong-willed Mary with her statue of a bleeding Christ and her long string of wooden beads, which she prayed over nightly.

No, he did not understand, and it did not make a difference. He loved these two children and their lovely little Gabriella. He was not prayerful in an orthodox way, but now, as he waved again at the windblown figure two chains of land away, he said simply, "Father in heaven, protect the lad from harm. Amen."

The sun climbed higher, giving an additional touch of warmth to the thawing landscape. Red fox and rabbit and squirrel were nudged from their winter haunts. It was good to be alive and healthy.

The fires that smoked all along the North Cape gave a sense of security to the day, and John felt it deeply as he sniffed the pungent ash.

Then, in the midst of his labors, he suddenly stopped; an unearthly silence seemed all at once to have descended on the cape. Squirrel and fox and rabbit were silent in the noonday. The chirping of wood thrush seemed strangled in mid-song.

John felt a trembling up the back of his spine as he straightened. He frowned, the lines running deep into his leathery forehead, and with squinting eyes and a puzzled look, he raised his head to listen to the oppressive silence. Then, as though on cue from some unseen baton, the silence broke into a squealing, squeaking chorus bursting from the groves of birch and shrub and hedge that stretched to the highroad and far beyond.

John turned toward the sound and waited in horror, sudden understanding causing his pulse to quicken and his heart to pump more rapidly.

The sun and spring thaw had awakened other inhabitants of the woods as well. The snow melting from the woodpiles and the heaped-up stacks of hay and Irish moss dripped like a warm and welcome liquid, disturbing creatures that, having hibernated throughout the dark, cold winter, now squirmed hungrily to life, squealing forth from rotted tree trunks and wood dwellings.

At first it was only the squealing that he heard, but as the sound rose to a shrieking pitch, the fields were suddenly filled with the tiny black bodies of field mice. They poured in ravenous columns onto the fields, devouring the new grass with a voracious greed that left only bare soil in their wake.

His mouth went dry. He tried desperately to swallow. Words formed on his lips, but he had difficulty shouting them. His heart pounded louder in his ears until he thought its thunder would split his eardrums. Finally, he managed to shout to Mary, who was looking idly out to sea, "Mary, Mary, mice. Field mice. Go back to the cabin. Go back!"

She turned to him and then to the swarming fields. It was too late; the path between the two fields was a black, furry cluster of thousands of squirming, creeping rodents.

Mary's eyes opened wide in terror. "Oh, Mother of Christ, help us." As she shrieked her prayer to the heavens, the roving columns, their little teeth knifing through the grass, clung to her long skirt and covered her laced boots. Her world spun dizzily before her, and she felt herself losing her balance. God, she could not fall. She must not. If she fell to the ground, they would cover her body in seconds. She summoned all the strength she could and began kicking them from her boots and snapping her skirt, flinging the beasts in squeaking flight. They were so filthy-looking they brought a shivering to her voice as she backed away from them. "Ahhhh, ahhhh, ahhhhh, ahhhhh," was all she could say as she swiped and flailed away.

The more she fought, the more quickly they advanced. If they kept up their tenacious attack, she would have to jump the thirty-odd feet to the sand below.

Suddenly, Bill Profitt's voice broke through the shrieking. She looked over her shoulder to see him and his sons racing through the tall grass, wading hip-high through the black, furry bodies, smashing at them with long sticks, shouting at her, "This way. Mary. This way."

She stumbled off in their direction as the nibbling rodents tore at her dress and climbed and fell over each other, their short, black, wirelike tails swinging in agitation and impatience. It was as though some unseen piper were controlling them, urging them on with some monstrous tune.

Sweat ran in streaks down her cheeks as she joined the Profitts, still wailing her shivering "ahhhhhh."

"Mary, get hold of yourself. You'll be all right," Bill commanded. "Come out of it, woman. Snap out of it." But he could see she was in some kind of shock, and all his words would be of no avail. He tried shaking her, but she continued her blank, glazed stare until he struck her fiercely across the face with the open palm of his right hand. She sprang to life then, shaking her head as though waking from a bad dream.

She rubbed her stinging face, bewildered for a moment. "Oh, good God, Mr. Profitt, is it the end of the world?"

"Mice, Mary, so hungry they will eat anything in sight. Their number must be so large they cannot feed themselves. The thaw has brought them down on us."

"Good God, what are we to do?" Her eyes, no longer fixed in horror, moved now as the black, clumsy bodies crept and darted and stumbled, their squeaking one great shriek from one end of the cape to the other.

The people of the valley fought back as best they could, smashing, banging, striking at the tiny bodies. Fires blazed and fields faded behind clouds of smoke.

"Come, lads, light your torches," Bill shouted to his boys. Like acolytes, they held their lighted staffs in front of them and tossed them into the screeching hordes.

"Good. Now take the high ground on the cape until the wind takes the fire west."

They climbed the bald knoll of earth and jagged rock that jutted out to the Strait and watched as the fire was caught by the wind and dug itself into the dry straw below the thick marram grass.

Clouds of smoke blew in ghostly waves; the vanguard of the unswerving, marching legions of mice faltered and burned, flames and smoke suffocating them, yet they persisted in their tenacious wedge of attack until they reached the sandy borders of the fields and fell into the icy waters, their full bellies bloated and burning as they drowned in the midday tide.

Below the ridge where Mary stood with the Profitts, John Wallace smashed wildly at the unrelenting battalions until his hands were bloody. Rodents climbed his legs and tore at his woolen trousers. He began a slow but steady retreat to the cabin, striking at everything in his path with weary arms, his breath choking in his throat. A pain shot up his left arm, and his mouth was as dry as paper.

Gradually gaining ground on the mice, he reached his cabin and yanked open the heavy storm door. He ran to his bed and tore a blanket from the rumpled mattress, ripped it apart with his bleeding hands, and tied it to a shovel. He soaked the cloth with oil from the lamp and torched it from the smoldering fireplace. It caught almost instantly, and he wielded it above his head and raced outside, where he hurled it into the rapacious pack eating its way toward him. The grass caught, and smoke and flame ripped across the field in a gray and orange fury, roaring headlong into the Profitt fire. The entire cape was now an inferno, a conflagration that spiraled and rolled in the wind that flew out to the Strait.

The sound of crackling bodies and the whimpering squeals of dying rodents echoed throughout the valley.

John turned to see still another phalanx of the enemy veering off to his cabin and the open door. "No, no, you bloody bastards. Not my house. Stay out of my house."

His chest was heaving with emotion and exertion as he stumbled after the filthy little nibbling creatures. But his right foot found a hole left from a dislodged stump, and he fell, his ankle twisted under him. The horde, fire-singed and smoking, continued its instinctive surge. Their sickening black bodies, tails as stiff as masts, crawled over the fallen man, biting and chewing with their tiny teeth until he bled from his face and torso. He lay, breathing rapidly, unable to move. A sudden pain raced up his left arm, and a tremendous blow smashed hard against his heart. He rolled over, trying to brush the devilish monsters from his face, but his arm was too heavy. He saw a patch of blue sky, and then there was a second stab of pain in his chest and everything turned black.

The fields along the cape erupted in booming, gusting flame, and a mixture of French curses, Micmac supplication, and Anglo commands filled the air as the flaming rodents continued their fiery surge over the bluffs and into the Northumberland Strait. Dead and smoking bodies floated on the tips of the waves. And those that did not make the water's edge blackened the red clay shore for miles and miles up and down the strand.

Mary and Bill and his sons stood exhausted, breathing with difficulty in the wake of the billowing smoke. They coughed uncontrollably, and their faces, black with soot and streaked with sweat, were worn and haggard. The rampage was over, and all that was left of the green, moist valley were charred, blackened hillocks and the stench of burning flesh.

Mary breathed fast and hard, her words choking in her throat. "Will they—will they be back, Mr. Profitt?" she managed.

"No, Mary, they won't come again. At least not this year. Maybe next. And if not mice, it could be locusts or grasshoppers or scald. This is hard country, Mary. It is not easy to own a piece of this land. But we will win out in the end." He smiled, and his good, open face lit up.

And then, in a sudden flash of memory, Mary blurted out, "Jesus, Mary, and Joseph. Gabriella! I just remembered Gabriella. My God, I must go to her." She lifted her skirts and ran down the brow of the cape, through the smoke, in the direction of the cabin.

"Go with her lads," Bill commanded his sons, "and Mary," he called after her, "be careful of the fires. The wind is changing." She heard him but paid no heed as she raced in a direct route to the house. Her sudden fear, worse than the mice or the fires, drove her on. Flames flew up at her, and she brushed them away with battered hands. The hem of her skirt was singed and smoking, and everywhere underfoot were the thousands of dead mice, their glassy eyes peering up at her as from some child's horrible nightmare.

She lurched forward onto the little side porch and threw open

the door. Her hands flew up to her face in terror as she saw hundreds
of the furry beasts swarming across the floor. The baby's crib was
infested with squirming black bodies that clung to each other like
bees in a hive. Her throat constricted as she tore into them, flailing at
them and shaking their filthy bodies from the blanket.

She clutched the baby in her arms and kicked the crib with her
boot. It rolled over, and mice toppled from the blankets and slipped
and crawled on clumsy, flat paws across the floor.

"Oh, oh, you filthy black scum. You bloody bastards." She
screamed and shouted and cursed for courage as Seth Profitt ran
past her with a fiery stick and forced the rodents into the hearth or
out through the open door.

His younger brother, swept the bodies off into the fields as Bill
torched the land adjacent to the cabin.

For the rest of the day they watched the burning fields, smoke
spiraling in billowing circles from Nail Pond, Tignish, and all the way
past St. Louis out to Miminegash Harbour.

"They must have eaten their way clear across the cape, Pa," Seth
the tall, rawboned towhead, said to Bill.

"They'll be floating in the water for days. I've seen the time when
there were so many of 'em that boats had trouble plowing through
their bloated bodies. Hold on now, Seth," he said, suddenly nodding
in the direction of John Wallace's cabin.

Three Micmac men wearing the skins of the winter hunt on Cape
Breton Island approached, carrying John's blackened body.

Bill shook his head sadly as the oldest Indian crossed himself and
stepped back. The two younger ones gently placed the body on the
ground in front of the cabin.

They all turned to Mary, who leaned in the open doorway. Her
blue eyes brimmed over with tears as she went to the lifeless form.
Kneeling, she wiped the dirt and grime from his face and lowered
her head to kiss John Wallace on the cheek. She stroked the white
hair and brushed it back from his forehead. Then she rose and stepped
back.

"Holy Mother of God, bless this good and gentle man. Son of
God, suffering Christ, protect this dear and good man for all eternity."

The wind silently blew the smoke out to the Strait. There was a
hush in the fields.

"Nearest priest is at Malpeque," the oldest Indian said solemnly,
breaking the quiet. He was the Micmac chief, and he had fished the
great waters and hunted the dark woods with John Wallace years
before.

"I know," Bill Profitt answered, his voice betraying his sorrow. "I
think John would want you to say the prayers for the dead, Padenuque. You and him was like brothers, eh?"

The chief narrowed his eyes, and the only lines in his olive face
appeared like bird scratches that stretched to the temples.

He was not a man given to public tears, and it would be un-
seemly if he were to sob openly in front of the two younger members

of his tribe. So he narrowed his eyes as though in pain until he knew he was in control.

"It would be my honor, Bill Profitt. My honor. Come, lift him to your shoulders. We will find a place untouched by fire. We will face him to the sea he loved so much."

The string of mourners passed through the black, smoldering fields, and the ugly hand of despair closed over Mary. The day that had begun with such promise was now a depressing midnight of gloom. Around her, devastation and death curled up from the ravaged fields in a smoking stench, and up ahead of her, his arms hanging limply as he was carried to his final rest, John Wallace, her only hope, her only support and protection, lay dead. The finality seemed to crush the very breath of life from her.

In the two weeks that followed John Wallace's death, Mary was like a creature driven mad by some intangible, satanic force. Voices whispered to her in the night. The voice of her father back in Galway counseled her in a soft, gentle tone to come home. Brendan instructed her to be firm and courageous, reminding her that it was only in the ownership of land that a family could attain dignity. There was also the thin voice of Abigail Parsons, the Yankee farm girl whom Mary had befriended in Evansborough. They had been closer than sisters, these two young women from such divergent, often warring cultures. It was Abby, dead of consumption, who spoke to Mary in her blackest hours. It was the voice from the grave. There were so many voices. Sometimes they all shouted into her ears at once, like some demented chorus of keening banshees.

The one voice she tried desperately, but unsuccessfully, to discern above all the others was that of Florilla Russell, the leader of the Evansborough mill strike, the strongest woman Mary had ever met. It was Florilla, who had candidly told Mary to stop feeling sorry for herself after Abigail died, to stand up and be counted, to be tough and independent. It was this voice she tried to hear and tried to follow, but in the din of madness that roared through her head she could not grasp its message.

With the voices came the memories: Evansborough and the young mill owner, Channing Evans. He was handsome in a sharp, craggy way, with a lean body and confident stride. Had he been so cruel really? To be sure, he had allowed the Irish canal laborers and their families to live in worse squalor than the tinkers of Ireland. But wasn't that really the fault of the lazy, good-for-nothing, drinking, brawling Irishmen for whom she felt such disdain and disgust?

If she had remained and assimilated herself into the Yankee world, would she not have captured Channing Evans as a husband? No. She shook her head violently as she thought: Do not delude yourself as you sit on the edge of the world here on this Godforsaken island of red clay. No, he would never have taken a Galway farm girl for a wife. But who knows? She might have become his mistress. He would have seen that she was well clothed and well fed. She blanched at the realization that she was reducing herself to the depths of prostitution. Her religion, her upbringing warred inside her as she secretly admitted that if she had the decision to make now, at this moment in her forlorn life, she would sell her love for material comfort.

It happened, too, that during those long nights the voices would be interrupted by the deep, hacking cough of her child, tenaciously sucking the air for breath. Only the choking cough stilled the voices and brought mother and child together in the midnight gloom of the cabin, slowly rocking the night away.

And so it was on this particular morning, as Mary half-somnolently rocked her Gabriella back and forth, back and forth, that another voice called out to her. "Mary? Mary? Are you awake?" Isabella Profitt peered in over the open half of the Dutch door.

Mary started in momentary alarm and shook herself awake. "Oh, forgive me, Mrs. Profitt, the baby cried most of the night. Her cough is getting worse. It's the croup." Mary rose slowly from the rocker. She seemed feeble, old, unable to move with any dexterity. Isabella knew the signs of depression well. Hadn't she, too, suffered from it her first year on the island?

"Do you have any grease, Mary?"

"I do, Mrs. Profitt. I do. In that tub near the hearth."

"Good. Here, give over Gabriella to me. That's the lovely girl. There now. Gabriella and Isabella. Our names are like a song."

Isabella Profitt opened the child's woolen nightie and applied the goose grease to her chest in a soothing and gentle rotating motion as Mary watched in a strangely detached way. Then Isabella tore off a piece of wool from the hem of her skirts, covered the baby's chest, buttoned her gown, and placed her back in the cradle.

"Sit, Mary."

Mary stumbled back to the rocker. It was as though she were paralyzed from shock or stroke.

"I brought us some tea, Mary. We shall sip a bit and chat. I'll just boil some water here." The fire was gray and lifeless with just a hint of flame.

"Let me poke your fire a bit, Mary. It seems to have given up its life. Fires are like people, you know: They have to be given attention, and they have to breathe and glow. They must be active." Wisps of smoke stirred in the ash, and red points of flame appeared as Isabella turned and approached the rocker. She placed her hand gently on Mary's shoulder. "That fire was all but dead. Don't you think it's about time we brought it back to life? If only so the baby might feel its warmth?" Her soft Northumberland accent rose and fell in the morning stillness of the cabin, interrupted only by Gabriella's contented breathing.

Mary's hands came suddenly to her face, and she began shaking uncontrollably, her sobs robbing her of air and almost throwing her into convulsions. All the sadness of the past, the long Canadian nights alone, the disappointments, despair, and frustration erupted from her bent and trembling body.

Isabella busied herself at the hearth, allowing this most necessary of purgations. The fire responded in orange flame to her quick hands, and the room took on a warm glow.

"There, I think we have life again," Isabella intoned softly, and then turned to Mary, whose sobbing had ceased. "Feel better?"

"Oh, I am so ashamed, Mrs. Profitt. So very ashamed."

"There is nothing to be ashamed of, Mary, and please, for heaven's sake, call me Isabella. Bill and I are neighbors, and I hope we will be neighbors for a long time to come." She lowered the iron pot over the fire, smiling. "I remember my first year on the island. I never had a dry eye, and *I* had a husband with me." She continued to build the fire with thicker chunks of wood while she talked.

"I want you to know that you have us, all of us. How do you think we managed through the frost and snow and droughts? I remember once after a terrible blight we had only the last year's rotten potatoes to eat and I was seven months along with Seth. I was weak and tired and full of despair and I was looking out at the rolling Strait, wishing I were on a ship back to England, when I saw a Micmac steal up to the house and leave a long pole by the entrance. At first I was afraid to go see what it was, and Bill was in the fields. But I screwed up my courage and went out. Attached to the pole were five freshly killed rabbits. Oh, we had such a stew that night. I remember we both cried as we enjoyed that repast. Now that Micmac became one of our dearest friends. He was like a brother to John Wallace, and he will be like a father to you. But he must know that you wish help. He is a very sensitive and shy man."

Mary looked up for the first time. She seemed more composed and soothed by the graceful offer of help.

"You mean Padenuque?"

"Yes, Padenuque. He is a marvelous Christian man, very devoted to his people and to God. So you see we are islanders—Acadian, English, Scots, and Indian—and islanders help one another." She patted Mary's hand, and Mary, in a sudden burst of affection and gratitude, took Isabella's hand and rubbed it against her tear-stained cheek.

"All right, Mary McMahon, now let us have that cup of tea."

Early the next morning a hunched figure began to dig up the moist earth with a one-handled wooden plow. She stopped momentarily and wiped her brow with the back of her hand. Her hair was pinned back, severe but practical, and the wind did not disturb it.

Out in the strait blue herons played on the tips of the waves. She watched for a moment and then returned to her plow and her field.

CHAPTER XII

THE YELLOW LIGHT of a deck lantern danced giddily along the deck of the *Aileen Donan* in the chilled wind of early June, and the night tide lapped against her wooden sides as Robert Fraser, Eamon, Totem Paul, and Brendan hugged the dark shadows in a futile attempt to retreat from the inevitable. Fraser cleared his throat and said almost coldly, in a sharp, curt command, "All right, if you are to be off, then be about it. There be no sense in dragging your boots. Come now, be quick."

"Aye, aye," they grumbled into their chests, and stalked resolutely to the wide plank that connected the bobbing ship to the wharf.

Fraser, unable to conceal his fondness for Brendan, called out apprehensively, "Be careful, Brendan. Take care of him, Frenchman, you hear me."

Brendan turned and offered a half wave, then ducked under taut ropes and bounced quickly down the shaky plank.

"We be very careful Captain Fraser, sir," Totem Paul roared back.

As Fraser watched them disappear into the sea mist that drifted along the quays, Eamon turned to his captain. Fraser, reading the unspoken question in his mate's wild eyes, said simply, "Yes. Go. You've been wanting to ask me for weeks. Go and Godspeed."

Without a word, Eamon raced along the deck and down the plank and was engulfed almost immediately in fog and mist.

Robert Fraser smiled from the shadows as Eamon's deep voice echoed along the dock. "Hey, Brendan, and you, you French mountain, wait for me. I'll lend you some real help."

They would start south at once. It was wiser to travel in darkness. The highroads were well populated with itinerants and wayfarers, gypsies and tinkers, starving families, and those being sought by the British for having stolen corn or grain to see them through another day. It would be best to avoid social intercourse, especially when they approached Galway, for surprise was their most powerful weapon. They must surprise the Douglas if they hoped to free Cathleen—if, please God, she was still alive.

It was this thought that sustained Brendan in the first week as they worked their way south. As he lay in a heaped-up field or wheat-stacked barn, he tried to ease Mary and Gabriella from his mind by allowing himself the luxury of a powerful fantasy, the rescue of his dear sister. There were nights, though, that saw the black fates and terrors visiting him in legions. He would awake with a start, shouting her name, and Paul or Eamon would cover his mouth with a mighty hand. Yes, the fear was there, the real, plausible fear that she could be dead. If so, of course, he would hunt the Douglas until he found him—"and if it takes a lifetime, then so be it," he muttered into the dark.

On the sixth day of their journey they rested by the side of the highroad in the thick, tangled hedgerows that grew in deep, impenetrable clusters on the outskirts of Galway City and feasted on the wild red berries that were abundant in this southern neck of Ireland.

Caravans passed throughout the day, and occasionally a pair of horsemen sporting English saddles and gleaming, diamond-studded riding crops that slapped and stung the sweating flanks of their mounts.

"The bloody bastards," Brendan hissed as they flew by, leaving the brown dust curling in dry wisps behind them. His mouth and tongue seemed to drip blood as he sucked on the red juice of a fat red berry. He gestured from his prone position with a berry red finger. "Those bloody bastards are raping this country, and when they've taken all there is to take, they will leave us starving and dying."

At that moment a jaunty, pinched-faced horseman flashed by in pursuit of the others, and with no provocation, he snapped out his whip at the driver of an approaching tinker caravan. The driver's hand flew up to his face in immediate pain.

"You see? You see that? God damn his English eyes. You see what I mean? They sport with us. We are their playthings."

"Easy, lad," Eamon soothed.

Paul, crouching low on his giant haunches, snapped a gnarled branch in his dirty hands. "Like this, I snap their English necks. Just like this," and the branch cracked in the silent grove.

"Hush," Brendan whispered hoarsely. His anger was stilled and replaced now by a smile as three other caravans passed. "Jesus, that's Greta and Nicholas. We are in luck, lads. God has smiled on us this day. Come, we must be quick. Those tinkers are my friends. They will hide us. Come, be quick, I say."

He crawled out of the dense grove and trotted up the trail, Paul and Eamon barreling along behind him.

When he reached the clearing, he was beyond the caravans, and he waited until the first one had passed before cupping his hands and yelling in staccato bursts, "*Nicholas, Nicholas, Nicholas.*" The driver of the second caravan jerked his head up from a half sleep and pulled up on the reins, halting the filthy, mud-spattered horse.

"What? Who be you?" the driver asked cautiously. And then the grin, the wide grin, appeared beneath the dust and grime. "Brendan, you rogue, Brendan McMahon." He leaped from his wooden seat and stumbled over to Brendan to pump his hand vigorously. "We often talk of you. Look." He turned to the next wagon. It was as red as the wild berries and shaped like an overturned keg. It was clearly cleaner than the others, and sitting with the reins loosely held in her hands was Greta, her blond hair straight and reaching to her lower back, her green, wild eyes menacing as she glowered down at the group.

"What a woman!" Eamon exclaimed hoarsely.

"She is a fiery-looking bitch," Paul responded.

"Look, Greta, remember the McMahon?"

Greta jumped from the wagon and walked directly to Brendan, pushing Nicholas aside. He was clearly nothing more to her than a traveling companion, and her harsh treatment of him emphasized that. She breathed deeply, and then she threw her arms around Brendan and covered his mouth with hers, opening and closing it in one long and passionate kiss.

"I have missed you, McMahon. We had a good night once." Then she stepped back and, with a sweeping open hand, struck him a stinging blow across the face. "That is because you did not come back."

"Oh, there is some *wooman*." Paul whistled through his broken teeth.

Brendan rubbed his cheek. "You bitch out of hell. I should break your bloody arms."

"Why not try to break my body, if you can, McMahon? Come. Come to my wagon. Nicholas, take the other two." And she strode off with a swagger.

Nicholas's wagon sagged and listed like a ship in a storm as the two great bulks climbed into the wooden hovel in the back, while Brendan followed Greta reluctantly, his fury subsiding slowly.

She snapped the reins, and they were on their way, Brendan sitting beside her on the high seat. Her body was close to him, and one firm, round breast rubbed against his arm.

"You *like* the feel of my body next to you, McMahon." It was not a question.

He could only nod, painfully aware of her teasing breast on his arm.

"We will camp outside Galway City this night. We have an encampment of travelers already there. The English landlords do not bother us as long as we do not camp on their farms. I think they are afraid we will put a curse on them." She smiled and added, "You will stay with me, McMahon. We will share a bed this night." And she thrust her breast deeper into him. He could feel the flames igniting his face and loins and a rush of shame and guilt as he remembered Mary and their baby. Christ, how was he to fight this temptation? Wasn't he thousands of miles away? Mary would never know, and oh, didn't he want to mount this untamed bitch and ride her bareback in the rocking stable of her caravan.

At a bend in the road a slight incline rose to meet them, and as they dipped into a grassy valley, they could see other caravans dotting a large, square pasture. Connemara ponies, volcanic and as fierce-eyed as their tinker owners, roamed the stone-glutted fields, their screams and shrieks splitting the late-afternoon stillness.

"We will camp here for the night. Come, McMahon, step down and join my people around the fire. We will drink and dance, and later we will make love in the bed of my wagon."

Brendan's heart pounded with lust. He wanted her, and nothing would keep him from having her this night—not Mary, not the baby, not the shame and sin of it.

He followed her over to the large iron pot that smoked and hissed on the open fire.

Nicholas, with a dirty gray beard and dirtier hands and face and neck, ladled out scalding potato soup into grimy pewter bowls. One toothless old wifey, her gums yellowed and swollen, her cheeks like an airless bellows, held out her bowl and lisped, "Dith is your turn to therve our travelerth, Nicholath?" Her tone was sweetly ironic.

"No," he answered simply. "It is Greta's turn, but she will be busy with her friend this night." And he smiled sardonically in the direction of Greta and Brendan.

The night was soft and filled with the murmur of birds and the throaty, guttural sighs of contented ponies.

The amber haze of evening lingered under white puffed-out clouds, and Brendan could see Greta's deep, penetrating eyes peering catlike at him as she curled sensuously in the corner of the wagon. Her arms reached out, and he slid alongside her, his mouth opening and closing over hers. His hands found her breasts and covered them. Their hardness matched his as he tore open her dress.

"Who is the wild one now, Brendan McMahon?"

"I am, you devil out of hell. I am." And his hands found her naked breasts, the nipples hard beneath his fingers.

"You are a thirsty one, this night. Which do you prefer, the poteen or me?" she whispered coquettishly, throwing him into an even greater frenzy. He was like a raging and ferocious beast as she squirmed and humped her way toward him in the straw.

"I cannot wait any longer, Greta. I must have you now." And he entered her fiercely, penetrating deeply and feeling her close over him and tighten around him. He drove savagely into her as her body rose and ground into his. He held her buttocks in his hands, forcing himself deeper until his entire torso seemed to explode in a volcanic release and he came forth into her. Outside the bucking wagon, ponies grunted in sleepy satisfaction.

Slowly, drained by the explosion, Brendan left her and lay by her side. She smiled into his eyes. "McMahon, you have improved since last we lay in each other's arms. There have been many women since?"

And then it came, the flutter of depression around the heart that turned quickly into a dull ache. Mary. The child. Conscience, massive and immovable, like a giant stone, crushed his chest. Mary. God, what have I done? Why? Jesus, forgive me. I'm so bloody weak.

"You do not answer, McMahon. How many have there been since me?"

"Christ, woman, stop it. Do you hear me? Stop it."

"Oh, so there is one special one. In this Canada? Am I right? One very special one, your eyes tell me."

"Yes. Yes. Yes, one special one. God damn your heathen eyes, my wife! My wife, do you hear me?" He snarled in anger, threw his tunic on, and crawled out into the black night. He picked his way between the wagons until he found Nicholas crouching on his haunches by a gray, dying fire. He was drunk, an empty earthenware jug by his side.

"It is empty," he said huskily as Brendan reached for it.

"Where can I get more, Nicholas? I have a need for it this night."

The traveler only then turned his attention directly on Brendan. "What is wrong with you, McMahon? You have the woman. You are safe here with us. What do I read in your troubled face?"

"I feel shame, my friend. Deep shame. I am sorry, and I am not sorry. Do you understand?"

"No, I do not. I never did with your people. Your priests have destroyed you. You want excitement. You want a woman. You want a drink. And when you partake, you whine and snivel and cry to the heavens for forgiveness. I have no patience with your kind of church, your false sanctity and suffering. Be a man or be a woman, my friend."

Brendan accepted the drunken criticism with puzzlement. Was he a hypocrite, the product of a woman's church?

It was too much to consider, and he just grunted, "Where is the poteen?"

Nicholas jerked his head to the wagon behind them. "In there, your Frenchman sleeps with a woman. He has some. He is a giant of a man with a giant swallow. He finished an entire jug by himself while the one called Eamon struggled into the farther wagon. He sleeps the sleep of the dead."

Brendan walked off, leaving the bearded tinker to stare reflectively into the smoking gray ash. He was a deep and troubled man, this Nicholas. Brendan could learn much from him if he did not have to leave in the morning.

Deep, thunderous snoring rose and fell in the blackness of the wagon as Brendan parted the canvas and felt for the stone jug that Paul's hand gripped fiercely even in sleep.

Brendan jerked the jug loose, and as he did so, the powerful body rose up. "Who be there, who be it?" he roared. "What stinking gypsy steals Paul's grog? I'll whip your gypsy arse, hear me?" His roars echoed through the encampment, rustling tinkers from their beds and straightening those who hunched by midnight fires. Paul leaped from the wagon, bellowing, until he saw in the flickering firelight the face of Brendan, swallowing huge drafts of poteen.

"Damn you, Irishman, never steal into a man's wagon at night. And never when he sleeps with a gypsy woman."

Several tinkers circled around them. One of them was Nicholas, and he spoke in quiet anger. "Frenchman, we are not stinking gypsies. We are not even gypsies. We are people who choose the road. We have a tradition, and if you are to live through this night, we wait for you to tell us you ask our forgiveness." The circle closed in on them.

The massive man stared into their glazed and drunken eyes and then at their hands, which hooked around the daggers at their belts. The settlement was as silent as an old grave. Paul's anger seethed. He knew he could destroy three or four with a mighty flailing of his fists but there was too much at stake here. The caravan would be their safe passage to Galway City, and that, of course, was their mission. He bit hard on his lip, shrugged with resignation at Brendan, and said solemnly, in a deep whiskey voice, "the Frenchman, he ask you to forgive him. It is the whiskey that speaks, not Totem Paul."

The circle broke, and the tinkers stepped back, dropping their hands to their sides and smiling.

"Come." Nicholas grinned with satisfaction that their manhood had been tested and prevailed. "Come, our French friend, we shall drink by the fire. Here, someone throw more faggots on and bring light and warmth to these midnight hours. We must sit and drink with our friends."

Brendan did not return to Greta's arms or to her wagon. He walked through the hazlewood and down to the silvery pond and let the poteen dull itself and him as he sat on the thick grass, contemplating the wise words of Nicholas, the bearded one. It had to be one way or the other. Either he was one of them—a tinker, who lived from one pleasure to the next, from fiery sunrise to glorious and glowing sunset—or he was Brendan McMahon, a husband and father. "Yes," he shouted to the pond.

He awoke cold and shivering in the clammy gray morning. A light rain was falling, and he jumped quickly to his feet and stumbled through the bush and up to the campsite, which was already bristling with early-morning activity. Ponies whinnied and screamed, their white teeth chomping the air in yawning salute. Fires smoked, and the smell of turnip bubbling in the iron pots turned his stomach. He knelt before Nicholas's fire and rubbed his hands as though applying flint to flint. The warmth gradually restored him.

"You have been among the missing, my friend," the bearded one spoke.

"Why? Who was in search of me?"

"Greta," he answered simply. "She was in a rage. I told her I did not know your whereabouts. I spoke the truth. I knew you were troubled. Maybe I talked too much. It was the drink. Forgive me, my friend."

"There is nothing to forgive, Nicholas. You gave me your wisdom. You were right. No man can serve two masters. I am better for my sin."

The camp was filling up with tinkers now as they approached the pots and served themselves the steaming turnip soup. Eamon and

Paul, red-eyed and plodding, staggered over. Paul sat down heavily on the sodden ground. "Ahhhh, Nicholas, I have met the match of my life, and I have lost to a jug of poteen. Ahhhhh." And he spit into the earth with disgust.

"More than one jug, my French friend. Three."

"Three? Oh-oh, no wonder I feel hoofbeats of wild horses in my head."

Nicholas and Brendan, in spite of the wet, gray morning, smiled in amusement at the big man.

Totem Paul held his head in his hands. "Now we have more trouble. Look, that woman, like no other I have saw, she comes this way."

Brendan and Nicholas turned to see Greta striding toward the blazing fire, her eyes brighter than the flames. She slapped a short, stubby, black hawthorn stick against the palm of her hand.

"McMahon," she growled, her voice like an attacking snake. "Mc-Mahon, you did not return to my wagon last night. I waited for you."

"I slept elsewhere, Greta."

"But I waited for you. No man does that to Greta, no man. Do you hear me?" Her ruddy, windblown face turned scarlet, and she struck him a lightning-quick stroke with the stick. It ripped open the skin below his right eye. Brendan stood his ground, blood streaming down his cheek. He did not move or flinch as she raised the stick for a second attack. His expression did not change. The attack did not come. Greta stared into his eyes for several seconds and then slowly released her hold on the stick. It fell to the mud beside her boots.

The camp was silent except for a barking dog somewhere in the hills above them. Greta moved closer to Brendan and wiped the blood from his face with the hem of her skirts. "Why do you take punishment from me, McMahon? Why is it you do not fight me? Beat me? Others would." And she looked at Nicholas. "Or they would try to."

"Because I deserved a beating at your hands, Greta. It is myself who is in the wrong. Forgive me."

The tinkers who had stood in silence in the background now began to mumble and go back about their business around the camp-fire.

It was soon decided that the caravan would make its way into Galway City and the three guests were quickly hidden in each of three wagons.

"Good-bye, McMahon," was all Greta of the burning cat-green eyes would say. "I do not understand your kind." And she swaggered off to her own wagon, her sensuous hips swaying provocatively.

"I do not understand *myself*," he whispered as he watched her climb into the high seat and pull on the reins with firm command.

CHAPTER XIII

THE ROAD TO Galway was strewn with men, women, and children wandering in search of food, some hoping to gain a day's work unloading the great barques that regurgitated foreign goods onto the wooden quays of Galway Harbor, others looking with dead eyes for a patch of earth that might yield a forgotten potato. Even the tinkers, abused and abhorred by Irish and English alike, seemed to live better for all their oppression than those who considered themselves true Irish.

Brendan watched the stringy procession through a crack in the canvas. They were more like mourners at a county funeral than peasants on their way to market. And of course, mourners they were, with no more future than those who already lay under the Celtic crosses in the village cemeteries.

And still some harbored a secret hope that a boat bound for America or Australia or Canada might be in need of a cabin boy or a steward or a common seaman. Anything would do so long as there was the chance to set sail for a sunny port and a country where a man could work and eat and love.

Brendan had seen the look before, in the eyes of the bright-eyed immigrants arriving on the teeming docks of Boston Harbor, only to be sent as slave labor to dig the great canals that powered Yankee mills. Jesus, he thought, as he lay in the semidarkness of the bouncing wagon, the bloody tinkers live better than most of the Irish in the States. He choked with bitterness and clenched his fists in anger. His single purpose was clear. He personally would break the neck of the Douglas.

They were at the outskirts of Galway City now. He sensed the distant roar of the market crowds and the horses' hooves clopping over the cobblestoned streets of the Old Town.

Only too vividly did the night of his escape from the clutches of the Douglas and his horde come back to him. Mary had been standing in the midst of the immigrants heading for America, and there was he, Brendan McMahon, hiding like some cowering animal behind a pile of kegs on the Galway docks. He called to her, softly at first, then screaming her name in frustration over the plaintive and melancholic singing of those who were boarding the ship and leaving home forever. At that moment the shouts and cries thundered along the quays. "There he is! McMahon! Get him! Take the bloody, murdering bastard." The Douglas raised his pistol, but before he could squeeze the trigger, Brendan was flying through the air and cutting through the waters of the harbor, losing himself in the murky dark. . . .

He wondered how Mary was getting along on the farm. Dignity of ownership, Daniel O'Connell had called it. To stand straight and tall on one's own land.

The wagon lurched and jerked, and the frightened horse reared. Brendan thought he would slide out into the streets of Galway. He held firmly onto the sides, feeling himself slip as the wagon began to tilt. But then they were upright again, and the horse, in a frenzy, tore off past the docks and finally halted in a grove at the far end of the harbor.

"Psssssst. Psssssst!" The driver squinted down from his high seat, a toothless smile cracking the worn face. "Come, McMahon. You will be safe here. There is no one about except us. The others will follow soon."

Soon they did follow, and when they arrived, Paul and Eamon jumped, rumpled and disheveled from their individual wagons, Paul looking as though a mountain had fallen on a mountain.

"By God, I have never felt so bad, Brendan. You Irish drink poison and do not know it."

The two drivers, impatient now to join their friends of the road, wanted to be off, perhaps to try what the McMahon had tried. To share the bouncing wagon with Greta.

"Thank you, friends, you have done us a great service. We will never forget you. Peace on your journey and peace in your lives." Brendan saluted them, touching his index finger to his forehead. They nodded in return and then quickly spirited their horses off to the red fires that were already burning in the wagon encampment on the outskirts of Athenry.

"Well, we are here," Brendan said to the wake of dust from the departing wagons. "Now we must plan."

Strong, sharp bites of briny air blew in from the cluttered, ship-choked harbor. The tall masts and rounded, proud bowed barques were suddenly reminiscent of Saint John and Canada, and Brendan felt a tug of loneliness at his heart. He sighed deeply and with obvious effort said, "Come, there is a spit of land with a grove of trees. It is just over the crown of that hill."

Paul, of the wise eyes, patted him on the shoulder. "We will be home like the geese, Brendan. Do not worry."

They clambered over the hill and descended to a stretch of wrinkled beach. They rested in an islet of trees until the night rode in with the tide.

"It is time for me to go," Brendan whispered into the dark. A lemon moon hung out over Galway Bay and reflected off the shimmering pale waters. Somewhere beyond those curling, rounded waves, thousands of watery miles away, Mary and Gabriella awaited him. God grant that he would return to them.

"Be careful, Brendan," Eamon said simply.

Totem Paul grunted, "Very careful."

"Now, remember, if I am not back by dawn, contact Michael Burke on the quays. He works at the Saddle Shoppe. Burke will take you to Daniel O'Connell's Galway headquarters. There you will receive help. I'm off."

And he faded off along the beach.

Back on the highroad he kept to the shadows, trotting along the empty streets, finally swallowed up by the dark. The moon was barely visible now behind a gray haze of cloud. Good, he thought. I shall be across the field and into the courtyard before the moon reappears.

He raced the trailing clouds and found himself at the back door of the Rectory of Saint Bridget's just as the courtyard was flooded with pale gold. He gave three sharp raps and waited, listening. Nothing. He tapped again, and this time he heard a stirring, then saw the yellow flicker of a tallow candle as it moved from an upstairs window and finally spread itself under the doorway. "Who is there? Who be you?" Father Nelligan's voice was alert but suspicious.

Brendan cupped his hands over his mouth. "Brendan McMahon, Father. The McMahon."

A wooden slat slid along on the other side, a bolt snapped, and the door opened on the rumpled form of priest.

"God be glorified. You have come all this way out of love for your sister. Quick, lad, come in through to the church."

Brendan followed the dancing flame as they crossed into the damp, stony silence of the country church. The sanctuary candle burned inside a russet glass globe, signifying the presence of The Blessed Sacrament. They each genuflected before it, Brendan feeling a moment of guilt for his sin with Greta. He bowed, and blessed himself, as he rose.

The old priest led Brendan to the sacristy, where he handed him the candle and pushed aside a rose-colored rug. He reached down and pulled at an iron ring in the floor. A trap door squeaked open. Brendan stared in disbelief. "Follow me down, Brendan McMahon." The priest reached for the candle and descended the wooden stairs.

The candle's flame was vertical in the dusty room below. The priest held it out until he located two more that were resting on either side of a tarnished tabernacle. When he lighted the candles, spidery fingers of light climbed the whitewashed walls.

"This stone altar was placed here by my predecessor when we could not say mass in the church. But lately, with the Kerryman speaking out for us, the English have not interfered with our worship."

"Aye, O'Connell is the hope of Ireland, Father. But, tell me"—and he breathed deeply in fear of what the priest might tell him—"my sister, is she alive?"

"Aye, Brendan, my lad, she is that. The Douglas has her confined."

"Where, Father? Tell me if you know."

The old man rested his back against the stone slab of altar. His sad eyes, exaggerated by the candlelight, drooped wearily. The cracks and ruts in his cheeks and under his puffy eyes told a history of sadness. His ministry, like Ireland's history, had been one long series of defeats.

There was fatigue in his tone as well. "Just off the Clifden Road there is an island owned by the Douglas. Inishturbot. He and his sinning, barbarous sportsmen go there to do all manner of evil things. It is said they hold a black mass there—for sport—God forgive them. It is there that Cathleen is being held."

"You are sure?"

"Yes, I am sure. A man who cares for our little church and digs our graves, he told me. He does work for the Douglas, too."

"This man—is he here at the church? Can he be trusted? What's his name?"

"No, he is not here. He lives in the village. Can he be trusted, you ask? Can anyone with an ache in the belly be trusted these days? His name is Thomas Falvey. Do you know the name?" The old man shrugged, his bony shoulders bowed.

"No. I do not. All right, then. I shall stay here until just before daybreak. Then I'll join my friends and make contact with O'Connell's men. They are still in the Old Town, yes?"

"Aye, the same place. On the quays. They have been a help to us. They are quiet about their work. Sometimes I must turn my head. I feel as though I live in two worlds."

"You are right to turn your head, Father. If you did not, you would no longer be their priest. Is that not so?"

"Aye, that is so. I know the sins of the English. But I can only guess at the sins of our own people. Two English soldiers were found dead last month. Their bodies washed up on the shore, and their capsized boat was found on a deserted beach off Spiddal. There was talk, of course. But nothing was ever proved. Still, my ears, old as they are, they hear things. That is one of the times I turned my head away."

"Where are the soldiers quartered these days?" In the past the English garrison had been only a few miles outside Galway, and that was too close if he and the others had to make a run for it.

"They have moved to Loughrea. O'Connell had a monster rally there three months ago, and the English looked for trouble under every rock. None occurred, but there they sit, and we are better for it here."

"That pleases me. We, at least, will not have them to contend with."

"You mention 'we.' Who is the 'we,' my son?" It was the first time his tired voice had belied any affection.

"My friends, Father. With the help of the Kerryman and his followers, we will take my sister out of that place. I swear it on this

altar stone." And he placed his hand on the smoothed, time-worn half-
moon of stone beneath which lay a relic of Saint Bridget.

The priest raised his hand over Brendan's head in blessing and
whispered, "*Benedicat vos omnipotens Deus, Pater, et Filius, et Spiritus Sanctus,*" then quickly departed. Brendan watched the stooped
figure ascend the fieldstone steps, and then he turned slowly, taking
in his surroundings. The floor of the room was hard-packed dirt, and
there was a narrow crawl space that led away from the altar. A passageway, an escape route, he thought. In case the English blocked
egress from the trap door, there had to be another way out. Brendan
reached for one of the altar candles, blew out the other one, and
crawled on his knees until the flame leaped up to his face. A slight
breeze rustled through a crack in the peat-smelling earth. There it
was, a large boulder to be rolled out of the way when necessity de-
manded. There was a large gap between the boulder and the eroding
earth. He raised the candle and realized he could look out on the
huddled cottages above the graveyard. He could see the tilted crosses,
and he knew many of those graves contained the rotting remains of
friends and relatives. Somewhere, out there, Mary's dear sister Gabriella, called away in her eighth year, lay in the clay of eternity.

He snuffed out the candle with his coarse fingers and propped
himself against the dirt wall. He would sleep until daybreak, and then
he would return to Eamon and Paul. Now that he knew where Cathleen was, he knew he could get help from O'Connell.

A long, thin hand reached up to the grinning rider perched
high in his English saddle. The hand trembled and shook. The rider
dropped the coins just beyond the outstretched hand and laughed
quietly as Thomas Falvey knelt in the predawn shadows, digging into
the muck for his coppers.

"That will buy you and your sniveling brats a few meals, Judas
Iscariot." John Douglas taunted him as he leered at Donal McCann
and the four other horsemen. "Didn't I tell you about your Irish,
McCann? Yellow bastards who can be bought. All of you."

McCann looked off in the direction of the village; the ambivalence
he felt both enraged and confused him.

The horses exhaled ghostly wisps of air, and the Douglas stroked
his mount gently. "There now, easy. We will not have much longer to
wait, my friend. Then you will be fed and made warm."

They were secluded beyond the church to the north of the graveyard, and as John Douglas purred into the ear of his horse, McCann
broke in, "There he is. There he is, John, crouching behind that cross.
You see, now. Yes, there. There he is." McCann's voice rose with excitement, his ambivalence gone. His finger traced Brendan's route like
a rifle barrel.

"Good. I have waited for this moment. I have been patient. Come,
we have him." He thumped his boots into the horse's flanks and sprang
out of the grove, the others quickly following.

Brendan was just emerging from behind a newly dug grave when he heard the morning explode with the pounding of murderous hoof-beats. He jerked his head in the direction of the riders, and his heart seemed to fall away. Jesus, they have me, he thought. He bolted from the graveyard and raced along the deserted, rutted alleys of Oranmore, but the horsemen were too quick for him. They blasted along behind until he stopped in the center of the village, his hands clenched, wait-ing for the inevitable.

Horses swarmed around him. His flying fists flailed uselessly until a riding crop smashed against his skull and he felt his knees buckle. He shook his head to free himself of the dizziness. Blood oozed from the gaping wound as he reeled under a second attack, and the black ground came up to meet him.

Wagons clattered; horses pounded past; children raced in teams of six and seven, kicking a round metal object between them. The mist cleared, and the day was almost pleasant, a pale pink streaking the deep blue that seemed to touch the horizon far out in Galway Bay. And still Brendan had not returned.

"I'm worried," Eamon said nervously. He was ripping dry leaves from a broken bough, and his hands worked unconsciously but with grim emphasis. "Where could he be? Do they have him?"

"The sun climbs; he should be here. He would not walk streets in daylight." Paul's forehead showed deep lines of concern.

"Unless he *cannot* walk," Eamon said in a low voice. "Come, we will find this Michael Burke."

They were a formidable twosome as they strode along the quays. Sailors and shopkeepers, dock handlers and farmers looked up as they passed. They were bulky with bull necks and long, sloping shoulders. Paul at six feet six was the taller, but Eamon, his meaty hands clenched and ready at his sides, was thick and muscular. Together they created a picture of awesome power.

They found the Saddle Shoppe, teetering on the edge of the quays. A bell jingled from above the door, signaling their presence. The interior of the shop was dark and smelled richly of leather. Sad-dles, stitched cowhide bags, and bleached skins hung from the walls.

"Is no one about?" Eamon asked.

"Aye, I am about." And a little man with a head that resembled a well-polished bowling ball appeared, stepping up from the back room, which looked out over the murky harbor. He wore a dirty and tattered leather apron that made him look as though he had no legs.

A smile cracked his gray face. "Well, I suggest you keep your head down while you are in here, my friend, or you will knock your-self out on the beams."

Paul, who was already in an exaggerated crouch, bent even lower. "What can I do for you, mates?"

"It concerns a friend of ours," Eamon said cautiously.

"What is your friend's name?" The polished head bobbed above the apron, eyes squinting.

Eamon looked quickly in the direction of Paul, and the Frenchman nodded slowly in return.

"McMahon," Eamon said quickly but in a soft whisper. "Brendan McMahon," he added unnecessarily, because already the little man had bustled to the door to bolt it and draw down the shade. The room was thrown suddenly into half shadows.

"Come through to the back, and mind the steps." His sharp command was firm and unexpected. He suddenly grew inches as he gestured for them to sit on the rough-hewn benches. "There. Sit and listen. McMahon is taken. It happened this morning at the church. An informer turned him in. We know who. We can take care of that, and we will. But now listen closely. I do not want you in the shop too long. There are people about, Irish as well as English. We must be careful. The McMahon has been taken to a small island, Inishturbot, a mile off the Connemara road. Tonight you will meet with O'Connell's men. They will help you. I can say no more now. Leave by the dockside door."

"But where do we meet them?"

"Powers Pub, in Dame Street. Eight o'clock. Go now." And the little man who had grown so large ushered them out onto the teeming docks.

Inishturbot rose out of the desolate mud flats of Connemara, a stone fortress in a bleak, sodden night. It had sat on this peninsula of the same name for four centuries, originally owned by an English duke who had shocked the crown of Britain by marrying an Irish peasant woman. Ownership was quickly and vehemently torn from his grasp by an outraged king. And for favors and loyalty to Mother England, John Douglas became the subsequent heir and squire. Following his death, the elder son, John, became master of the tiny island. And master he was as he drunkenly stormed the stone corridors and commandeered those of lesser rank to join him in infamous sacrilege.

Dressed in the confiscated clerical garments of Roman Catholic priests, they paraded up and down the great banquet room, their liquored voices raised in profanation of the Latin mass. John Douglas, leering stupidly, held the white host of communion high before his eyes. Cathleen, tied to an oak chair, pressed her eyes closed at the desecration.

"To the deity of Satan," Douglas intoned as an accomplice to his right waved the burning censor under the nose of Brendan, who pulled and jerked uselessly at the tight leather straps that circled his chest and arms and legs.

"You filthy, rotten butchers. You have stolen the blessed host. God forgive your sin."

"Pater Noster, love and devotion to Satan, king of the world and the oceans and mountains that surround us."

Their sick laughter roared throughout the stone room as the other members of the band slapped the tables and shouted their approval. Donal McCann stood in the shadows, his eyes lowered in shame.

The Douglas, wearing the white amice and knotted cincture, continued his sacrilege, devouring the wafer and washing it down with a mouthful of poteen.

"Just like all their drunken, misfit priests. I am no different and they are no different or better than I. No different. And now, McMahon, I will direct my sermon to you and allow my congregation the delight of deciding whether your head should leave its shoulders." His face glowed demoniacally in the wavering light of the flambeaux that hung from the walls.

As the Douglas was climbing heavily onto a chair and then to the tankard-cluttered table, eight men beached their curraghs silently on the sand below and stole cautiously along the west wall of the fortress in the shadow of the black hand that had snuffed out the moon.

"Up there, that window. Quick, on my shoulders, Irishman." And a stocky, swollen-bellied follower of Dan O'Connell grinned apishly and climbed the palmed hands of Totem Paul, who boosted him high into the air. He grasped the square stone turret ten feet above the ground and stood for a moment, frozen, in the black night.

"Come out of it, lad, get moving," Eamon whispered up to him.

The portly man, his stomach distended from too many days of seeing less food than the pigs, stood suddenly above it all, above the starvation and poverty, the landlords and the blighted earth.

"For the sake of Christ Himself, man, move."

A wide grin split his gray face, and he grabbed the rope that Paul flipped up to him. He tied two thick and sturdy hawthorn sticks to it and passed them through the bars in the window casement. A mighty jerk, once, twice, and then on the third pull the bars twisted and came forward to crack the stone and fly with the rope over their heads to the wet sand below.

The shadowy band smiled in the darkness. Then the Irishman at the top of the world secured another rope to the ramparts, and they climbed it silently, one hand over the next, until they all were secure atop the rampart.

"One by one, we swing in through that opening," Paul ordered.

"Let's hope you can fit that bulk through, Frenchman." Eamon smiled in the dark.

"If I don't, I break that goddamn wall with my hands."

They dropped softly to the landing, and Paul, with the agility of a far smaller man, led them down the winding stone passage, past the open iron doors of the foul-smelling cells. As he approached each one, he stopped, checking quickly to be sure it was empty.

Suddenly, as he inched around a corner, he sensed with the practiced instincts of the hunter the presence of the enemy. He stiffened, waved the others back, and ever so slowly pressed his face to the wall. They had reached the castle keep, and in a flash he saw his prey, a large man, no doubt a guard, with a pistol jutting from his belt and a broadsword in his hand. Paul inhaled once, deeply. Then, like a panther, he sprang forward. He wrapped his right hand around the sentinel's neck while he brought his left arm up behind the head, slowly bending it back until there was a sickening snap as the man's neck broke. Paul lowered the body to the floor, reaching for the dangling broadsword as he did. It all took no more than ten seconds. The others appeared, awestruck at this man who was more powerful than the legendary Brian Boru. Only Eamon smiled. He had felt Paul's strength before.

"Come, we follow the passageway. Stay close; there is not much light."

A smoking torch gave desultory light to the lower landing, but it was enough to show them the way.

Paul stopped abruptly as a voice, a strangely wailing and emotionally charged voice, rang and echoed along the floor below. He stepped out noiselessly for such a big man and found himself in an alcove that was just off a large banquet room. The alcove was in darkness, but the hall was grotesquely illuminated by flaring, garish candelabra which threw weird, fingery patterns against the wall and the ceiling.

A man rose up, then down on his toes, a candle held so close to his face that all Paul could see was a large, orange moon of distorted expression. The smell was incense, and it smoked from iron pots and from the clinking censor that was being raised, chain hitting censor in that salutary papist ritual of blessing. The censor was held by the same pinched-faced dandy who had slapped his whip across the tinker's face on the Galway Road.

"Jesus Christ Almighty," the portly Irishman said, peering around Totem Paul at the unholy scene.

"Jesus," the portly one said again, "it's a black mass."

"Be quiet, man, listen." Eamon jabbed him with his drawn pistol.

"And I suppose you would ask mercy from this Christian congregation, McMahon, mercy for you and your slut of a sister. It has been declared around the countryside that my father fell on his knife when he engaged you in a fight. My father, a good man who never hurt a soul, not even a bloody black papist soul. Where was your gratitude to him for allowing you and your pig family to squat in his cottage and to work his fields? Where was it, McMahon?"

The voice had an insane ring to it, and the drunken parishioners in this most unholy congregation sipped their rum slowly, the red anger of hate glowing in their already florid faces.

The Douglas lowered himself clumsily from his unsteady perch on the banquet table and turned to his acolytes.

"Well, what is your Christian verdict for this heathen bastard, this killer of fathers, this ungrateful bloody coward? What say you?"

"I say, cut his head off. Cut it off and stuff it." Drunken, bloated laughter from a fat-faced, jowl-shaking lackey.

"A pike up his arse first. Then stuff his bloody head."

"Cut off the hands that harmed your dear father," from a more obsequious landlord.

"Hang his head above the hearth."

The Douglas smiled at this. He had promised himself that McMahon's black curls and Irish peasant face would adorn his father's hearthside. But not here, in this cold and isolated corner of nowhere. No. Not here, where stones grew more abundantly than grass. English lords and ladies did not come to Connemara. But they did come to Galway City.

The fantasy of sitting before a roaring fire, sipping imported French wines at Glenverness and pointing to the head of the McMahon as it peered down with the eyes of a dead fish and recounting the story of how he, the Douglas, had lured the infidel back from across the seas, tried him for murder, and slain him with his own sword, oh, what fine talk, what entertainment that would afford the ladies. John Douglas let his eyes drift to Cathleen, whose almost bare breasts rose and heaved with emotion. She, of course, would give herself to him to save her brother. And after he was satisfied, he would throw her to the pigs. Because that's where they all belonged. But not until he had squeezed out of her everything she could give him. And she would give him everything. She would do anything to keep her brother's head from leaving his body.

"Yes." Their cries warmed him.

"Well, Cathleen, it is either you or your brother. Only you can save him. What say you to that?"

Cathleen's shoulders sagged as Brendan spoke for the first time.

"Do not, Cathleen. Do not give in for me. I beg you. I would rather lose my life than know that he touched you."

"Oh, that is good. That is very noble, McMahon. Do you not think that is noble, gentlemen? He is a proper brother and a proper bloody papist." The Douglas shoved the candle into Brendan's face, and the smell of burning hair filled the room.

"Oh, Mother of God, forgive me, but take me, John Douglas. Take me and do what you will. I will not resist."

"Oh, for the sake of the Almighty, no, Cathleen. I did not come all these miles to see you become the Douglas's whore."

"It is a small price I pay for your life, my dear brother. Small indeed. I say take me, landlord." She screamed the last, and her voice startled the congregation.

"Take her. Take her. Take her," they shouted in drunken orgiastic unison.

The Douglas let the candles lick at her ropes, and they burned free and loose but not without burning Cathleen McMahon. Although the heat of the flame seared and pained, she said nothing.

She rose from her chair, rubbing the numbness left by her bonds, and then she grimaced from the burns of the candle.

"Come, my dear, to my chamber. I will soothe your hurt."

She followed him out to the stairway, looking back once at her anguished brother and then they disappeared in the dark.

"Now we get these drunken bastards," Paul whispered. "Do not wait more. Pick a man. Go."

Paul was the first, and he raced through the great room unseen until the pinched-faced one turned to place his burning censor on the table and reach for a tankard.

"Bastard," Paul hissed as the dandy looked up in sudden fright. "Bastard." And his great hands began to squeeze the pinched one's head in at the temples. The rush of pain was about to burst into a terrified scream when a large hand covered his mouth. The pinched face turned red, then purple, then white. Paul's quick action was not lost on the rest as they tore across the room, their long knives stabbing and cutting into the rum-sodden bodies of the congregation. Not one had enough time to rise and reach for a pistol or sword.

Within five minutes those would-be lords-over-all lay in a crumpled heap of torn flesh and English finery. Some still had their tankards fixed in the death grasp of their hands.

"Cut the lad free. Hurry," Paul barked.

Brendan's grin lit the room. "Here, lad, you'll want this." And Eamon threw him a knife.

"Thank you, Eamon, but I have these." And he produced two white-knuckled fists. "I'll be back with my sister." He flipped the knife back to his friend and flew out of the room in search of the baronial chamber.

Feeling his way along the walls, he could hear no screams. She would be as good as her word. Then the coaxing, sensual tone of a wheedling animal traveled along the corridor. "Come to me, my lovely Cathleen. Come, and no harm will come to your brother."

The voice brought Brendan closer, and then he heard Cathleen's disgust and contempt. "You filthy scum. You deserve to be torn apart by wild dogs."

"Leave the room, Cathleen."

Brendan's voice cut like a knife into the back of John Douglas. "Is this some bloody joke? Are those bastards making some kind of fool of me? I'll have *their* heads."

"Their heads have already been taken. Leave, Cathleen, join my friends below."

"Where is Donal McCann? Where is my brother, Roderick? Where are the others?" His voice was unnaturally high and strident.

"The same place you were going to send me, landlord."

Brendan hesitated for a moment at the idea of attacking a man dressed in holy garments. He was not ready when the Douglas pulled a knife from beneath his priestly robe, and it flashed through the air and caught the McMahon in the lower stomach. The blood flowed instantly, and Brendan instinctively cupped his hand over the wound.

Furiously angry at his own lack of vigilance, he sidestepped the next attack and grabbed the flying, knife-wielding hand.

The hand shook, trembled, and then wavered as Brendan turned the knife back. There was a long moment when nothing in the room moved, and then Brendan thrust the knife into the Douglas's heart, and he pitched forward onto it, dying as his father had died.

Then Brendan fell out the door and stumbled to the top of the stairs before his legs failed him and the darkness closed in.

For nearly a week Brendan McMahon lay, drenched in perspiration, drifting in and out of consciousness. Cathleen never left his bed-side. She cleaned and dressed the wound, applying an Indian corn poultice, an old country remedy, that drew and sucked the poison from the deep pocket of pain, while singing in a lilting Gaelic of hem-lock groves, green fields and Druid kings and of the hazelnut and the dark and mysterious world of the fairie.

"You are a fine woman and a devoted sister if I may be so bold to say."

The voice startled her in the half darkness of the Kerry manse where they had been taken soon after Brendan's bleeding had ceased.

She rose instinctively as any Irish maiden would at the sound of an educated and articulate voice.

"Please, sir, I do not know who you are."

The tone softened from its usual deep resonance. "I am Daniel O'Connell, a friend, and you are, of course, Cathleen McMahon."

"Dear God, the King of the Beggars," she blurted. "Forgive the way I look, Mr. O'Connell."

"I would say you look quite lovely, my child but do I dare? After all, I am a married man. But, Patrick, what do you say? You're a bachelor. There is nothing preventing your comments."

Patrick Leary, dark and quiet, came in behind the great man and bowed shyly to Cathleen, who curtsied in return. Truly, she was lovely, Patrick thought, but all he had the courage to say was: "Ah, ah, yes, Daniel."

"Ah, ah? Well, now, how is that for an artful dodge? The man's tongue obviously has been clamped tight by your beauty."

"Please, Daniel." Leary, usually the poetic and politically articu-late right-hand man, always a match for the great O'Connell's wit, was nonetheless nonplussed in the presence of the woman.

"All right, my wallflower friend, I shall not embarrass you fur-ther." And then, turning quickly to the question at hand: "How is our young comrade?"

"He is still unconscious, Mr. O'Connell, but we hope and pray he will come back to us."

"Come into the other room, my dear, and sit. I must talk with you."

The sitting room was of an elegance Cathleen had never experi-enced. The rich mauve draperies trailed to the inlay of the shining oak floor. Lowboys held vases of wild flowers the fragrance of which brought early summer wafting into the room. The beamed ceilings were dark and masculine, made darker still by the white stuccoed walls and brightly colored rugs.

On the day they arrived from the Saddle Shoppe, where they had been secured until Brendan was able to travel, Cathleen had met only Patrick, the fine-looking one now gazing shyly off to the wide win-dows that framed the green and undulating fields of Kerry and the silver lakes beyond.

"I am sorry I was not here to greet you before this, my dear, and my lovely wife is off visiting in Wexford; but you will be seeing her soon, and I shall be home here at Derrynane till Sunday week. With God's help, and that of your fine nursing and lovely voice, the lad will recover. Rest assured that if he has stayed with us so long, he is over the worst. He will pull through. Now we must make tea. Patrick, be a good lad, and call Nora to bring in the tray. I have longed for one of her buttered scones for a month." He smiled ruefully and patted the soft pillow of rolling flesh above his belt line.

O'Connell's voice rang bell-like throughout the sprawling, comfortable room. Cathleen had never heard a voice like it. It rose and fell, sometimes in a rich, golden resonance, and then trailed off in a lilting, soothing whisper. She was clearly in awe of him, and as she watched Patrick move swiftly through the doorway in search of Nora, she felt herself stiffen at the idea of being in the room alone with such a great man.

O'Connell, blustery at times, but also uncommonly sensitive to the feelings of others, set out to ease her nervousness.

He leaned forward in his chair and took her hands in his. "Forgive me, dear, for the bit of a tease I am. Patrick is such a shy one that I have great difficulty combating the insidious temptation to ruffle his peacock feathers once in a while. I love Patrick intensely, but my gracious, he is so serious. It's fine to be dedicated to the cause of Ireland —God knows, we all are—but the lad would do well to smile more. He needs the twinkle of an Irishwoman's blue eyes." He patted her hands, smiled, rose, and drew the draperies, shutting out the Kerry countryside. "There, that's better. The taking of afternoon tea should be intimate and warm, do you not agree, Cathleen?

"Oh, here we are. Nora, you are a veritable savior. Look at those lovely scones."

Nora, bent and thin as a stick, pushed the tea trolley across the room, followed by a grim-faced and introspective Patrick.

"You have a golden tongue, they say, Daniel O'Connell. Eat hearty, but do not use your blather on me." The old woman's wrinkled face was smiling, and O'Connell chuckled loudly.

"Oh, Nora, I thank God you are not at the rallies. Sure I wouldn't move you to give a halfpenny to our cause."

She poured the tea dutifully and passed a steaming bone china cup to each of them. "I've given more than a ha'penny to Ireland. That's for sure. But you can serve the scones yourself, Daniel O'Connell. I have other things to attend to in the scullery." And she was off and gone, her trolley rattling over the polished floor.

An awkward silence filled the room until Patrick stammered, "Daniel took her out of the poorhouse in Galway, and she would die for him."

"Oh, do not be so dramatic, Patrick. The woman was in need, as, alas, are so many in our beloved country."

Patrick studied a crisp scone intently before attacking its buttery goodness.

"You see, Cathleen, I tend to make jokes about Patrick, but he is —well, I know it may seem a bit bombastic to say, but nevertheless, I shall venture to continue—he is Ireland."

"Oh, for God's sake, he is blatherin' now, Cathleen." Embarrassment reddened Patrick's cheeks. He had never called her by her first name before, at least not to her face, but he had lain in bed, whispering it to the night, listening for its curved lilt. Cathleen. Cath-leeeen. He had said to the dark, "Cath-leeen, you are the loveliest woman I have ever seen and I love you. Oh, my God, but I love you."

"I mean, excuse me, Miss McMahon," Patrick blurted.

O'Connell smiled into his hand and stirred his tea. "Well, I may be overdoing it, Cathleen, if I may call you that"—and O'Connell's eyes twinkled in the direction of Patrick, who studied another bite in a sudden, intense scholarship of scones—"but Ireland has such need. Such need." He sighed in fatigue. "We need all of our sons and daughters."

"And you will have them. You will have all of us, Daniel O'Connell." The voice was hardly more than a whisper, but there was a subtle and convincing power to it. "You have me."

They turned to the doorway in surprise and saw Brendan, gray-faced, his hand clutching his side, but nonetheless standing and smiling. "You have me, Daniel. I am a son of Ireland and honored, sure, to do the bidding of Ireland's King of the Beggars."

CHAPTER XIV

The wind whipped a creamy froth across the rounded waves that spun in and curled along the beach, leaving a marble-washed trail in the blood red sand. The evening was warm for mid-September, and Mary wore only a light homespun frock with a shawl thrown over her shoulders. She enjoyed the solitude of her journey into Tignish for the weekly social. Lately her heart had not hung as heavily as it had when Brendan's letter arrived. She was thankful that he was safe and that Cathleen was free, to be sure, but Brendan's passionate plea for her understanding had brought bitter tears to her eyes. Understand? Understand that a husband and father had chosen to march for a futile cause thousands of miles from home?

Ireland needs me, Mary, my beloved. Ireland needs all of her sons and daughters, and God knows I owe Daniel O'Connell that much. It will not be long. When I feel that I have paid my debt to my country and my benefactor, I shall return and never leave again. So help me.

At the time, in her bitterness, she had wanted to tell him never to bother coming home again. She would do as well without him. But she did not. She did not even bother to answer until he wrote again, begging from her. Then she said simply:

Your wife and daughter will be here. Your farm prospers, and I have had much help from my island neighbors. These are good and generous people, and I shall enjoy my life among them.
Love,
Mary

And she was enjoying the tidy, hard-working little community. She had Isabella for guidance and friendship. And even this golden night she had the contentment of knowing that Gabriella was safe in the arms of Isabella Profitt.

She had worked long, mean days in the fields under the blazing sun, readying her red mounds of earth for the harvest, forking the hay into the outbuilding that had been John Wallace's home, and gathering seaweed and sea lettuce from the long stretch of beach below the North Cape.

Mary Roark McMahon was a farm girl from the day of her birth. The soil was in her blood. To be sure, she had wanted to bathe herself clean of it, to wash the smell of dung and cow flap from her memory. That was what had driven her to Evansborough and the mills. But there she had encountered another smell, the odor of greed. It was no different from the exploitation of Ireland's tenant farmers, except that it was disguised in finely tailored clothes and delicate Yankee manners. She knew now that she was where she belonged, and as she looked out at the dark blue line of the horizon and breathed deeply of the salty air, she felt good about herself. She was surviving, and she had learned a lot. Not of the soil, because that was part of her soul, but of the sea, rich in food she had never known before. She had dug quahog and snail and caught crab and lobster and, with Isabella's counsel, had learned to prepare not only nutritious meals but festive delicacies. She was learning, and the broad, straight line of her shoulders bespoke a woman who would not be daunted, by nature, circumstance, man, or men.

She crossed at the wooden footbridge that spanned a salt-water pond and was on the Tignish Road, the water to her back.

The road rang with the wooden wheels of crowded carts, all heading in the direction of the parish hall of Saint Edmund's. To shouts of "Take a lift with us, Mary" and "Climb aboard, ma'am," she answered with a wide smile and a nod and "No, thanks. I enjoy the walk."

"Suit yourself, Mary." And they clattered and clamored on.

The festivities were already in progress when she arrived. Violins and tin whistles sped the dancers across the room in great, stomping steps. There was no shyness here, no cautious waiting for the party to warm up. These were islanders, and they had worked a long, hard day. They could not afford to be extravagant with time.

Mary, too, began clapping and tapping her buckled boot, pointing her toes, and swaying her lovely dark head to the sprightly music.

"You're looking lovely this evening, as usual, Mary McMahon." Father Gautier, the balding, round-bellied priest with soup stains on his soutane, smiled at her through crooked teeth. He was, by all observations, a very unattractive man, an ugly man. Yet his warmth and compassion, the ever-ready smile and shine to his eyes dispelled any displeasure one might have with his appearance.

"Oh, Father, if I didn't know better, I would swear you were Irish, with your silken tongue." She beamed at seeing him. He was so solid a fixture in their little community.

"And since when does a Frenchman have trouble speaking with the ladies? Tell me, how is our Gabriella?"

"She is wonderful, thank God. She grows and prospers every day."

"And Brendan, what news is there from that quarter?" His eyes became serious and his manner more pastoral. This was, after all, his flock; he laughed with them, wept with them, prayed with them, and above all, he cared for them.

But Mary's bright eyes continued to shine, and the priest recognized the strength in her. "He is still in Ireland. He has become a very close friend of Daniel O'Connell. He will be home when he feels his work is complete. Now I must raise my skirts and do my heart good with some dancing."

"Good for you, Mary. Enjoy your evening."

And she did. She swung in and out of the circles and squares, going from one outstretched hand to the next. The hall was a dizzying blur, and on she danced and tapped her toes and heels, clapping in a giddy quick time until the music wound down and someone shouted, "Punch bowl's ready." And everyone cheered and made his or her way to the long wooden table laden with cakes and breads and assorted pastries.

The next morning, she reflected on the festivities. The dance had been a welcome change for her, although Brendan's presence would have made it complete. Never mind, she thought, that was last night. This is a new day.

So she took to her task with renewed vigor and added energy. She strapped Gabriella to her back, papoose-style, and they set out to milk the goat. "How is my angel today?" she asked over her shoulder, but Gabriella was already asleep.

The island had already settled into autumn now. The Strait was ink black this morning, and long shadows rippled across its surface as a chill sun rose over the horizon. If it turns cold this early, it will be a long Canadian winter, Mary thought grimly.

The day seemed to cloud up suddenly, and as she turned to gaze at the sky, she saw a black-suited figure approaching from the direction of the cabin.

Mary turned and walked halfway up the path to greet him. "Good morning, sir, what can I do for you?"

The man was unusually lean. His long hands, brittle and knobby, fell out of the sleeves of the black coat and reached below his knees. In his right hand he held a piece of paper.

"Are you Mrs. Wallace?" His voice had a dry edge that seemed in keeping with his bony frame.

"Mrs. Wallace? No, there is no Mrs. Wallace here."

"Well then, who are you?"

"I'm Mrs. McMahon," she offered too quickly, caught off guard by his rapid questioning.

"Where's the Wallace family?"

"They are both dead. There." And she pointed to the south field.

"Well then, what be your business here?"

Mary felt the flames igniting and her Celtic blood beginning to boil.

"Let me ask you the same question. What is *your* business here?"

"I am the land agent for all these lots, and I have an unpaid tax bill here for John Wallace."

"John Wallace does not own this land. My husband and I own it. John Wallace gave the land to us."

The gaunt features exposed more bone as he laughed and shook his head. "A man can't go over to giving his land to anybody. He does not have that right. This is government land. What is your name?"

Mary felt a sudden uneasiness. "McMahon, Brendan and Mary McMahon."

"I have never heard any such name registered with the Land Commission."

"Look, my husband sent three pounds for the taxes, and he sent them directly to the Land Commission office in Charlottetown."

"If that be the case, your tax money was never recorded because the only name on our records is John Wallace. So your tax money is worthless because the land is not yours. It is the government's. It reverts to the crown upon the death of the lessee."

"What are you telling me? What are you saying? Are you mad? Come with me." And Mary raced up the path, the jarring and jostling waking the sleeping child and frightening her into choking sobs. "Be still, Gabriella, be still, my little angel," she commanded sternly.

The agent could not keep up with her, and Mary was already standing on the porch with the yellowed parchment in her shaking hand when he arrived, out of breath and perspiring.

"Here, read this. Read it." She pushed the paper against his scrawny chest.

He held it up in front of him and read it, his mouth making a whistling sound. Finished, he handed it back to her. "This paper is completely invalid. This land never passed hands officially."

Mary's crimson face burned in anger and shock. "What are you saying to me? What in God's name are you saying?"

"I am saying that you have twenty-four hours to clear off this lot, or I shall have you arrested for squatting on land that is not yours. I will bring the government constable back tomorrow to be certain you are gone. Now good day."

He turned abruptly and wove his bony form up the path to the highroad and his carriage.

She watched the black horse and equally black chaise roll along the road like a departing hearse. A wind seemed to ripple across the black waters of the Strait, and she trembled in the sudden chill.

The next morning she stood with Bill Profitt and Isabella, holding Gabriella close to her heaving chest, as the constable slapped pasteboards on the door and gatepost of the home she had loved so dearly. The message read, "Off Limits—Government Property—Crown Land."

The constable shook his head as he passed. His eyes seemed to say, "I have a job to do. I'm sorry, but I am powerless."

The land agent waited in his hearse-like carriage until the constable was done, and then they were gone.

"I'm not taking it lying down. Government or no government, I will fight them. They have taken our home away. I have lived with this bloody injustice all of my bloody life. It is always the same, the bloody crown against the peasant. Well, this time I will go to the government and state my case. And the bastards would do well to listen." Tears of frustration and grief rolled down her fiery cheeks. "Take good care of my baby, Isabella. I shall miss her enough to die. But I know what I have to do and I will do it."

PART TWO

THE LAND

1834–1835

CHAPTER XV

Charlottetown, in 1834, was a busy and bustling market town, full of vendors and hucksters shouting their goods from under the pagoda-shaped roof of the old Market House. Cries of "Spruce and ginger beer, homemade molasses candy, apples, and fruits" rose out of the wet, gray October afternoon and fluttered like slapping banners in the wind across the square as Mary Roark McMahon, jostled and bumped by hurrying shoppers intent on getting under cover, stood, a stoic statue, buffeted by wind and rain. She had not seen so many people since leaving Evansborough. But even in Evansborough activity was confined to the brick-walled fortress of the mills, while here the chattering, lively shoppers glowed fresh and red-faced from the world outdoors, the world of farms and valleys and oceans.

The women, simply dressed in homespun duffels, stuffs, and druggets, dyed mostly blue, streamed in and out of the booths and stalls and butcher shops, their packages tied securely and held almost fondly under their arms. High-collared men talked and bartered and conducted business on every street corner. It was the most excitement Mary had experienced since leaving the United States. And although her heart was heavy with loneliness for Gabriella and Brendan and with despair and frustration over the rightful ownership of their land, she was swept up in the swirl and swell of surging humanity and found herself almost carried by the crowds across the muddy street.

A sign above a confectioner's read, "Digger Shanley's Sweets." She smiled, a warm glow lighting her face. It was here that Father Gautier had directed her. Digger Shanley was an Irishman who, while respecting all his Charlottetown neighbors, managed to keep a glowing place in his affections for his own special countrymen. He was a Connemara man, and although no one would challenge his love of Canada and the island, the rugged and ravaged territory of Connaught was chiseled on his heart and brain. His blood pumped Irish through artery and vein, and when he greeted Mary, a broad, expansive smile as wide as the river Shannon itself broke across his face. He was a big-framed man with a thatch of brownish hair that was sprinkled a peppery gray. His stomach hung out over his belt, hard and round, a tribute to numberless kegs of ale consumed over the years.

"So, Galway it is. Oranmore. Sure I know it well, and I know the Roark name. Step in here out of the damp."

Mary was still standing in the doorway, directing her questions to him in a shout.

"Of course, I am the Digger Shanley. Don't I have Ireland's own map all over my face?"

Mary's spirits lifted at his welcome. He had the tongue of her people, and the song in his voice brought Brendan and her own father into the sweet shop.

"Sit." And his coarse red hand guided her to a rough straight-backed chair. "Here, let me take your satchel."

"Sure, everything I have in there is as wet as an Irish wash." She smiled. His brogue brought out her own, and she chuckled at her sudden response to the Irish.

"Aye, you are a Galway lass, that's for certain. I'll bring these into the back. Through that curtain is our living quarters. Two floors and plenty of space. Do you need a place?" But before she could answer, he had rushed clumsily through the red curtain, almost tearing it from its rod.

He was gone for several minutes, leaving her in a glow of warmth to savor the sugared aroma of colorful beans and nut brown chocolate and ginger sticks and molasses bars.

Above the door she had just entered, a cracked and worn painting of the Savior hung crookedly. The suffering Christ with bleeding heart exposed reminded her of all the farmhouses, churches, and hovels in Ireland where the same picture glowed in the light of a flickering candle. She was home again, and this man who did not even know her or the nature of her need had offered her, a perfect stranger, a place to stay. Tears built up and spilled down her cheeks, and she brushed them away. She had promised herself that she would be strong, no matter what happened.

"Here we are now, and what do you make of this lovely colleen, Una?"

The Digger thrust the curtain aside with theatrical exaggeration. "There." He pointed to Mary.

Una Shanley, a great-bosomed woman as square-shouldered and strong as her husband, flashed an enormous smile, a smile as sweet as the shop.

"Well"—she bustled over to Mary, who was still enthroned in the straight-backed chair and feeling almost regal—"a Galway lass. What brings you to us, dear? What can the Shanleys do for one of their own?"

Mary's eyes filled with tears again. God, what is wrong with me that I cannot control myself? she thought.

"Oh, lass, what is it? What be wrong with ye?" Suddenly the Irish again, across the miles of ocean, the rolling green, the boreens piled high with peat, the tin whistles, the jigs, the highroad bowling, the

smell of farms and smoking fires and animals. But also the smell of
death and the stench of poverty. The Irish lilt could lull you away
from reality.

Mary forced back the tears. "They have taken our land away, and
I mean to get it back." There, the momentary sentiment was gone. She
stood tall and said, "I am Mary McMahon, wife of Brendan McMahon,
I have a baby girl, Gabriella. Father Gautier told me to come here."
She inhaled a long, determined breath and continued. "Yes, you can
help me. I need a place to stay, and I have no money. But I am a
good, strong worker."

The big woman placed her two large red hands on Mary's shoulders. "I am Una Shanley, the Digger's wife. We have plenty of room,
and employment will be no problem. Now sit and tell us all."

Mary began her story in Ireland with her desire for a better life,
her move to the Evansborough mill town and the subsequent flight
north when Brendan, involved too deeply in the mill strike, realized
they would never be able to live in Evansborough in peace and, more
important, that their lives there would be suffocating.

"Brendan had this deed." She produced it from the bosom of her
dress and handed it to Digger. "The government man says it is useless,
that the land was only lent to the original name on the lease and that
upon his death it reverts to the government."

"The bloody land question," Digger roared. "Are we to go to our
eternal graves fighting the land problem?"

"Be calm, Mr. Shanley." Una smiled and took the faded deed from
his clenched fist. "Sure he's apt to break a blood vessel when he loses
his temper. But he's right, of course. The crown is like a contrary
schoolgirl, fickle one day, stubborn the next. We have had our own
disputes over land, you may be sure of that."

"Tell me, Mary Roark, your man John Wallace, was he given a
king's grant or did he buy outright from a proprietor, or were he or his
forebears proprietors themselves? These are points you must know if
you are to fight this. Even now, you tell us no one is working the
farm?" Digger's brow knotted in curiosity.

"I was ordered off the land. The house is vacant."

"You see, by leaving, you played right into the hands of the agent.
Obviously he means to sell the lot again, probably to a buyer in England. There was a case years back of an ex-soldier who had drawn one
hundred acres on lot thirty-two, not far from here in Queens County.
He was promised title, so he constructed his house and lived in it for
two years, which was the requirement, and he waited for the deed.
The deed did not come. After leaving for a short time on business, he
discovered, upon returning, that his house had been burned down.
When he sought justice, he was told the land was no longer his because he had left it unattended."

Mary gasped, "You don't mean to tell me they would burn our
home to the ground?"

"I don't mean to alarm you, Mary. I mean simply to tell you that
evil has been done even here on our lovely island."

The bell over the door clanged, and a customer came in, the rain gusting and blowing behind him.

"Una, take the child to the back. We'll talk later, Mary. Get some rest." He bounded exuberantly behind the counter. "Well, my good sir, some sweets for the missus or someone else equally as special?"

During the month that followed Mary wrote letters to members of the Assembly and the governor himself. Each day she took an hour to sit in the ladder-back chair and write her forthright reasons for being allowed a hearing of her case. No day went by that her insistent and urgent quill did not scratch across the white parchment, sometimes in desperation. And each day Digger was there for advice if she needed it.

"You are a charitable and kind man, Digger," she said one night. "A fine and stalwart man."

"Oh, bless you, lass. It's just that charity should be subtle as summer tides, washing quietly in and stealing ever so quietly out. I think sometimes I am too noisy about it." The poetry hung in the room, and neither said anything for some precious, golden moments, and then his face turned red again and he stuttered, "Did, did, did I ever tell you how I got the name Digger?"

"No. Tell me. Tell me now."

"Well, sit for a moment. It's not yet closing time, but sure it's running along to eleven. It's a raw night. Not likely to see many shoppers now." He sat down on the barrel he'd been moving.

"When I came to Canada over twenty years ago, I was twenty-two years old, and I'm ashamed to admit that I couldn't even write my own name. I could find no work as a store clerk because I couldn't read the labels on the boxes. I couldn't deliver orders. I couldn't do inventory on the docks. I could do nothing that required education. So, you say, why not be a farmer? I hate the farm. The farm killed my parents and gave back nothing for all the hours they slaved for it. So I walked the roads of Nova Scotia and New Brunswick, doing odd jobs, clearing fields, chopping and selling wood to those as ignorant as I. I came to the island only because a ship was heading this way. I stepped on to the red soil of Bedeque Bay township and almost immediately I was approached by a French priest. He observed correctly that I was not at the moment employed and asked if I would like to work for him. I said that I might be interested and asked what type of employment he was offering. 'Digging,' was all he said. So, not questioning him further, I followed him to the parish house, whereupon he handed me a shovel. I followed him to the rear of the church, he pointed to a half-dug grave and said 'Finish that.'"

Mary could tell it must have been one of his favorite stories because he told it with such relish, inflection, and dramatic pause.

"I said to the priest, 'You are hiring me as a gravedigger?'

"'Oui,' he said, 'you have some objection? The pay is two shillings a grave.'

" 'What happened to the fellow who began digging this one?' I asked. 'Did he lose the job?'

" 'No.' The priest smiled. 'He lost his life. Gravedigging is difficult, *n'est-ce pas*? This will be his grave when you finish.'

"So I became a gravedigger, and I began to study the tombstones with help from the priest, who later taught me to write and read.

"I was young and strong, and I lived at the rectory in a little barn behind the church. When anyone came to call on the priest and he wasn't there, I would take down the message. They would usually say, 'Who are you? What do you do here?' I would say, 'I am the grave-digger,' and they would look at me in shock, as though I had said, 'I am the village hangman.' After a bit, when I would go into town, I would hear people whisper, 'He's the gravedigger.' Then, as I got to know people, they would shout, 'Hello, Digger, let anyone down to-day?' It was all good fun, and I made many friends. With the priest's counsel, I bought a wagon and began traveling the roads. I bought my goods right off the brigs from England or the West Indies, and then I went house to house, bartering for other goods or money. Why, I stocked everything from boxes of Liverpool soap, puncheons, molasses, jars, hogsheads of sherry, port, scotch whiskey, sugar, Holland gin, and even Demerara rum. I never mentioned the brew to the priest, of course. I didn't want to upset him.

"Then I took my savings, hired a young Irish lad to travel the roads—always expand, you see, don't sell a thriving business that's your bread and butter—and I came to Charlottetown, met my won-derful Una, and now we have five shops. But look, I've given you a life history along with the origin of my name. It's almost closing time. You must be tired. I know old Digger is."

"No, Digger, I loved the story. You've worked hard for what you have, and that was our dream, too. We wanted to work hard for our land. To be sure, it was given to us, but it was not a gift we treated lightly." She looked off at the hanging Savior.

"I know, Mary. But you must fight for what is rightfully yours. And fight you will. You have had no response to your letters. What do you plan to do now?"

"With your permission, I would appreciate a few hours off each day so I can go to the Governor's Chambers. I will see him and state my case even if I have to break the doors down."

"Good for you, Mary McMahon. Go along now. I'll blow out the lamps."

As she made her way through the curtains that separated shop from home, he called to her, "By the way, Mary, can you guess who that priest was?"

"No," she said, puzzled.

"Father Gautier. Good night."

Though still November, it was already winter as Mary clutched the collar of her woolen coat and flew along the streets of Charlottetown. She crossed the wind-swept, icy concourse with a stinging snow biting her face, her breath leaving white puffs of cloud in its wake.

She had done everything that seemed reasonable. She had written to the seven members of the governor's Advisory Council, and to the governor himself, asking for a chance to state her case, "an appointment to discuss this most delicate and unjust situation which confronts me. I am sure that in all your compassion and understanding you will be just and restore my land to me."

Their response to her efforts was an arrogant, despotic silence. And so her mission was clear. She would go to them.

It was a Wednesday, market day, and already the frozen streets were cluttered with shoppers. The stalls spilled over with sugar, salt, oatmeal, kerosene oil, seeds, fertilizer, and meat. Makeshift signs announced the arrival of new shipments: "Just Arrived by Brig. *Manchester* from London, Liverpool and Glasgow 40 Quarter Casks Dark, Pale Brandy, 500 doz. Edinburgh Ale, 60 doz. Guinness Porter, and 200 Chests and ½ Chests of Congo Tea, Sugar, Salt, Candles, Honeydew Tobacco—Ship Bread, Gross Black Lead."

Out on the frozen, glassy Hillsborough River, sledlike wagons filled with more goods were pushed and slid and slipped along to the awaiting docks. This was a growing, expansive country, this Canada, and this island had food and shelter and fuel in abundance for its citizens. Mary McMahon observed it only too well, and her grimly set mouth and firm, jutting jaw announced to anyone who took the time to look that she and her family would be part of that growth and no bloody bureaucrat in frock coat and pleated trousers would take away her full title to all that Canada had to offer.

She passed the Round Market, its twelve bays jammed with more shoppers, topped off by a cupola. But it was not this thriving gazebolike structure that commanded her attention. It was the building next to it: the government building, a rather anonymous gray, stolid, and square structure, a building that seemed to say, coldly and brusquely, "State your business and leave." Her heart quickened as she climbed the stone steps and turned the brass doorknob. Kerosene lamps were smoking on the tables along the long stone corridor. No one was about as she walked past the closed committee room doors. For a moment she felt how completely alone she really was. If only Brendan were with her. Where was he? What was he doing at this moment in their separated lives?

"Yes, may I help you?" The sharp voice cut cleanly into her reverie, and she turned to face a tall, slim, and impeccably dressed man in his early thirties. The man straightened his cravat with his thumb and index finger.

The interior of the building held a lingering, bone-numbing chill, and the sudden appearance of this man seemed to emphasize its coldness.

"I wish to find the Assembly Room."

"The Assembly Room is up that staircase, but you cannot go in."

He began to walk away, as though his statement were a final decision and dismissal.

"Just a moment, sir."

He turned on his heels, knitting his brow as though irked by some inconsequential problem, "Yes?" he asked acidly.

"Why?" She was equally terse.

"Why what?" The brow was a straight line now.

"Why is it I cannot go in?"

"Why can't you?" There was weariness in the voice. "Because they are in session, and they do not wish to be disturbed by"—he fluttered his right hand in a gesture of dismissal—"outsiders."

"Outsiders, is it? They sit in chambers *because* of these outsiders, as you call them. Are you saying the people of Prince Edward Island are outsiders to their own representatives?"

Before he could respond, she had her skirts raised and had begun a quick ascent of the staircase.

At the top she turned left and came abruptly to a halt before a pair of great oak doors. A young clerk with plastered-down hair, wearing a wrinkled white shirt and high tie boots, stiffened as she approached.

"I would like to go in, let me pass."

"Sorry, madam, only members and no women."

"Excuse me. Did you say no women?"

"That's correct, madam. Only on certain occasions, and today is not one of them." At fifteen years of age the youth had already been consigned to the lowly world of a civil servant, armed with the ready answers of the unbending and categorical world of bureaucracy.

Just then two aging, gray-mustachioed gentlemen came along and passed through the doors without so much as a nod.

Through the open door, Mary caught a glimpse of a group of men sitting attentively at what appeared to be school desks. The assembly area was cordoned off by a red velvet rope. The door closed with a click.

"Are they members?" She nodded in the direction of the two who had just entered.

"I do not know, madam."

Overcome by frustration and anger, she pulled open the door and barged into the Assembly Room.

"Say, you can't go—" But the youth's voice was left on the other side of the door as she closed it behind her.

Startled faces looked up from polished desks. The figure on the dais stopped in mid-sentence, his head darting about in perplexed motion. "Here now, what is the meaning of this?" he finally managed, his red jowls and two chins shaking and twitching. "What do you want, young woman? This is an outrage."

"I wish to state my case. I wish to discuss the land question, which *I* find an outrage." Her voice was steady and sure.

Murmurs ran along the rows. "The land question!"

"Here, here, you have no right to speak. Call the clerk. Remove this woman from these chambers. This is unheard-of."

The door swung open again, and the clerk lurched in, his hands extended in some sort of attempt to pluck Mary from the chamber. But she was too strong and too quick. She pushed him aside, and he careened into a desk, toppling a bespectacled representative from his chair.

She faced the gawking Assembly members and announced, "I will be back, and you will hear me, mark me. You will hear me." Then she left, the door banging on its hinges.

"Who is that woman? Does anyone know? Who is she? And what does she want with us?" The governor stepped down from his podium, purple veins criss-crossing his red face, his hand groping for the lace handkerchief which hung limply from his breast pocket. "My God, the next thing we know the people will be telling *us* how to vote."

Mary did not linger in that dull gray building; she could feel the clutch of its cold, damp hand. She would not win a fight here, not in these male-dominated surroundings. Not today, but she would be back. She would be heard. For the present she had other ideas and another plan. She would sit on the frozen grass in front of Government House, the focal point of all the Charlottetown citizens, who were continually strolling by to study the newly constructed home of the governor.

She had remarked with interest in the past month the delight all Charlottetowners took in watching the governor's house expand and spread its wings over the harbor as it slowly developed into an elegant symbol of their capital. The people of the town were proud of their landmark, and now, when they came to look, they would see Mary Roark McMahon sitting on the rolling, grassy hill and holding her sign: "*Responsible* Government—Not Just *Representative* Government."

And that was what they saw just before noon on that bleak November day.

Crowds gathered outside the iron gates, as much in awe of Mary as of the white pillars and ornate gables that graced the sprawling clapboard mansion.

"What's she doing?"

"What is she up to?"

"Why, she should be ashamed of herself, the brazen hussy. A disgrace to women."

"Good for her."

"She's saying it for all of us." They shouted and glared at each other. They lined the fence, and Mary could hear their comments; but she remained seated on the frozen earth, her fingers numb and cold, holding tightly to the sign she had fashioned that morning in Digger's shop.

As the afternoon sky turned to slate under low, threatening

clouds, and the gawking citizens returned to their homes, Mary, still clutching her sign, marched down the winding drive just as the governor's carriage bounced jauntily into view.

The purple veins on his fleshy face broke out again over the bridge of the nose and in violet pockets under the eyes, and he shot a quick, exasperated glance at Mary, who stared right through him. His eyes lighted on the sign, and then he swiveled back to address his companion.

She turned to look after them as the carriage disappeared around the back to the stables and she recognized the other occupant as the imperious man she had met in the corridor. She could still hear his curt, dismissive tone: "They do not wish to be disturbed by outsiders." Outsiders! The words hung in the air and brought a fresh flush of anger to her face. She felt less an outsider here in Canada than she had in America, the land of her dreams. America had not been ready for foreigners, although professing an open and generous spirit to all people. But Canada had been. Canada was young and vibrant and open to growth. Outsider be damned! The day had turned cold and dank, and reluctantly Mary decided to end her vigil with the vow that she would be back. So she continued her walk down the drive, stopping for a moment to watch a flock of birds strutting along the grass, almost in martial file, like a medieval army ready to do battle. Enchanted by the birds' black hoods and gray-white tunics, she was momentarily startled by their sudden, noisy flight and did not realize at first that it had been prompted by the voice ringing out behind her. "What do you want? Here now, what are you about on these premises?"

She turned, the sign propped almost comically in front of her. The imperious young man was trotting down the hill, cupping his hands over his mouth and shouting as he approached.

When he was only yards away, he stopped and stood with his hands on his hips. He wore no coat, as though summoned in the middle of the night to meet some catastrophe, and he shivered from the cold.

"Well, you are a pretty sight," Mary said, more like a concerned parent than the offender whom he was upbraiding. "I'm more warmly dressed than you, and I am one of those outsiders."

"Yes, yes. I—I—forgive me for that remark. That really, well, that was rather stupid of me. But really, I mean, really, what in God's name are you doing here? Why do you call attention to yourself like this? You could be put in jail for trespassing." His voice was almost begging, and for a moment Mary felt sorry for him. He looked so cold.

"I'm here to get my land back, but if I have to go to jail, I will. I will do anything to get my land back."

"But really, it simply isn't fitting. Surely this is a matter a man should be handling."

"Who are you?"

It was a challenge, and there was a moment's silence before he answered, "I am the governor's secretary. My name is Byron Jelfe, and may I be so bold as to ask yours?"

"Mary McMahon, and my only man is a husband who is thousands of miles from my difficulty, so I fight for both of us. And you should have a coat on—you could catch cold."

He seemed to soften in spite of himself. A smile twitched at the corners of his mouth. "You sound like my mother." His smile was honest, and it warmed her despite the late-afternoon chill.

"So you do know how to smile? I am surprised. This morning there was only the gray face and the drawn mouth." She could hear the brogue creeping into her speech.

He no longer stuttered. He stood straight, and he seemed transformed. "Well, yes, I know how to smile. Perhaps I am not what you might think." The smile widened. "Look, let me get my coat, and I shall walk you to the edge of town if I may, and then you can tell me your problem. Fair enough?"

She thought for a minute. "All right. On the condition that you promise to help."

He was grave again and guarded. "No. I make no promises I cannot keep. But I am an honest listener. Well?"

"Fair enough." And to Byron Jelfe her smile was like a very warm overcoat of fur.

She watched him trot off toward the house. The hooded battalion of birds appeared then, veered in liquid motion, landed quietly on the grass, and resumed its military formation. This time he did not disturb them as he ran down the hill.

"They are quite beautiful, are they not?"

"Yes, they are. I love all nature."

"Especially the land." He smiled. They walked off almost cordially, and it seemed to Mary that they had done this all before. It was strange. There was no embarrassment about their being together, and they were well into the discussion before they even reached the massive iron gates. Mary had launched immediately into her story, and the hatless Jelfe, hands stuffed deeply into his overcoat pockets, lowered his head in intense interest.

By the time they arrived at Digger Shanley's Mary had explained it all.

"Well, that's it. And this is where I live."

"Oh, the Sweet Shoppe." His shiny black hair blew softly in the wind.

"You know it?"

"Of course. I often come to make a purchase here."

"Oh." She sounded disappointed and mentally chided herself for it. She had been too lonely lately, and his gentleness reminded her of Brendan. Of course, he purchased sweets for his wife or lady friend, and what finer shop than Digger Shanley's?

"I must confess to something." He looked boyish in his penitence. His green eyes dropped soulfully.

"What? What is it? You seem troubled," Mary responded with genuine concern.

"I am. I must tell you something. I have a vice, and I fight it, but to no avail." His discomfort was becoming more abject.

"A vice? What is it, Mr. Jelfe?"

"I am addicted to sweets, Mrs. McMahon." And then, slowly and ever so subtly, the now familiar grin broke across his face.

Mary did not react immediately; but when she did, she laughed that throaty, bubbly laugh, and in her exuberance she clutched his arm. "You devil. You teasing devil. I thought you had a problem with the drink or evil women. You are a devil, Mr. Jelfe."

They both laughed until he looked down and, noticing her hand on his arm, quickly resumed his businesslike demeanor.

"Ah, then, what began as an anxious day turned out well, I am sure. Tell me, Mrs. McMahon, will you be at the Chambers again in the morning? Or Government House in the afternoon?"

"Neither, for the time being, Mr. Jelfe. I will wait to see if I receive a reply to my letters now that I have made a proper nuisance of myself."

"Well, it was a delight meeting you, Mrs. McMahon. I shall convey your problem to the governor."

"Thank you, Mr. Jelfe. Good evening." And she curtsied to his formal bow.

Digger Shanley, watching from the upstairs window, frowned momentarily as he watched the scene unfold below him, and then he shrugged and descended the stairs to meet Mary as she came through the living quarters from the shop.

"Well, Mary, tell me about your day. I have been told you are the talk of Charlottetown."

"Oh, I hope I have not embarrassed you, Digger."

"Embarrassed me, lass? I am proud of your Irish courage. There are not many who would do what you did today. Man or woman." But his voice carried no authority, she observed.

"Thank you. There were times when I felt very awkward, especially with all those people staring at me. What does Una think? Does she share your feelings?"

"Well, now let us not get into that. Why do you ask? And why might you think she would feel any different?"

"Because she remained silent this morning while I fashioned my sign. She did not say aye or nay to what I was doing. Maybe I should leave your house, Digger Shanley. I do not wish to come between you and Una. You both have been too good to me."

"Don't talk such nonsense, Mary. Una is just a bit frightened because of the business. She is right, of course. We would not want to destroy all that we have worked to build up. But surely that will not happen."

"Let us hope not, Digger. Let us hope not."

Una appeared at the top of the stairs. Her face was serious but by no means angry.

"You understand, Mary, we have nothing against you, God forgive us. But people, well, you know how people are." She walked down the narrow staircase, holding her long skirt by the hem.

"What are you saying, Una Shanley? I do not get your drift."

"I am saying, Digger, that I think Mary should find another place to live, God forgive me."

"God forgive you, surely, if He can find it in His bleeding heart to do so." And he bowed in the direction of the portrait of the Savior that hung out there behind the dark curtains separating them from the shop.

"Digger Shanley, we have worked ourselves morning, noon, and night. Are we going to throw it all away now?" She took Mary's hands. "You understand, Mary, I know you do. Would you please explain it to him?"

"She's right, you know. Your business could suffer, and you both have been too kind for me to cause you any problem or inconvenience. I will leave in the morning, and I thank you both for everything." She ascended the stairs to her room, and then she turned to look down at them. "I am sincere when I say you will always be my friends. I understand. Believe me, I understand."

"Oh, Mary, you are one of a kind, bless you." Una's eyes filled with tears. She was sorry, yes, but she was thankful.

It was only a few minutes later that a soft rap on the door brought Mary from her desk where she was composing a letter to Isabella.

"Who is it?"

"It's the Digger, Mary. I have something for you." His voice was muffled on the other side of the oak door.

"Yes, Digger," she said as she opened it.

He stood with a tray in his hands and a crooked smile on his face.

"Una made you a bit of supper. You must be starving after your day in the cold. Oh, and there is a letter for you. Goodnight, Mary."

"Thank you, Digger, and thank Una for me. She is a good woman. You must not be angry with her."

"No, I will not be angry, Mary." He paused a moment before handing her the tray.

"Yes?"

"I saw you tonight from the window. How is it you know Mr. Jelfe?"

"I met him at Government House. I explained my situation. Why do you ask, Digger?"

"No reason. I would not wish to see you get hurt. You are alone and very vulnerable." He smiled. "I suppose I am acting like a father."

"No need to worry. I know how to take care of myself. But thank you for your concern." She closed the door with her shoulder and placed the tray on the desk. The inviting aroma of the steaming, well-seasoned stew brought her taste buds alive. She ate with alacrity, fin-

ishing off with brown bread and tea and a mint jelly and smiling at
the four pieces of chocolate Una had included. Poor Una was suffering such guilt. She is a good woman. They are both good people, she
thought.

She cleared the tray from the desk and sat down with anticipation to read her letter from Isabella Profitt. It was bulky, and inside
was another letter, this one from Brendan. Her heart leaped with joy.
She sat back and read Isabella's letter first, saving her husband's.

My deare Mary,
    My letter writing is not so goode. Pleeze forgave me. Yore
little angel is fine and full of chear. No one lives at yore house. So
that is goode. We look all the time. The agent does not return so
far. Many people in Tignish are angree for what hapened to you
and yore farm. God bles you. Hear is a letter from yore huzbend.
                                                    Isabella Profitt

The simple sentiments brought tears to her eyes. The goodness
and kindness of the woman were so evident in her honesty, and thank
God Gabriella, her angel, was well and happy.

Brendan's letter bore the postmark Derrynane, Cahirciveen,
County Kerry. She held it to her bosom, kissed the envelope softly,
and then opened it carefully. The paper was precious to her. Brendan
had touched it and addressed it. Had he pictured, as he wrote the
address, what the farm looked like; had he seen her and Gabriella in
his thoughts? God, how she missed him. Were they both crazy, she
and Brendan, off on their separate missions? She could not help feeling that *his* was one of misplaced allegiance. At least she was fighting
for *their* land, for something that could be *theirs*, something tangible
that *they* could work and walk on and nourish, something that would
grow with the years, not for that empty dream of Irish peasants: the
invisible and unattainable gift of freedom.

Her hand trembled as she removed the thin white parchment.
The letter was long, and she settled down to it as though she were
actually talking to him.

When she was done, she sat back in silent contemplation. Brendan's enthusiasm for O'Connell and the cause of Ireland frightened
her. This passion could consume him, as it appeared it was already
doing. What if he decided to stay indefinitely? What madness was
this? Her face flushed, and an angry flame began to burn inside her.
The whole thing, this entire situation, was beginning to become clear
to her. He was off slaying dragons like some visionary in a dream, and
she was fighting for their land and their survival.

Glory be to God—she managed a wry smile—always Irish in spite
of it all! Thanks be to God O'Connell's not a woman, I'd be afraid
Brendan would want to propose marriage.

CHAPTER XVI

IN THE WEEKS that followed, Byron Jelfe was never far from Mary's side. He counseled her and advised her on what government records she needed for verification that a legal conveyance had taken place. He wrote an official inquiry to the Land Commission in London, and they both waited patiently for the official records of John Wallace's legal ownership to be sent back to Charlottetown.

Meanwhile, Mary was working in a small woolen mill that employed only a dozen or so people. More than once did she smile at the irony that found her skilled hands working the loom and carding machine. At times it seemed she had never left Evansborough. But her determination was fierce, and she worked long hours. The money would come in handy as a nest egg when she returned to Tignish. She did not squander her money, but she did manage to buy a few dresses and a navy bonnet that brought out the blue in her eyes.

It was this fetching bonnet that she wore on the Sunday before Christmas. Byron Jelfe was competing in the Tandem Club race. The gentlemen of Charlottetown chose partners and shared the reins of large horse-drawn sleighs. They charged along the snow-packed hills and streaked across the ice of the Hillsborough River to the finish line and the awaiting trophy. It was a gala event that brightened those first, bitter-cold days of winter and put everyone into a gay mood for the Christmas week to come. Colorful banners and bunting decorated houses and shops. Brightly colored sleigh robes and gleaming fur rugs covered the drivers as they jockeyed for position, and shouts of encouragement filled the snowy air. The red-eyed horses pranced and bucked, vaporous streams issuing from their large, open mouths and smoking nostrils. The ladies' costumes were a potpourri of riotous color. Male spectators doffed tall hats and derbies, seemingly oblivious to the weather.

Mary stood in the bone-jarring cold, bundled in a heavy woolen coat, the blue bonnet setting off her long black hair. Her skin was flushed, and her smile flashed radiantly as Byron's horse pranced by.

Sitting with him in the cab was a rotund and full-faced man

whom Mary remembered having seen in the Government Chambers. He was a successful barrister and also a representative to the governor's Advisory Council. Mary did not like him. He had a cruel, grim mouth, and she had seen him upbraid one of the young clerks in a most unmerciful tirade because the clerk's boots were spotted with mud. His name, she recalled, was Bard, Francis Bard.

Mary squeezed through the crowds that lined the racecourse in time to greet Byron with a tentative wave, and Jelfe beamed when he saw her.

The crowds leaned out, peering at the starting line, and then a booming official voice shouted, "Ready. On your marks, get set, go." The sleighs shot out as whips cracked and snapped like frozen twigs breaking underfoot.

Gloved hands offered muffled applause as the cheering, shouting spectators broke from their ranks and rushed to the other side of the street to watch the sleighs turn the bend below the hill.

Byron and his rider fell into third place, and Mary, caught up in the excitement, screamed her encouragement. They were approaching the river now, the most dangerous point in the race. This first contact with the ice had to be made cautiously, lest the sleigh skid and go off course or simply topple over.

The first team did just that. The driver did not rein in his horse quickly enough, and the great, panting beast faltered and slid on the mirrored surface, unable to get any footing. The sleigh was turned sideways and careened off into the thick banking. Both passengers were thrown out but tumbled swiftly to their feet, smiling and indicating to the onlookers that they were unharmed. Meanwhile, the horse dragged the overturned sleigh off downriver.

The next pair took the ice more slowly, their horse digging into the smooth surface and seemingly gliding along; but Byron Jelfe's sleigh was close behind, and his horse stepped out smartly and dashed on past.

The cheers mounted as Byron snapped his whip and coaxed the beast with expert hands on the reins. They drove the required three hundred yards, almost sliding into the red markers and veering off course; but at the last minute the bulk of the overweight Francis Bard leaned left, and a collision was avoided. The horse seemed to fly from ice to land, digging hooves into the snow, flinging great white divots into the air behind.

The harness bells jingled like cut glass as Byron urged the horse on to the finish line, and the remaining sleighs rumbled across, their hopes of winning the Tandem Trophy dashed for another year.

The race master climbed the windy wooden platform and announced the winners as the crowd cheered, drowning out their names, "Mr. Jelfe and Mr. Bard." People pressed in to the platform as the victorious tandem held up their gleaming trophy for all to see. Then the race master announced, "Hot buttered rum and food of all kinds right behind me, folks, in the basement of Saint Paul's Church. Go and get it."

Mary hung back, suddenly made shy by the press of the crowd, but Byron saw her out of the corner of his eye, and handing the trophy to Bard, he jumped to the ground and worked his way toward her, smiling and nodding, shaking hands and accepting congratulations as he went.

"Well, you are a very popular man today, Mr. Jelfe."

His smile faded, and he affected a childish pout. "Why, Mary, I thought we were all over that formal business. I won that race just for you, and still you dare call me Mr. Jelfe. I am going to tell them I default and give the trophy to the runner-up." He turned abruptly and began to move back toward the platform.

"Byron! Come back here," she shouted, and then caught herself, putting her gloved hand over her mouth in embarrassment as several people turned to her and laughed good-humoredly.

"Now that's better." He smiled broadly. "Come, let us have some hot buttered rum to warm us up."

"You are a tease, Byron Jelfe. I almost believed you."

They huddled off to Saint Paul's. The snow was slanting now, drifting in powdery heaps along the streets, and out on the Hillsborough River the silver glaze of the ice was covered by a soft cushion of white, which had already buried the tracks of the sleighs.

The parish hall was a bedlam of noise, talk, music, and singing. All faces were reddened and wind-lashed, and steam rose from cups of hot coffee, tea, and buttered rum.

Ducking into the bustling, bursting hall, they were greeted by a round of applause that caused Mary to step back self-consciously. She and Byron were friends, but she did not wish it to appear that they were anything else.

He gestured for silence. "It was the horse. I have a magnificent horse, very intelligent." He laughed and tapped the side of his head.

"I think it was the girth of your partner that saved the day," a voice shouted, and more laughter followed.

The warmth stung their faces, and their eyes sparkled as they sipped their hot buttered rum.

Byron joined a group in the far corner of the room, and Mary walked over to the overburdened food table to try some of the freshly baked little cakes.

"It's been quite a day," a voice said at her back. She turned to the robust form of Digger Shanley.

"Why, Digger, you're a sight for sore eyes. I haven't seen you or Una for a fortnight. Is she with you?"

"No. The cold was too much for her. She hasn't been feeling too good the past few days."

"Oh, I'm sorry to hear that. Is there something I can do?"

"Oh, heavens, no. She'll be fine. Just a bit of the rheumatism, I expect. She couldn't think of coming out on a day like this. How is your battle progressing?"

More racing enthusiasts stormed into the hall then, and Mary lost sight of Byron in the crowd.

"Well, I'm waiting to hear from London. It should be soon now."

"Soon, is it? You have been here over two months already. Are they going to keep you away from your child for the winter?" He squinted at the word *child*, and his voice rose slightly. "I do not like to see a mother separated too long from her family. It is not healthy, Mary." He reminded her of a country priest.

"I do not like the separation either, Digger, but what can I do?"

"What does your friend Mr. Jelfe have to say in the matter?" She thought she caught a suggestion of sharpness at the mention of Byron's name, and it angered her.

"Mr. Jelfe, or Byron, as I call him, has done everything he could for me. He is waiting to hear from the Land Commission, and then I shall take my case to Province House."

Digger sipped his rum. "Yes, I'm sure Jelfe has been very, very helpful."

"Are you suggesting something, Digger Shanley? I know that Galway cuteness. What are you trying to say?" She moved closer to him, trying not to shout in the crowded, boisterous hall.

"I am not saying it well, Mary. But you know I have great respect and admiration for you."

"Be assured, Digger Shanley, Byron Jelfe and I are just good friends."

"I hope so, Mary. I would not want to see you hurt. I told you that before. I said you are vulnerable, and you are becoming more so each day. It's difficult for a woman as young and lovely as you to be away from her husband. And, Mary—" He did not continue.

"What? What is it, Digger?"

"It is nothing, Mary. Nothing at all." He shook his round head.

"You have something to say. Then say it."

"Well then, I will. Has it ever occurred to you that you might have finished your business with the government weeks ago if you had continued to embarrass the governor by sitting out your vigil at Government House? I just wonder if Mr. Jelfe's interest is in *your* best interest or the governor's."

Her cheeks were aflame with temper. "Now you listen to me. Byron Jelfe has done everything for me, and when I walk my own land again, it will be him I shall thank."

"I hope so, Mary. But do not forget, you're dealing with an Englishman. Have ye not a short memory?"

"Don't be throwing the Irish at me, Digger. This is Charlottetown, not Galway or London. I'll be leaving now, and I'll be thanking you to mind your own business." She turned away and then turned back. "I hope Una is feeling better. Give her my best."

She made her way through the chattering crowd to the other side of the room and a cluster of young women who were helping to serve the refreshments. "Yes, miss, what would you like, eh?" A pretty young thing, Mary thought.

"I'll have a mug of hot rum, if you please."

The girl crooked her head. It was not usual for a young woman to be seen drinking spirits in public, and she questioned Mary again, "Did you say rum, miss?"

"I did. Do I need my mother's permission?" Mary shot back hotly.

"Oh, goodness gracious, no," the girl sputtered with embarrassment.

Several people turned then to stare openly at Mary. Such public display of anger was seldom seen in Charlottetown, and certainly never from proper women.

Mary's anger at Digger's implication still nettled her, and she drank the rum quickly, its warmth oozing down her throat and igniting a fire in her stomach. Her elbows tingled, and a bright glow shone in her face. "That was very good. Thank you. I will have another."

She became aware of a murmuring in the crowd and knew they were talking about her. But a numbness was creeping over her, and she no longer cared. This time she sipped more slowly. She was not accustomed to spirits, although she had on several occasions tasted a thimbleful of poteen to help ease the shyness she always felt in the initial stages of making love to Brendan.

Her body was humming with life, and she sauntered over to Byron, whom she could now see holding court with a half dozen cronies from the Tandem Club.

He saw her coming, and he excused himself, leaving a trail of knowing smirks and nodding heads behind him. "I was about to join you, Mary. I see you have a mug of rum. It is delicious, is it not?"

"It is that." She giggled, her face lighting up.

He studied her for a moment. She was so strikingly beautiful that he wanted to reach out and touch her creamy cheeks, stroke the silk of her black hair.

"Take me for a ride in your sleigh, Byron," she said suddenly. "I feel full of excitement."

"I would be honored, Mary. You do seem particularly exuberant. Could it be from the rum?"

"I do not know. No. Yes. Yes, of course, it is the rum, and the day, and the race and the colors, and everything."

He followed her out of the hall, and their departure did not go unnoticed, particularly by Digger Shanley.

Byron helped her into the sleigh and then wrapped the fur rug around her, touching her hips as he tucked it securely about her.

The horse whinnied and shook its thick mane, and bells jingled and sprinkled their high-pitched song over the drifting snow.

White, furry flakes lay on her lashes, and as he took the reins with one hand, he gently stroked them away. It was a spontaneous and delicate gesture that brought embarrassment to neither one. It was as though they had always touched. She smiled at him and said nothing. Some moments were better left undisturbed, she thought.

The sleigh glided along the icy, snowbound streets in a world of white silence. He could feel her body beside him, and the thrill of her so close to him brought a hot and raging flush of desire. How he had longed for her ever since the first day that he saw her. But she had never given him reason to believe that she would have any interest in him beyond the quick and respectful friendship that had sprung up between them.

The afternoon was turning dark. Candles and lamps flickered a spangle of gold across the snow, and the harness bells of other sleighs chimed in a crackling winter key, their rippling whisper tumbling over the swathed, alabaster town.

Mary's body tingled with excitement under the protection of the fur rug. She clasped her hands in her lap contentedly as the sleigh moved smoothly down to the whirling, swirling, snowflaked harbor.

"It is truly a magic evening, Mary. The snow is splendid in its silence."

"It is, Byron. It is indeed a magic evening."

He pulled on the reins, and they sat in the silvery quiet. "You know this rug is black bear, but it looks more polar bear at the moment."

She laughed her throaty, robust laugh, breaking the night's silence.

"I love to hear you laugh, Mary. It's so genuine. You don't hold back. Where did you learn such confidence?"

"The laugh is sincere enough to be sure, but the confidence is indeed strained. I have made myself do many things, like coming here to fight for my land, but there are few nights I do not awake in fear and trembling. I ask myself what will happen if I do not get the land and cabin back. Where will I turn? What will happen to my family? Oh, Byron, I may appear to be strong and independent, but there are times when I feel so weak and helpless."

He looked away when she mentioned family. They were always there, and there was no denying it: a husband and a child.

He made a clucking sound with his tongue, slapped the reins lightly, and the horse shuffled off.

Her shoulder was touching his arm, and her nearness was so palpable that he battled with the idea of sweeping her up into his arms. It seemed she read his deepest thoughts, for she sighed and sank lower under the fur rug.

"Would you like to come to my rooms for tea?" The invitation was spontaneous and delivered clumsily.

"I think that would be lovely," she said evenly, and smiled.

"You would?" His reaction was boyish, and Mary laughed heartily.

The mare was snapped into action as Byron urged the beast on with the sting of the lash.

His rooms were just beyond the harbor and within walking distance of Government House, where he could arrive quickly in the event the governor needed him.

There were three apartments, and his was in the basement of a large stone house. "The government owns the house, and for a nominal fee civil servants, I being one"—he fumbled with his key—"there we are, can rent out the flats." The door swung open, and the sudden rush of heat from the stove made her shudder.

"Goodness, it was colder out there than I realized."

"Here, step over to the fire. I'll bring it to life." He reached for the black leather bellows, and the whoosh of air brought an orange flame licking at the thick oak log.

"Ah, ah, she'll be driving us out of the room in a few minutes." He replaced the bellows.

The flame threw the darkened room into shadowy relief.

He turned up two lamps, and a pale light bathed the apartment. "Let me take your coat and shawl and that lovely bonnet, Mary. I'll place them by the fire where they'll dry off and be warm for you when you go."

"You are very kind, Byron. A true gentleman."

"I thought you might say 'English gentleman' for a moment." He took her wet things and hung them on the back of a large leather chair.

"I suppose there are a few English gentlemen—that is, besides yourself. I love your rooms. How many do you have?"

"Four, the parlor, where we are now," he added unnecessarily, "my office, through there, the bedroom, and the scullery. By the way, I must prepare the tea. You sit by the fire, and I'll have things ready in no time." He went to the scullery, and she could hear him rattling around with cups and saucers and plates.

"May I help you, Byron?"

"No, of course not. You're my guest. I'll be done in a moment."

The room had a quiet elegance about it. A sturdy bookcase held many leather-bound volumes of Chaucer, Shakespeare, Donne, Milton, and Fielding. Leather chairs and a damask love seat complemented each other like man and wife.

"Do you like my library?" He carried a pewter tray into the room and settled it on the low table by the fireside. "I just received this from my mother, *Poems of William Wordsworth*. They say he is quite good." He held the book in his hands with a gentle fondness. "I love poetry, don't you, Mary?"

"I suppose I do. After all, I come from a land of poets and story-tellers. . . . I think I'll sit on the floor by the fire." And she sat at the open hearth, taking the cup and saucer he offered her.

"There is some sweet bread and a honey cake that is awfully good."

"Yes, I'll take both. I'm hungry from the weather and the rum, I suspect. Did you know I was becoming a bit tipsy from the drink? I hope you didn't think me bold for asking you to take me on a sleigh ride."

"Bold? It has been the grandest day of my life, thanks to you and the rum. I shall always keep a warm place in my heart for hot buttered rum." The ticking of a grandfather clock lent a feeling of contentment to the room.

"Byron, I must ask you something, and I hope you will not be disturbed by my question."

He placed his cup and saucer on the table, his brows knit in quiz-zical lines. "Why, what is it, Mary? You seem so serious all of a sudden. Of course, you may ask me anything you wish."

"It has been said to me . . ." She hesitated and stared into the fire.

"Go on," he whispered gently.

"It has been said that by aiding me in my fight for what is rightfully mine, you are really acting in the interest of the governor."

"I don't understand. How could that help the governor?"

"Well, if I had continued to embarrass him in public, he might already have given me rightful ownership and I would be gone."

"Gone. So you would. Yes, you would be gone, and I make no secret that I do not wish to see you go. But that day you were sitting on the grass, I thought he would have apoplexy. He ordered me to 'get that fool of a woman off the property, and I do not care how you do it.'" Byron's voice became a raging, stentorian baritone in his impression of the governor. "So I told you I would listen to your problem. But by the time I walked you back to the Sweet Shoppe, I knew I would do all I could to help you. I have said nothing to the governor about your case. I have done it all on my own. But I do have a confession to make to you. The guilt has been oppressive, and now it is you who must promise not to be angry. Stay there a moment."

He rose and walked into his office and came back with a very formal-looking white paper. "Here, Mary."

She took it from him and read it to herself, the large script dancing on the page in the firelight.

She read slowly, glancing up once, her face drained of its healthy pink. When she finished, she folded the paper and slipped it into the pocket of her brown woolen dress.

"Why, Byron? Why did you not tell me you had heard from the Land Commission?"

He left his chair and knelt beside her on the floor and took her hands in his. "Because I love you. I love you more than my own life, and I knew that once I gave you this paper, you would soon be gone, and I would never see you again. I wanted to keep you here for as long as possible."

"Oh, Byron, you mustn't. Please don't say such things."

"I can't help myself. I am in constant misery and loneliness when I am away from you. And when I'm with you, I feel buoyant and alive. The world is mine for the asking. You bring out everything that is good in me. Please don't be angry, Mary. The commission only verifies ownership and leaves the disposition of the case up to the local authorities. We still have a fight. In my selfishness and madness I was just trying to postpone things for a time. Damn me, Mary, but I love you so."

His eyes penetrated hers, and slowly he reached out and she was locked in his embrace. His hands framed her face, and he kissed her tenderly. His right hand fell softly on her hair to stroke it as though he were feeling some rare silk. He kissed her again and continued to gaze, in awe, at her beauty. He smoothed her face and felt the ivory of her neck. Every touch was soft, almost trembling in its approach.

His hand brushed against her breast as he kissed her again. He lay down beside her, resting his head in her lap, and stared into the dark blue of her eyes. She bent down and kissed him then. Her breasts grazed his cheek, and his hands came up to cup them.

"Oh, for the love of Christ, what's happening to me?" she cried out, tears of anger and frustration streaking down her cheeks.

"What is it, Mary? Why do you cry, my sweetheart, my angel?"

"I cry because I am half a woman. I cry because I have a husband who is too distant for me to love. I cry because I want love, yet my conscience will not allow me the freedom to have it. I cry because you are the sweetest, gentlest man I have ever met and I cannot give myself to you. I think I love you, too, Byron, in a different way. I love your tenderness and kindness; but I have taken a vow, and I am determined that I shall be true to that vow, so help me God."

He brushed her tears away, kissing her forehead as he did so. "Do not be so hard on yourself, Mary. I understand. I truly do. I shall always love you. No one can take that from me. I shall love you through eternity. Please do not cry. Finish your tea, it's getting cold. Then I shall see you home. Are you better now?"

She sighed deeply. "Yes, I am better now, thanks to you, Byron. I will be all right now, my gentle, understanding friend."

The next morning Mary sat at her window and, with heavy heart, contemplated the awkwardness of her position. She was at a crossroads in her young life. She knew she could easily and willingly give herself to Byron Jelfe, but where would that leave them? She would be caught in the trap of having to decide between two men. It was just the mental anguish of Brendan's being so far away. Damn O'Connell, damn his eyes and his bloody cause! Oh, God, help me persevere in all that I must do, she begged.

Distracted from these unhappy thoughts by an urgent rapping at her door, Mary rose to find Mrs. Morley, her skittery, hen-faced landlady, hovering impatiently on the landing. "Here, for you, brought by messenger. I'll be off. I have more important things to do than delivering love notes."

"Why, what do you mean?"

"You know what I'm talking about. I don't want you bringing menfolk around here in the night, do you understand that?" Her beak-like nose quivered with indignation.

"The gentleman was simply escorting me to my door." Mary felt weak in the knees at this sudden scolding.

"I saw the two of you from the parlor window, kissing and carrying on. I won't have it, and you a married woman. Your poor husband should take a stick to you. Good day."

She skittered down the hall, leaving Mary feeling naked and soiled.

True, he had kissed her again, but with love and understanding, softly on the lips and then on the forehead, and he was gone. Did no one understand her plight? She closed the door and opened the note. Although she, too, had assumed it was from Byron, this was far from a love note.

Mary,
     Una is growing worse. I need help. Can you come immediately?

                                                  Digger Shanley

She was bundled up and out the door in minutes.

The shop, surprisingly, was locked this Monday morning, but Digger answered her knock almost immediately, raising the green shade as he opened up to her.

"Bless you, Mary." He took her mittened hands in his. "May God bless you for coming so quickly. I didn't know who to call. I didn't want to bother those with family responsibilities."

"I'm pleased you would ask my help. Is she upstairs?"

"Yes. Here, give me your shawl."

As they ascended the steep staircase, Mary could hear the deep rattle of Una's breathing. "Have you sent for the doctor, Digger?"

"Yes, but with the storm and the freezing weather all the doctors are busy. There was a shipwreck off the shoals early this morning. Frozen bodies have washed up with the tides. The Medical College is already overloaded. They said they would send someone as soon as possible."

The bedroom door was open, and Mary was instantly taken aback by Una's appearance. Normally a big, robust worker of a woman, Una Shanley had been reduced to a choking, wheezing, tallow-faced invalid.

Mary approached the square four-poster bed. She sat on the edge, taking one waxen hand in hers. "Has she been able to take soup or any liquids?"

"She cannot even raise her head. Her poor heart must be aching from all the choking she has gone through. God be with her." Digger clutched nervously at his throat as though he, too, were choking.

"Digger, do you have any goose grease?"

"Not goose grease, but I have grease for the vaults. It's cooking grease."

"Fine, that will do. Bring it to me with some strips of wool."

Mary watched him leave, and then she pulled the blankets back. Una's eyes opened and moved glassily around in her head. She reached out feebly for Mary's hand. "There now, Una, we'll have you well in no time." The woman's head slowly nodded back and forth. "Please, Una, you must *want* to get well."

Una's shaking hand summoned Mary closer until Mary's ear was next to the sick woman's mouth. "Take care of Digger . . . not do any . . . thing for hims—" She could not finish, so taken was she by a violent racking coughing attack. Her sunken jaws and trembling mouth sucked for air.

Mary untied the pink bow of Una's nightgown, exposing the perspiring chest. Her once large breasts lay flat and sagging, sweat glistening from the heaving flesh.

Digger came back then, carrying the tub of grease and pieces of wool. He saw his wife's exposed breasts, and embarrassed before Mary, he turned to the frosted window. Mary seemed not to notice. She applied the grease to Una's chest and, lifting her gently, to the back. She then covered her with the pieces of cloth.

"There, now rest, and do not speak or upset yourself. The doctor will be along shortly. Come along, Digger. Let her sleep."

Digger looked down at his suffering wife, bent to kiss her sallow cheek, and then followed Mary downstairs after he shut the door behind him.

"Let me make you a cup of tea, Digger," she said to him as he sat heavily at the kitchen table.

"Will you be having one, Mary?"

"Yes, I'll join you. There's much friendship in a cup of tea, my mother used to say."

"What is her illness, Mary, would you be knowing?"

Mary began boiling the water. She had seen this consumptive death before. And she had seen the look of death in Una's eyes. Should she tell him? He was like so many men—physically strong and rugged but emotionally unable to cope at moments of family crisis.

He hovered over the table like a dumb animal, continuing to clutch his throat nervously.

"Well, Mary, what do you think? She will get well, will she not?"

She faced him squarely. He was not a child, and he should be prepared.

"She is very sick, Digger, very sick."

"Jesus, woman, what do you think it is?"

"She has all the symptoms of tuberculosis."

"Tuberculosis? I thought it myself but I dared not believe it." The word was like a curse, one of those words one heard as a child and repeated over and over in the dark mystery of one's bedroom, words that had some adult meaning and were almost always connected with evil.

"Tuberculosis?" he repeated.

"Surely I cannot be certain. I am no doctor or nurse, but my own dear sister had the same symptoms. Many a night I rocked her little body as she struggled to fill her lungs with air. And I had a friend in Evansborough who had the same thing. She caught it from the lint and the stuffiness of the mill."

"Did—did they—did they live?" His hand went to his neck again.

She placed a hand on his bull-like shoulder. "No," she said simply.

"Oh, Mary, what would I do without my Una? Without her I would be lost. I swear I could not manage by myself."

"Please, Digger, let us wait for the doctor."

And wait they did, all through the bitter-cold day until, a little after four, the doctor arrived, stamping his feet loudly on the porch mat.

He was a gruff, colorless man in a black greatcoat and carrying a bag to match. Digger led him up the stairs and waited outside. A few moments later the doctor came out.

"Well, Doctor, what is it?" Digger's voice was cracked and strained.

"Tuberculosis." He shook his head in that universal movement common to all men of medicine. "She is too sick to be moved. I'll leave you this medicine. She must take it every two hours, two spoonfuls. Who applied the grease to her chest and back?"

"Er, our—our friend, Mary."

"Good. Do it often. I will be back by midweek. Good day."

Digger followed the doctor down the stairs and to the door. "Thank you for coming, Doctor, thank you." The doctor grunted something indistinguishable, stepped into the cold, and made his way to his carriage.

Mary watched the black carriage disappear around a bend in the road as Digger joined her.

"You were right, Mary. Thank you for telling me. I was at least a bit prepared. And now I must work day and night to save her."

"I'll stay with you. That way one of us can rest while the other keeps the vigil. Now have another cup of tea."

"God bless you, Mary. God bless you."

And a constant vigil it was as they took turns sitting by Una's bedside. There was no time for Mary to take her case to the Assembly; she never left the shop.

On Wednesday the doctor returned and saw evidence of ever so slight an improvement. "Continue what you are doing," was his terse comment, and he was gone.

Thursday a note arrived from a frantic Byron Jelfe.

Mary,

I have looked everywhere for you. Mrs. Morley gave me no satisfaction. She barely gave me a minute, saying she did not know where you were and didn't care. Fortunately I met Miss Gillis, one of your co-workers, and she said a note had been delivered this morning, stating family illness as the reason for your absence.

I was further told that Mrs. Shanley is quite ill and you are helping. How sweet and good of you. This has been a beastly week. I have barely had time to think. The governor is on one of his rampages, piling up the work before Christmas. Do you have any plans for Christmas? Do write to me.

Your devoted servant,
Byron

In all the worry and concern for Una she had put everything out of her mind: the land, Brendan and Gabriella, Byron, even her position at the mill. Christmas was even a dim memory. As lonely as it had been without family, she thought she would never forget the dull ache that stabbed her heart during the early morning mass at the Cathedral. The Assembly. She had even forgotten her appearance the following Monday before the Assembly. She had to get there; but she could not leave Una, and she was so drained mentally and physically she did not think she had the strength to deliver her speech to the Assembly even if she were given the opportunity.

But all her frustration ended on Friday morning as she sat, half dozing in a cane chair by Una's bed. A wheezing, whistling cough shrieked through the room, jolting Mary upright. She stood and leaned over the bed. Dawn was streaking a cold winter pink across the room, and the early sunlight lit up Una Shanley's face. A slight smile of peace crossed her mouth. Una was at rest.

The black funeral cortege was a tribute to Digger as well as to Una. They were good, charitable people, and Charlottetown did not forget. The church was filled on Monday morning with people who had been helped at one time or another by the Shanleys.

The priest intoned the ancient Latin, and the congregation walked by the pale wooden casket, touching it for the last time.

Mary stayed with Digger throughout the ordeal and acted as hostess to the friends who came back for tea and biscuits. It was not until everyone had left that the universal stillness brought on by a death in the house crept along the corridors and across the rooms. Digger sat with his head in his hands in the empty parlor.

"Digger, I must go out. Will you be all right by yourself?"

He looked up, his eyes red-rimmed and tear-stained. "I will, Mary. I would rather pass this day alone with my grief. How can I ever thank you for what you have done? You have been an angel of mercy."

"Digger, you were so kind to me. Both of you. It is small recompense." She leaned over and kissed his cheek. "I will be back for teatime." She tiptoed out of the kitchen as though her footsteps would disturb the very death that was in the still air.

It was midafternoon, and not many people were about on the snow-crusted streets of Charlottetown. Mary's scarf hung loose over her black hair, and her coat was opened at the collar, so oblivious was she to the fierce blasts of winter cold that blew across the square.

Horses brayed and stomped the cold earth in front of the government building as she approached. There were many carriages, some with drivers sitting solemnly, the reins held loosely in their hands. Good, she thought, the Assembly is in session. She breathed deeply and lowered the shawl to her shoulders, allowing her hair to fall freely. Her cheeks were pink from the weather, and if it were not for the narrowing of her eyes, she would have appeared nothing more than a lovely, windblown creature on a random visit to the seat of island government.

She mounted the stairs quickly, her high-buttoned boots echoing over the stone. In front of the closed chamber doors, a clerk—not the same one she had encountered before—sat perched behind the mahogany desk. This time she would not comment to him one way or another. She would bolt right past and seat herself immediately. If they wanted to remove her, they would have to carry her out.

"Good day." The clerk smiled at her. She did not answer but turned the polished doorknob and went in before he had time to climb down from his sentinel's post.

"Say you can't . . . I say—"

But she shut his voice off with the door and, without hesitation, seated herself at a vacant desk. She was aware that her presence would cause immediate consternation.

"Madam, you have been told before, you are not allowed in these chambers." The governor's perenially crimson face colored even more deeply as Byron Jelfe half rose from his chair. "Jelfe, you know this woman. Get her out."

Byron whispered something in the governor's ear as the entire Assembly turned to stare in her direction.

"I have come to speak to you, and you will listen to me this time. You will not send me away because I am a woman."

"If she doesn't leave, then I will," one representative roared to the others.

"Aye."

"Aye."

And they began to rise from their chairs, led by the rotund Francis Bard, who squeezed his corpulent frame along the narrow aisle between the desks, his mouth quivering as he berated her to the others. "You foreigner, have you no manners, no decorum, no sense of decency?" This last he shot more at Byron than at Mary.

"Enough. Enough of your talk, Bard. I will not have you talk to the lady that way." Byron shook a finger at the portly figure.

"Lady? Whoever said she was a lady? This whole city knows she is a married woman and the only reason she *submits*"—he spit out the word *submits* as though it were something distasteful in his mouth—"to you is to see how much she can get out of you. Jelfe, you're the laughingstock of Charlottetown. Didn't you know that?"

Byron started in Bard's direction but was blocked by two other members of the Assembly, one of whom, an angular and patrician-featured man named Charles Andrews, addressed the governor in a voice that was used to commanding attention. "Excellency, we are a governing body. We are here, or so I was given to believe, to represent the people of this island. Surely we can declare the formal Assembly closed and reopen it informally to allow this young woman an opportunity to speak."

The governor gaveled the members back to order. "Gentlemen, take your seats. The woman has a problem with her land, Mr. Jelfe informs me."

"More like a problem with Jelfe." Bard's laugh was more like a squeak.

"That will be quite enough, Mr. Bard. Your innuendo is not appreciated in these chambers."

"Hear, hear," came from others. Byron Jelfe was much too respected and admired to be abused in such fashion. Bard's obvious envy of anyone else's success was common knowledge and the subject of constant amusement, but these scurrilous attacks on a peer were not to be suffered.

"Would you step forward and identify yourself, please, madam?"

Mary stood up and walked slowly to the front of the chamber. Tiny fires burned in her eyes, and the straight line of her back announced determination. A long red velvet cord separated her from the twenty men who sat before her.

"My name is Mary Roark McMahon, and I am a Canadian like all of you. My husband was given a deed by the former owner of our land. The deed is here in my hand. It bears the signature of the person to whom the deed belonged.

"He met my husband on a sea voyage, liked him, and desired to make a gift of his land and buildings, as evidenced by the deed itself." She spoke without hesitation but in a quiet voice that brought some of them forward in their chairs.

"The man was John Wallace of Tignish, a good man who passed away several months ago. The farm had been in his family for nearly one hundred years.

"A government land agent came to collect back taxes, taxes we had paid but which were obviously not recorded in our name—McMahon—because the register of deeds did not have us listed as landowners.

"I explained all this to the agent, who told me this piece of paper was worthless and proceeded to order me off my land. He called in the constable and hung signs stating that the land was now government property."

"It was his right to do so," Bard shouted, and pounded his desk, looking to the others, unsuccessfully, for approval.

Mary's eyes narrowed almost to closing. "I am speaking, *sir*, and when I am finished, you or any of your colleagues may speak, but not until then. Is that quite clear?"

Her bell-like voice rang throughout the chamber, her eyes riveted on the fleshy face. The silence that followed was palpable in the room, and Mary allowed it to continue for a long moment before going on.

"It was *not* his right to do so. He did not prove to my satisfaction that the government owned the land. I had more proof of our ownership than he had of the government's. It was only my respect for the law that allowed him to drive me from my own land. But I find I am losing that respect.

"Now I am told that I have probably lost the land anyway because I have left it, because I have left it only to save it." Her words were deliberate and measured, and the question in her voice indicated disbelief.

"I ask you, gentlemen, what kind of injustice is being preached by this government? I came to this country to escape injustice. There was no dream of my owning land as a citizen of Ireland. Ah, but in Canada anything was possible, or so I thought, and so I was told. Gentlemen, do not turn Canada into another Ireland, where the laws are so contrary they change from day to day and place to place, only to suit those who are in high places. And do not be so rigid that you cannot listen to the individual pleas of your people.

"I lived for a time in the United States, and I saw there how people of wealth and power manipulated the common worker. I saw injustice and disgraceful working conditions in the textile mills, and I watched the hypocrites who owned them and who cloaked their greed in philanthropy." She paused, smiled, then continued. "You seem surprised, gentlemen, that I am able to speak so, but you see, that was the plan of the mill owners, to work the girls in the daylight hours and bring them culture by way of lectures at night. Oh, we all became quite educated. Of course, we were always so tired we never had time to question the injustices of inadequate wages and inhuman hours. We worked and we listened.

"But I managed to come to Canada, where the air was clear of factory smoke and the farms were green and rich." The poetry of her words brought the lilt back into her voice.

"Do not be like our neighbors to the south. Do not allow the power that you have here in this Assembly to turn you into dictators. Show strength when you must, but mercy whenever you can."

A gust of wind shook and rattled the windows, and when it passed, the chamber was hushed. Mary stood firm, her shoulders back, her high cheekbones pink with inner fire. A few of the members turned slowly to each other and breathed deeply, but they did not speak, nor did they nod aye or nay.

Then the governor came forward. The purple veins were not as pronounced, and the floridity of his face had lightened considerably.

"May I see your deed?" he asked simply.

"Yes, sir," she answered, and slowly passed the parchment to him, as though she were handling the sacred Eucharist itself.

He studied the paper and then passed it on to Charles Andrews, who read it closely, his patrician brow furrowed in concentration.

He looked up and addressed the others, tapping the deed against the tips of his fingers. "My honored colleagues, as a barrister I see nothing illegal in this document."

"Let me see that piece of paper," Bard snarled.

"Why, surely, but be careful with it, Francis. It is obviously the young woman's only proof of ownership." He bowed and smiled slightly in the direction of Mary.

Her heart pounded so she could hear it in her own ears, and she felt a sudden dizziness at being so close to her goal. But she swallowed hard and maintained her composure, nodding slightly in return.

"Well, Francis, it's as strong a document as you probably possess in evidence of ownership of your own property. Or do you have such evidence?" It was the first time the Assembly had stirred since Mary had finished speaking, and the comic relief brought the members smiling and laughing out of their private thoughts.

"Here." Bard thrust the deed back to Andrews and slumped back in his chair.

"Mrs. McMahon"—the governor took the deed from Andrews and returned it to Mary—"Mrs. McMahon, would you kindly wait outside while this Assembly meets in executive session? We will have an answer for you presently."

Mary, almost afraid she would stumble, so rigidly firm she had been, turned slowly and left the chamber. Once outside, she held onto the wall for support. The clerk, as much in awe as in puzzlement, asked, "Are you all right, madam? May I bring you a chair?"

"No, no. I am fine. I am just a mite dizzy, is all. Thank you, lad. I'm fine now."

She walked the length of the stone corridor, gathering her strength. What had she said? It all was a blur now. For so long, so many nights as she lay alone in her bed, she had rehearsed what she would say and how she would say it. But it had come out wrong, she knew it. She had not said at all what she had intended. Oh, God, how inadequate she felt. How alone. If only Brendan had been there, he would have known what to say. What did she know? A woman in a man's world. How presumptuous of her to think that by her single efforts she could regain their land.

A door clicked open at the far end of the corridor, and Charles Andrews stepped out. He looked about until he saw her, nodded in recognition, and came forward briskly. His eyes were narrowed and his mouth was grimly set.

"Mrs. McMahon, we have discussed your situation, and what bothers some of us most is your allusion to the power of this Assembly. Many of us have been appointed members for quite some time, and I—we—some of us wonder how much and for how long we have been arrogant in the disposition of our duties to the citizens of this island. You have certainly given us reason for thought. I never wish to be a hypocrite; it is the most evil of human traits. Oh, and by the way —here I am going on like a true man of politics—the land is yours. You have proved ownership. The Land Commission will be notified. The tax money you paid will be credited to you, and the governor will write a personal letter to the agent in Tignish, explaining that he is to leave you alone. But most important, it will include a reprimand. Many of these agents are nothing more than hoodlums and criminals, and they must be investigated. The land question was not settled today, Mrs. McMahon, but possibly, because of your eloquence, we have made a beginning."

Mary, who seemed too often to vow not to cry, let the tears of joy stream down her cheeks. She could not speak; a stone was lodged in her throat.

"I understand, Mrs. McMahon. I understand, and may I say, I admire you greatly." He bowed, turned on his heel, and walked back to the chamber.

The bells of the Summerside coach seemed to herald the new year—1835—a year of rebirth, as Mary sat huddled in the corner with her ambivalent thoughts. Saying good-bye to Byron and to Digger had not been easy. For Digger, in his sorrow, she felt only compassion. "I will throw myself into my work, Mary," he had said. "I will build a business empire if only to lose myself and my thoughts. I shall never marry again. My business will be my family. And, Mary, if ever you need me for anything, I will always be here." She had kissed him gently and joined Byron in the chaise that was to take her to the coach. Their parting was brief, as if they had known that to linger would be to stay forever.

"I shall love you always, Mary."

"And I, too, shall love you in a special way, Byron, my dear, dear friend."

Their lips touched, and then, like two birds in flight, they parted forever.

The coach lurched and shook her out of her reverie. "Tignish Village, ma'am." The coachman peered down from his seat into the dark velvet interior.

Mary's heart thumped with excitement, any lingering doubts instantly dissolved as, breathless, she stood by the gate to her own home.

CHAPTER XVII

A SPRING RAIN lashed and whipped the blackened fields all across the southern face of Ireland, and with its wet attack a driving wind tore through the huddled villages of County Kerry, leaving illness and starvation in its cruel wake. The fields were thick with muck, and what little planting there was fell victim to nature gone wild.

Cathleen McMahon stood at the wide parlor window of Derrynane and watched the caravan of horses, their sodden backs twitching and trembling from the bone-jarring chill of the rain and wind.

"I will be on my way now, Cathleen. Weather or not, we must move on. The people expect Daniel, and we must not disappoint them."

"Aye." She turned to him, her eyes bright with a joy that turned their deep blue to azure, and she smiled.

"You seem happy that I am leaving," he said almost boyishly.

"It is not happy I am that you are leaving, Patrick. God knows I shall miss you. But it is always happy I am when you are near."

He took her hands in his and kissed them. "Why has God blessed me so, Cathleen?"

"And thus blessed me in return," she answered.

He held her softly in his arms and lifted her chin and kissed her gently. "You do love me, Cathleen, do you not?"

"Why must you always ask, Patrick? Is there something that I do or do not do that causes you such doubt?"

"Because I am foolish. I am like the melancholic bard who wants to feel sorry for himself and wants to suffer and has so little confidence in himself when it comes to loving a woman. I do not have Daniel's way with words, and I do not have the great strength of your brother, the McMahon. I use my brain too much and my hands and tongue too little."

"And did you ever think that could be the reason I love you so?"

He smiled into the sparkling blue pools of her eyes and kissed her again. "I thank God for you every day of my life."

"And I the same."

"Come summer we will be man and wife. I live for that day,

Cathleen. Now I must be off." He released her reluctantly and left her standing by the streaming window.

All through that dismal day the caravan slipped and slid along the wheel-rutted roads above Bantry Bay, until finally, bone-weary, they arrived outside the village of Sneem just as the wind shifted and blew the rain out to sea.

In moments, it seemed, the evening had changed as a yellow glow of descending sun flashed along the sparkling lanes and boreens that wove in and out of the village. And standing in a halo of gold, like someone from a Celtic myth, was Brendan McMahon.

He smiled brightly at O'Connell and Patrick Leary as he approached the mud-spattered chaise. "Well, Daniel, I know you are a man of much power, but to command the heavens is more than I expected. Here, let me help you." And his powerful grip supported the portly O'Connell out of the swaying coach.

"Where are we lodged, Brendan?" O'Connell asked as he surveyed the little town, hardly more than a few odd shops, a water trough that gurgled and overflowed from the violent rains, and a gray Celtic cross in the center of the square.

"Down that close. Last stone house on the left. Come, your man awaits with a hot meal. The rally will begin within the hour. The field is already filled with people awaiting your arrival."

O'Connell's weariness could be seen in the gray puffs under the eyes but was even more noticeable in his manner. When he suffered from fatigue, he was short-tempered, abrupt, and quick to order and manipulate those around him. Exhaustion robbed him of his usual diplomatic demeanor.

"You have seen to it that the churches have collected the sums as I have instructed?" he snapped out sharply.

"Yes, Daniel." Brendan nodded dutifully.

"Good. Make sure the clergy in this town are aware of my gratitude. You go to them. I have no time for it myself."

Brendan wanted to disagree with this quick dismissal of the village priests, for whom a personal visit from Daniel O'Connell would be a memory cherished. The priests, after all, had their parishioners, like birds, eating from their hands, and any group, any band, was a help to the cause. Brendan decided to accept in silence the curt orders from his exhausted leader. If O'Connell was manipulative, he was no different, in that way, from other great leaders who used manipulation as a tool to further their causes.

They did not dally over the meal but ate quickly and heartily and were on their way, leaving several members of the caravan to unpack and bed down the horses.

The cheering rose in a familiar wave that grew and broke across the Kerry field as O'Connell walked among the people, touching them and squeezing their outstretched hands, on his way to the platform.

Silence fell over them as he prepared to speak, and even the wild crows that cawed and squawked in the hawthorn trees were stilled.

"Irishmen and Irishwomen, Catholic Emancipation has proven itself a success. Your coppers have parted the angry seas between Ireland and England. England is listening. She is under the careful scrutiny of the rest of the world. She must release Ireland from slavery. No more will we be shackled and bound like Babylonian captives. New recognition is being shown each day."

"What are ye doin' with all the gold that crosses yer palms, O'Connell? Spendin' it in London on food and drink?"

The voice, sharp with accusation, cut like a scythe into the soft, velvet tone of O'Connell's rhetoric. It came so quickly, its timing so awkward, so uncalled for, that O'Connell stepped back instinctively, suddenly at a loss for any quick rejoinder.

There were other shouts then, from the rear and the middle and the sides of the assemblage. They came like the stinging snap of a whip, and they came so rapidly O'Connell's curly head swung back and forth as though he were dodging fists.

The rest of the crowd had been struck as dumb as O'Connell, but now they broke from their shock and launched their own attack.

"Who are ye, you blatherin' bastard?" a dirty-faced old man shouted.

"God damn yer eyes," came from another.

"Tell us, O'Connell, what do you really do with the hard-earned money that these poor, starving farm folk give you?" The words were clipped, and although there was an attempt at coarseness, the educated tone was evident.

Brendan, who glared along with Paul and Eamon, noticed a bulge in the man's sleeve.

"Step up on the platform, sir, and we shall discuss your suspicions. I have nothing to hide. Please come up and identify yourself." O'Connell had regained his composure, and he welcomed the heckler with his hand.

But debate was obviously not the intention of all the hecklers, who began pushing through the crowd, shouting epithets and slander.

Brendan sensed what was coming. It happened so fast, and since it had never happened to O'Connell before, no one was prepared for it. But Brendan knew what to do. He had to get to that heckler before the field erupted in a violent bloodbath.

He flew off the platform, springing, catlike, directly into the man's chest. They both toppled to the ground, and as the heckler rolled over, he tugged at the sleeve of his coat. A lead pipe fell beside his outstretched hand. He reached for it, but too late. Brendan's boot dug into the hand. The man screamed in pain as Brendan dug harder and then swung the other boot full force into the heckler's face.

The crowd moved back as the other hecklers lunged and pushed toward Brendan, brandishing clubs and lead pipes. But Eamon and Paul had been quick to follow Brendan into battle. Paul twisted the arm of one more behind his back, breaking it with a snap, as Eamon felled another with a solid blow to the throat.

Now the crowd began to strike out. Fists smashed into flesh and bone, and clubs and pipes cracked heads and backs. Brendan picked another heckler out of the swaying, crunching sea of swinging fists and toppled him with a series of short, rapid blows to the face and a right-hand smash to the jaw.

O'Connell, flushed with anger, shouted for order from his platform. But order did not come until the dozen or so hecklers crawled to their feet and took flight across the flat Kerry field as the mob, like a victorious army, cheered their retreat.

O'Connell allowed the emotion of battle to subside. He was not happy with the victory and wasted no time in stating his displeasure.

"I have never preached violence. Moderation is the character of genuine patriotism, not the passion of hate that enslaves the human soul and poisons the human spirit. Violence and physical force are stepchildren to defeat. Violence debilitates. Ireland cannot win her fight for independence from a position of weakness, and weakness will surely result from violent revolution."

"But, Daniel," an old man called up to him, "those rogues deliberately planned to break up this rally. You saw them. They came armed for a fight. It was just lucky your men surprised them before they ever got started."

O'Connell looked over at Brendan and then back at the worn-out, whey-faced farmer. "I could have stopped it with debate. Fists were not necessary. Look at your patriots of the past. Where are they when we need them? Lord Fitzgerald dead. Wolfe Tone dead by his own hand. What good this martyrdom? What good this revolution? We look for a nation of strong and vibrant people who can rise above their hate and become a moral force no British army or British Parliament could ever defeat. Be big enough to put the toys and clubs of children behind you, and I swear to the God above me that Ireland's moral courage will crush any aggressor. So help me."

His words wove magic, and the crowd responded with an outpouring of hope and feeling, their cheers exploding again and again across the glistening field.

As was his duty, Brendan brought them back to reality by passing tin boxes among the crowd. Their coppers rang against the tin and then fell with a thud as the boxes filled up with the pennies of the poor. This should have ended his duties, but this night he was struck by O'Connell's eloquence, even though the great man had arched his eyebrow in sharp reprimand of Brendan for his swift attack on the hecklers. He felt the words surging and growing inside of him, and his mouth was parched as he looked out at them, a bedraggled people whose only hope in life rested on the mighty words of Daniel O'Connell. Brendan marveled at what it was like to be a molder of people's dreams, the leader of an entire nation.

Before he realized what he was doing, he had raised his hands and called them back to the platform. They turned in the midst of departure and lifted their heads to him.

"Irishmen and Irishwomen," he shouted, "Daniel is right. Do not weaken yourselves with revenge and bitterness. Be like the Christian martyrs who, by their moral example, converted Rome to Christianity. A man's wants are simple: a wife, a family, and a patch of his own land to plow. And by your patience and your trust in the great King of the Beggars these things you will have, as God is my judge."

His face was flushed, and his palms were wet with nervousness as he turned to Paul and Eamon, who were gazing at him oddly. "Come," he said, embarrassed now, "we shall join Daniel."

But then a strange thing happened. The crowd began cheering again, their fists punching the air as they chanted, "O'Connell, O'Connell, O'Connell." Brendan felt a glow of pride well up inside him. They were cheering O'Connell, to be sure, but it was his words that had stirred them up again.

For the next two nights, as he lay awake staring at the beamed ceiling of a croft a few miles above Derrynane in the lush, rolling hills of Kerry, Brendan heard his own words ring out like cathedral bells tolling the call of Sabbath. The thrill of moving a mob of people dominated his being, and he knew he would never be quite the same again. He smiled in the dark, remembering Paul's words: "Brendan, king of bastards."

He had laughed good-naturedly at the time, but now, alone in the midnight dark of his room, he felt the tight vise of conflict gripping him. He had a wife, an infant daughter, and land back in Canada. His duties were there. He had been gone for more than a year, and he was torn between his responsibility to the cause of freedom for Ireland and his responsibilities as a father and husband.

No, that was not it entirely. He reluctantly acknowledged in the silence of the black night that he had enjoyed the adulation and cheers that greeted his brief but inspiring words to the crowd. His blood had pumped with excitement then, and it did now as he lay remembering his golden moment. No. He could not go back yet; there was still too much he had to do for his native land. So for days he put thoughts of fatherhood out of his mind. Mary would be proud of him surely, he told himself.

From then on, at each of the monster rallies that filled the fields and boreens of southwestern Ireland, Brendan McMahon managed to say a few words to the crowds either before O'Connell's arrival or after the great man's carriage had disappeared down the country road in spiraling clouds of dust.

He began to swagger, and his wide chest seemed even more expansive these days. His voice, always harmoniously pitched, now snapped and spit out orders to the others who followed O'Connell.

His sudden arrogance did not go unnoticed. Eamon and Paul discussed it one night as they sat in a stone, shepherd's hut dug deep in the Kerry hills.

"McMahon seems like another man, Irishman, n'est-ce pas?"

"Aye, he does that, Paul. I do not like the change that has come over him. He is a good lad, but I think he is too much in the power of O'Connell. Sure O'Connell is a fine man. We all know that. But the

McMahon is becoming a very likeness of the man. And in such a young lad that is not good."

"There is danger, too. People are asking who is this McMahon. It will not be too long before they put McMahon at the scene of the Douglas."

"Aye. We have been lucky so far. O'Connell covered us nicely with rumors of a wild band of Scandinavian pirates doing in the Douglas, but the more the McMahon's name comes up, the greater the danger of discovery."

"What then you say we do, Eamon?"

"We will wait and watch, my friend. Wait and watch."

It was not a long wait, and the decision to take Brendan aside and give him some fatherly advice came one evening in the village of Kilrush.

During the day an advance group had fanned out across the countryside with broadsides announcing the coming of Daniel O'Connell, and late in the afternoon Brendan, Paul, and Eamon found an alehouse down one of the cobblestoned lanes in the old town.

The McMahon pushed his way up to the bar and ordered three ales. "Bring them over to the table like a good man," he ordered the publican.

"Bring them over yourself. Do ye think ye are in some fine Dublin hotel? Here." And he handed the pewter mugs to Brendan, who flushed with embarrassment in front of his friends.

Eamon and Paul said nothing as Brendan joined them at the table. "The bloody bastard. Doesn't he know who I am? Who *we* are," he corrected himself.

Eamon quaffed the foaming ale, wiped his mouth with the sleeve of his tunic, and sat back. He looked at Paul, who nodded in return, both of them knowing instinctively that this was the moment.

"Brendan, lad, we have something to say to you, Paul and I."

"Aye, well speak your piece, man," the McMahon snapped at him.

"What you just said, are you aware of it, lad?"

"What I just said? What are you talking about?"

Brendan was tired, and his tone lacked patience. He is becoming more like O'Connell every day, Eamon thought.

"What you said at this table, about the bloody bastard not knowing who you are. *Should* he know who you are? And may I ask you, McMahon, just who the hell are you?"

Brendan's eyes flew open, and his jaw dropped.

"You see, Paul and I have been watching you. And ever since you delivered that little speech in Sneem, you have been as cocky as a farmyard rooster. Others have noticed it. It's getting away from you, Brendan lad. It pains me to say these things to you, but I think you are losing sight of who you are. Am I right, Paul?"

"*Oui*, you are certainly right, Irishman. It is for your own good we tell you, Brendan. You are beginning to think you are the O'Connell. This is his country. It is no longer yours."

"I—I don't understand. It's for the cause I speak. It is the cause that is important." Brendan's confidence was shaken, and his voice had lost its sharpness.

"Brendan," Eamon said gently, "I think you have become bigger than the cause. If you stay here much longer, you will lose yourself. Have you not considered your other responsibilities: your wife and child?"

"Of course I have. What makes you think I do not consider my responsibilities? You are an Irishman. Do you not consider the cause more important than anything else in the world?"

"No, I do not think it is the most important thing in the world. I think a man's family is."

"Brendan, Eamon and I will leave. Our job is done. Come home with us before you forget where your home is."

"Come, Paul, let us leave the lad to think."

Brendan sat late into the night, swallowing rum and washing it down with ale. His mind was jumbled and confused, yet somewhere behind the alcoholic veil he knew there was wisdom in the words of his friends. He finally stumbled to his feet, blurted an apology to the publican, who did not hear him, and lurched out into the dark street.

He reeled back to his rented room above the livery stable and fell onto the straw bed. As he drifted off to a noisy sleep, he saw himself addressing thousands of cheering followers.

Just before dawn he awoke with a start. His mouth seemed full of cotton, and his head throbbed. Good, he thought, I deserve to be sick. What a big feeling bastard I've been. But oh, Jesus, what a headache.

Three days later, his head clear and his mind made up, Brendan hiked through the thick grass, hopping across icy streams and jumping from one knoll to the next, with the words of Eamon and Paul still ringing in his ears: "It takes a man to admit he was wrong and a real man to do something about it."

His heart was light, and images of Mary and Gabriella warmed him. He was going home. He would never leave them again.

Daniel O'Connell's great house spread out like a stone giant in the warm sun. Winter was fading slowly. The moist, fresh smell of good earth was underfoot, wild flowers pinched at the nostrils, and it was a blessing to be alive.

Nora opened the door, and he threw his arms around her. "Nora, you are a beauty. Is my dear sister about?"

"Here now, be ye some wild man down from the mountains? Mind yerself, Brendan McMahon." But she smiled briefly and then whisked him away with her French linen apron. "Your sister is off for an evening canter with her intended."

"Oh, good for her. It is Daniel I wish to see anyway. Is he about?"

"Aye, he is in the large parlor."

"Fine. I shall find him, you needn't bother."

"Bother, is it? Sure, I had no intention of bothering myself with anything. Oh, but look," she called after him, "he has guests, you cannot be going in there now."

"Oh, nonsense, he will be happy to see me." And in all his excitement and boyish enthusiasm, Brendan hurried along the corridor and found himself almost immediately in the midst of several men who were standing in front of a roaring hearth, sipping delicately from Waterford crystal glasses.

"McMahon," O'Connell blurted out, "what is the meaning of this intrusion?"

Brendan, taken aback by the coldness in his voice, glanced quickly from one guest to another, their tweeds and white ruffled shirts in obvious contrast with his own tattered clothing and dirty boots.

"Come with me," O'Connell said, leading Brendan into an anteroom and closing the door on his guests.

"Now, what has brought you bursting in here like a wild man?" The acerbic tone cut deeply, and O'Connell's aristocratic bearing, which Brendan had chosen to dismiss on other occasions, was very much in evidence now.

Brendan, his enthusiasm all but banished by O'Connell's haughty manner, answered quickly but with determination, "I have decided to return home. To Canada."

O'Connell leaned forward, and his voice softened considerably. "Rubbish, my lad. Your place is here in Ireland. Ireland is your home."

Brendan realized that the softened tone, the affectionate choice of "my lad," something O'Connell had never called him before, were, once again, the tools of a manipulator; only this time O'Connell's eyes were not tired.

Brendan thrust his hands into his pockets and prepared to stand his ground. He could be just as stubborn as O'Connell in support of his convictions "I shall be leaving in the morning."

The older man was clearly unused to being contradicted by one of his own. "You are a selfish young man, McMahon."

The flame of temper burned hotly, and Brendan was quick to retaliate. "If selfish it is to go home to a wife and child, then let it be so. But let me tell you a thing or two, Daniel O'Connell, there are ragged and starving farmers who would be quick to nod yes to an invitation to drink whiskey or rum beside your warm hearth this night. And there are those who might say you are becoming soft and fat on English promises. Look to yourself, Daniel, before you question the motives of others." Brendan's eyes shot fiery sparks, and then he turned on his heel and left by a side door, but not without delivering one final barb: "I'll go out this way. I'm not dressed well enough for that crowd."

In the bleak gray of a wet dawn, Brendan, Eamon, and Totem Paul said their simple farewells to Cathleen and Patrick. "God bless you, dear sister, and may the Lord smile on your marriage," Brendan added. Cathleen stood on tiptoes as he leaned from his saddle and brushed her forehead with a kiss. "Take good care of her, Patrick, as I know you will."

In the oval courtyard the horses brayed and stomped the damp earth as the wide French doors swung open and O'Connell appeared. His brown, curly hair was tousled, and one suspender, draped across his fleshy shoulder, held up his trousers. The elegance of the previous evening was no longer in evidence.

He descended to the grassy forecourt and extended his hand to the McMahon. "I shall be forever grateful to you, Brendan, Paul, Eamon, and so, too, shall Ireland. But above all, I thank you for your sharp reminder last evening. It was a jolt I needed. I believe I was beginning to forget who I am. I was forgetting the beggars and befriending the bastards." He smiled.

"Ireland is blessed to have you, Daniel O'Connell. Good-bye and good luck." Brendan raised a hand to his forehead in salute, and then they spurred their horses along the road to Killarney, to the sea, and to home.

"You have done well, Mary. Your hands have hardened to the task of planting and plowing, but you have not lost that lovely blush to your cheeks." Isabella smiled softly as the evening sun played across the red waters of the Strait. They were sitting on Mary's little porch, enjoying the gentle breeze. Mary looked down at her hands. Yes, they were calloused from hard work; nonetheless, they moved deftly over the white-gray fluff as she carded the dirt and seeds free from the raw wool with the quick, strong brushing strokes of her steel comb.

"I have done well," she said reflectively. "Yes, I agree, Isabella. But I have done well because of you and Bill and Padenuque and the others. You all have been like family. Better than family," she added almost in a whisper.

"Brendan will be surprised at our little home and our plantings and our few sheep. You know, Isabella, I would never admit this to anyone else, but some nights when I lay awake thinking of him, I have difficulty remembering his face. Glory to God, I sometimes forget what he looks like, and I strain to see him in my thoughts. I suppose that sounds sinful for a wife to say about her own husband."

"Nay, it's being honest, is all it is. But when will he be coming back, if you forgive my asking? Soon now, I hope."

"Maybe a few more months, maybe by summer's end or at least before the snow flies, God willing."

"Aye, God willing. Well, I must be about my business. There are still chores to be done before I take to my bed. My lads are in Charlottetown at market. I will be bidding you good eve, Mary."

"Good night, Isabella. I think I'll sit here for a while longer."

The mention of Charlottetown had triggered memories of fine houses and restaurants and fancy clothes; the excitement of market day and the mix of people; parties, Government House, the sleigh race, and Byron Jelfe. Byron. Her heart fluttered briefly.

She watched Isabella set off down the path and across the hunch-backed fields to her own farm. What a wonderful friend to have, she thought. She did not know how long she sat there, but stars blinked overhead and the night was black around her by the time she rose to go inside.

The next afternoon Brendan McMahon was wending his way up to the North Cape. A warm late spring had brought the beauty of the lady's slipper a trifle early to the island, its large oval leaves rising from the moist red earth in a pinkish bloom, rioting throughout field and valley. A sweet-smelling growth; flower and grass, rolled across the dipping meadows and enveloped the land and imbued Brendan with enormous energy and joy.

Farmers were bending to the toil of laying roads; fallen tree trunks lay like felled monoliths in the dirt. Their thick backs serving as traction for carriage and cart alike. The scent of the freshly cut wood blended with the sweet aroma of blooming, unleashed nature.

Oh, God, he thought, exhaling deeply, oh, God, it is a blessing to be home. He felt like a boy again, but even as a boy back in Galway he had never experienced such joy in the bounty of life. He scrambled up the jutting cape, his heart and mind racing at the thought of holding his beloved Mary in his arms again.

A twilight breeze tossed his black hair back off his forehead. The night was closing fast now, and he hurried on until he saw the rounded shoulder of the cape bowing over the beach. He stopped for a moment and wiped the perspiration from his brow with the back of his hand before making his way to the crest of the cape. There, off in the distance, was the farm, and inside were his wife and child. His eyes filled with tears. "I will never leave this island again unless we are together," he vowed aloud to the night.

A thin slate marker which he did not remember having seen before rose from the ground just below the cape. He approached it and bent to read the name chiseled there: JOHN WALLACE 1765–1833. Beside it an older stone, the one he did remember, was almost covered by the earth. So John had died the year he left, and Mary had never mentioned it in any of the few letters he had received. He had just assumed that John was by her side, helping her, guiding her, counseling her, and supporting her. "Jesus," he whispered into the dark. "God forgive me." He bowed in front of the modest wind-worn slab, muttered a silent prayer, crossed himself, and moved off through the fields.

Before him, the sudden glow of a candle filled the seaside window of the cottage. He squared his shoulders in response to its welcoming flicker of light and hurried on.

He stepped up on to the porch, his heart thundering in his ears, and rapped lightly on the wooden door. At first there was no movement within. He rapped more forcefully then, and he could hear a chair move and a voice call out, "I'll be there in a moment." Her voice, as soft and lilting as he remembered it.

Through a crack in the log wall he could see the wavering candle moving across the room. The bolt slid back slowly, and Mary stood in the open doorway. "Yes?"

"Mary." Her name caught in his throat, and tears obscured his vision of her.

"Bren—holy Mother of God—Brendan, is it? Is it really you? Have you—have you really come back to us?"

His voice cracked as he stood awkwardly before her. "I'm home, Mary, home to stay." He stepped toward her timidly, a shy country schoolboy. "Oh, Mary, I love you."

And then they were in each other's arms, the candle falling from her hand to the wooden porch. As he brought her to him, he heeled the flame with his boot, and they embraced in the darkness that curled about them.

A week after Brendan's arrival the neighbors descended on the McMahon house with food and drink and music and song. In wagons and carts, on horseback and on foot, they swarmed across the fields.

"It's a fulling frolic." Isabella said to the bewildered couple who stood on the porch. "They've come to help you make homespun cloth, but I suspect"—she winked—"it's just an excuse for the ladies to get together and the gents to have a bit of the drink. Come, Mary, Brendan, say hello to your neighbors. Come, Brendan McMahon, they've come to welcome you home."

Throughout the morning and into the early afternoon, the men helped Brendan dislodge tree stumps and plow out a new patch of lowland field. Wool, which had been woven into a web of cloth containing fifteen or twenty yards of material and had for months been soaking in soap and water, was now placed on a long table and pulled, twisted, turned, and pounded into cloth as Mary and the other women sang and hummed familiar island tunes. Occasionally, Brendan would catch the glint and smile in his wife's eyes and thank God he had persisted in bringing her to this place.

As the afternoon waned and the work of the day was done, the men broke out the stone jugs and passed them from one sweaty hand to the next. The women, closer to the house, set out homemade wooden tables bedecked with the good, natural food of the farm. There were meats, potatoes, turnips and cabbages, fresh-caught fish, homemade jams, and all varieties of breads and pastries.

Brendan stood among his neighbors, his stomach warm and glowing from the poteen that burned and smoldered with its own special fire. He felt his tongue loosening for talk, and the only talk that consumed him was the talk of land.

Since the night of his return and Mary's detailed account of her fight in the Charlottetown Assembly, he could not discuss anything else. The land was on his mind before he fell to sleep and flashed across it upon awaking.

He felt himself filled with oratory, the drink having more than done its service.

"We, many of us," he was saying, "come from a country where most men will never know the joy of working their own patch of land. Here, on the island, we have cleared the land, built our homes with our very own hands." He knew that he had their attention and felt again the thrill he had experienced addressing the crowd in that Kerry field. Flushed with the power of his own rhetoric, he plunged on. "We need a government that is responsible to us and to our needs. Any day any one of us could have our farm taken away. Some of you do not even have proper deeds, and you will never have proper deeds if the land question is not settled. You could go to your beds at night and find yourselves out on the highroad in the morning—at the mercy of an uncaring crown and the greedy, grasping hands of a land agent."

While Brendan spoke, Jean Pierre Morell inched his way closer to the front of the group. An Acadian fisherman who lived alone in a teetering shack that overlooked Seacow Pond on the gulf side of the North Cape, he was as removed from such concerns as a man could be. He was, however, very much interested in Mary McMahon.

Morell, his tongue thick with poteen, listened to the words unwind from the golden spool of Brendan's tongue. The drink urged Brendan on. "When I walked along the beach this morning and listened to the mighty thunder of the waves beating against the shore, my shore, I thanked God Almighty for this jeweled garden surrounded by water, and I vowed to the heavens above that I would fight until my last ounce of blood was shed before I would ever release my hold on my land. And that vow extends to you. I will fight for you as well as for myself, so help me, God." He could hear his words pounding in his ears, and he suddenly brought himself up short. He lowered his voice, summing up quickly. "And so neighbors"—he paused to pull on the jug proffered by an outstretched hand—"make sure you have proper deeds." He took another pull. "Brrrrr, ah, ah, Jesus, men, that's a fiery taste. The devil himself must have brewed it."

They all laughed good-naturedly, then, some patting him on the back as they passed the jug along.

"Hey, McMahon, there no need *you* worry for a deed, they tell me, eh? Your wife there, she get your farm back for you, eh?"

Brendan smiled widely, although the harsh whiskey was at that very moment tearing a hole in his stomach and scalding the roof of his mouth.

"Aye, Morell, she did that. She's a great woman, she is."

Morell stepped forward, the others still grinning and passing the jug. "Ya, up there in Charlottetown, the gov'ment men, they think she one good woman, too, eh?" Morell grabbed for the jug as it made its rounds. He hooked his thumb through the handle, cocked the stone jar, and quaffed a healthy swallow. He did not blink an eye as he passed it on, throwing back his black head in a deep bass of a laugh. The laugh had a derisive ring to it, but it was lost on Brendan. It was not lost, however, on the others who knew Morell, and they paused. Bill Profitt did not pass the jug.

Brendan answered with a trace of pride in his voice, "Aye, they met their match in Mary, all right. They didn't know how to handle her."

"Huh?" Morell looked around with an exaggerated puzzlement creeping over his whiskered face. "Huh?" he repeated. "I hear tell they handle her pretty good, eh?"

Brendan, his reason dimmed somewhat by the poteen, nevertheless began to catch the sardonic tone in the dark Frenchman's voice. An uneasy silence settled over the group. Someone coughed. The shrill cry of children at play drifted toward them.

Brendan held his smile; but it was not as wide now, and thin lines formed across his forehead. "Slow down, Morell, I do not think I understand you."

The others began shifting from foot to foot as Bill broke in. "What Morell means is they took care of Mary because she is intelligent and an independent woman."

Brendan's eyes narrowed, and he stared into the black-bearded face. "Is that what you meant, Morell?" There was a moment of silence, and Brendan pressed the point. "I am asking you, Morell, is that what you meant?"

"I mean, McMahon"—and he spit the words out—"they take care for her, and she take care for them, eh? Hey, if that what she must do to get the land, good luck for her."

There was no trace of smile now on Brendan's grim face. "Why, you filthy bastard." He bit off the words and sprang at Morell, catching him with two rapid left hands to the head and a staggering uppercut. The Frenchman did not go down, but his thick head rolled from side to side and then was jolted backward. He straightened, his great chest heaving as he came in close, stopping the next flurry of blows with his forearms. He managed to get inside the arc of the blows and wrap his powerful arms around the McMahon's chest.

Brendan could not free himself to land a punch.

"I will break this Irishman's body with bare hands, eh!"

The crowd stepped back. As long as it was a fair fight no one would interfere.

Mary looked across the field and saw the ring of men but nothing else, and she returned to the cabin to fetch more hot water for the tea.

Brendan was slowly losing his breath as the arms tightened in a vise around him. He would have to act quickly, or it would all be over. He stretched his right leg behind Morell's left and curled it around the joint of the knee. The Frenchman lost his balance and toppled backward, Brendan falling heavily on top of him. The powerful arms released their grip momentarily, and Brendan jumped to his feet. He would not allow the Frenchman to get so close again.

"Get up, Morell, get up." He growled it through gritted teeth.

Morell climbed slowly to his feet, resting for a moment on his knee. A sneer of a smile crossed his face. Then he was poised and ready, his arms spread out. "I break your head open like a walnut, Irishman."

"Then come and do it, Frenchman. I'm ready for you."

Morell tried to get inside again, but this time the McMahon was ready. He threw two quick jabs and two rapid hooks and danced back out of range.

Blood dripped in a thin red ribbon from Morell's nose, and when he wiped it away with his hand, he stopped for a moment and studied it. The sight of his blood seemed to propel him into an insane fury, and he looked wildly from the ring of bystanders back to Brendan. His eyes turned cold, and he charged, this time like a bull, his hard black skull pointed for that spot just below the chest.

Brendan sidestepped and hung two quick shots to the side of the Frenchman's head, spinning him around.

But Morell was not done yet. He waded in, forearms raised to cover his face. Brendan threw two more lefts and a right, but they were easily repelled, and then Morell unleashed a roundhouse right that drove full force against Brendan's left cheekbone. There was a dull snap of breaking bone, and Brendan almost buckled from the blow. But he managed to stay on his feet, fists still raised.

They were getting dangerously close to the edge of the cape now, and Brendan knew he had to act quickly. Morell pressed in closer, throwing wild lefts and rights. He landed two powerful blows to Brendan's head and face, and now it was Brendan who saw the red blur of his own blood. Morell laughed with glee as he saw the river of red streaming from the Irishman's nose and face.

In his fury Brendan threw caution to the wind, ducked inside the man's bulk, and dug his fists into the area around the heart and the solar plexis. He felt the hulking body shake and heard Morell suck for air. He stepped back and ripped four, five, six quick jabs, a smashing hook, and a right that came up, it seemed, from the red clay itself.

Morell stood like the mute animal he was, blood oozing from his nose and mouth and ears, but still he came on.

Brendan's arms were like lead. The bull-like man was bloodied and losing, but he was wearing Brendan down. Brendan fired everything he had. A volley of lefts, a right-hand blow to the head, followed by another and then another, until he stepped inside one more time and shot a lightning bolt to Morell's heart. The Frenchman staggered and pitched forward. He rolled down the red sand of the bluff and lay still with the blue waters of the Northumberland tide licking at his boots.

Brendan slid down the hill to the beach as the men, now joined by their screaming women, lined the cape above.

He dragged Morell into the water, shoved his head below the waves, then released it and walked back to shore.

Morell came sputtering to the surface; the blood that had washed away streamed new and fresh again.

"I'm here, Morell, if you want any more." The McMahon stood with legs parted, hands on hips.

Morell stumbled through the breaking tide, stared at Brendan blankly for a moment, and then staggered off in the direction of Seacow Pond. Brendan watched him go. The Frenchman did not look back.

Mary was still in the cottage when Isabella hurried to tell her about the fight.

"Where is he? My God, is he hurt?"

"Hurt? No. I do not think so. I saw him walk off to the new patch of lowland."

Mary lifted her skirts and raced through the fields to find Brendan crouched beside a narrow silvery stream. His tattered shirt hung like a battle flag as he cupped the cold water and splashed it onto his face.

"Here, let me do that for you." She tore off her apron, dipped it into the water, then applied it to the red apple blush of his cheek and the bleeding nose and mouth.

"Won't you ever grow up, Brendan McMahon? Am I to be wife and mother to you forever?"

"Just wife will do," he said with a sharp, cutting edge to his voice.

She stopped and looked at him. "What do you mean by that?"

He stood up and tucked in what was left of his shirt. "Is it true? Is it true what that Acadian bastard said?"

She seemed astonished. "What—what did he say?"

Brendan swallowed hard, apparently at a loss for words, and then he blurted it out. "That you had to *give* yourself in return for the deed to our land."

The stream gurgled and insects buzzed. Sounds of laughter from the party that was supposed to be for them—for Brendan's return home—drifted on the breeze.

Mary rose from the wet grass and walked slowly to her husband. She looked deep into his eyes and then struck him a stinging openhanded blow across the face. The blood flowed freely again from his mouth.

"Never accuse me of that again, Brendan McMahon. I had my opportunities for love. I do not deny that. You were gone almost two years, and a woman has her desires. I was always faithful to you. But I'll tell *you* something, you golden-tongued orator and saloon brawler: As much as I wondered if you were always faithful to me, I would not dignify such suspicions by asking you. Now clean off your bloody face, and come back to the party—such as it is now that you have ruined it."

PART THREE

———

THE
ISLANDERS

1848–1872

CHAPTER XVIII

BRENDAN MCMAHON walked the heaped rows of red earth, his hear
soaring under a blazing July sun. For as far as he could see, as he
scanned his land from east to west and north to south, his one golden
legacy from Ireland lay in the row after row of cobblers that graced
their land.

Thirteen years before, when Brendan left Ireland for the last time,
Patrick Leary had counseled him, "Potatoes, Brendan, plant them. Do
not turn your back entirely on your heritage. For sure, the potato has
turned black and rotten on a blighted plant. But when the harvest is
good, you are safe for a year, and your family will have full bellies.
Better than gold," Patrick had said. "Gold is too easily spent."

The Strait sparkled and twinkled and the blue canvas of Canadian
sky promised fair weather. The cottage reached out to him as he
ambled in silent pride across his fields.

The years had brought five children: After the lovely Gabriella
came Peter, Daniel, Abigail, and James.

There had been good harvests which could be traded for goods
and sold for money. John Wallace's little cottage was now raised to a
second floor, and four outbuildings had been added, to house potatoes,
hay, animals, and farm tools. Each building, including the original
house, was painted a fresh eggshell white with deep red trim.

Everything had such definition, he thought, and color. He turned
to see three half-naked little bodies clamber up the cape, their tanned
skins still glistening with sea water from their romp in the ocean. He
roared a hearty laugh as the little one, James, tried desperately to
keep up with his two older brothers.

Brendan was a Canadian now and, above all, an islander, and as
he followed his children to the house for the noon meal, he felt true
contentment.

Dennis Hurley answered the insistent banging that thudded
against his cottage door. Dennis, generally a calm and kindly man to
his wife and two children, was this day unusually vexed. He had been

called away from the fields to make minor repairs on a window broken when his ten-year-old son sent a rock hurtling through the air in an effort to frighten a skunk.

The banging continued.

"Hold your bloody horses, I'm coming," he snapped. "Are we expecting visitors?" he shouted with annoyance over his shoulder at his wife.

"No," she said simply, and continued dipping cotton wicks into melted tallow.

The thumping increased. "I'd like to take one of your candles, light it, and put it down that jackass's pants."

"What if it's a woman?" Ellen Hurley giggled.

"Ah, woman," he shouted as he threw open the door.

There standing in front of him was Ian Kemp, the land agent and rent collector for Lord Powiss.

Kemp was young as land agents went, and some said his sister had been more than friendly to certain magistrates in Summerside. No agents were welcome on the farms; but some were anathema, and Kemp was one. His mistreatment of farmers had more than once been reported, but it seemed the complaints had fallen on deaf ears.

"What do you want from us, Kemp? Say your piece, and be on your way. This is a workday. And if I don't work, I cannot pay your bloody high taxes. What is it?"

Kemp's skin was soft and peach-colored, and it matched his hair. The combination served to produce a pale and vacant young man. But there was no softness in his nature. He was arrogant, ruthless, and unreasonable, and most of all, he was protected by crown and constable. In consequence, too many farmers had merely to stand with their mouths closed in frustration and anger and accept the abuse and injustice heaped on them.

"Your taxes are due. Are you forgetting the day and month of the year, or are you too involved with your woman on this workday, as you call it?"

Hurley, a shy man and, like most of his Irish neighbors, modest in matters of women, blushed with embarrassment and anger at the crude insinuation.

"You keep your twisted tongue to yourself, Kemp. And stay on the other side of the door. I have your payment. Hold there." And Dennis fumed and grumbled his anger as he went into the far bedroom for his tin box.

Kemp's eyes played with the buxom form of Ellen Hurley as she continued to dip the candles. She could feel his evil eyes studying her, and as she looked up, her face reddened under the persistent scrutiny of his gaze.

Dennis Hurley saw the exchange as he stepped back into the room. "Here you are, five pounds. Count it if you like."

"Oh, I will, Hurley. I will." Kemp shifted his attention from the woman to the coins that Dennis dropped heavily into his upturned palm. He fingered each one gingerly as though the thick copper might carry disease.

"Wait, now, wait a moment there, Hurley. What do we have here? These three shilling pieces and four penny pieces. Where did ya get 'em from, the Micmacs?"

"Why, what do you mean?"

"Why, they're counterfeit, and surely you must know it."

Hurley grabbed them out of the outstretched hand and brushed past Kemp to the dooryard, where he held the pieces up to the sparkling sun. "There be nothing wrong with these pieces, Kemp. You're just making things difficult, as is your bloody custom."

"Be careful, Hurley. I could find flaws in all your coins if I so chose. However, you just replace these, and I will be on my way."

It was all Dennis Hurley could do to control his anger. "I have no more coin in the house."

"Well then, where does that leave us now?" Kemp said smugly, his eyes moving about the cottage, the farm, and the barn. Abruptly his gaze halted, and he smiled, pointing. "There, I'll take that black mare. She looks healthy enough. Yes. That will do it. These coins and the mare, and you're paid up for another year."

He sauntered over to the horse, confident and satisfied he had made a deal acceptable to both.

"You bloody well don't touch that animal, Kemp. You mind yourself, and I will return in a few minutes. I'll be to a neighbor's for a loan of coin. You mind, and I will be back." Before Hurley left, however, he went into the house and when he came back out into the sunlight the iron bolt fell into place behind him with a sharp clack.

Dennis returned quickly, his breath coming in quick gasps. "Here, that should take care of my taxes. Now take it and be gone off my property until your *business* brings you here again."

Kemp took the coins and held them out in front of him. "Hurley, these are Spanish coins. Surely these are worthless," he said, shaking his head.

"Worthless? Worthless? They are coin of the realm."

"Yes, but the wrong realm, foreign currency from a fifth-class country. Worthless."

"But—but that is all I have until I sell my crops at market." His tone held both exasperation and despair.

"Well, it's either your farm, and I do not expect you want the government to take that away or"—and he smiled—"the mare. I am a charitable man, Hurley. I will take the mare as additional payment."

"You rotten scoundrel. I will break your blody neck with my bare hands."

Kemp stepped back, and as he did, he was joined by two young toughs who had apparently been waiting behind a row of birch for just such an outburst. Kemp had learned early in his tenure that his abrasiveness and arrogance might require the kind of backing that could be bought for a few coppers and a pint of rum.

"I wouldn't do that, Hurley, or it might be your own bloody neck that gets broken."

Dennis Hurley had to work, and he had to work every day, long hard hours, every day of his life. An injury, a broken hand or arm, would lay his land useless and unproductive. He swallowed hard. He looked at the mare, which he had nurtured from a foal, and then back at the grinning land agent.

"Wait. Wait for a moment. I may have a few more coins buried away. Wait." He tapped on the door, and the bolt was raised from the inside.

Ellen saw the look on her husband's face and was struck with immediate fear. "What? What are you about to do, Dennis?"

He did not answer her. He looked straight ahead, his fierce eyes half-closed as though in pain. He reached for his musket, which hung in its place above the fieldstone hearth, and rested it against the fireplace. He took a long, thin bayonet from the wooden mantel and attached it to the piece.

"Oh, good God in His Heaven, please, Dennis. Please give them what they want. Holy Mary, Mother of God. It is not worth it. Give them what they want. I plead with you, my husband. If not for me, then for the children."

It was as though he did not see or hear her as he walked to the door, opened it, and shuffled out into the sunlight. He raised the musket and said simply, "Get off. Get off my land, Kemp. And do not come back. You will have your tax money when I earn it. Leave. Now."

"You're crazy, Hurley. You must know we will be back, and then you'll be forced off your land. We'll send you packing right off to jail."

"Do what you will, but remove yourselves from my land. I was sent packing once before, and that was from the land of my birth. I made another life once. I will do it again if need be. Now move." He tightened his grip on the musket as they backed off slowly.

"The only life you will make for yourself is behind the bars of a jail, Hurley. And tell me who will take care of your buxom wife while you are rotting in your cell?" The agent's peach face shone at that, and a sickly grin parted his lips sardonically.

"Why, you miserable heathen bastard, you will be sorry you ever came here today." Hurley's wrath, stifled for so long, flamed at last. He jumped forward to drive the bayonet into Kemp's stomach. Kemp doubled up in pain, and Dennis Hurley, his pent-up frustration finally unleashed, pulled the bayonet out and struck him with a series of short, rapid jabs, one of which dug deep into his heart. The two thugs, who had been looking on in horror, broke suddenly from their stupor and raced off into the woods, Ellen Hurley's anguished screams echoing in their ears.

When word reached Brendan, he was just finishing his apple cake while James, the five-year-old, ruddy as a tinker, played in his lap.

"Father, you should be as strict with James as you were with the rest of us. We never could leave our chairs during meals." Gabriella had Mary's dark hair and Brendan's high forehead, and she seemed always to have a smile in her speech.

"Oh, now, Gabriella, he is the baby, sure, and all he looks for is a bit of attention." Brendan chuckled at his eldest child, who was becoming quite the young lady and a fine young lady at that.

But it had not been always so. The first few years following Brendan's return, the child had been shy and almost speechless. When her father gathered her into his arms, she was taken to sudden crying. And even when Mary attempted to console the girl, Gabriella was slow in responding to the softness of her mother's voice. Both parents bore the guilt of having been too long away when she was just a baby.

It had pained them both to see the child retreating from them, and sensitive to the widening breach, they lavished her with love and affection. Brendan sat her alongside him in the cart when he went to market, and Mary sat for long hours telling the child stories of her own youth.

Gradually the child began once more to giggle in joy or sigh with excitement and wonder, and the family circle drew closer in love and companionship.

Peter, now twelve, was more serious, more quietly industrious. He had the eyes of an old man, knowing and contemplative. "Maybe he will be a priest," Mary had said one night, and Brendan had answered stoically, thinking of his need for two strong arms on the farm, "If that is what God wants for him, then it will be so."

Peter raised his head to his mother as she stood over him, forking out two large hot potatoes onto his plate. "Thank you, Mother," he said softly.

Eight-year-old Abigail was having her meal with the Profitts. She was Isabella's little doll and constant companion now that her own boys were grown and off farming several miles away. So far neither of the Profitt boys had married, and Isabella had given up all hope of grandchildren.

"How does the crop look, Brendan?" Mary took her place at the other end of the table. A light breeze blew in from the ocean, causing the muslin curtains to dance and wave.

"It will be a bumper crop, Mary Roark, a banner crop. The good Lord has blessed the island with rain and sun this year. We couldn't have asked for better."

"What is better, rain or sun, Father?" Nine-year-old Daniel, dark and slight, with long, artistic fingers that were reminders of his father's before the toil of farm life had knotted and calloused them, looked up from his plate, a frown knitting his boyish brow.

Brendan smiled at this curious lad, whom he would often find sitting on a distant cape, peering far out at the ocean.

"Both, lad, one is no good without the other. One *complements* the other. It is like a marriage." And he winked at his lovely Mary, who nodded back in affectionate acceptance of his simple wisdom.

"Well, in *your* marriage, *yours* and *Mother's*, who is the rain and who is the sun?"

Brendan's eyes filled with laughter, and he roared as the others joined in. Daniel did not laugh but simply waited for an answer.

"Well, Father?" His sensitive greenish blue eyes were like the sea.

"Eh? Ah, well, now, *there* is one that even your namesake Daniel O'Connell would have had trouble answering."

"Well, what is the answer, Brendan McMahon?" Mary quizzed him coquettishly.

"The answer is—the answer is that in our marriage there is rain and sunshine together, and you know what that means, Daniel."

"No, Father, what does it mean?"

"It means that our marriage is a rainbow."

"Ah, oh, ah." They smiled warmly.

"That's very beautiful, Father." Gabriella held her mother's hand.

"Be off with you, Brendan McMahon, with your blarney." Mary blushed, but more from pleasure than embarrassment. "Sometimes I think you should be giving speeches instead of planting potatoes. Come now, children, let's be finishing up; there's a long afternoon ahead of us. Where will you be if I'm needing you, Brendan?"

Before he could answer, there was a rapping at the parlor window on the west side of the house.

"Who could that be, and what a strange place to be knocking?" Brendan said as he placed James back in his chair.

He hurried off to find out and saw below the window Dennis Hurley's frantic face. Dennis's mouth was twisted, and his eyes were strange as they darted back and forth in his head.

Brendan pushed the window up. "Dennis, what is it, that brings you calling in midday like a stranger?"

"Brendan," he muttered, "I need your help, and I need it now."

"Well, Jesus, man, come around to the front door and stop acting like a bloody thief."

Brendan met him on the side porch. "Here, Dennis, sit. You look as though banshees had chased you through a bog. Quiet yourself, and tell me what is the matter."

Dennis refused the chair, preferring to pace back and forth as he told his story.

Brendan sat transfixed. He did not nod or shake his head. He simply remembered a fight with a Scottish landlord who had taken a whip to him for having attended Daniel O'Connell's rally. His hand went instinctively to the scar under his left cheekbone. Then there was the dull memory of John Douglas falling on his own knife. It was all so long ago, and to Brendan no longer than yesterday.

When Dennis had finished and the only sound was that of wild birds shrieking and squabbling in the low bush behind the house, Brendan finally spoke. "You will have to flee, Dennis. You will not receive mercy from any magistrate on this island. We must hide you and your family until we can get you off. Where are Ellen and the children?"

"Ah, the, ah, house, back at the house," he said absently.

"Dennis, put it out of mind. The man provoked the attack. When in God's heaven will they leave us alone to do our chores and smoke our pipes with our families? . . . Look, you must go to Padenuque. He is old, but he is wise. Tell him I sent you. Stay with him until I bring Ellen and the children. Do as he says, hear me! Dennis, for God's sake, man, snap out of your trance. You must, for the sake of your family."

Brendan shook him by the shoulders, and a trace of color came back into Hurley's face. "Aye, Brendan. I will do exactly as the old man tells me. But you be careful. The militia will be on the way, make no mistake of that."

"Aye. Now be off."

As he watched the once proud man duck off into the high grass like a frightened squirrel, he saw himself, skulking across the stone-glutted fields of Galway with the baying hounds at his heels. Would it be always thus? Was it so much for a man to ask to own a patch of his own land? He turned in anger to find Mary already in the hall-way. His explanation was brief.

"But, Brendan, he killed a man. Surely you cannot condone that?"

"I do not condone it, Mary Roark. But I understand it."

"Should you get involved?" Her frown annoyed him.

"Mary, he is a neighbor. He cleared the south pasture with me, shared the milk of his one cow with us when ours had dried up from the sickness. He is an Irishman who is always kind and gentle. Jesus, woman, involved? It could be me. I'll be home by evening." Sometimes he wondered if Mary ever remembered her own heritage.

He took the cart, and it swayed and bounced over the fields, down to the beach and along the wide expanse that extended out to a sand bar and the three hunchbacked rocks that marked the boundary of Dennis Hurley's land. The Hurley farm was unusual because it included so much beach and, at the same time, some of the densest growth on the island. Dennis, gentle among flowers and trees, had allowed little islands and inlets of growth to remain as shade and places of quiet.

Brendan approached from the beach side, secured horse and cart in the deep, thick growth adjacent to barn and home, and listened to the silence of the lazy summer afternoon. When he was sure no one was about, he moved into the clearing in front of the house.

His eyes fixed on the figure stretched out on its back beside the barn. The big black mare whinnied and pawed the ground, sending reddish brown clouds rising in the still air. Brendan reached down and rolled the body over. A tiny trickle of blood ran from the corner of the mouth, and the vest and white shirt were covered with holes and blood-soaked stains. The ants and insects had already begun their ritual attack on Ian Kemp's face. Brendan brushed them away with his hand, and some of the vermin disappeared down the collar of the dead man's shirt.

Brendan stood up, crossed himself, and walked to the house.

He knocked on the door. No one answered, but he thought he heard the sound of keening, occasionally broken by loud sobbing. This time he knocked fiercely. "Ellen, open this door, it's Brendan McMahon. Come, woman, there's not much time. We must hurry. The militia will be here." Finally, the door opened, and Ellen Hurley stepped back, her arms wrapped around her ten-year-old son and eight-year-old daughter. Her body shook and her hands trembled as she directed the children to the far bedroom.

He took her hands in his. "Ellen, you must be brave. We have only minutes before we must leave this house for good. Take the few things you feel you must have, and leave everything else behind."

"Leave? Leave my home for good? Oh, I cannot," she sobbed, her shoulders shaking uncontrollably.

"I know, I know, Ellen. It is understandable. You and Dennis have worked hard to build up this farm. Believe me, I understand. But if you want Dennis alive, you have no choice. You must leave now. Quick, take only what you need for one night. I will go out to the highroad to keep watch for the militia."

She looked once about the room, tears rolling down her cheeks, and then, with great resignation, she sighed and called her children to join her in packing.

Beyond the house, Brendan lay in the high grass. The sun was warm on his face.

The Tignish Road stretched out in a fairly straight line for several miles. The nearest militia station, with a garrison of ten enlisted men and an officer, was several miles away in Saint Felix. If Kemp's two followers had raced directly there, the militia would soon be coming down that road.

He glanced back at the well-cared-for farm. Dennis Hurley, having come destitute and broken from a barren patch on Achill Island, had forged and dug and labored day and night to turn these overgrown fields which no one wanted into a prosperous farm. And now, in a matter of hours, the man was on the run, his house and belongings left for auction or, worse, a land agent's torch.

Brendan's gaze returned to the road, and his heart skipped a beat. From three miles away, dust coiled and curled in a red spiral behind at least a dozen horses, and to judge by the speed with which they approached, they were not out for a pleasant midweek canter.

He jumped to his feet and ran back to the house.

The door opened just as he got there, and Ellen, with her two children, stood framed in the doorway. It was an agonizing moment, but Brendan knew he could not allow it to continue. "When I say, 'run,' head for the birch arbor. Do not look to your right," he warned the children, "and do not look back," he emphasized to Ellen. The three nodded.

"Run."

They rushed for the thick stand of white trees, their canvas and burlap bags thumping at their backs.

Brendan could now hear the roar of approaching riders.

He raced after Ellen and the children and bundled them all into the cart. Once on the wet sand, packed hard from the morning tide, he let out the reins and spirited the horse in a wild race down the deserted strand and back to his own cape.

It was fully one hour later that a dozen riders trotted out to him as he was attempting to dislodge a great stone from the south field. He used a thick oak bough for a wedge; but the thousand-year-old boulder had slept too long beneath the grass, and it would take hours more of laborious coaxing before he could bring it forth from its earthen grave. The cart and horse stood idly by. Sweat poured from his body. He wore no shirt, and his brown back glistened with perspiration.

As the men drew nearer, he straightened, rubbing his lower spine and smiling up at them. "Now, that is what I call neighborly, you fellows come to lend a hand?"

The officer smiled and tipped the peak of his black helmet.

"I'm afraid not, Mr. McMahon. We have matters of a more serious nature to investigate."

"Oh, well, maybe another time. What is it you'll be looking for? Maybe I can help."

"I hope so. I certainly hope so, sir. We are looking for Dennis Hurley, your neighbor. He killed a man."

"Dennis?" Brendan had been leaning on the bough, but now he straightened up. "Dennis Hurley killed a man? Why, that's . . . I can't believe . . . Dennis. Are you sure? Who was the man?"

The officer smoothed out his lobster red tunic with his hand as he looked around at his men. He seemed to be judging their reaction to Brendan's surprise.

"The man was Kemp, the land agent, and yes, we are certain Hurley killed him. We have two eyewitnesses, and it appears that Hurley and his family have vanished like a puff of smoke."

The officer was studying the horse and cart. Wiping the sweat from his forehead, Brendan followed his gaze. The wheels and sides of the cart were splattered and caked with the red mud of the wet clay beach. The path from the beach led directly to the boulder and the cart. Those tracks could be easily followed directly to the Hurleys' place. Brendan would have to think fast.

"But I was with him only a few hours ago, and nothing seemed wrong. He was in such good spirits. Why should he do such a thing?"

"You were with him?" The officer sat up in his saddle.

"Why, yes, I drove the cart over because he told me he needed help clearing his lower pasture."

"Did you work long with him?"

"No. I did not work with him at all." Brendan's answers came quickly but still with that casual curiosity that said Dennis Hurley could never have committed such an act of evil.

"Dennis Hurley is a gentle man, Captain. I find it hard to believe he could kill another living soul."

The officer scrutinized the cart. "You say you drove the cart to Hurley's?"

"Yes. Why?"

"Oh, nothing. I intended to ask you just that question, but obviously that won't be necessary now." The captain's English accent connoted education and breeding, and he sat his horse like a gentleman. Brendan had the distinct impression that the officer was suspicious of him, but the man's voice remained courteous and his expression ingenuous.

"Well, Mr. McMahon, if there is nothing else you can tell us, we will bid you good day, sir." He saluted, pulled the horse away, and cantered off, the others following in close pursuit.

Brendan returned to his struggle with the great stone until he was certain they were gone, and then he started slowly for the beach. He set off at a steady jog until he reached the base of the cape where the Micmacs camped during the summer months, close to the sea. There were plans to be made, and they had to be made now. Dennis Hurley and his family had no time to waste. They would have to leave the island as soon as possible. At the moment the militia was confused, riding in circles; but in another day there would be platoons assigned to various areas, and either they would flush the Hurleys out of their Micmac hiding place or the roads would be impossible to travel undetected.

A reddish orange flame licked the black shroud of the sky. Sharp pins of white stars blinked and winked over the Northumberland Strait. Two dozen people sat inside the warm circle of heat that smoked and sparked from the driftwood bonfire.

Although the day had been hot and sunny, a chill Canadian wind now blew across the water. Blankets were tucked more securely around sleeping children as the little band traded stories and tales of the great Canadian Northwest, a land so vast and so untraveled that fact became legend and legend fact around the heaped-up red-streaked wood.

"We will be very obvious. We will make no pretense," Brendan was saying to the assembly in a low but distinct voice.

"Patenaude tells me there are militiamen all over the highroad. Another garrison has been called in from Cascumpeeque. Is that not so, Patenaude?"

"It is so, Brendan McMahon. My people have been about this night, and they have seen much activity." Patenaude's copper face shone in the flame of the fire. He was speaking for his father, Padenuque, whose age dictated that he retire early to his bed in the triangular tent that commanded the high bluff.

Brendan walked slowly among them. The Profitts sat next to Mary and the children. Next to them were several members of the O'Neil family. They all were arranged in a circle and huddled in blankets.

Almost inconspicuous to any onlooker were Dennis Hurley, Ellen, and the two children, who were staggered between the O'Neils and the Gaudets.

"How are you keeping, Dennis? Ellen?" Brendan's tone was soothing without being overly solicitous.

"Good enough, Brendan, for a man on the run." His voice seemed faraway and broken.

"None of that now. You are safe with your people. Have faith. You will make another life for yourself and your family."

"What is your plan, Brendan? How do we escape? Padenuque would tell us nothing except to join his son and come here." The woman's voice cracked with fear.

"Rest easy, Ellen. I expect that the militia will see our fire and pay us a visit. When they do, we will be singing and laughing and spinning yarns. Patenaude's sons are lying in the high grass near the Tignish Road. They will alert us of any approaching horsemen."

"But then what? We do not understand." Ellen looked over at her husband, who was staring, glassy-eyed, into the orange flames. She studied him for a moment, and tears formed in her eyes as she shook her head solemnly.

Brendan took her hands in his as he crouched down beside her. "He will be all right, Ellen, as soon as you are on your way and free. And you must help him to get over the guilt he is feeling. When the militia arrives and is satisfied that we are just simple folk sitting around a settlement bonfire, they will leave and search elsewhere. We will know where they are, and they will leave us to ourselves. Then the Micmacs will bring the canoes, and you will board them."

"Where are they taking us, Brendan?"

"To Lennox Island. There is a Micmac village there. You will be cared for until you feel safe enough to go on."

Brendan's conversation was suddenly interrupted by the rustle of bodies pushing through the high grass of the cape above.

Two young Micmacs slid down the sand to the beach and whispered something to Patenaude.

Patenaude nodded, slapped them on the back, and sauntered over to Brendan. He spoke softly for a big man, and his message was brief: "They come."

"All right, let us have laughter and song." Michael O'Neil uncovered his fiddle from the gray blanket that was wrapped about him and his wife and began a lively and spirited island tune. "When Johnny, ye comes a-courtin, I will be settin' on the porch awaitin'." Some hummed and others sang the words as Howard Shea joined in with a tin whistle.

The drumming gallop of horses thundered along the strand, and slowly the song, the fiddle, and the whistle faded in the smoke and blackness of the night.

Sweating, frothing horses pulled up before the glare of the fire, which etched their stiff black figures in bas-relief.

"Well, what have we here, Mr. McMahon?"

"Good evening, Captain. You are a tireless man. Do you never rest?" Brendan reached up and shook hands, mildly surprised by the steel grip of the Englishman.

"I will rest when I have my murderer in irons." His gaze swept over the huddled group, scrutinizing each face intently before moving along to the next. His eyes settled on the lovely Ellen Hurley, and she felt her heart sink and the strength drain from her body. His eyes moved on.

"Are you having a celebration of sorts, Mr. McMahon?"

"No, Captain, just a get-together. We have them often. This is a busy time in the fields, so the night and the bonfire bring us together to share in our stories and local history. Perhaps you would join us and tell a yarn or two."

"That is kind of you, Mr. McMahon, but we still have some riding to do before the night is done. I know I can count on any one of you coming to me with information on this Hurley, if you hear or see anything."

"Well, of course, Captain. Is that not so, neighbors?" They mumbled and murmured their assent, and the captain touched fingers to his cap and bade them good-night.

Brendan and the others watched the horses fade behind the black curtain of night. No one moved for a long while.

"All right, we have no time to lose. Patenaude, are they ready?"

"Yes. I shall give them the signal." He reached for a fiery chunk of wood and waved it back and forth and then up and down, forming the sign of the cross.

Four canoes slipped through the waves, the moon coloring their white bark sides with a pale yellow. The silhouetted Micmacs slapped at the waves, bringing the boats about and riding the curling foam until they were beached. Watching them, Brendan's mind traveled back almost seventeen years, to the time when an Aran Island fisherman named Thomas Gill had rescued him, his mother and two sisters from the clutches of John Douglas and his men. Then the craft had been the sleek tar-bottomed boat of the Aran Islands. Abruptly he forced himself back to the present.

"Come, Dennis, the lads await you. Keep the blankets, you will need them."

"Brendan, I don't know what to say. I'm thankful and I'm sorry. My temper caused a man to die."

"Dennis, there is not a person here who would judge you. Live your life, man. You have a wife, a family and a future. Now get a hold on yourself. Go now, Godspeed and safe home."

They were helped into the boats, and almost immediately the Indians pushed the canoes out into the open surf. Dennis Hurley sat next to his wife in one boat while their children shared another. Tears rolled down the gentle Irishman's cheeks as his wife buried her head in his shoulder. Then they were gone, riding the crest of the waves through the dark of the night tide.

Brendan and his neighbors stood quietly at the edge of the surf,

peering after the departing family. No one spoke, but they all understood only too well the significance of the Hurleys' plight. They all
had left a home once, and they all could share in that displacement.
None had left a home twice, but if it could happen to a gentle man
like Dennis, could it not happen to any one of them? That which had
always seemed so certain was suddenly no longer so.

They turned back to the roaring, spark-spitting fire and began to
gather up their blankets and shuffle for home. But they did not get
far before a voice commanded them to sit. "I have words to say this
night and those words are for you, my neighbors and friends."

They looked back and forth at one another, their faces quizzical
as they arranged the blankets again.

Brendan stood before the fire, his face burnished a ruddy, orange-
copper and his black hair fanning out behind him. They mumbled to
each other as Mary, hugging Abigail and Daniel, squeezing warmth
into their little shoulders, frowned at him. Her own husband, yet at
this moment she did not seem to know him. His eyes danced with a
devil's fire.

"Neighbors, my heart grieves for Dennis Hurley and his family
this night, as I'm sure you all grieve. He came here to a land that was
choked wtih trees and stone. He worked that land as a hired man for
Pierre Dumas, and when Pierre decided to go to Nova Scotia, he drew
up a clear, notarized deed, and Dennis signed it and bought four lots
from him. The deed, unlike many of ours, read pure and simple, and
it was signed by two Summerside magistrates."

"We all have heard the story before, Brendan," Reginald Gaudet
interrupted. "What is the point of repeating it now? We are tired and
cold, and tomorrow will be hot and long."

"The point, Gaudet, is this." Brendan's voice had an edge to it.
"Dennis had a good, firm title of his land. Yet he is gone, his home
left behind to blow away in the wind and storm or, worse, to be taken
over by the government. And what of us? Many of us have deeds that
are not as firm; what will happen to us at the hands of arbitrary agents
and government people?"

They all leaned forward, the fire casting their faces into a copper
luster.

"There is a question long unanswered in this province as well as
other provinces across Canada. And that question concerns land. Land,
neighbors, yours and mine. There are still proprietors back in England
who, if the spirit so moved them, would call our deeds into question,
squatters' rights or no. We have a representative government that rep-
resents its own interests, but not the interests of the whole island.
Some of the largest landowners on this island are the members of the
governor's Advisory Council and the governor himself."

"What do you propose we do, Brendan?" Bill Profitt asked quietly.

"I propose that we begin to work for a new and responsible government, one that is responsive to all our needs. I say we form a new
party. And I have been thinking for a long while that we need a
louder voice, a voice that will reach all the islanders. We need a news-

paper that can list our demands and speak out our frustrations. We
need a voice that will shout out to the government in Charlottetown.
We *will* be heard. We *must* be heard, or we will forever be clearing
land and planting seeds while looking over our shoulders for an evic-
tion notice. I came to this island to stay, and I have no intention of
being forced to move on."

"Hear, hear."

"Agreed."

"For certain," they chorused.

"But, Brendan, who would operate this newspaper?" Mary asked,
her voice sharp and her head cocked. "Surely you have a farm to take
care of." She had heard his newspaper notion before, but he had never
acted on it, so she had dismissed it as simply a notion. Now he seemed
adamant. All this talk of politics and newspapers brought a sharpness
to his voice that worried her. She had seen Brendan's passion for the
political arena years before, when he had trailed after Daniel O'Connell for the dead cause of a suffering Ireland. She did not wish to see
that zeal again, for it would surely take him from his home and family.

He smiled at his wife to reassure her. "*I* certainly cannot run it,
but there is an Irish lad I'm told, name of Edward Ahearn, working
on a newspaper in Nova Scotia, the *Caledonian*. He's highly respected
for his writing, and if I had the support of the good people of Tignish,
I would write to him and ask if he would be interested in forming a
paper here, in Prince County. . . . Well, do I have your support? Do
we fight for what is our right, or do we wait day after day to have
our land taken from us?"

"How much would such a venture cost, McMahon?" It was Angus
MacHattie, who operated the only blacksmith shop from Tignish to
Summerside. The sleeves had been cut from his shirt to accommodate
his well-developed biceps, but the evening chill did not seem to pene-
trate his beefy frame.

"Ah, the Scotsman always gets down to money," Brendan said
with a chuckle.

"Aye, that may be the truth of it, but it will be *this* Scotsman
who will pay more than his share as usual." Of course, it was true;
MacHattie was the wealthiest man in the county, and he questioned
the price of everything and bargained to the hilt of the sword; but
once he gave his word, it was a bond never to be broken. And he did
contribute more than any of the others to any worthy cause because
he knew he had been blessed with abundance, and he did not mind
sharing, as long as the price was fair.

"I'm told one pound ten a week."

MacHattie, his thick arms crossing his wide chest, thought for a
moment. His head bobbed slowly at first, and then his assent was
obvious. "One pound five, yes, one pound five per week, a princely
sum from a princely county." He smiled at his own turn of phrase.
"Yes, a princely sum for anyone who does not use his back to make a
living," he added.

"You're a hard man, MacHattie, a hard man when it comes to

money. We will establish a cooperative, whereby each citizen of Tignish and the neighboring towns will contribute a sum to be agreed on."

"How do you know the people of this county will agree to your proposal, Brendan?" O'Neil said in a whistle through the gaps between his teeth.

"Because we have talked about it. It is not a new idea. It is just that we are isolated up here on the North Cape and we have always felt protected and smug, tucked away from the rest of the county. I have heard it said of us many times in my travels to Summerside. And possibly they are correct in their assessment of us. Well, we can see after this day how isolated we are, how protected we are. If we are not careful, we all could be driven off our land and off our beloved island like the Acadians before us. The crown does not have our interest at heart. The crown thinks only of the crown." His voice rang across the breaking surf and came back to him on the tide. For one brief moment he remembered the eloquence of Daniel O'Connell.

"Brendan, you are a fine speaker. Have you never thought of standing for the legislature yourself?"

"Be sensible, Angus, I've enough to do caring for a family and a farm."

Mary sat up suddenly and straightened. Her shawl fell off her shoulders, and she rearranged it.

"The autumn election will be on us before we know it. Talk is that Old Man Perrault will not stand for another term. Ach, the man's infirm, forgetful, and a pawn on the Assembly's chessboard. But you, McMahon, you are a man of strength. Of course, like all the Irish, you talk too much and love the sound of your own voice, but you would be good for the people of Prince County. I will give you that much." MacHattie suppressed a chuckle. He admired Brendan, not only for his strength of body but also for his gentle strength of soul. MacHattie, childless all these years, with a good but sometimes sad-faced wife, had watched on many occasions from the smithy's forge as Brendan tramped by with young Daniel draped over his shoulders like a colt that had thrown a shoe. The Scotsman was a deep man who saw the world without confusion or clutter; things were either good or bad. People were either good or bad. Dennis Hurley was a good man. Brendan McMahon was a good man. Nothing else need be said.

"Well, what say you, McMahon? What say you? There is a chill in the air. We cannot wait all night."

"Yes, Brendan, consider it." Bill Profitt joined in, as did O'Neil and the others. Isabella said nothing but swayed back and forth with the sleeping Abigail bundled in a blanket and nestled snugly in her lap, her head resting on Isabella's shoulder. Isabella rocked slowly and managed a discreet glance at Mary, whose face was as hard as marble.

Brendan's chest swelled. He had never considered politics. He was a farmer, heaven knows. What did he know about sitting in the Assembly? No, no. It was inconceivable.

But they continued now, swept up in the idea as though it had always been on their minds, as though Brendan McMahon of Tignish

Parish, Prince County, Prince Edward Island had been destined from birth to be their representative.

"You must, Brendan, for the sake of your neighbors," Profitt insisted as Isabella bit hard on her lips.

"Let's hear it for the McMahon." O'Neil whistled through his teeth.

They clapped and cheered, and the sound raced along the cape like a speeding herald.

Then Patenaude walked to the center of the group. He bowed solemnly to them and turned to Brendan, and in the way that was most natural to him, he spoke simply. "You have no choice, Brendan McMahon; your neighbors have spoken." He bowed then to Brendan, nodded to the others, and walked off in the direction of his village on the high cape, his two sons following at a respectful distance.

No one spoke, but their eyes trailed after the departing figure. Then Brendan, feigning a chuckle to cover the embarrassment he felt at the solemnity of the moment, answered them. "I judge then it is settled. I shall stand for election to the Assembly this autumn."

They cheered once again and came up to him, one by one, to thump his strong, broad back. As they did, he looked at Mary, but she was already moving up the path, holding the sleeping Daniel in her arms.

It was fully an hour before Brendan's heavy boots stamped across the wide boards of the porch as he entered the sleeping house. After taking a lighted candle from the sconce beside the door, he ducked under the archway of the living room and on into the kitchen. Out and beyond the slumbering farm, the Strait hissed and rolled in the quiet night. He placed the candle in a jar on the kitchen table and reached for the stone jug of poteen, to throw back his head and swallow hard. He felt warm and good, and the glow of the poteen mixed with the glow of pride he felt at the confidence his neighbors had shown him.

"Well, aren't you the proper Irishman? Loaded with golden words and burning poteen." Mary stood with arms folded across her ample bosom.

Turning to her, he smiled tentatively only to be met by an icy stare. The smile died on his lips. "What is it you are saying, woman?"

"I am saying that you have the gall of an English landlord to tell those people you would stand for election to the Assembly." She jerked her head in the direction of the beach and the scene of his recent victory.

"Gall, is it? I did not go seeking their support. They came to me. You saw it. Damn it, woman, you were there."

"Aye. I was there all right, and I saw the chin jut out and the shoulders straighten with your overblown pride. The young Daniel O'Connell I suppose they will be calling you." Her voice was as sharp as a blade. Her folded arms seemed to be holding in the anger that rose slowly in her voice. "And now you come home and drink that bellywash, and you with a day's farm work ahead of you. Where the hell is your head, man? Is it so stuffed up with pride that you cannot think straight?"

"Who the Christ do you think you are talking to, some child? I happen to think that it is my duty and responsibility to stand for election."

"Your duty and responsibility are here on this farm with your wife and children. That's where your duty lies, not in Charlottetown."

"You seemed to think for a time that you belonged in Charlotte-town if I remember correctly."

"Aye. That I did, because you were off playing the Irish hero. Someone had to fight for what was ours."

"I suppose I will hear that story until they shovel me under the clay."

"Rest assured you will. And be damned thankful for what I did."

"Tell me, what are you so fired up about?"

"I'll tell you why I am fired up. Did you have to say yes to those people before consulting me? Does your wife have no say in the matter?"

"So that's what's been eating at you, is it? Can't you get it through your thick Galway head that what you and I want means nothing? Are you such a country girl you can't see that this is for the good of the island?"

"Thick, is it? You bloody bastard, you're nothing but a dreamer, like all Irishmen. You can't see beyond your next drink. You remember this, and remember it well: This farm comes first. It comes before any high and mighty talk about the island."

"Damn your eyes, damn you, you're a stubborn bitch, you are."

Her right hand swung out and slapped him a stinging blow across the face. His own fist was cocked and raised on instinct, but he caught himself from throwing it. He turned, picked up the stone jug and pushed on past her.

"Where are you going now with that jug? Where?"

"To the barn. I couldn't share a bed with you this night. I'd be afraid that I would choke the bloody breath out of you."

Summer came to the valleys and dingles of Prince County, sprinkling rain and sun over the potato fields, and by the time August arrived the Irish cobblers were bulging under their red mounds of earth.

Brendan McMahon left nothing to chance. His determination was evident in the grim set of his jaw as, from the placid Northumberland Strait on one side of the high capes to the gusty, moody gulf on the other, he brought the word.

"Land. Your land, my land. Dignity of ownership"—this was his message, and the farmers and fishermen listened and agreed.

The relationship between Mary and Brendan remained cool. Although he had returned to their bed, their tongues lashed more than once, sending the children into hiding in the high grass or behind the barn. But Brendan tried to stay abreast of his duties, and she did respect him for that. On one occasion Mary, fatigued from a day of churning butter, preserving wild berry jelly in the root cellar, and feeding and administering to a family of seven, seemed to lose all control and shouted down the very timbers of the house as Brendan trudged wearily into the kitchen long after the evening meal was over.

"Jesus, Mary, and Joseph, what am I, some Micmac woman ready at all hours of the day and night to feed you hot broth from my wooden spoon? Where have you been? Your children are all washed and in their beds. The livestock has been fed, and you come in here like some Irish aristocrat."

"Be easy, woman. I've walked a lifetime today. I am tired. I'll get something for myself. Do not bother yourself. Go to your bed and rest."

"Oh, aren't we the poor suffering martyr? I can smell whiskey on your breath. Wouldn't that be part of your fatigue?"

Her tongue hissed like a viper's, and he felt its poisonous sting. But he said nothing as he helped himself to fish chowder from the deep black pot.

"Answer me, isn't it the drink that has you weary tonight?"

"No. It is not," he answered abruptly.

"You are a farmer, Brendan McMahon, and all you have done this summer is walk the farms of others. If you did not have good, hard-working children, this farm would be sliding into the ocean. You preach about the land. What about *our* land?"

"They are good children, to be sure, and they understand what their father is doing. It is for their land that I am doing this. And what is this nonsense? I have not shirked my duties here."

"Oh, so that's it. The children understand, but I do not. I am the wicked one."

"Jesus, woman, I did not say that. Now be off. I do not wish to argue with you. I must be about early in the morning."

"To do your farming, I trust."

"No. Not my farming this time." His voice was rising. He could feel the temper beginning to surge inside him, and he made a conscious effort to bury it.

But Mary would not let up. The farm, and the long, hot summer, and Brendan's increasing absences from home—all contributed to a growing resentment that she was finding more difficult to control each day.

"If not farming, then what?"

He began eating, dipping thick slices of bread into the chowder. His stomach was empty, and he ate heartily. The food soothed him momentarily, and his anger died.

"This chowder is good. It is very good."

"Never mind the chowder. What are you about early in the morning if I may ask?" She stood in the doorway of the kitchen, poised as if to leave, but she did not. Instead, she walked back into the room and sat at the far end of the table. "I do have that right, do I not?"

"You may ask," he said patiently. "Jarrod Murdock has sent word he wishes to speak to me."

"Jarrod Murdock, the shipbuilder and merchant?"

"Aye."

"You are to go to him? Why, that'll be a day's journey. Port Loyal? Is that not where he lives?"

"Aye."

"You will not set foot back on this farm until midnight. Good God, man, how long am I to put up with this foolishness?"

"Foolishness? Foolishness, is it?" He pounded the table with his fist, and the shock sent the bowl crashing to the floor. "You call it foolishness, and I know in my heart and brain this is the only way to save our land from a government that allows us no responsible representation."

"Don't give one of your speeches to me. Oh, you are so high and mighty since a few Indians and neighbor farmers decided to look on you as another savior. Well, I'm telling you, I think you are nothing but a beggar on horseback."

"Do you even know what you are saying, woman? Or are you so starved for a man's conversation you will force it by argument if need be?"

"Do not hold yourself in such high esteem. You may be able to blather the wives of ignorant farmers, but I am not so easy to convince."

"Well, then, what in hell is it you want from me?"

"I want you to stop this nonsense and return to the earth like any good and self-respecting Irishman. Know your place. Your place is here."

"Oh, Christ, woman, you are thick. Thick as a cow. Can't you understand that this place, my place, as you call it, may not be here if I do not do something about it and soon?"

"Who ordained you to this sacred ministry? Who, I ask you?" Her voice, sharp and shrieking, cut through the kitchen. Her eyes blazed, and he picked up the bowl from the floor and hurled it against the wall.

"Keep your bloody chowder," he spit back at her, and rushed for the door, but before he could leave, the sound of a small voice, sobbing and trembling, stopped him in his tracks.

"Father, why are you and Mother fighting? Pl-please, st-stop. Pl-ease?" It was the sensitive Daniel who stood in the half-light of the hallway, timidly drawing back into the shadows.

Brendan bent to pick the boy up in his great arms. "Oh, my little man, your mother and I are tired. I was silly, and I dropped my bowl of lovely fish chowder. Wasn't that a clumsy father? Come, my little man, I will put you back into your bed."

"Are you going to bed, Mother?" The little voice cracked and sobbed.

"I am. Get your rest now, Daniel. Your mama loves you."

Brendan hugged his son and ascended the stairs.

"Good night, Brendan," Mary whispered, her voice drained of emotion, "will you be sleeping in the barn this night?"

"No, I'll be sleeping in my own bed."

"Good," was all she said.

Jarrod Murdock was as squat and thick as a tree trunk. He stood on bow legs, and all his strength seemed to be concentrated into one small area from chest to neck. He was known to have raised a loaded cart with his bare hands. But then there were many stories of Jarrod Murdock's feats. The least apocryphal of these had to do with his capacity for drink.

On one occasion, apparently stupefied and numb from a night's drinking in Charlottetown, he slept away the better part of the next day. A ship's captain entered the saloon and proclaimed to all his disgust for the lack of ambition he encountered on the island. He was to have received a cargo of timber from up north, and none was forthcoming.

The barman, pointing to the sleeping Murdock, said, "If it's a cargo you want delivered with the speed of a fox, there is your man, there."

The captain downed his rum with even more disgust and was about to depart when Murdock jumped to his feet and announced that he would have the timber delivered by sailing time. The captain somehow agreed, and Murdock rode all night back to Port Loyal, rousing his debtors out of their beds before dawn and intimidating them into bringing the timber to the inland rivers in time to be shipped by raft up to Charlottetown. Jarrod Murdock was a businessman, ruthless, aggressive, demanding, and arrogant. He had no time for sentiment and all the time in the world for money.

There was, though, one weak bone in his body. Although he had three grown sons, he kept a special place under the cold stone of his heart for his ten-year-old daughter, Margaret, or Little Peg, as he affectionately referred to her.

And on this particular September morning, as he strode the green sweep of his front yard with Margaret in a long white gown by his side, he was imbued with a rising contentment. Life was a smooth voyage these days, devoid of storms or unseen barrier reefs, and he was determined to keep it that way. He turned in his reverie and gazed back at the house. It was a sprawling but expertly designed building with wide windows and extended porches. Its white clapboard and black witch's trim contrasted neatly with the lush green of the lawn and the red dust of the wagon path that meandered through an oak and birch arborway directly to the far white pillars of the front portico.

The house was like Jarrod Murdock, solid and strong, practical and conservative. Its widow's walk was a reminder of the few grand houses back in West Devon, where he had scratched out a sickly, impoverished childhood along the craggy, bleak English coast.

Through luck and determination to pull himself up by the bootstraps, he had worked his passage to Canada, gained employment cutting lumber, stolen it by night, sold it on the docks at Charlottetown on Sabbath days, become a supervisor of a lumber camp and general store, and finally been paid his back wages not in money, but in acreage considered worthless by his absentee and retiring London employer. Yes, it had been a difficult struggle; but succeed he had, and with the acquisition of mile after mile of prime inland waterways, shipbuilding had seemed a natural outgrowth of his lumber business.

The Assembly came next. It gave Jarrod Murdock, known to many as the Robber Baron of Port Loyal, the mark of acceptance and dignity for which his grasping nature starved. Life sang for him this golden morning; it sang along with the yellow warblers that had already begun their migration southward to the warmth of South America. He watched them high over the russet and yellow sun-drenched leaves, driven by some blind primordial instinct on their preordained journey. Go, my feathered friends, he thought, but while you are gone, your nests will be assaulted and destroyed, and then you will have to rebuild in the spring.

There was no spring in Jarrod Murdock's life. He was in the early winter of his years as he approached his fiftieth birthday. There could be no rebuilding. He must continue to build what he had, and with his continued devotion to business and hard work, he saw hmiself as a man who one day might be the wealthiest citizen on the island. There seemed to be no obstacles to this plan.

No obstacles except one. This McMahon from Tignish, lately there was much said of him: a man of the people who would fight British absentee ownership of land, who saw as the only solution to the island's problems a confederation with the rest of Canada.

Confederation. The word was anathema to Murdock. With confederation came regulations, bureaucratic snooping, notarized deeds, surveying of land and waterways, and government inspection of merchant ships. Jarrod Murdock ran his little kingdom by his own rules, and he did not relish any outside intervention.

He must talk to this McMahon, who seemed to have no considerable opposition in the election now that Old Man Perrault had decided not to stand for a third term.

McMahon, if he won, and it now appeared certain that he would, might well be in a position to cast the deciding vote if confederation ever came before the Assembly.

The sun climbed high over Port Loyal, sending yellow shafts of light through the leafy grove of trees. The noonday warmth was more like summer, and even the departing birds seemed to hesitate in midflight over the blue waters of the Port Loyal boatyard as though in some seasonal confusion.

Murdock watched them veer off over the skeletal hull of a halfbuilt barque perched high above the water's surface on its rough oak supports. The sound of hammer and logger's saw and the thumping and banging of the long wooden pegs and iron nails echoed along a shoreline that was black with the laboring, bending figures of shipwrights, craftsmen, and day laborers.

On this bright Indian summer day Port Loyal resounded with the exuberance and vitality of growth and production. Murdock did not squander time and money on building the inland and river rigs, the schooners that sailed from one island port to another, with less lucrative cargo. The construction of schooners took place in the harbors and inlets of New London, New Glasgow, Rustico, Murray Harbour, and Souris, where the concern was with fishing and coastal trade. Jarrod Murdock had long since abandoned such parochial thinking. His product was as natural to the island as its red, rich soil; his product was timber. It built the barques, and it was the cargo that English brokers eagerly awaited on the teeming docks of Liverpool.

But it did not end there, because Murdock's counterpart in England, at Appledore, the sequestered and sheltered seaside shipbuilding town in the Bideford area of Devon, was none other than his eldest son, Graham. Graham Murdock, tall and lank, had not inherited his father's build, but he had inherited everything else. Graham Murdock was a shrewd and aggressive businessman who ran the Devon adventure as if his father were straddling the ocean and looking down on him, watching every move.

It had taken sweat and sacrifice; but the experiment had succeeded, and Jarrod Murdock watched his business grow on both sides of the Atlantic with an obsessiveness that burned like fire in the black pit of his soul.

"When will they come back, Father?"

Margaret's voice was a lyrical contrast with the harsh sounds that rose in the still air from the boatyard below.

"Huh? What? Did you say something, Little Peg?" He took her delicate white hand in his gnarled brown one and studied the rosy pink tips of her fingers. "You have the softest and loveliest little fingers I have ever seen, my gem. I suspect that someday you will be a fine artist."

"Do you think so, Father? Why, if I do become an artist, I will paint your portrait and we shall have it hung over the fireplace, and when guests arrive, I shall say, 'That is my handsome father.'"

"Oh, now wait a moment, my little bird, you may say 'my *successful* father,' but to say 'handsome' would be stretching the truth from here to Charlottetown."

Murdock was quite aware of the names summoned up, not only by his business practices but also by his squat, dark appearance. The Black Poker was one he had gotten wind of. His spine, paralyzed from a childhood illness, rendered his Napoleonic form permanently rigid, and the lack of flexibility showed in the black lines of his forehead and the sharp downward strokes at his mouth.

"You are handsome to my eyes, Father." Her innocent brown eyes were clear and honest. She was delicate like her deceased mother, gone now these four years.

"No man ever had a more precious child. I sometimes wonder why I have been so blessed." By way of fact, Murdock did wonder many nights as he lay alone and lonely in the large brass bed in the master bedroom that looked out over the hulking masts in the estuary, why

God had given him such a child. He was not totally oblivious of his shortcomings as a human being, just as he was quite aware of his genius in matters of business.

"Who is this coming through the grove, Father?" Margaret's pink finger pointed to the arborway just as a tall, broad-shouldered man, perhaps in his mid- to late-thirties, emerged into the full, glowing halo of the sun.

The visitor halted a few feet from father and daughter. He grinned crookedly and gestured toward the grove. "I seem to have lost the rest of the path. I left my cart and horse at the bend."

"It is a common occurrence," Murdock said, his black scowl like a tightly drawn mask.

"Much of the grass has grown up around it," Margaret said brightly. "You can see it better in winter. Isn't that so, Father?"

"Yes, my little sparrow." The mask softened. "What can I do for you, stranger?" Murdock put his question brusquely, at the same time studying the muddy boots, the sweat-soaked woolen shirt, and the grime that streaked Brendan McMahon's face.

"I am looking for Jarrod Murdock. I was told I could find him here."

"You have found him, but if it is work you seek, you must go below to the boatyard and speak with the superintendent."

"Oh, how do you do, Mr. Murdock." Brendan extended his hand and withdrew it quickly when he found that Murdock's had remained resolutely at his side.

"Yes. How do you do. Well, good day, they will take care of you below. You look strong enough."

"Excuse me, sir, but I am Brendan McMahon from Tignish Parish. I was told you wished to speak with me. I already have a job." Brendan did not smile. The man's manner irritated him.

The mask loosened entirely then, and Murdock thrust out his beefy hand. For a few interminable seconds Brendan almost succumbed to the spite he was feeling; but it was short-lived, and he shook the hand of the small, blocky man, though with less enthusiasm than usual.

"Forgive me, Mr. McMahon, I do not know what I was thinking. Surely I knew you were coming today; one of your farmer friends relayed your message to me. Come inside out of the sun. You must be thirsty. Can I get you some ale?"

"No, thank you, Mr. Murdock, but I would like a cup of water. And could I use your pump? I'd like to soak this head and face of mine."

"By all means. Margaret, show Mr. McMahon to the pump. You will find something in the stable to dry yourself off. Help the man, my sparrow. I will have Mrs. Dawson prepare a light lunch." He walked off to the house, his stiff body moving only from the waist down. Brendan, watching him, could not help comparing Murdock to the wind-up doll he had once seen in a shop in Summerside.

Refreshed after a good dousing under the pump and a healthy rub of his head and face with a fine cotton cloth, Brendan ducked into the dark cool of the kitchen, where a long, ruggedly functional table dominated much of the room. Murdock sat at the hearthside end while Mrs. Dawson placed cold pork and greens and a dish of cold potatoes in the center of the table. There was also bread and jam and white butter and ginger cookies and a large pitcher of cold spring water.

Mrs. Dawson poured some of the water into a pewter cup, and Brendan, after his five hours' jarring ride over rutted roads, felt a ball of cotton forming in his mouth. But his pride would not allow him to reach for the cup. He sat, clearing his throat and stealing a glance at the cool droplets gliding slowly down the side of the jug.

The room was simply but comfortably furnished. A horsehair love seat stood under the wide window that framed the deep blue of the river beyond. Staircases rose from either end of the kitchen to the upstairs chambers. Lace antimacassars adorned the backs of chairs, and the floor was of smooth stone. There was nothing ostentatious about it, but there was an obvious comfort and space. A man could walk a house like this in much the same way he could pace the fields of his own land.

"Drink, Mr. McMahon, do not stand on ceremony with me. I had a late-morning meal. I've been about since four this lovely morning."

"That's an early hour for a man to rise, Mr. Murdock. Surely you do not have to feed your livestock. A man of your means must have someone to do that for you." There was no sarcasm in his voice, but there was just enough edge in it to make Jarrod Murdock take a closer measure of the man at the other end of the table.

Brendan's lips were cracked and parched. He wished he had drunk more from the cold water of the pump, but there again he had not wished to show his weakness in the presence of the little girl.

"No, I was not interested in the stock. True, I have someone whose duty that is. No. My occupation at that early hour was to observe who was present to load the barque *Devon* for her journey to Liverpool. I trust the care of animals to those who have lived with them, but the care and responsibility of my shipping business I trust to no one but myself."

"Were your observations satisfactory?" Brendan reached for the pewter cup and lifted it to his lips but returned it to the table without drinking.

"Yes, they were. Four slugabeds arrived at fifteen and twenty minutes past the hour. Naturally they are no longer in my service, and unfortunately they were living on Murdock homesteads."

"What does that mean, Mr. Murdock?"

"It means, Mr. McMahon, that as of this moment they are *no longer* living on my homesteads."

Brendan raised the cup again, and this time he swallowed, the cold water soothing the rough, raw skin of his palate. He drank again, and as he put the cup down, Mrs. Dawson arrived from nowhere and filled it.

Murdock, apparently engrossed in his tale, did not seem to notice what Brendan was doing.

Brendan drank again, this time quaffing the water in one great swallow. The little pleasures, he thought.

"But that is all over now. Let us get back to my reasons for wishing to meet you, Mr. McMahon. May I call you Brendan? It seems foolish for us to continue this formality when we, no doubt, will be sharing the responsibility of representing the constituency of Prince County. And please call me Jarrod."

"Jarrod it is. "

"Good. Very good. Now, Brendan, I have been very impressed with your interest in the land question. This is an area where we must tread lightly, but you are perfectly correct in bringing it out into the light of day, so to speak."

Brendan sat up and cut a piece of pork, then smoothed butter over a potato and ate while Murdock continued praising him and his stand on forcing elected officials in the Assembly to define the right of ownership and to organize a certain table of rules by which a man or woman would abide in order to be certain of his or her actual ownership of land.

"And that is a very good idea, one that has not escaped my own thinking. There are so many problems before the Assembly, however, that the monumental task of facing and solving the land question is almost insurmountable at this time. But you will see that for yourself when you are elected." He chuckled into his chest.

"What makes you so certain I will be elected, Jarrod?"

"Oh, come now, Brendan McMahon, your name is on everyone's lips. You are the new man of the people."

Brandon blanched and continued eating. Such praise could be destructive if one allowed oneself to believe it. Daniel O'Connell had said that more than once, and although the great man had passed away, his seventy-odd years of struggle in a suffering nation over, nevertheless his would always be the voice that spoke to Brendan when he was in need of counsel. Dan O'Connell would never trust a man who evicted poor people from their cottages for such puny reasons as this Murdock cited.

Brendan pushed his chair back. "Now that was good. Good and filling. You are fortunate in having such a fine cook for a wife, Jarrod." Mrs. Dawson raised her head from the scullery in the far corner of the room as Brendan bowed in her direction. She raised her eyebrows almost comically, and he smiled in puzzlement.

"Mrs. Dawson is my housekeeper. Her man works for me at the yard. My wife died of consumption four years ago." Murdock lowered his head, and Brendan stuttered an embarrassed apology.

"No need, my friend, we have managed well." He walked to the window, and when he spoke, it was the voice of a different man. "You see—out there—my life runs like a free spirit over the grass. I call her my bird, my Little Peg. She is one of two loves."

"What is the other?" Brendan asked softly, not wishing to tread insensitively on the feeling of the moment.

Jarrod Murdock turned from the window, and the softness was

gone from his face, the tight mask once more in place. "My business," he said coldly. He returned to his seat, poured water from the pitcher, and drank. He placed the cup on the table and looked directly into Brendan's eyes. "I have worked a lifetime for what I have achieved, and I will fight with the last drop of my blood to protect my possessions. Nothing will ever get in my way, and if something"—he paused for emphasis—"or someone ever does, I will destroy him." He allowed the ringing of the words to hang in the air, and Brendan looked over at Mrs. Dawson, whose narrowed eyes and grim expression told only too well the misery that Jarrod Murdock could cause.

"Now, McMahon, I expect you will take my advice on certain matters once you sit in the Assembly." The friendly tone had changed abruptly, and Brendan was certain now that the voice of Daniel O'Connell in his ear was, as usual, correct.

"What certain matters are you referring to, Murdock?" Brendan did not enjoy being referred to by his last name, and the only logical way for him to express his displeasure at this lack of courtesy was to counter in the same manner.

Murdock. There it was before them. Brendan would be treated as an equal or he would not be treated at all. It was only a name; but it was a gauntlet hurled at the feet of Jarrod Murdock, and he did not mistake its significance. So be it, he thought; if McMahon is my obstacle, then I will destroy him. "Well, McMahon, I think we understand each other. The next time I see you I suspect you will be representing your district in the Assembly."

"I prefer to say I will be in a position of *responsibility* to my district. Good day, sir. And thank you for the pleasant repast." He stood and bowed again in the direction of Mrs. Dawson and then to the tight-faced Jarrod Murdock. "You needn't show me out. Again, good day."

They watched his broad back disappear through the door, and Mrs. Dawson's mouth broke into a subtle smile as Jarrod Murdock fired his pewter mug into the cold ash of the fireplace.

CHAPTER XIX

"WILL THE SENIOR representative from Prince County be so good as to introduce the junior member from Tignish?" It was a courteous and formal request, its tone confident and firm.

Byron Jelfe leaned forward in the cherry wood chairman's seat, his eyes scanning the rows for Brendan McMahon. Then he repeated for emphasis, "Mr. Murdock, will you be kind enough to introduce Mr. McMahon?"

Jarrod Murdock's poker-stiff body carried him to the podium of the Assembly. The gallery was filled this day, the first full meeting following the autumn election. Women were dressed gaily in bonnets of various colors, with long coats that covered, in some cases, unseasonable but colorful flowered dresses. There were smiling faces full of outright pride for the husbands, fathers, and sons who sat below them in the section of polished chairs marked off by a gothic printed sign that read simply: "Members of the Assembly—Only."

Mary Roark felt the excitement for more than one reason. There, sitting as chairman of the Assembly, was Byron Jelfe, a trace of gray hair now curling over his ears, his creamy English face still fresh and open. Still handsome and gentlemanly, courteous and even of voice, he sat as though he had not moved from that chair in thirteen years. The governor was a new one, to be sure, but still, it seemed, dependent on the quick mind and parliamentary procedures that Byron executed with such facility.

It was here that Mary Roark had risen to her golden moment. She had stood up to this Assembly, and she had won. So many things had happened since then. She had seen Byron only the night before for the first time in thirteen years. Digger Shanley had hosted a party for Brendan. It seemed all Charlottetown had turned out for the occasion, and as Mary sat in Digger's parlor remembering all too clearly the sadness of another time, a voice spoke over her shoulder, "You haven't changed in the slightest since last we met, Mrs. McMahon."

She turned to the voice she had never forgotten. People were laughing and talking in clusters, and Byron, finding an unoccupied chair, brought it next to her and sat. "Byron Jelfe, you have not changed either." She held out her hand, and he patted it affectionately.

"How have you been, Mary? Digger tells me you have a growing family and a husband who works from dawn to dusk on one of the finest farms in the western part of the island. I am happy for you."

"Thank you, Byron. I trust you are happy in your work."

"Oh, yes, reasonably so. I could be happier." He smiled, his clear eyes sparkling. "But couldn't we all?" he added hastily.

"To be sure, to be sure," she said, her eyes downcast.

"But why are you alone in the midst of a party, a beautiful woman like you?" His words were like a soothing hand softly stroking her brow. They seemed to bring back the moments of romance she had dreamed of as a girl in Ireland and even her brief interlude with the Yankee mill owner in Evansborough. And of course there was the memory of Byron himself and their magic, snow-filled evening together so many work-weary years before. She'd had more opportunities for an easy life than most women, yet, as though fated by some Celtic curse, she found herself destined to live the demanding life of the farm, from one farm to another, from one island to another. At times like this, with the rising music in another room and the sound of a gentleman's voice in her ear, she longed to spring the trap free and waltz across the sparkling floor of a fancy Charlottetown hotel, seeking her gliding reflection in a hundred mirrors.

"My husband is in the kitchen with the menfolk, or at least some of them." She smiled. "Irishmen love the talk and the tall tales and, of course, the whiskey that loosens those long tongues of theirs . . . though I've seldom met an Irishman who needed much help to say a few words."

"Come then," he said almost impetuously. "Come for a walk. The evening is sharp but clear, and there's a moon that bids for perfection. Where is your wrap?"

Before she could protest, he had pulled her to her feet, and together they made their way through the crowd. Her coat hung on the mirrored clothes stand by the door, and she lifted it off its peg and slipped outside.

The night was crisp and refreshingly cool after the warmth of Digger's crowded parlor.

"Have you ever seen such a clear night? Everything seems so brittle."

"You are becoming a poet, Byron. You must be keeping company with the Irish."

"It is odd you say that, Mary. Very odd indeed." They crossed Queen Street, gathering outer garments about them in protection from a sudden blast of cold air.

"Why is it odd, Byron? Surely you know that all the greatest poets of the world are Irish."

He held her elbow gently, guiding her past the shadowed marketplace, where the Round Market huddled like a giant mushroom, and on by Saint Paul's Church.

"Remember your impassioned plea before the Assembly, Mary?" He gestured with his gloved hand at the sandstone buildings. "I was very proud of you that day. I knew then that you were a remarkable woman."

She smiled up at him, the moon catching her hair in its glow.

"When I saw you up there, your lovely blue eyes flashing, your soft voice rising in emotion, I said, 'There is the most beautiful woman in the world.' And of course, I knew I could never have you for my own."

"But, Byron, you knew we would always have something special between us—"

"Shhhh! For just a moment, my lovely Mary." He put a finger to her pouting mouth.

"I thought I would lose my senses with desire for you. I tried, I desperately tried day after day, year after year, to put you out of my mind. I buried myself in my work. I was on constant alert to the governor. I was there to arrange his pillows if he turned over in his bed at night. But nothing helped, nothing. Until . . ." He smiled broadly, the smile seeming to light up the darkened lanes of Queen Square.

"Yes? Until what, Byron?"

He stopped in front of the Old Courthouse and took her hands in his. "That's it, Mary, the irony I spoke of earlier. How odd that you should mention my being in the company of Irish people. Because, my lovely Mary, you see, I have been. I have been almost solely in the company of one Irish person for a year now. Her name is Molly Donovan, and we are to be married in the spring. I do not know when I have ever been happier. I must confess she looks very much like you. She has your eyes and raven hair and your quick wit and lyrical voice. But she is not as independent as you. She is a simple person with very simple needs. Do you not feel great happiness for me, Mary?" His joy manifested itself in the intense glow of his face.

Mary smiled stiffly in return, and her response to his happiness was perfunctory. "Why, of course, I am happy for you, Byron. Naturally, why wouldn't I be? It's silly of you even to ask."

"Oh, I knew you would be joyous at my good fortune, Mary. You were so right to discourage anything between us. Who knows? If we had allowed our emotions to overcome our good judgment, we both would be very unhappy today."

Her mouth quivered slightly. "I do not understand what you mean, Byron. Why are you so certain we would have been unhappy?"

"Because you are a married woman, God knows, and one doesn't quickly dissolve a marriage based on the love that is between you and your husband."

"You said this—this Molly—is that her name?"

"Yes."

"You said she is a simple person with simple needs and not like me. Am I not a person of simple needs then?" She was having trouble disguising her anger, and though surprised by her own reaction, she could not help herself.

"Why, of course, Mary, of course you are."

"Did I not choose to go back to the farm and leave the city behind? I could have stayed in Charlottetown. I could have worked in a shop. I could have worked for Digger. I could have worn fine clothes. I could have had you, Byron Jelfe. But I chose to go back to a desolate farm in a Godforsaken corner of this island. Isn't that being a person of simple needs? Isn't it? Well, answer me, isn't it?" Her question rang in the dark.

The joy on his face turned to shock and incredulity at her response.

"Why, Mary, you seem so angry. Surely I never intended to upset you."

"Upset me? Nonsense. I am not upset, Byron. I am just disappointed that you would find me anything *but* simple. I chose the simple life. Your Molly person will be the one living the fine life of a city woman."

"Oh, Mary, that's just the point. You are the strong one. You're the one independent enough to *make* a life on a farm. Molly needs me. You never needed me. If anything, I needed you. I needed *your* strength. And that is not good for a man."

"Why does this Molly need you, Byron? What cruel blows has life dealt her that she needs your protection?" Her sarcasm was no less biting through the overt anger.

"She has lost all her family from sickness and starvation. Your country suffers much these days, Mary. Molly had nowhere to go and very little money. She had a few bits and pieces she sold to gain enough money for passage to Canada. She wanted to go to America where she had relatives, but she had enough passage money only for Canada. We both were fortunate that her lack of means brought her here. A priest in Saint John arranged for her to work for a family in Charlottetown. I met her at the Tandem Races a year ago."

The Tandem Races—that had been *their* magic day, hers and Byron's, and now it belonged to someone else.

"I'm sorry she has had so much sorrow. I know of Ireland's suffering. Crops have not been good." She changed the subject quickly. "My father has written me that Galway is a city of desperation. Each day the docks swarm with the homeless looking for an escape." Mention of Ireland and her father seemed to quench the fires of Mary's resentment, and almost immediately she was overcome with embarrassment at the childish envy that had gripped her just moments before.

"Take me back to Digger's, Byron. My husband will be wondering where I have gone."

The King's Gate Hotel, sequestered among aging oak trees and gardens and adjacent to the south bend of the Hillsborough River, was to have been a luxury Mary and Brendan gave each other.

Digger had offered them lodging, but they politely refused his kindness for an evening by themselves. The summer had been bitter, filled with the sharp and biting antagonisms, and although this tryst had not been discussed as an evening of healing recent wounds, each hoped it would be a time for renewal.

But as Mary stood by the window gazing at the silver ribbon of the river unwinding south, she knew the evening had been a failure. Her cheeks still burned with embarrassment at her reaction to Byron's joyous news. Why should he not enjoy the love of a woman? Who was Mary McMahon to stand in his way? Oh, God, she thought, I must be the most selfish woman in the world.

She slid quietly into the window seat and watched the moon stroke the river with a silent hand. Behind her Brendan slept peacefully, content with his success. He had enjoyed the companionship of his friends, but too much whiskey had sent him off to sleep almost immediately.

She listened to his steady breathing. The night below her window was tomb-silent, and her mind flooded with images and thoughts of the past.

Surely she did not love Byron Jelfe, not, at least, as a lover. Byron was a good and gentle friend, and he had flattered her with his affection and devotion when she needed it. But if she were to be sincerely honest with herself, she must confess that it was the romance of sharing forbidden moments that had most excited her. The silent snow and the warmth of Byron's apartment, the feeling of him beside her at the Tandem Races—all of it came back to her. It had been an honest joy, a romance, vague and suggestive and pure, not muddied and soiled, but a bright and shining memory. That was it, of course; it was a *memory* she was trying to hold onto. And why not? The memory was pure and certainly nothing of which to be ashamed. How much romance does one need in a lifetime? For Mary, it seemed, more than most women. But possibly she was just being honest with herself. Maybe she was no different from most women who, in the midnight hours, asked themselves, "What would life have been like had I married another man?"

She loved Brendan; of that she was sure, no matter what problems they might have had over the long, dusty summer. Suddenly it was all very clear to her. She had been a Galway farm girl who had dreamed of cities and fine dresses, and instead of realizing those dreams, she had found herself back on the farm she had hoped to flee. Byron Jelfe had been a respite, a brief break with routine and daily struggle, and it had been their interlude, as much as the man himself, that had spawned her romantic memories.

And hadn't Byron been right? She *was* strong, and her independence had taken her back to the farm because, she, Mary Roark McMahon, could manage there. She could bring up a strong and healthy family where many women could not. And with that thought she smiled, it seemed for the first time in months.

The night was turning from black to gray and the curtains billowed in the soft breeze of approaching dawn as she rose and stood beside the bed.

"Brendan, are you awake?"

"I am," he answered almost immediately, and his voice startled her. "I have been watching the curve of your back in the moonlight. I wanted to come to you, but I was not sure you would want me. I love you, Mary. Surely you must know that."

"I know it, Brendan. We have had a difficult summer, the two of us. I am to blame."

"No, I am as much to blame, stubborn Irishman that I am. Will you be coming back to your bed, Mary?"

"I will. Yes." Her voice held a tremor as she allowed her night-dress to fall to the floor. Her body seemed to glisten as he beheld her in the early-morning light.

"I love you, my husband," she whispered as she slipped in beside him.

"And I love you," he said as he took her into his arms.

"Will the junior member from Prince County step forward?" The gruff voice of Jarrod Murdock fell over the gallery as some leaned forward for a closer look at the tall, dark-haired Irishman with the broad shoulders and back.

Brendan walked to the podium and nodded to the chairman and governor in that order. He then offered his hand to Murdock, who diplomatically grasped it and smiled to the respectful assemblage.

"May I introduce my newest colleague from the great Prince County, Mr. Brendan McMahon?"

Mary's heart pounded with excitement as she stood with the others in the balcony, applauding mightily for her husband. Byron Jelfe looked up at Mary, her eyes brimming with tearful pride, and he smiled. He allowed the applause to engulf Brendan before gaveling for silence and a call for the next representative to step forward and command the podium.

The New Brunswick ferry, the *Saint Laurent*, bumped idly against the Summerside docks. Sea gulls squawked and fought overhead before their poised descent for the scraps that departing passengers tossed across the water for that very purpose. Great legions of flapping birds filled the sky, casting a spreading and hovering shadow over Edward Ahearn's raised head. His face, young and fresh, had a bemused expression. He seemed to delight in the fluidity of motion as the gulls in full, lazy flight speared the water with their sharp yellow beaks, and ascended with their prize to light on the sail lofts, the gabled roofs of which looked out over the harbor. He had never been to the island before, and one new sensation after another vied for his attention.

Summerside was more lethargic than Saint John as it slumbered in the late-afternoon April sun. People were about in carriages, on horseback, and on foot, but there was little noise or commotion. Ahearn had a sense of peace as he stood on the dock, his carpetbag by his side and his nostrils pinched by the bite of the salt air. Even the color of the water fascinated him as it lapped against the ferry, for below its blue surface was the red tint of the sandy bottom.

There was no one to greet him, yet he did not seem concerned.

Fishing boats glided in with the tide, and the French and English commands to pull in lines and secure ropes roused in him even more the excitement he was experiencing on this new adventure. He picked up his bag and rummaged through it until he brought out a loaf of bread. He tore off chunks and stuffed the thick white pieces into his mouth. He walked to the stone quays that served as a protective sea wall, and sitting above the curving tide that splashed against the rock, he pondered his decision. A Mr. McMahon had written to him in the fall of the year, asking if he would be interested in forming a newspaper in an area where one had never before existed. The salary was fair, not exorbitant but equitable, and the promise of a new career and a new challenge in a new place added to Edward's excitement. His publisher and employer at the *Caledonian*, Mr. Charles Dobbler, was as excited for Edward as a father would be for a son. He would appreciate Edward's helping him through spring, and then he would give his blessing, sad though it was, for Edward's happiness and success.

Edward Ahearn had left Ireland as a boy, working his passage across by scrubbing pots and pans and decks and every inch of a ship whose captain had an intense fear of disease and sickness. Many a night the lad had sat, exhausted but happy, straddling a barrel of molasses on the swaying deck, his long legs dangling as he wrote verses about the stars, the moon, the sea, and the entire universe. When the night grew late or cold or stormy, he stuffed the poems into his pocket and joined the others belowdecks. The captain so liked him that he refused Edward the privilege of going ashore, afraid the boy would jump ship. And that is, of course, exactly what he did one moonless night as they were anchored off Saint John. Into the frigid waves he dived, then stroked for shore, where he found quarters in a French chapel and was discovered by a sleepy curate the next morning. The priest put him to work, but deciding the boy needed paid employment, he placed him as a printer's devil with Mr. Dobbler. Edward made amazing progress, and before long he was writing full-length editorials on the price of fish, the treatment of the Micmacs by profiteering English companies, and the land question as the single most significant evil in Canada.

His editorials were widely read and discussed. Many times he was criticized, and many times he was praised; but whatever public opinion was, Edward Ahearn was generally at the center of it.

He broke out of his reverie by throwing a stale crust into the water, where it was immediately set upon by a wise old gull with a hood more gray than white.

"Excuse me, young man. Have you seen anyone waiting about? Someone with a satchel or two? Probably my age or more?"

Brendan McMahon slipped from the driver's side of the square, mud spattered cart and walked lightly across the dock. He looked about him as he spoke, but he saw no one except the lad on the wall.

"No, sir, there's just myself. The passengers disembarked more than an hour ago."

"Blast it," Brendan cursed. "That bloody Frenchman," he mumbled.

"Excuse me, sir?" Ahearn said.

"Oh, nothing, lad. Look, was there no one hanging about immediate to the ferry's arrival?"

"No, sir. I can't say there was. I'm the only one who is waiting about, it seems."

"Did you come over on the ferry, lad?"

"Yes, sir. I did. A lovely crossing it was, smooth as an old coin."

"Did you hear tell of an Edward Ahearn on board?"

"Ah, yes, sir, that I did."

"Oh, good lad, there's a copper in it if you can tell me where he went—in what direction?"

"Oh, I know that, sir." Edward held his hand out, and Brendan approached him and slapped the copper piece into his open palm.

"Well, which way, lad? Come out with it."

"He did not go in any direction." He smiled, pocketing the coin.

"What? This is no time for riddles. I'm later than I expected already." The McMahon's usual good humor was buried in his impatience.

"It is no riddle, sir. I am Edward Ahearn, and you must be Brendan McMahon." He jumped from the wall and pumped the surprised Brendan by the hand.

"But you? You're—you're only a boy. Jesus, lad, how old are you?"

"I am nineteen, sir, but I will be twenty in five months."

"Nineteen?" Brendan's hopes and dreams for a liberal, educated, and experienced voice were dashed to the wooden dock.

"You seem disappointed, Mr. McMahon. I do not understand why." He was not hurt or sensitive; he was just puzzled. There was barely the trace of a line in his forehead, but those there were wrinkled into a bewildered frown.

"Look, lad, I blame myself for bringing you this distance. I never thought . . . I never even gave a thought to your age."

"What does my age have to do with it, Mr.McMahon? I am a newspaper writer, not a horse."

The quick and unexpected wit brought Brendan up short. He smiled, and then he caught himself. "You see, we are looking for experience. How much newspaper experience could a nineteen-year-old boy have?"

"Nineteen and seven months," he corrected. "I have been associated with the *Caledonian* in New Brunswick for more than seven years. I have my articles to prove it and a letter from Mr. Dobbler, the publisher. He told me my youthful appearance might cause skepticism."

He passed over the letter, which Brendan read, and then two newspapers bearing editorials by Edward Ahearn. One of the articles concerned the land question. Brendan read slowly, occasionally taking the lad's measure with his eyes.

"You wrote these editorials?"

"Yes, but I must confess something."

Brendan's mouth turned even grimmer. Naturally the lad was confessing to receiving help or worse, that he had put his name to someone else's work.

"All right, lad, let's have it all then."

Edward looked down at his satchel for a moment, and then he said, "I was only seventeen when those were written. They really are not too well done. However, I do think I have improved since then."

Brendan looked at Ahearn's open face, at the newspapers, then back at the face again. He could truthfully never remember meeting anyone the age of this lad having so much confidence. But it was not a cocky and arrogant confidence; it was a very matter-of-fact and casual assessment of what he, Edward Ahearn, felt capable of doing.

"I believe you really mean what you say, Mr. Ahearn. I bloody well believe you are serious."

"I am quite serious, Mr. McMahon. If you want a newspaper— a liberal newspaper—then you shall have one. But I must warn you, Mr. McMahon, I believe in the freedom of the fourth estate. I will not have you or anyone else telling me what to write. Oh, I don't mean that I wouldn't make the church socials sound more exciting than they usually are. I don't regard those events as important to an editorial policy. After all, everyone wants to think a good time was had by all. But when it comes to editorial policy, gossip versus truth, truth will always win out in my newspaper, even if the truth hurts me *or* you. Do we understand each other, Mr. McMahon?"

Brendan's head was spinning. He had just come from a visit at Totem Paul's Ferry Slip and they both had consumed too much rum, trading yarns of O'Connell and the seabound Eamon. Good talk it was, to be sure; but there was a bit of fuzz in his head, and this Ahearn of the boy's body and the old man's wisdom was becoming too much for him.

"I would always hope you would, ah, write, ah, the truth, my lad," Brendan stammered. "Well, you certainly have me convinced. Shall we be off to the North Cape and your new newspaper?" Brendan chuckled and snapped the reins.

CHAPTER XX

FOR THE NEXT three years, growth was the watchword of the island. Fields green with sweet grass and brown with potato beds stretched from one point to the other. Farmhouses, whitewashed and sun-washed, dotted the land. And the land itself fulfilled all its fertile promise. Farmers tilled the soil, harvested their crops, and drove their goods to the market to be exported to Britain or to America. There was excitement and vitality and prosperity, and families grew along with them. Gabriella, with the satin black hair of her mother, was approaching twenty years of age, followed by the serious and gangling Peter at sixteen. Daniel, at thirteen, was growing in his dark mysticism and James, good with his hands, was almost nine. And then there was twelve-year-old Abigail, visitor to all neighboring farms, apple-cheeked, cheerful, and loved by everyone. Brendan and Mary loved their children's dark good looks and felt immense pride when the entire family sat in the Tignish church of Saint Edmund's on Sunday mornings.

Brendan, too, grew and prospered. He bought two shops in Tignish on Digger's advice and with his financial help. Digger, a willing mentor to any Irishman who desired to make something of himself, saw in Brendan a clear mind and a strong body, capable of work and single-mindedness. And along with his entrance into the world of finance, Brendan McMahon was making a reputation for himself in the minds and hearts of the voters of Prince County. Many nights he sat at the kitchen table, a candle flickering at either side of his bobbing head as he read the minutes of a recent meeting of the Assembly or pored over the agendas of future meetings. He believed in being prepared at all times. And that preparation was the very characteristic which impressed the people of his county. Of course, the editorial assistance of Edward Ahearn's blistering, liberal pen had been of no little significance in the rise of Brendan McMahon, businessman and member of the island Assembly.

It was strange how Edward had settled in so quickly, and been accepted so readily, as though he had lived on the island all his life.

It had taken the mere stroke of his golden quill to arouse and ignite the citizenry. His editorials were read throughout the island, and his never-ending fight for a solution to the land question threatened the very stone and mortar of island government. Edward Ahearn was a man to be reckoned with.

It was not unusual for Edward to take even Brendan to task on his vote pertaining to a particular bill before the Assembly, and on those occasions he paced by the window of the *Sentinel* office in the block of stores on the main road leading out of Tignish, waiting for the fiery-eyed McMahon to barge into the office, newspaper held high and protesting mightily. "What the bloody hell does a twenty-two-year old child know about the inland river revenue anyway?"

Those horn-to-horn verbal battles always ended with a jug of poteen sitting empty in front of them and the sentimental history of Ireland lamented across the ink-smudged printer's table.

There were other moments of joy for Edward, who felt for Brendan the kind of kinship he had never had the opportunity to share in his youth. There were those moments of joy spent with the raven-haired Gabriella.

Their friendship had grown slowly, and their love even more so, as was the way of the island.

But there was finally that day when a picnic brought all the young people of Saint Edmund's Parish together on the vast stretches of sandy beach. Father Gautier organized games and songfests and the day melted down with the orange sun streaking everything light pink as the bonfires flew off in a thousand sparks like Chinese fireworks. They boiled clams in giant pots and heralded the night with song.

Edward whispered in Gabriella's ear, and before either knew it, they were standing on a far cape, watching the night descend on the rippled surface of the Strait.

"Well, with the sun gone, we are like two people in a darkened room," Edward said.

"Yes. It was a grand day, Edward. I love happy days. Do you not?"

"I love you," he said simply, without embarrassment at their intimacy.

"And I love you," she replied as simply as he.

Their embrace was soft and gentle, but when he kissed her and urged her body close, he felt that it was the most natural thing in the world for both of them. The evening slipped away as they lay in the high grass, their lips moist and parted in love.

"I cannot wait until the night we share each other completely, Gabriella. May I speak of marriage to your parents?"

"Yes, Edward, I am sure my father would rather have you in the family so he could argue with you more often. But come, we must join the others. The morning will find us with a clearer conscience if we leave now."

So it was that Brendan and Mary, lovers themselves only yesterday, it seemed, now prepared for the marriage of their first child to a young man of prominence and intelligence, a young man on the rise who was more like a son to Brendan than a son-in-law. As for Mary, she saw in her black-haired daughter, all the zest for life and love that she herself had once felt. But Gabriella was different from her mother. Where Mary had always harbored a deep yearning for the excitement of city life, Gabriella loved the meadows, streams, and woods of the island. She and Edward were a perfect couple. It was a marriage arranged in heaven, most people said when they saw the two of them racing along the windy beach or sharing wild blackberries in the back of a hay-strewn wagon full of rollicking picnickers. Gabriella was the spirited and zesty celebrant of life whom Edward of the wise old mind and the boy's body needed to complement his own serious and missionary zeal for truth and justice.

Yes, life for the islanders was beautiful and full of growth. There was work, to be sure, long, tedious, backbreaking labor from the sun's pink rise to its fiery demise below the waves, but work that was a blessing because it showered the farmer and the fisherman with the rewards of honest labor. Harvests had been plentiful, and satisfaction showed in the beaming faces of the islanders.

But for Brendan McMahon, neither the bountiful harvest, as welcome as it was, nor the adulation of an impressed constituency, as satisfying as that also was, could fill the bottomless chasm of black despair that constantly gnawed at him. It was a purgatory of suffering, eating away and weakening his spirit at a time when he should have been holding out his hands in grateful acceptance of the golden harvest of life.

In 1852, while the islanders prospered, the men and women and children of Brendan McMahon's beloved Ireland had died daily by the thousands. The famine of 1849, like an Old Testament plague, brought on by an angry God, swept across the country and left in its wake even three years later the potato black and dead in the field. The blight, the curse of a punishing God, left its victims in the graveyards of every field in Ireland. Whole families died, one by one, leaving the survivors to bury the dead and then to die themselves, alone and unattended in the gutted, fetid fields of waste. Those who could took to the open roads in search of a greener field, one that had not yet turned black. But there were no such fields, and no such escape, and the open roads turned into open graves.

Letters arrived daily addressed to families all along the North Cape, informing of death and suffering and disease. Can you help? For the sake of Christ, help us. Help suffering Ireland and her children, your brothers and mothers and fathers and sisters, your nieces and nephews, your old friends. For the sake of Christ, do something.

Letters shouted, screeched, sobbed, and pleaded, and the islanders, guilt-ridden, to be sure, but grateful for their own prosperity as any human saved from death would be, continued to reap the harvest from the fertile red soil.

Brendan's mother, dead several years before, was at least saved this suffering, but his two sisters, Una and Cathleen, what of them?

He had written but had received no answer. Cathleen and Una, both married, with families of their own, were so caught up in the daily struggle for survival that they had no time for letter writing.

Many evenings he and Mary sat before the flaming hearth, talking about the plight of Ireland long after the children were asleep. "Look, Brendan, you have written, and you have had no answer. Why do you torture yourself with guilt? There is nothing more to do. My brothers are dead along with my father, and there are nieces and nephews I will never see again. There is nothing else *I* can do. *I* put it out of my mind. Canada is our country. I love Ireland, but I love my new country and my children—our children. Our family. We cannot go on day after day with your faraway look, jumping at the sound of every cart or horse on the Tignish Road."

"They are our people, Mary, and each day more of them die of starvation while England exports the little food that is left. England grows fat while Ireland starves to death. What kind of justice is there in the world? For the love of Christ, are we here in Canada to become another England? No. I will not settle for unanswered letters."

"All right, Brendan, you need not preach at me. God knows, I have feelings, too. Do not be so self-righteous. I am simply asking you to use your common sense. You cannot always be running off and leaving your family behind without good reason."

"Good reason! Christ, woman, what better reason is there than to help our own people?" he shouted in her face.

"Do not take the Lord's name in vain in this house, Brendan, and don't lose your temper with me. I said 'good reason' because you must be certain you can help before you expose yourself to sickness and disease. That is all I meant. So, please, do not deliver one of your fiery speeches. Just think, man. Think of all the consequences."

"All right, Mary, no speeches, but I do have some ideas."

"Well then, what are you going to do?"

"I will storm the Assembly. I will ask for money, for clothes, for food. Or a ship. Immigrant Irishmen are dying in quarantine off the shores of Quebec; fever is raging worse than it did two years ago. Our people need homes, food, and care, and I will do what I can to help them."

She could see in the set lines around his mouth the grim strain of determination.

And so it was that after weeks of deliberation, of writing proposals in that careful but slow hand of his, of reading his proposals aloud to the thundering wave-washed shores of the North Cape, Brendan was ready.

He spoke with Chairman Jelfe, for whom he had developed a fond but unspoken respect, regarding the agenda for the April sitting of the Assembly, and so it happened that on a bright day in early spring Byron Jelfe banged his gavel three times and spoke briefly to the representatives.

"Gentlemen, today, before we take up the particulars of our

planned agenda, it is urged by the governor and other humane parties of this chamber to grant Mr. Brendan McMahon from Prince County the right to speak as a private citizen. Mr. McMahon."

Brendan nodded gracefully and approached the rostrum. As he spread out the prepared text of his speech, a low mumbling passed along the rows of curious legislators. Then, and with no pretense at whispering, Jarrod Murdock spoke aloud to those in his immediate area. "For a private citizen, McMahon seems quite prepared, I dare say." Laughter rippled along the aisles among the sycophants who shamelessly allied themselves with the wealthy shipowner.

Brendan, smarting under the obvious sarcasm and feeling the anger creep up under the starched collar of his white shirt, offered to no one in particular as he fumbled with his papers, "I hope I am as articulate as many of the private citizens in the great communities of this island." The quick retort cut deeply, and those who were still smiling stiffened.

Jelfe suppressed a grin as Brendan began. "Your Excellency the Governor, Mr. Chairman, and most honored members of this Assembly, may I begin by thanking you for the opportunity to speak to you today on a most sensitive and pathetic situation." As he smoothed out the text before him, his eyes fell on the Assembly and then slowly moved to the balcony and back down to the far corners of the room. When the hush was to his liking, he continued. "Today, across the ocean Ireland begs from her bruised and swollen knees for our help. Daily we receive reports of mass starvation, of coffin ships that plow through the bodies of dead immigrants who braved the rigors of sea travel in hope of escape. The reports tell of fever, of death, of starvation, of conditions that no man, woman, or child should ever have to face on God's earth. These people are not sinners; they are sufferers, yet they have been consigned to the depths of hell. Families have been wiped out as though their very names had never existed on a parish baptismal record or on a marriage certificate. Those who cannot afford the passage to North America die a little each day.

"With the failure of the potato, there is no food left. Trevelyan continues a policy of exportation. 'Do not encourage the idea of prohibiting exports,' he says. 'Free trade is the right course.' These are the words of the man who is head of the English Treasury and chief organizer of the Relief Commission. He has a duty, a sacred obligation, to see that Ireland is fed. Instead he allows her people to die at his feet. They have suffered since 1845."

"What is your point, McMahon? Be out with it. This Assembly has important business." Murdock's finger punctuated the air.

Brendan kept his composure and addressed himself to Murdock.

"My point, Mr. Murdock, is just what you refer to. Important business. People. Human beings. Human suffering. Death. I want this Assembly to take under advisement an Irish relief fund that will enable us to send food, clothes, and medicine to the underfinanced quarantine areas off the coast of Quebec and to bring those suffering souls to *our* shores. I know we are not wealthy, and there may not be much we can do in Ireland; but in God's name, we can at least help those sick and starving wretches who lie in the rain and mud without bedding or Bible, waiting for the reaper to harvest his fevered crop."

"Oh, come now, McMahon. Such dramatics. Your exaggerated rhetoric is embarrassing this Assembly."

"If those people continue to die, this Assembly should indeed be embarrassed, and you along with it, Murdock. It is strange that you do not seem to show much interest in the lot of dying people since I had every intention of requesting the loan of a ship to transport goods to Grosse Isle in the middle of the Saint Lawrence. Surely, I felt, an emigrant like yourself from the poverty of West Devon, and a devoted and humane Canadian citizen, would want to help. Was I so wrong in believing this, Mr. Murdock? Was I so wrong in believing that a man of your means and success would lead this Assembly in an effort to help fellow human beings?"

Murdock rose at his desk, his mean mouth quivering in agitation. His lips trembled, but no words came. Spectators in the gallery, opened on this first session of the spring term, leaned forward almost as one. Brendan's words had touched them; many had relatives among the Irish dead and dying and they, too, felt a black despair in their souls. They hovered over Jarrod Murdock like a sinister black-robed tribunal.

"Well?" their powerful silence seemed to say. "What will you do to help those suffering people? *Murdock. Murdock. Murdock? Well? What? How? When?* Speak up, man. What will *you* do to help?"

Murdock leaned on his pudgy fists and waited to regain his composure.

Jarrod Murdock had not cheated and stolen land and timber from illiterate and desperate farmers all these years, becoming in the process one of the wealthiest men on the island, just to have some glib and golden-tongued Irishman embarrass him into making a bad business deal. For really, that was all it was, a very bad business transaction. Help these scum, and before long they would be neighbors, tilling little patches of rented land and squatting in filthy mud huts with pigs and ducks. They would bring fever and chaos, and the local citizenry would be diseased and disorganized. Irish immigrants and all their grim history would be a financial drain on the golden harvest of the island. No, no one would force Jarrod Murdock into that trap.

"Mr. McMahon"—Murdock's thin attempt at a smile cracked slightly at the corners of his mouth—"as I said, you state your case too dramatically, but of course, much of what you say is gospel truth. I have read of the difficulties of the Irish in the *Sentinel*, and I have much regard for our noted Prince County journalist, Mr. Ahearn; but for the good of all people and, I might add, especially for the people of our beloved Prince Edward Island, I must not allow myself to be swayed by your most powerful rhetoric, eloquent though it may be. We have been blessed here, to be sure, though not every harvest over the years has been bountiful, and we have had our plagues of insects and blight and field mice. We, too, have suffered, but we have prevailed in all that suffering. Except for a few isolated cases of cholera and fever, our collective health has been good. I, for one, am thankful to a merciful God, but I must caution against opening our doors to pestilence, sickness, and death."

There was a hum among those in the balcony, and Brendan felt the warm glow of his success grow suddenly cold. It would be difficult to counter Murdock without appearing more concerned with the plight of suffering immigrants than with his own island neighbors.

Brendan chastised himself slightly for his own naïveté. The rostrum, the rhetoric, the attention, and the sound of his own voice, all had worked against him. He had allowed himself to be seduced by the theatricality of the occasion, and when he singled out Murdock, he had made the mistake of thinking he had the man in a stranglehold. He had allowed himself to relax, and Murdock had crawled out from beneath his rock, coiled, and struck. Except that his venom was sweet. It appeared like a salve for the minds and hearts of an audience seeking guidance. It all had happened too quickly. Brendan had lost control of the situation, but now he tried to salvage what he could.

"But it is our duty as human beings," he stammered.

"We have a duty to our own people, Mr. McMahon." The voice was benign and gently understanding. "Do we not have a duty to the people of this island? Surely you know we do, whatever your noble intentions."

"Well, yes, of course, but that is not the point. If I had a ship, I could bring the poor souls back here to the island, and we could care for them and nurse them back to health, and they would become productive citizens."

"I laud your idealism, as does everyone in this chamber, is that not so, gentlemen?"

Murdock was extravagant in his praise, and several members shouted, "Hear, hear."

"But," he continued, "what if these poor unfortunate souls were to spread a disease that swept across our island? Certainly you would never forgive yourself."

"But I am talking only of those who pass quarantine and are legally and medically allowed into the country."

"Mr. McMahon, can there be any real guarantee that some who appear to be healthy are not, in fact, carrying typhus? *Typhus*," he repeated for the gallery, the word hissing from his snakelike tongue. "*Typhus*. Really, Mr. McMahon, no one wants that, not even you." His hands gestured in resignation. "But we could go on like this all day and I do not wish to attack a man of such virtue and idealism, even though I have only the very interests of our women and children at heart. May I then propose that this Assembly organize a volunteer relief fund to collect money, food, clothes, and blankets for the destitute Irish who are living on the shores and islands of Quebec."

"Hear, hear," shouted the sycophants now in unison. "Hear, hear."

The McMahon's shoulders sagged as the governor instructed the chairman to take up the business of the agenda. He crumpled up his speech with trembling fingers, wanting only to strike out and smash a fist into the ugly face of Jarrod Murdock. But fists were the weapons of drunks and small boys. Cool, calculated reason, common sense, and political savvy were the only real weapons of grown men. He had learned that bitter lesson this day.

Brendan nodded to the chair and slouched back to his place. Murdock bowed courteously to him as he passed. At least Mary had not been here to witness this disastrous defeat. That he could not have taken.

Byron Jelfe found him sitting alone at a table in the low-beamed White Swan Inn. A jug of Demerara rum, half-empty, stood alongside a pewter mug. The McMahon's eyes were fierce red coals, and he slouched back in his bowed-backed captain's chair. Midafternoon found few patrons sitting in the half-light.

"May I join you, Mr. McMahon?"

Brendan looked up slowly and gestured silently at a chair. Jelfe pulled it around until he was close to the McMahon's left elbow and signaled for a mug.

"Do you mind?" Jelfe nodded at the rum. A kerosene lamp flickered, casting a yellow glow across the earthen jug.

"Suit yourself," McMahon answered dully.

Jelfe poured, swished the mug around, smelled its contents, gulped it, and immediately poured and drank another.

Brendan McMahon straightened and studied Jelfe for a long minute. Then he spoke. "You don't seem the kind of man who swallows hard on a drink, Mr. Jelfe. Is there something troubling you?"

Byron smiled. "Might I ask you the same thing, Mr. McMahon?"

"What makes you think I am troubled?" The eyes flamed red again.

"Well now, you are sitting alone at a table in the Swan after a session of the Assembly when everyone knows the tradition is for assemblymen to hoist a rum or an ale at the Forge."

"The Forge is not to my liking. There are too many men of business draped over the tables, discussing money and the quickest way to make it."

"And too many politicians, too, I imagine?" It was general knowledge that Jarrod Murdock did his hardest drinking behind the swinging doors of the Forge.

Brendan poured a healthy rum and threw it down, the brew warming the pit of his stomach. Then he looked directly at Jelfe. "Aye, Mr. Jelfe, too many bloody politicians for my taste."

"I'll drink to that, Mr. McMahon." And Jelfe followed with his third as Brendan frowned.

"Are you really a drinking man, Mr. Jelfe, or am I to carry you home?"

"Do not worry about me, Mr. McMahon. I am capable of taking care of myself."

"Fair enough. Now, you joined me for a reason. What's on your mind, sir?"

Jelfe leaned forward. He was an immaculate man, not a hair out of place, and his fingers were long and slim as he slipped them around the mug.

"I am angry with you, McMahon." His stare was steady.

Brendan narrowed his eyes, his stare just as rigid. "So you are angry with me. Am I to ask you why?"

"That is it exactly, McMahon—with your last words, calm and balanced, you turn the question back to me. It is for me to say why you anger me. And of course, that is so discreet, so political of you. Why couldn't you have done that this morning, instead of playing your entire deck with Jarrod Murdock looking over your shoulder?"

"What happened this morning is my business, Jelfe. I had something to say, and I said it."

"Oh, you said it all right. But so did Murdock. He came out of that chamber the hero of the island, and not one drop of blood, your blood, was shed. Jarrod Murdock is a very clever man, McMahon. He commiserated with you and the *dreaded* Irish immigrant—no doubt there is much sympathy for them—but he spoke for the entire island, our freedom, our prosperity, and, above all, our continued good health."

McMahon almost spilled the rum as he poured it into his mug. "Murdock is a bloody charlatan, Jelfe. You know it, and most people in that Assembly know it."

"Of course, but he swayed public opinion, and many of those legislators today learned something about their constituents and the prevailing wind. The people of this island are good, hard-working folk. They help their neighbors, they worship their God, and they work their fields; but they love their children, and anything that threatens them is unacceptable. You could have won them over in spite of the threat of sickness, but you allowed Murdock the opportunity to speak. It was *your* speech, not *his*, but once he was given the opportunity, he knew what to do with it. So you see why I am angry with you, McMahon? You had the floor, and you surrendered it."

Brendan sucked in a breath. *Surrender* was not a word he was comfortable with. "I see. But I do not understand why you are so concerned." He breathed again, and his anger subsided. "Why are you so interested in my problems, Jelfe?"

"Let us just say I have my reasons. They are good reasons." Jelfe studied the lamp for a minute before continuing. "The question that remains is: What do you intend to do now?"

"Do? I do not understand. What can I do? I said my piece, and I said it poorly. Any support I could muster was lost in a few fleeting moments of stupidity. Oh, yes, we will get blankets and bread, but those miserable dying wretches need hope, a new life. Some of them are only children. Nothing but bloody starving children. God damn those English bastards!"

Jelfe poured Brendan a drink and then refilled his own tankard. He lifted his mug and tapped it against McMahon's. "Cheers," the Britisher said. "*Sláinte*," the Irishman answered.

"You see, McMahon, you have that thick temper, thick as a bog and just as useless. You can curse the English all you like, and other drunken Irishmen will agree; but in the meantime, Irish people are dying and sick and waiting for some kind of hope. If they cannot pass a doctor's inspection, they will be shipped back to Ireland. And how many of them can withstand another ocean voyage in their condition? For God's sake, man, forget your rhetoric or lack of it, and act now. The time for talk is over."

"Then what do you suggest, Jelfe?"

"I suggest you get your own ship. Jarrod Murdock will never give you the loan of one, no matter how much you offer to pay. And he can tie up every shipbuilder on the island. You know that. All he has to do is call in their debts. He has done that before, and he would do it again."

"Then, God Almighty, man, where in hell and damnation do I find a bloody ship?"

"You're not thinking, McMahon. Either it's your country temper again, or you are not the rum drinker I thought you were."

"It's not the rum, Jelfe—I could drink the Hillsborough River dry. I just do not know where to turn." He held the mug to his mouth with both hands and drank as though he were guzzling water in the heat of summer.

"Have you never given a thought to the most loyal and dedicated Irishman on the island?" Jelfe matched McMahon's healthy dispatch of the grog.

"Jesus." Brendan's red eyes brightened. "Digger Shanley. Old Digger himself. Of course. He has money and influence."

"And ships." Jelfe smiled. "Ships," he repeated into the empty mug.

"Damn my eyes. If I had not kept everything locked up inside of me, Digger would have known, and he would have come forward, I am sure of that."

"You cannot be waiting for people to come to you, McMahon. Go to him now, man. Go. I'll finish your grog for you."

Brendan jumped to his feet, although he felt a bit unsteady. He braced his left hand against the table and thrust out his right. "You're one fine man, Byron. For an Englishman," he added with a grin.

"You're not so bad yourself, Brendan, once you've lifted your head out of the bog." Their grips were firm and lasting. There was promise in such respect.

Brendan bolted for the door and almost ripped it off its hinges as he ducked out into the late afternoon.

Byron Jelfe watched him go and then pushed his tankard away and wavered to his feet. He stumbled to the rear exit in search of a quiet alley where he could be sick with some degree of dignity.

CHAPTER XXI

THE BRIAN BORU, proud as her kingly Irish name, stood braced against a pounding spring rain that pelted the docks of Summerside as two dozen squall-punished Canadian Irish raised their hands to cross themselves in prayer for the success of Brendan's mission of mercy to Quebec.

Father Gautier extended his hand in the ancient blessing while volunteer farmers—Irish, English, Micmac, and French—peered over the roped deck and listened.

"May God bless and protect them in their journey of mercy and charity. May God ease the prow of this vessel through the turbulent storm-tossed waters, and may God bless Digger Shanley and his kindness and charity to a suffering people." And then, because Father Gautier, knowing the tempo and the pulse of his island brethren, sensed that prayer for them should be as simple and as practical as their lives, he stuffed his hands into his long black coat and smiled at Digger, who shifted nervously and with embarrassment beside him.

"Well, Digger, you have come a long way in a few years, from gravedigger to merchant and shipowner. It just shows what a little wisdom from the clergy can do for all of us."

"Sure, and if I had listened to you, I would be head sexton by now."

The priest laughed and then turned to Brendan. Despite the jokes, they all were aware that it was a solemn moment. "God be with you, Brendan, and all of you," he said simply.

"Aye. Thank you, Father."

Brendan turned then and went to Mary and the children.

Mary's eyes looked into his. "I thought I would never be after saying good-byes to you again, my husband."

"I know, Mary Roark. I know. We've been over it enough. We do what we must."

"So be it," she said, and was then wrapped up in his powerful embrace.

The children, their tears mingling with the wet of the rain, crowded around the two of them. Gabriella, as the eldest, stood back, and Edward slipped his hand into hers. She smiled gratefully, reassured by his affection.

"Well, now, we must be on our way. Do not worry. We have an excellent captain in Liam Malley. His Irish luck has seen him through many a gale in the past. And of course, Paul can always push us to Quebec if need be. I must go. Take care of them, Edward. I'll be back for the wedding. Make your words ring across this island. Land. Land and dignity. Remember."

"Never mind preaching to me, Brendan. And do not be telling the fourth estate what it should be writing." The serious face glowed with a boyish grin.

"Good lad." Brendan patted Edward's thin shoulder.

"And, Peter, you are the oldest boy. You know you have duties and responsibilities. Take care of your mother and the others."

"Yes, Father. Do not worry."

"I will not, my son."

"Good-bye, Father." Abigail kissed him, joined then by Daniel, his deep eyes questioning and always, to Brendan the reminder of some deep melancholy.

"God bless, Daniel. You take care of James since you are closest in age."

"Yes, Father."

"All right, we are off. Look at that great Totem of a man beckoning me. He's as tall as the mast." He waved back at Paul, who was already flipping the long rope dockward.

"I'm off. God bless." And the McMahon, followed by a few others who had lingered over their good-byes, mounted the gangway to the deck of the *Brian Boru*.

Commands from ship to shore cut through the squalling rain, and soon the ship was inching away from Summerside and slowly slipping behind a curtain of rain. Her sheets billowed and clapped in the wind, and then she was no more than a gray speck against the swirling white water of the sea.

CHAPTER XXII

THERE WERE TWO distinct moments of joy in Jarrod Murdock's daily life. One was walking through Port Loyal with Margaret, chatting as though she were a wife or female companion. Their talk of nature, the painted landscape, the euphony of hidden birds were all somehow enhanced by the outside world they both loved so well. To strangers they appeared as lovers gliding in and out of sun and shadow. To be sure, her blossoming adulthood and fragile beauty stood out in obvious and immediate contrast with the pockmarked and granite meanness of Murdock's face. But the hum of their voices through the wood and the obvious joy one shared with the other seemed to erase the disparities of beauty and age.

That was one moment, bright and full of cheerfulness, but the other was a dark and mysterious ritual.

When the dinner hour was ended and Mrs. Dawson had cleared away the dishes and brought Murdock his rum and chicory flavored coffee, he excused himself, always abruptly, kissed Margaret on the forehead, and mounted the circular staircase to his bedroom.

He placed his coffee and rum on the roll-top desk, closed his door, turned the flickering lamp up, and seated himself in a straight-backed chair close to the window that looked out on pasture and river.

And then, with gentle fingers, he lifted the large Bible-like book from the top drawer. He held the book before him, like a priest entranced in a moment of sacred liturgy. The book was then placed on the altar of his desk and opened at random.

The curling, penned scrawl of his own hand spelled a history of mounting possessions. The hand was neat in deference to the white block paper that seemed to be calling for the entry of new acquisitions.

But on this particular evening as the rain struck and rattled the windows, Jarrod Murdock did not write. He read. And he read slowly and with zealous interest. His gaze crossed the wide pages, names burning into his brain: Reilly, Dalton, Hanley, Nelligan, Dorgan, Ready, Hogan, Shea. Irish names. Their counties, their origins, their children's names and ages, their possessions, but, most important, their debts. All entered on the pages before him. Their debts to the penny or the hours of labor they owed Mr. Jarrod Murdock.

"Bring dying immigrants to contaminate us with disease and sickness, will they? To weaken us in our dream of progress. We are not ministers to the sick." It was not unlike Murdock to hold long and impassioned conversations with himself in the holiness of his room while Mrs. Dawon shook her head on the landing and Margaret attempted to block out his ravings by busying herself with crewel work. These conversations became sermons, homilies to himself, the orisons by which he lived and acted.

Jarrod Murdock truly bore no grudge against race. If the victims of famine had been French or Indian or even English, he would have felt the same. He viewed these people, any people who would debilitate the strength and potential of the island, as enemies. As it so happened, however, the names before him were Irish names, many of them the names of those Prince County farmers who had thrown down spade and shovel and joined irrational and romantic ranks with Brendan McMahon.

There was no good in fighting this Shanley, he knew. Digger was too wealthy, too successful, and not dependent on Murdock merchant ships to bring foreign goods to his Charlottetown markets. But these farmers, many of them, owed him work or money.

Years before, he had realized that the true entrepreneur was the one who could extract labor for rents. For labor was a daily routine that built Murdock ships and plowed Murdock land and harvested Murdock potatoes and fished Murdock rivers and ponds. And it all was pure profit after the initial investment.

But now, because of some errant and poetic impulse, these farmers had taken it upon themselves to sail on some misguided mission, leaving their women and children responsible to the ledger. Impulse and poetry were strangers to the philosophy of Jarrod Murdock. Mercy and sensitivity never built a dynasty. The yellowed pages of history would attest to that.

He stirred his coffee, sipped it, poured rum into it, stirred it again, and swallowed. He poured in the remainder of the rum, swirled it around, stared into the cup, and formed the word *dynasty* as he licked his lips. Then he swallowed the last of it and closed the book. Tomorrow the Reillys, and then each of the others. "No one, McMahon or anyone else on this island, will ever defy me again."

The next morning glowed and sparkled as the sun stroked the dripping wood sorrel, the fern, the lady's-slipper, and the wild, shiny leaves of lily of the valley. It was a peaceful morning, still and tranquil, until the heavy hooves of Jarrod Murdock's mare resounded across the green, lush fields of the Reilly place. He was followed closely by two riders.

Elizabeth Reilly, bending before an outdoor fireplace, with fat and grease smoking in filmy clouds from a large black pot, added lye

to the soaking hardwood ashes. She was engulfed by smoke and un-
aware of Murdock's arrival until he reined in the horse several yards
behind her.

"Good morning, Mrs. Reilly." His greeting was friendly and warm.

She turned, startled at horse and rider having come so close without her knowledge. "Holy Mother of God, you frightened the devil
out of me, Mr. Murdock. Forgive me, sir. It's soap-makin' day, as you
can see, and I think my head must have been in the vat."

"Do not be alarmed, Mrs. Reilly. I was not expecting a formal
welcoming committee." He tried vainly to force a smile. "Tell me, is
your husband about?"

"Sure now he is not, Mr. Murdock. He's after goin' to Quebec
with the others to help our poor sufferin' people."

"He's not here?" The wooden smile was replaced by the familiar
and more characteristic grim lines around the mouth. "I do not understand, Mrs. Reilly, who is doing his *work*?" The word rose in a question, as though the speaker had found her answer preposterous.

"Oh, our oldest boy is pitchin' in."

"And how old would he be?" Murdock could have told her the
boy's name if need be, his memory of the ledger was so exact.

"He'd be ten, sir. A fine, hard-workin' lad, he is, too."

The other two riders trotted up behind Murdock's horse.

"I'm sure he is, Mrs. Reilly. But certainly he is no match for the
strength of Michael Reilly."

"Oh, go on with you now, Mr. Murdock," she bantered coquettishly, secretly proud of Murdock's estimate of her husband. "Himself is
not that strong a man."

"I do not treat this matter lightly, Mrs. Reilly. No ten-year-old
can do the work of a grown man." His voice deepened to its usual
gruffness, and the cheerful banter was instantly drained out of her.
The real Murdock, the one she knew, the one they all knew, had come
to life and glared down at her from the saddle. She wiped her hands
nervously on her cotton apron. "Well, Mrs. Reilly, who works this
farm?" He let the question go unanswered. "I have here something
that I should read to you."

He reached into the leather saddlebag resting securely by his hip
and brought out a black leather book.

"Do you know what this is, Mrs. Reilly?"

She looked up at him dumbly as chickens squawked and
scratched about in the barnyard dirt.

When he saw that she was not inclined to answer, he nodded.
"Very well. This, Mrs. Reilly, is my ledger, and I will read from it."
He held the book high, the golden shafts of sun streaking across the
paper.

" 'Reilly, Michael *et aux*. For one year's rent: Labor in the ship-
yards, sunup to sundown, Monday, Wednesday. Farming, dawn to
dusk, Tuesday, Thursday and Friday.'

"Today is Monday, Mrs. Reilly. Your husband is not at the yard.

Who will take his place? Certainly not the boy. He is no shipwright. No carpenter. Who then?

"And this farm. Will the boy plow and dig and clear land, mend fences, feed stock, plant seed the way his father would? I think not." He looked over his shoulder at the riders and then back at the woman, who was now struck dumb. "So you see, Mrs. Reilly, it is either labor or rent. Now, if you are prepared to give me ten pounds on the barrelhead, we can easily dispense with the labor." According to the records in front of him, the Reillys already owed 3 pounds 10 shillings to Jarrod Murdock's Port Loyal General Store.

"But, glory to God," she stammered, breaking out of her stupor, "I do not have that kind of money."

"Well then, Mrs. Reilly, an agreement is an agreement, and I will have to ask you and your family to vacate these premises."

"Vacate? Vacate these premises? You can't mean that, sir. Glory to God, where do we go?"

"Go, Mrs. Reilly? Why not Quebec? You have until dusk. I want this house empty. I have a grateful Scots family ready to move in. Come, men, we have much riding to do this day."

All up and down the county word was given and debts were called in. Dalton, Hanley, Nelligan, Dorgan, Ready, Horgan, Hogan— all caught the wrath of Jarrod Murdock's command. Pay up or move out. And all the women and children could do was cry on one another's shoulders and curse the mission ship, and their own husbands' thick, impetuous Irish pride.

Before nightfall the roads of Prince County swirled with the curling dust of wagons as women and children shuffled along in bewildered silence on their way to the North Cape and the McMahon farm.

"There is no place else for us to camp, Mary. You hold your deed free and clear. No one can tell us to get along from here."

"Rest yourselves, and camp near the ocean. My lads will help you build lean-tos. Did none of us foresee this happening? Are we so secure and forgetful of the old ways of landlords that we would allow ourselves to fall victim again to such tyranny?"

"Murdock never gave my man a command or a warning not to go. Himself is a loyal Irishman," Mrs. Nelligan said of her husband, "but he is not crazy. He would think of his family first."

"Aye," Mrs. Ready broke in, "they discussed the time they owed to that blody devil, but they said they could make it up. No one said they could not."

"Did you ask Murdock if they could?"

"Well, no," Mrs. Hanley said, "but Murdock knew of the plan to volunteer; it was common knowledge. If he was so against it, why did he not come forward and prohibit them from leaving?"

"Because he *wanted* them to go. Don't you see? Then he could step in and show this island that he is the king. Him and his sacred book. The ledger king. He keeps every square inch he owns recorded in that book. It is like a devil's book. Like Satan himself, he records every deed and debt of this island. It wouldn't surprise me if he wrote in blood. Mrs. Dawson, the poor old Scots lady who works for him, says he keeps the book closer to him than he did his wife. If sin took human form, it would be Jarrod Murdock walking the red soil of Prince County. But you must be tired. Go. Rest this night. Thoughts come easier with rest."

Mary Roark McMahon watched them straggle off to the hooded cape and then walked across the fields to Isabella Profitt's.

It was Bill who greeted her as she stepped up the path to the house. His face was gray, and he seemed thinner to her. Strange how he had aged without Mary's realizing it.

"Good evening, Mary, the weather stays a friend, does it not?"

"It does, Bill. Is Isabella about, or is Abigail running her in circles again?"

"Ah, she's a great little lady. She has those Irish good looks of her mother, she has. Ah, but the two of them are in there, preserving blackberry jam. She's a joy to us, Mary. She is the daughter we never had, with two dead at birth and one less than two months before the Creator took her. We are grateful to you for allowing her to come to us so often."

"I am happy she gives you so much joy. She is like a wild bird, flying from one nest to another. Forgive me if I must bring her home now. I will be needing her help in the morning."

Bill, taciturn as the Northumberland stone of his birthplace, had seen the weary travelers descend upon the McMahon fields, but he did not make mention of it until Mary did.

"You see, I have company in my fields this night, Bill."

"Eh," was all he returned. He would wait for Mary to tell him the whole story if she so pleased, as she did, and when her narrative was complete, he shrugged helplessly. "What manner of beast could commit such a deed? Is there no one to reason with him?"

"There are only women left, and he does not respect women."

"That is quite obvious. He would never attempt such a scheme if the husbands were here." His voice was weary, robbed of its usual clipped firmness. "But still, Mary, he is within his rights, no matter what we think."

"Aye, but strange rights they are. To be sure. Well, I've been away long enough. I must fetch that wild bird before she flies off again."

Bill Profitt could not sleep. He tossed in the square four-poster bed all night long. On several occasions he rose and walked to the window that looked out over the sloping capes and the Strait. Fires from the campsites sparked the serene black of the night sky, but the scene brought no warmth to his soul. He loved the island, and to see its peace and comfort and security destroyed in its turn destroyed him. Bill, all along, had been against confederation, and that was not a popular position to take, especially since his neighbor on the next

farm was a respected legislator who championed the cause of confederation as the only solution to the land problem and the nepotism that
now existed on the island. Confederation, a dreaded word to those
with vested interests like Murdock, who would be held accountable to
the rest of Canada; to such men it was anathema. But it was not fear
of accountability that troubled Bill Profitt. He was a quiet man, strong
and silent, but deep and thoughtful, a man who viewed the island as
a gift outright, a gift from the Almighty. He plowed his fields and
harvested his potatoes, and he was beholden to no man. He did not
enjoy the prospect of becoming a number among all the other citizens
in all the other provinces. Prince Edward Island had been good to him
and his family, and he had been good to it. He loved the land as he
would a friend, and he did not wish to see it appropriated by a bur-
geoning Canada. All these thoughts he had shared with Brendan over
many a cup of poteen. Bill Profitt was a man of conviction. He was a
man not easily swayed. But he was also a sensitive man and a man of
truth, and as he studied the fires of the homeless families on the cape,
he felt a lump stick in his throat. If only he were younger. If only he
were as strong as he once was. Lately he seemed to tire so quickly.
Isabella had mentioned it more than once when he walked in slowly
from the fields.

Finally, at three-fifteen in the morning, he made up his mind. He
dressed, kissed his sleeping wife, and left the house. He saddled his
horse and headed toward Port Loyal. Someone had to reason with
Jarrod Murdock, and it seemed—since he was one of the few men
left in the area—the task had fallen to him. He must summon his
strength for the journey he was now convinced he must make.

Once he had gained the highroad, he prodded his horse into a
gallop. Port Loyal was a good ride away. The early-morning air carried
a chill, and Bill, though warmly dressed in a heavy cable-stitched
sweater and woolen pants, found himself trembling with cold.

Even at this predawn hour, candles burned in farmhouse windows
as the men pulled on coveralls and straightened shoulder braces in
preparation for another day's digging. The huddled, peaceful farms
summoned in Bill Profitt a great sense of well-being and at the same
time a twinge of sadness for a way of life he knew must soon change.

Since the beginning the battle for land had not been easy, and it
was still an uphill fight. But each day of pulling on coveralls in the
predawn light was a day of independence and self-sufficiency. Or so
he had thought when he argued with friend and neighbor against
confederation. "They will try to own us. We will be subject to them,
to some government regulations simply because they help us build a
ferry to the mainland."

Oh, how he and Brendan and Edward Ahearn had argued and
cursed over their rum. He smiled at the thought of those nights.
Brendan and Edward were good friends. Bloody good friends, he
thought, solid men with solid principles and strong ideals. He rubbed
his left breast with his hand as he thought of the campfires in the
McMahon's fields. Those women, *they* had no independence, no pro-

tection. They were the victims of the greed of a cruel and possessive man who would own the entire island if he had the chance. This island had no room for kings; the islanders had had their fill of royalty, and so maybe Brendan and Edward were right after all. Maybe confederation would limit the island's independence, but Jarrod Murdock and people like him would destroy the islanders' freedom.

He would tell that to Murdock. He would say that he, Bill Profitt, and everyone opposed to confederation would muster to the man and join the ranks of the proconfederationists if those women were not returned to the warmth of their hearths by nightfall. Murdock would know he'd had a visitor *this* day.

His hand flew in twitching instinct to his left breast again. A knifelike pain dug into his heart, and he began to waver in the saddle. His world of farm and earth suddenly grew faint and vague before him. His hands fought with each other in an effort to push the pain away, and then suddenly the horse, sensing something strange, rose in panic and fear, and forced the rider backward as he slid motionless to the red clay. His eyes, pushed far back and white in his head, were like fixed pieces of glass.

The horse kicked at the soil, reins trailing in the dust, but the journey was over. Bill Profitt was gone, and the island had lost one of its dearest and most devoted friends.

CHAPTER XXIII

GROSSE ISLE lay in the verdant, lush center of the Saint Lawrence River. It had been a quarantine station since 1832, and in compliance with Quebec customs regulations, all incoming ships were required to stop there for medical inspection. Low white buildings seemed almost securely and peacefully burrowed into the earth. Shrubs and trees and wild grass extended to the water's edge, and a climate of balmy, breezy contentment rose in the spring air.

Brendan stood with Totem Paul, the sharp-faced Owen Hanley, and the rest of the Tignish volunteer farmers on the deck of the *Brian Boru*. The morning was quiet save for the screech of the herring gulls that flew above the *Boru's* broad-backed stern.

Brendan wondered as he had for weeks, if he might not find a relative or friend among the destitute immigrants. Might Una have made the journey, or Cathleen and Patrick? Yet Brendan was not the only one to reflect on whom he would find sick and suffering. The thought had been expressed by many of the volunteers on the journey as they milled about the decks in daylight or engaged in muffled conversation belowdecks just before falling off to sleep.

"Seems peaceful enough, McMahon." The sea-stitched face of Captain Liam Malley loosened slowly, and his blue eyes softened. Malley was a veteran of many seagoing catastrophes, and his experience at the wheel was etched in the deeply dug lines and ruts around his alert and startling eyes.

"We are grateful to you, Captain. We could never have done this if you had not come forward." Brendan's tone was honest and direct.

"I work for Digger, and I do what Digger says."

"I know you Clare men. Few words. I also know you turned down a fine opportunity to captain a brig twice the size of the *Boru*, and for a handsome stipend, I might add." Brendan winked.

"You Galway men have great imaginations, McMahon. That's why your fields are filled with rock. Too much dreaming and not enough work."

Hanley, close at Brendan's side and with Ballinasloe, County Galway, blood pumping through his veins, chuckled knowingly. "He's right, you know, Brendan. If we wrote fewer poems and did more digging, the rocks would be gone off packing with the snakes."

The feeling was good among them. They had enjoyed swapping county rivalries during the journey, but the real closeness was in their mission.

The sailing had been peaceful and without incident. The ice that could choke and strangle the Saint Lawrence even this late in the year had broken up early, and all that the *Boru* encountered was a thin glaze of crumbling crystals, which bumped and broke off against the cutting edge of her prow.

A camaraderie of song and anecdote had sprung up among the men. And Totem Paul, of course, had continued to startle everyone with his amazing strength. They all would go away from this journey singing his name to the four corners of the island, and Paul would be a living legend again, as he had been in Ireland.

Up beyond a bend in the river, hundreds of gulls hung above the green inlet, some occasionally spearing to the earth and then veering off with their beaks trembling, while others queued up, waiting their turn to dive.

Slowly, ever so slowly and with a subtlety that was not immediately noticeable, the wind shifted. Those who had been hanging over the sides of the ship turned to each other as they began to smell the aroma that carried on the new and sudden breeze.

The sun disappeared behind a gray cloud, and the gulls that had escorted the *Boru* landward changed now from those of the grayish black-tipped type to the thick-bodied black-backed scavengers that roamed the refuse heaps and raw sewage lagoons of the wide river.

The shoulder of land that spit out into the river was deserted except for the roofless shacks, and as the ship glided past the point, the stench of human waste drove the gawking islanders back against the bulkheads. Some gagged and vomited overboard while others hurried quickly belowdecks.

"Jesus, Captain, what in God's name—" Brendan could not finish his question as the smell reached the pit of his stomach and he felt he would be violently ill.

"Here, take this." Malley choked and thrust a handkerchief at him. "Cover your nose and mouth. Give yourself just enough air to breathe. I was afraid of this." He rolled up his charts and stuffed them into a long, narrow compartment under the wheelhouse.

Brendan tied the gaily colored kerchief around his head. His eyes, which had begun to water, blinked clear.

When the others saw the McMahon and Malley with faces covered, they followed suit, and those who had no kerchiefs ripped pieces of cloth from their shirts.

"Liam, what is it?" Brendan's mouth seemed not to move behind the cloth.

"Dysentery. I've experienced it before. The Gold Coast. Killed hundreds of tribesmen. You will grow used to the smell; but accustom yourself gradually, and prepare yourself for sickness even a Galway man could not imagine."

He left the railing and positioned himself in the center of the deck. "Men, I must warn you there is fever, probably typhus, ahead of us. I would fault no man who wished to stay on board. But if you choose to go ashore, cover your mouths when you can. *Do not, I repeat, do not* take any of our water ashore. We have kegs of it, but only one man will be in charge of it. No one else is to touch it. If I find any man taking water to the mainland, I will throw him in irons. And if *I* cannot manage it, I will find those who can."

"Why, Captain? Why the water? These people must *need* water." Hanley seemed perplexed.

"Because it can be contaminated too fast, and that can harm *us*. If we are sick, we cannot help those who need us. We will arrange for the sick and dying to get water, but we must do it sensibly. Men, I have seen this contagion before, and I have smelled this sick smell of dying before. We can be of service here. But we must be organized, and we must be cautious. You will see many people dying. You must not become personally involved. On this ship I am in command. Everything goes through me. Onshore the McMahon is in command, and everything goes through him."

"Oh, Christ, Captain, look at that."

Michael Reilly pointed starboard. A string of boats moved from five anchored brigs to the grassy shoreline, carrying cargoes of bodies heaped one on top of the other. Some, it seemed, were still alive, their cries carrying across the still water.

When the boats reached the shore's edge, handlers pulled the cadavers off and flung them onto the mud and rock. Those poor living souls who had come ashore among the dead, drew themselves up in horror, rising on bent and bony knees, their clothes no more than torn rags on their backs. Some, too weak to raise themselves, crawled among the corpses, screaming in fear and terror as they did so.

"Oh, Jesus Christ, have mercy on them," Hanley prayed to the gray skies, the tears streaming down his cheeks. The others joined him, and they approached the railing again. What they saw they knew to a man they would never forget. One bend in the river away was a halcyon green world, a vast pine-scented enclosure the cathedral ceiling of which was the blue and cloudless sky, and before them unfolded a living and dying hell of pestilence.

All along the grassy banks the living lay among the dead and dying. Kerchief-covered handlers went among the prone figures, pointing one to the other and rolling the lifeless in canvas or into boxlike coffins. Their carts teetered and listed over the rocks in a grim, squeaking procession to a treeless graveyard. A thousand crooked crosses already marked the place where people lay, finally at peace.

Floating among the ships were masses of filthy straw, remnants of foul beds, kegs, and barrels that contained human waste, rags, tattered and torn clothing, and the sickening solids of excreta.

Liam Malley shouted through the gloom of a day now turned a

chilly gray, "Heave to, mates, toss that line in. Someone will have to
drag it ashore and secure it. They forgot to build a bloody pier, and
I wouldn't wait for those fever boats to pull us in."

Hanley scampered fore, and Ready trotted aft, both uncoiling the
thick hemp, hurling it in to the water with a resounding splash and
diving in after it. When they surfaced, they shook off the spring cold
of the water and doggedly swam for shore with lines wrapped around
their thick shoulders. They stepped onto mossy rocks, secured the
lines, and waited for their mates.

The *Boru* sidled into the cove with the help of the crew, nudging
it home with long French paddles. The plank was dropped, and Brendan McMahon was the first to descend. It all was very quick, as though
to think about it, would result in no movement and no action at all.

The crew followed in single file, their kerchiefs tight about their
mouths and noses.

A long, mud-spattered white hut snaked along the upper embankment, and Brendan walked briskly toward it. A sign above the door
read "Hospital" in both French and English. Brendan ducked under
the low lintel and entered, leaving the others outside.

He was astonished to find only one person present. Sitting at a
battered oak desk, a man in thick spectacles peered at a piece of paper.
The man's hands shook, and his gaze seemed to go through and beyond
the paper. The man's face was not old, but his body was. He was
hunched and thin, with the bones of his shoulders protruding through
a filthy brown-spotted smock that was probably once a white tunic.

"Excuse me," Brendan said, clearing his throat as he looked
around the room. The floor was of dirt, and there was the gritty smell
of dust hanging in the small, confined area.

At first the man continued his paralyzed scrutiny of the paper, and
Brendan shuffled closer, clearing his throat again, this time pulling the
kerchief from his mouth so it hung about his neck, western-style.

Slowly, as though his head were too heavy for him, the man
straightened, placed the paper on the desk, and said almost meekly,
"Yes?"

Brendan pulled an official notice from his breast pocket and
handed it over as he explained. The man seemed not to have heard,
and Brendan repeated, ". . . from Prince Edward Island, member of
the Assembly, permission to escort those healthy enough to pass the
medical inspection—" He did not finish because the man cut him off.

"Yes, yes, take them, inspection or not. Take them all. You may as
well bury them. It will save us the trouble."

"You don't seem to hold much hope, Mr.?"

"Matthews," he answered.

"Do I detect an Irish accent, Mr. Matthews?"

"You may."

"What part?" Brendan continued.

"Dublin. What is it you wish, Mr. McMahon?"

"Why, we wish to help our people."

Matthews removed his glasses. "You wish to help. That is very noble, Mr. McMahon. I am sure you mean what you say. You see this?" He held up the piece of paper he had been reading when Brendan interrupted him.

"Yes."

"This paper. Let me read what it says. This is an official count as of one hour ago. The *Lamb*—an ironic name, I might add—had a total of two hundred forty passengers, and out of that number there are eighty-seven fever cases on board, twelve persons died on the voyage. The *Victory*, out of three hundred twelve passengers, forty-three died at sea, fifty-seven on board too sick to move.

"The *Egmont*, two hundred fifty-one passengers, twelve died at sea—a pleasant crossing, it should be noted—thirty-seven fewer cases.

"The *Charlmont*, a veritable conveyor of contagion, two hundred seventy-two passengers, ninety-seven died at sea and one hundred thirty-six fever cases.

"And the *Shannon*, named for that illustrious river that flows with the blood of dead Irish, fifty-seven buried on the high seas, eighty-three fever cases out of a grand total of two hundred ninety-five cramped and destitute souls.

"There you have it. The *Lamb*, the *Victory*, the *Egmont*, the *Charlmont*, and the *Shannon*, putrid, foul-smelling ships that stand forth in the bay at this moment while the dead and the dying are unloaded like so much timber from the bowels of their holds. This is the hospital, Mr. McMahon. We have room for two hundred and another fifty without beds, and right now we have more than four hundred crawling over the floors like so much vermin. Two of our doctors have died within this month, and I am the only one left."

"You are a doctor?"

"Yes." He smiled grimly. "Are you surprised? Did you expect a clean gown and monocle? I am sorry to disappoint you. You see, I stopped being a doctor weeks ago. I am what you might call the chief mortician, now that my colleagues are gone."

"I am sorry. I am truly sorry, Doctor."

"I am sorry, too, Mr. McMahon. There has been too much death. You must forgive me for my bitterness. It is really all I have left." He placed his spectacles on the bridge of his nose with a proper push of thumb and index finger and rose behind the desk. He was a much larger man than Brendan would have expected, over six feet in height.

He came around to the other side of the desk and extended his hand. Brendan shook it warmly. The doctor smiled.

Brendan followed him out into the foul air, and he pointed to the boats coming in. "If you and your men wish to help, then help those poor souls from the boats, those who still have a spark of life in them. It is really quite simple: Separate the living from the dead, and try to make the living as comfortable as possible. They need cleanliness. Over there. Those boiling pots. There is hot water and soap. Do you have water on board? Clean, fresh water?"

"Yes, we do."

"Good. Each fever case should have small quantities of water. They must build up their strength."

"We have blankets and clothes, Doctor."

"God bless you. Bathe them, give them drink, and warm them. It is all we can do. It is as simple as the Bible."

Brendan sent parties back to the ship to bring the woolen blankets, the clothes, and the water. The water, guarded by Mick Dalton, was not released until Liam Malley nodded to the request.

All through the rancid days they worked, bathing the dirty, fevered souls. The women, too sick and weak to guard their modesty, lay naked as the islanders washed and cleaned them with the gentleness and tenderness that strong men sometimes have a capacity for showing.

For one full week their routine never altered, and indeed, there were improvements enough to give them all hope that their coming had been more than an impulsive and adventurous act.

The bay was free now of the glut of passenger ships the presence of which had only been a grim reminder of the death voyage that had brought these ravaged souls from their homeland to the outback of this stinking island. When the last ship, the *Charlmont*, slipped beyond the bend in the river, those who were strong enough rose from their blankets on skeletal elbows and smiled through cracked and swollen lips, a thin ray of light glimmering faintly in their eyes. "The devil has left us. God be praised," cried one old man.

The sound of ax and crosscut saw and the smell of liquid sap from fallen trees drifted over the island, making the stench of death and sickness almost tolerable. Islanders cleared land for graves, but they left a roof of intermingled branches to form a quiet and spiritual place for those whose only home now would be the clay. With the felled trees, they set about building more sheds to house those whose only roof had been the stars.

"I don't know what we would have done without you and the islanders, Mr. McMahon." Dr. Matthews sat at the long wooden table in the galley of the *Boru*, sipping a bowl of hot broth. There was a glow about the man that Brendan had seen before but could not identify. Liam Malley sat beside him, his clay pipe sending acrid drafts of Indian weed curling about the low-beamed room.

"And I don't know what those people would have done without you, Dr. Matthews."

"I have had help. The government has sent many people, and many have died like saints administering to the sick. You know, gentlemen, what troubles me the most?" He put the pewter bowl down and leaned on his elbows. "Since I have been here, I have seen other immigrant ships sail past on their way to less crowded and nondiseased quarantine centers, and I see the decks of these ships crowded with neatly dressed, laughing faces. A German vessel went upriver a week or so ago, and the fair-haired girls and handsome pink-cheeked men sang hymns. When the ship disappeared, I am not ashamed to admit

I went into the hospital and wept. Oh, the injustice that is visited upon our people. Will it ever stop?"

"Why are the other ships so clean and healthy? Why the bloody difference, Doctor?" Malley's teeth bit tightly on the clay stem of the pipe.

"Because the English have raped Ireland, ravaged her like some innocent maiden, and now when Ireland is heavy with the burden of Ireland's child, England solves her problem by shipping mother and child away on any vessel that can gain breakwater.

"What you have seen, and I say this with all due respect to your gracious charity, is mild. I have walked through the stinking slop of the holds of those floating graveyards and seen, as though I could *touch* it with my hands, the dense steam of foul air issuing from the sleeping quarters of those miserable souls.

"There are English ship brokers who have sold space to entire families for three pounds, ten shillings just to fill the ships so they would not sail the sea empty of cargo, be it lumber or human beings.

"But do they not know what lies ahead?" Brendan's unbelieving eyes were those of a naïve and innocent schoolboy.

"Oh, Mr. McMahon, there are passenger agents, landlords, and every imaginable scum trading bodies for pound notes on the docks of Cobh, Galway, Castletown, Bearhaven, and any port that can put a ship between there and here. They tell the poor, unsuspecting beggars of a world of opportunity and gold and food and great homes, of streets that are paved with jewels."

"And they believe it? My countrymen believe these lies? Why have they changed so? I would not have believed such tall tales."

"You would not? If you had one germ-infested potato to feed you for one full week, would you not begin to believe anything you were told of riches and food and warmth and escape?" He allowed the words to hang in the air. The only sounds were the creaking of the wooden ship and Liam Malley's agitated biting of his pipe.

"Aye, you would believe it, Mr. McMahon. Any man would if he thought he could save himself and his family."

"Drink your broth, Doctor." Malley smiled. "On board my ship you follow the captain's orders, not the doctor's."

Above them, suddenly, loud hobnailed boots thumped and rumbled along the decks, and voices thundered and echoed down the gangways until Hanley's beaked face peered in at them.

"Captain, Brendan, excuse me, but it's Paul. He's terrible sick, and we can't get him to lie down and rest. Jesus, but he is like an animal gone wild. Come, quick."

Brendan sprinted across the plank and up into the clearing where the newly dug graves were piled with mounds of fresh earth.

Several of the islanders were backed up against the trees as the mighty bear of a man flailed about with his great arms.

They looked at Brendan with relief and relaxed their caution momentarily as the McMahon stepped forward into the clearing.

"Paul, what are you about, man? Are you pulling the trees down with your hands? Showing off your strength again, old friend?"

Paul's face was gray and twisted, and his fists were bunched as though fighting some internal enemy. "Oh, Brendan, I do not feel good, *n'est-ce pas?*"

"Aye. Well, my strong friend, sit and relax. You have not slept. You have served many of the sick for long hours. You have not rested like me and the others." Brendan knew that only by acknowledgment of Paul's superior strength could he convince his friend to rest from his labors.

"Eh? You have rested, Brendan? Good. I sit for a minute. My head, it hurts."

He began to waver, and the others rushed to help him.

"No," Brendan shouted. "Leave him be. Going to rest a wee bit, Paul?"

"Aye, Brendan. I rest." His large right hand held onto the bark of an oak, and he steadied himself long enough to get down to his knees gradually, and then he keeled over on his back.

"Quick. Blankets, scalding water, and rip those bloody clothes off. He's been so busy working he has not changed into clean clothes."

Brendan decided against moving Paul to the hospital. Instead, they fashioned a makeshift lean-to of branches and leaves that kept the sun and weather from his pallid face.

Throughout the long night, Brendan sat beside the outstretched giant, listening to his labored breathing while sponging the hot sweat from his forehead. Occasionally, Paul would lapse into conversation, recalling their days with O'Connell and their monumental drinking bouts before Brendan became a serious-minded representative to the Assembly. "Brendan, when will we have grog again? Eh? You forget them people in Charlottetown for two days, and we will drink together like before when you were as crazy as Paul, eh?"

"Aye, you bloody mountain. I will drink you right into the Northumberland Strait."

"*Arrr, arrr.*" The Frenchman laughed from deep down; it was a crouping sound, and it seemed Paul's chest rattled from it.

"Brendan. You are there, no?"

"Of course, I am right here. Shhh. Sleep. You will be better in the morning."

"Brendan, listen, remember the woman in Ireland? Greta? Hey, she was one woman, eh? Brendan. Eh?"

"She was. She was one woman, Greta was. Sleep now, my friend. Sleep."

The wood turned quiet, the great man's breathing steadied, and Brendan fell asleep, only to wake with a jolt to the gray dawn. He sat upright and looked around to get his bearings. A hazy mist rose from the surface of the river. Birds warbled to life and rustled from branch to branch overhead. Paul. Suddenly Brendan remembered the sick Frenchman. Jumping to his feet, he leaned into the enclosure. The giant body lay still under the blanket, but the bearded face appeared to have more color. Brendan dropped to his friend's side, placing his hand over the heart. Its beat was faint but steady.

Oh, Jesus, Mary, and Joseph, thank God. He will come through it. He is too strong even for death.

Brendan stroked Paul's forehead and brushed the brown hair back out of his eyes.

"Sleep, my friend. We have many tankards to raise in the years to come."

By the end of two weeks the island had begun to recover. There would be no miracles; of that everyone was certain. Ships would continue to come upriver with diseased passengers until the blight and famine in Ireland were over. But at least the staff on Grosse Isle had been given a lift.

"We are expecting another shipload today, Brendan. I suggest you take those well enough to travel and go back home. You have done all you can. I count two hundred thirty-one people who are well enough to travel and can pass the medical inspection. Take them. Give them a new life. God knows they deserve it. Sail with the tide. If you stay, you will only become further involved. There will be others who will come to help. And the word from Ireland is that the worst is over."

So, later that day, Brendan bade farewell to Dr. Matthews and his quiet and anonymous helpers and began transporting the immigrants to the *Boru* who clasped the rope rails on either side of the gangplank with trembling but determined hands.

Some did not want to make the journey. "I will never board a ship again. I would prefer to die here on this island than ever to stand on the deck of a ship."

Then there were those who heard the one dreaded word from Captain Liam Malley's lips: *farming.* "I will never, ever again plant a seed in the earth. The earth has brought us nothing but sickness, suffering, and death. Keep your bloody farms. Give me the brick and mortar of the city."

But many did take the opportunity and boarded without trepidation. When all seemed ready, Brendan made one last trip alone to the pine grove under the canopy of oak. He prayed for those who had not survived and walked slowly along the shore, still sad but proud of the work his men had done.

Yet another ship was already displacing its cargo of sickly immigrants into the same square boats they had seen on the day they arrived. All along the shore bodies lay on blankets again, but at least now there *were* blankets, water, and newly constructed sheds on the hill.

Brendan did not watch the hellish routine but continued, afraid that he would commit himself to a fresh batch of sick and that the survivors on the *Brian Boru* would face disappointment again.

In his path a boy—or so the emaciated form appeared—crawled in the oozing mud. With sunken cheeks and black, indented pits under the eyes, he looked up at Brendan in a mournful plea for help. The lips crusted with sores formed words but did not speak them. Brendan, his heart breaking with pity, pulled the lad up out of the mud and propped him against the green banking.

The boy was six or seven, and he tried to speak.

"What is it, lad? What is it you wish to say?"

Finally, the words stuttered from his mouth: "Mama, Mama. There. Take me to Mama." The little finger pointed at a blanket several yards away where a woman lay among the others.

"You were separated from your mother, little lad. Here, let me carry you over to her."

Brendan picked the fragile body up and carried the lad to the woman's blanket. She looked up gratefully as the McMahon placed the boy beside her. He smiled down at her and was about to say a few words of comfort when Hanley shouted from the plank that all was ready. He turned from the mother and child and began to walk away only to be stopped by a voice calling his name: "Brendan. Brendan." The voice managed to summon some inner resource of strength. "Brendan."

He went back and knelt beside the woman. "Did you call me? Was that my name you called?"

"Yes, dear sweet Jesus, yes. It is I, Brendan, Cathleen, your sister. Thanks be to God I have found you."

He looked in shock at his once beautiful sister. Her gray face was sunken to bone, and her raven hair the color of dirty snow.

"Oh, my God, my dearest Cathleen. Oh, my God, what have the bastards done to you?" He took her gently in his arms, while reaching out for the lad as tears stung his cheeks in a fiery stream.

One day out of Summerside, Cathleen McMahon Leary lifted her head from the pillow. There was only the slightest suggestion of color on her gaunt cheeks; but color it was, and Brendan thanked God for it as he stood anxiously at the foot of the bed.

"I'm afraid I have taken your bed away from you, my dearest brother."

"It is happy I am to give it up to you, Cathleen. You look so much better. You had us worried." Her hair was so white, he thought.

"My son? Sean, he is well? Oh, God. Tell me he is well, Brendan."

"He is more than well. He is at this moment turning the wheel with Captain Malley."

"It is the second time you have saved my life, Brendan. I have been a terrible burden to you."

"You have been no burden at all. We have Dr. Matthews to thank for releasing you, sick as you were. But tell me, what news do you have of Una?"

"Last I heard she was well. The Arans have the fish to eat, God bless them. She is married with two fine sons." Her eyes took on a far-away look, and she turned her head to the bulkhead of the neat and polished mate's cabin.

"Do you wish to talk about it, Cathleen? It may be good for you."

Her voice cracked in a stifled sob, and she nodded her head. "Aye, it might be best. Patrick and the two children, a boy and a girl, died within days of each other. There was no food, and Patrick went everywhere in search of it. He came back empty-handed. Oh, Brendan, he cried like a child because he said he had failed his family. Fever and starvation took him and the two children. Sean and I did our best to bury them. We burned the cottage and took to the road. Tinkers, God bless them, had mercy on us and pulled us from a ditch and fed us what little they had."

"Where was the leadership? Couldn't you go to someone for help?"

"Brendan, an Irishman is like no other in the world. Patrick was too proud. He had left O'Connell for me and the children, and he would not go back a broken and starving man. He knew the leadership resented his leaving. O'Connell had told them as much before he died."

"But you said in a letter—it must have been years ago, now—that it was O'Connell's suggestion that Patrick stay at home with his family."

"It was. Daniel loved Patrick like a son. But Patrick had the notion that Daniel said only what he thought he must say and that Patrick should have turned down the suggestion."

"Oh, the thickness of it all. Such self-righteous pride. It is a curse laid down on all of us. Then how did you manage passage on that foul ship?"

"I had a ring. Daniel O'Connell gave it as a wedding gift, and when the tinkers left us in Cork, I found a captain who would take us here. I did not know where Canada was, but I knew that you were here. The agents on the docks told of clear air and fresh water and food. And I thought by some miracle I would find you. I knew I must find you. And a miracle it was. Dear Patrick and the children must be watching over Sean and me. I felt certain if we could make it to Canada, we could get to Prince Edward Island."

"Aye." He nodded solemnly, and then, to change the subject, he added, "But surely a ring that Daniel gave as a wedding present was worth fifty times the price of passage on that death carrier that brought you here."

"Aye, but Captain Vinson said his ship was the best on the line and there was abundant food and water aboard." Her mouth twisted in contempt. "The food was salt pork, and to eat it was to invite an unquenchable thirst. And when we asked for water, they poured it from the same kegs the salt pork was packed in, and the thirst became unbearable. The only other water was dirty, and at first we could not drink it, but God knows we had to drink something. I think that is when sickness struck the passengers first. Bodies were tossed over the sides every day without even a prayer or a moment for proper burial.

"One woman near Sean and me hid the body of her dead daughter for three days. She made us promise not to tell anyone. God forgive me, the smell became so bad even the rats stayed away. When Vinson found out, he was furious and took all rations away from all of us for two days. As though he were taking much of anything."

Brendan's anger and disbelief served only to remind him of Jarrod Murdock and his kind. He would declare war on the Murdocks of this world, and by God, he would win.

"Well, my dear Cathleen, you have said quite enough. You must rest. You will soon be home with Mary and your nieces and nephews. Lie back. I will send a young lad in with some hot broth. He has been trying to knock the door of this cabin down for days now."

He bent over and kissed her forehead, straightened the blankets, and began to leave. Then he turned, his dark brows knitting quizzically, and asked, "Tell me, dear sister, what was the name of this Captain Vinson's ship?"

"Why, the *Antonia*, Brendan. Why do you ask?"

"Oh, no reason. Rest now, and prepare to meet your little lad."

The Summerside docks spilled over with wives and children, who crowded together in a silent but anxious vigil as the *Brian Boru*, her decks mobbed, sailed serenely home on a glassy sea. Word had traveled overland by trapper and hunter and sailor that the *Boru's* mission was accomplished and that she would be urged into port with the tide on June 8.

There were shouts and tears and cries of exultation that fathers and husbands had returned safely, and there were introductions of immigrants to the families who would be sharing their bread and board until some employment and living quarters could be arranged.

Brendan was the last to leave, thanking Liam Malley and promising to meet sometime for a tumbler of good grog in Charlottetown.

Cathleen was on Brendan's arm as they walked down the gangplank of the *Boru*. She leaned heavily on her brother, still weak and unsteady on her legs.

Mary, with her children, stood somewhat apart from the rest of the chattering mob. Her eyebrows raised, she watched her husband disembark with a strange woman and a little boy.

The children, of course, had eyes only for their father. Daniel was the first to reach him, but James whispered a muted prayer and then crossed himself in thanksgiving.

"Well, well, how is my Daniel?" The young boy with the deep-set eyes, gathered up in the powerful arms of his father, smiled darkly.

Mary came forward almost timidly, and Brendan kissed her softly. "I have missed you, Mary Roark."

"I have missed you, Brendan."

"But can you ever believe who this is?"

Mary looked puzzled. "No, Brendan, I cannot."

"Oh, good God, Mary," he shouted, "it is my sister Cathleen. She comes to us as one of God's miracles. Oh, but come, I have much to tell you. I shall tell you all in the carriage. Jesus, but I missed Tignish."

Mary, hesitant at first, stepped forward and embraced her sister-in-law. "God bless you, Cathleen. And who is this little man we have here?"

Cathleen took Mary's two hands in hers and patted them lovingly.

"I have heard so much about you, Mary. My brother talks of no one else. And he was wrong. You are more beautiful than he said you were. This is my son, Sean."

"Oh, sure you sound like Brendan, but tell me, are you feeling fit? You seem weak. You are ill? Children, this is your aunt Cathleen. Take her to the wagon, and make her comfortable. And, Daniel, take the lad in tow. Go along with you now. I must talk to Brendan, Cathleen. I shall be quick about it, and then we shall have you home and into a comfortable bed where you belong."

"She is much older than I ever thought," Mary said as she watched the group go off to the wagons.

"She is younger than I by almost four years. She has been through so much, Mary. Please help me to help her."

"Why, of course, Brendan."

"I missed you so, Mary." He squeezed her hand and said softly, "I think we should retire early." He winked. "It has been such a tedious journey."

"Well, then surely you will need your sleep, Brendan. I would not wish to disturb you." Her head was cocked in that coquettish and teasing fashion of hers.

"You are a difficult woman, Mary Roark, but I will change that beneath the quilt this night."

"Why, Brendan McMahon, you are sounding like a wild man."

"I am wild with desire for you." His heart thumped with passion for her. He wished they were alone and could ride along the shore and he could take her in his arms and make love to her beside the thrashing sea.

Her face flushed. "Well, I suppose you shouldn't go to sleep too early." She smiled. And then her tone became serious. "Brendan, I do not wish to spoil your homecoming, and I do long to lie beside you also, my dearest. But I must tell you something, and it grieves me to have to do so. We all missed you, you will never know how much, but there has been much grief and suffering since you left."

"Grief and suffering? What do you mean?"

"The day after you sailed for Quebec Jarrod Murdock called in all debts from families of those men who sailed with you. There were many who could not pay, and he sent them packing along the highroad. They came to our farm because they knew we had no debts with him and we had a deed that was free and clear, God bless dear John Wallace for his kindness."

"And you, dear wife, for your courage to fight for our land." He put his arm affectionately around her shoulder. "Oh, that bloody Murdock, what kind of evil eats away inside him that he could do that to women and children? What manner of beast is he?"

"I do not know, Brendan, but I do know there will be trouble as soon as the women tell their menfolk. Murdock has the militia behind him because his ledger is proof of the debts."

"That damn ledger of his. He worships it like an idol. Is that all that the man lives for, his possessions? Even his little Margaret, I would not be surprised if her name appeared in the book as another possession of his."

"What are you going to do, Brendan? Something must be done before there is bloodshed."

At that moment, as if her words were a herald of what was to come, Reilly and Ready broke from the ranks of their loving families and headed for Brendan and Mary. Mary's eyes widened as she looked to Brendan. "They know, they have already been told."

"Brendan, has your missus informed you of what Murdock has done to our families?" Reilly's face was the color of red clay.

"Aye, now pass the word. We must not act without good, hard talk."

"Talk? Talk is cheap, McMahon. We must act. We must act now. We should tear Murdock apart with our hands. These hands that have ripped and torn at *his* soil on *his* land. These hands that have worked for *him*, to fill *his* pockets, have become strong. He will know the feel of strong Irish hands on his throat." Reilly's cocked fists were like steel hammers, ready to pound Murdock senseless.

"Enough," Brendan growled. He did not want to call attention to this high emotion, justified though it was. He must find some way to get them through the initial shock of their anger. In a day or two it would subside enough so he could plot out a plan of action. "Look, Michael, I know how you feel. There is not an Irishman on this island who has not experienced the anger of being forced from hearth or home or even country for that matter. But you must swallow your anger and think. Violence never solved anything." Gradually, it seemed, he was adopting O'Connell's philosophy.

"But for the sake of Christ, Brendan, what—"

"Stop, I say. Stop it now. We are home. We have saved many of our people. We should be thankful. Tonight we will celebrate at my farm, and then we will talk. Good talk. Not talk of fists and blood. Hard talk of a plan to get you and the others back to the land. Now, please, trust me. Tonight. Go now, join your families. You have been too long away from them."

CHAPTER XXIV

THE SOUND OF tin whistle and fiddle filled the North Cape. There was dancing and whirling about, the clapping of hands, and broad smiles of excitement on the faces of the newly arrived immigrants, who stood almost fearfully in front of the tables of bread and molasses and pastries and vegetables, stews, cheese, fish, and jellies.

"Go on, lad, eat something," Brendan whispered to Sean as the boy seemed to back away from the feast.

"I have never seen such amounts of food before, Uncle Brendan. Never in my life."

"Well, you're seeing it now. Feed yourself full. God has been good to the island this year. Enjoy His blessings."

Brendan and Mary and the other islanders walked among the timid and almost embarrassed newcomers and urged them to the tables. "Come now, try some stew and some of my bread; it's the best on the island, is it not, Mary McMahon?" Mrs. Dalton, a good-natured, great-bosomed woman, bellowed out to one and all.

"Aye, it is, Mrs. Dalton, next to me own." Mary laughed and put on the brogue.

And little by little they began to move up and help themselves to plentiful servings, their eyes moist with gratitude as their lips formed shy thank-yous.

One person not forgotten by Brendan was Bill Profitt. As the whistle and fiddle summoned those with the strength to dance, Brendan and Mary slipped across the brook to the Profitt house where Isabella, in the soothing calm of early evening, shared her thoughts with an affectionate and companionable Abigail McMahon.

"I hope we are not intruding on you two," Brendan said as he and Mary approached their comfortable corner on the porch. His pretense at light-heartedness did not hide his feelings.

"Oh, no, Father. Mrs. Profitt and I were just talking about the Irish people."

Brendan nodded and went to Isabella, who extended her hands to him. He took them and kissed her gently on the forehead. "I am truly sorry about Bill, Isabella. His kindness and counsel saw us through many a difficult time. I would have been over sooner, but as you know, we have brought people back with us, Irish people who are sick."

"I know, Brendan, I know. Bill so loved you both. He was a quiet man, but his feelings ran as deep as a well."

"Isabella, I know it will not appear callous to you that we are having a celebration only two fields away."

"He announced it before I told him of Bill, Isabella," Mary said. "I did not encourage Brendan to cancel it. I knew you would understand."

"If Bill was here, you can just bet he would be standing among the menfolk, swapping a yarn or two and stoking that grand old pipe of his. And you know, Brendan, how you and Bill would argue over confederation?"

"Aye." Brendan smiled in fond memory of the long debates that sometimes slipped on well past midnight.

"You should know, Brendan, he was very troubled over Jarrod Murdock's treatment of those women and their children. He was not for confederation, but he told me that night that if he had to choose between it and the Murdocks of the world, he would choose confederation. How he wanted to talk to you that night. He did not sleep. He could not. It all bothered him so. Let us hope he is happy now. We buried him beyond the far bluff. He would like that. Once he told me how happy John Wallace must be to lie within touching distance of the sea."

"Bill was a good and gentle man, Isabella. He is happy with God. Of that I have no doubt."

Isabella, strong and never one to dwell on her own misery or misfortune, released her hands from his. Her face clouded now in the oncoming darkness, but her soft tone was reassuring. "What would I do without my little friend? You have shared such a wonderful treasure with me. Now go back to your people. God knows you have reason to celebrate, from what I have been told by my little gossip bird here."

They left Isabella once more to the care and companionship of their daughter and walked back down the stone-bordered path, their fingers joined in a tender touch.

The night was filled with the fragrance of lady's-slippers. June was in full bloom, and the island tingled and trembled with new life. The lyric of whistle and fiddle, the sweetness of the flowered evening, the flutter of unseen birds, and the call of the breaking surf spoke for them. No words were necessary to suggest a walk to the shore. Already a moon, apple-round and a subtle gold, sent pale sparkles across the waves.

Mary's body beside him brought back all the feelings of love and desire Brendan had held for her in the days he was away. He turned to her upturned face and kissed her warm lips softly. He did not hold her at first. Instead, he kept his hands by his sides and kissed her until her lips became moist and his desire for her burned inside him. Then slowly their bodies touched. His hands slipped from her back to her buttocks, and he pulled her in closer to him. "My Mary, my dearest Mary, my wife."

She returned his kiss and spoke for them both. "We are one, Brendan, we are one."

His hands explored her breasts, and he felt like a bridegroom again. He slipped her summer frock from her shoulders and kissed the rounded tops of her breasts. Her chest was hard to his moving hands. The dress fell to her ankles, and she stepped out of it and picked it up from the damp sand. He took her hand, and they walked beneath the overhang of the cape. With one pull of the satin ribbon, her white shift was open, and he slowly brought the straps from her shoulders. Now she was naked to the waist, and his hands found her again, gently and with love. She rose to his touch, and soon their bodies joined. When the first ecstasy slowly and sweetly departed, they lay under the shadows of the moon, their hands clasped again in the tender affection of man and wife.

"I suppose they will wonder where we are, my husband."

"If they cannot guess, then they do not know Brendan McMahon very well. It was common gossip on the voyage that I studied the waves as though your portrait were painted on each and every one. But I suspect you are right, my wife, we should be starting back. I want to talk to Reilly and the others before the poteen makes more sense to them than my words."

They left their warm and secure burrow beneath the cape and climbed to the field above.

Brendan motioned to Reilly with a shake of his head, and Reilly, not as flushed as earlier in the day, threaded his way through and around the revelers. "Aye, Brendan, would you be needin' me for anything?"

Brendan slapped the man on the shoulder. "I'm happy to see your eyes are clear of red, Michael. I think it is time we assembled our people and decided on the direction we must take, eh?"

"Aye, Brendan. I have had time to think. After all, if I broke that bloody bastard's neck, there'd only be another to take his place."

"I'm impressed with your reasoning, Michael. I never knew you were such a thinking man." Others were gathered around them now, and they began to chuckle.

"Well, I thought it over, and it seemed the wisest course."

"Don't believe the blackguard, Brendan. He is only saying what Mrs. Reilly told him to say," Dalton roared.

"The devil you say, Dalton. Sure there's no man on this island more twisted around the apron strings of a wife than you are."

There was great howling and camaraderie, and the spirit was infectious and optimistic. Even the tight, fleshless masks of the immigrants were illuminated in smiles.

Brendan ascended the shoulder of a hill, and the crowd began slowly to assemble around him.

When he was certain everyone was close enough, he spoke, not in a rhetorical fashion, but more as though he were speaking over a back fence or out in a pasture while helping a neighbor clear a field from a grove of birch.

"It is a blessing that we all are here this night," he began. Peter McMahon advanced closer to his father, a torch held in his hand. The father smiled at his son's aid, and throughout the crowd other torches were lighted and held high so that the vast pasture was bathed in a wash of orange flame.

Brendan looked out on the rough outdoor faces, gouged and lined from weather and sewn tight by blazing summer suns, but on this night also expectant.

"I wanted you to know that we are not accepting the treatment of Jarrod Murdock like a pack of trained dogs doing the bidding of their master. I will return to the Assembly Monday week, and I will shout this injustice from every corner of the chamber. Embarrassment before his peers will force Murdock to back down. You will be working the land again, mark me."

"Begging your pardon, Brendan, but Murdock does not strike me as a man who could be embarrassed so easily. He seems beyond that. I have attacked him on every issue that relates to the land and the farmer, and he continues to act according to his own whimsy." Edward Ahearn stepped into the torchlight, and his usually pale face took on the hue of burnished copper.

"Aye, so you have, Edward. The *Sentinel* has been the one true voice for all of us, and we thank you for it. But now you must see, as I know you do, that our only answer to Murdock is confederation. I will pursue confederation until he sees me in his sleep."

"I agree, Brendan. I—"

Before Edward could finish, Ready's voice boomed out from the darkened shadows of the crowd.

"That is good, what you plan, Brendan. And I am sure you have the backing of every one here, but that could take days, months, years, for God's sake. We are farmers. We must do something now. Brendan, I am not a violent man by nature, but it seems to me that we have a right to work and feed, house, and clothe our families, and if physical force is the answer, then I say we should march like an army on that bloody, unscrupulous bastard."

"Hear."

"Hear."

"Hear."

They joined in with enthusiasm, moving up and down in flaming, rebellious agreement, but their cheers sent chills up and down the spines of Mary and the other women. There had been enough misery and suffering in their lives. Brendan would take their fight to the Assembly and win, but not with bloodletting, not with physical force.

The McMahon allowed the cheering to run its course, and then he spoke more deliberately, his tone no longer that of back fence or pasture. "I will never be a party to violence. What did violence gain

Dennis Hurley? For one moment of satisfaction, he had to uproot his family and leave his farm behind. Is that what you want? To be run into the sea by the militia? We are not soldiers, we are farmers. There are other ways of doing this, and we will decide together the best and most peaceful solution."

"Please sir. Please, sir, if I may make a suggestion?" The voice belonged to a girl, no more than twelve years of age, who was barely visible in the thick of the tightly packed crowd.

"What is it, lass? Come forward. Come. Some of you help the lass to the front. There, there we are. Now, lass, what is on your mind? You have as much a right to speak as anyone. You're an islander now. What is your name?"

"I am called Nora. Nora Collins, sir."

"Well, Nora Collins, you seem a bright-eyed one. What do you wish to say to this wild band of farmers?"

"Well, sir, my da and brothers worked a croft for Lord Dunning. And the man, sir, was very mean to the da."

"Yes, where in Ireland, lass?"

"In Connemara, sir, near Maam Cross."

"Aye, go on with your story."

The girl looked around at the strangers staring out of the glowering and flickering night.

"Don't be afraid, Nora, we are all friends here. We make a lot of noise, but we really are good friends. Is that not so, Lawrence?"

Ready grunted, "Aye," with some degree of irritated embarrassment.

"Well, Lord Dunning had many acres of farmland, and he worked the men and women of his crofts without mercy all day into the black of night. And then when tax time came each year, he raised the tax they had to pay for the privilege of working his land. My da and the others decided one year that they would not pay the taxes. Your man says, says he, 'All right, no taxes, no work.' And Da and the others decided that was fine with them. Da got the others together, the way you are here, and told them the landlord needed them more than they needed the landlord. So they did as the da requested; they did not work."

Brendan smiled. The story was not unfamiliar to him; he had been told of this somewhere before. "Yes, Nora, go on, we all are listening to you."

She seemed more relaxed now as she turned to face them. "Well, the word went out all over Connemara, and farmers threw down their tools and let the fields remain idle. Soon after, the landlords got together; there were some good ones, and they forced Lord Dunning to lower his taxes. The word went out after that, and any time a landlord raised taxes or was meaner than usual, the farmers did a dunning. They dunned him, and he soon backed down."

"Are you suggesting, lass, that we do the same to Murdock? That we do, as you call it, a dunning?" The anger was gone from Ready's voice.

"I'm sorry, sir, I do not know your island. I should not have spoken. It was not my place to do so."

"Aye, but it *was* your place to do so. I think it is an excellent idea." Brendan reached down and patted the girl's head.

"What do you think, neighbors? Has little Nora Collins solved our problem? Should we not do a dunning on Jarrod Murdock? Should we not let him feel the pinch in his pocketbook? When not a bloody nail is pounded into those ships of his, and his fields turn to dust and weed, will he not rue the day he forced women and children to the open road?"

"He will," they roared, their flame red faces staring up at Brendan while their fists punctuated the briny mist that rolled in off the Northumberland Strait. "He will. He will" echoed along the sand and surf only to be swept up by the night sea.

Daniel McMahon had watched it all from the tufts of high grass that grew along the marshy hills overlooking the lower level of the field where Brendan stood silhoutted against the sky. The little girl had helped with her words, and *she* was just an urchin from the stone hills of Ireland. But what could he do? He was not like the others, to carry pitchforks and march as he had seen them doing this very morning. They had banded together all along the Tignish Road, the dust spiraling in red clouds under their boots, women and men, old people and children. But Daniel was always embarrassed by such obvious display. He was a boy who could sit alone and ponder oceans and rivers and skies for hours at a time and never desire the companionship of another living soul. But in this effort of all the Tignish citizens, he wanted desperately to share, to show his father that he, too, could make a contribution. Still, he just could not bring himself to join a group of irate and marching people. All night he had lain awake under the wide oak eaves while his brothers and sisters sighed and breathed deeply in their sleep.

The other children had joined Brendan and Mary the next morning, but Daniel did not. Mary had insisted he be a part of it, and she had her own reasons for feeling thus. But Brendan had said, "Leave the boy. It is his decision, and if he chooses to stay at home, then so be it."

So, as the band of farmers and shipwrights and laborers ambled off to show Murdock their strength, Daniel outlined his own plan. His father would be proud of him; he would make certain of that.

The thought had struck him like a bolt of lightning in the hours before dawn. The ledger. He, Daniel McMahon, would steal Murdock's precious ledger. He would travel along the shore below the road, keeping the band of marchers in front of him and in view, and when Murdock was summoned from his house, Daniel would somehow slip inside and find the ledger. It was common knowledge that Murdock retired to his room after dinner to study the new entries. Finding Jarrod Murdock's room would not be difficult.

Daniel was a man now, almost fourteen years old, a man by any standards and certainly a man by the standards of the island. He walked barefoot along the strand, splashing in and out of shallow, sun-reflecting pools to cool his feet. His spirits were high because for the first time in his life he was doing something on his own, something for all of them. He knew they thought of him as different somehow. And he agreed with them; he was. But he was never sure of the way in which he *was* different. He watched his brothers and sisters sitting at the table, chatting their play-day stories, and he never had anything to say. Surely, he was as alive as they; but his vitality lay within, deeply within, and there were nights, as he stood above the bluff and looked out to the ocean, thinking of his father, whom he loved deeply, that mysteriously and without warning he would cry. These moments of periodic melancholia gripped him fiercely, and at times the despair they brought left him a crumpled and weeping figure in the dark night.

It was not that he did not love his mother—he did—but his love for his father was a deeper emotion. It had been easy when he was a boy, accepting his father's strong embrace and whiskey-scented kiss. He could love and kiss the rough-whiskered face in return. But now he was a young man, and with that realization came all the attendant manly trappings. He did not hug and kiss his father anymore, and Brendan did not embrace and kiss him. They lived in the world of the unsaid and the undone.

But now this glorious morning he had his own plan, and it was no one else's.

On through the morning sun they marched the highroad, and Daniel ambled discreetly behind them, excitement and a sense of quiet adventure rising inside him.

Just before noon he stopped and ate the corn muffins he had secured deep in the pockets of his coveralls. Before him now he could see the marchers ascend the rolling hill of Port Loyal. His father was at the head of the crowd, and as Daniel crouched and crawled through the thick growth, he saw Jarrod Murdock's rigid body appear on the terrace above.

Murdock and McMahon did not speak until the shuffling crowd came to rest. Then Murdock, his face drained of color, moved forward a few feet. He was still standing the high ground, and his squat, imposing frame hovered above the rawboned figure of the McMahon. "You all are trespassing on my property. If you do not leave, I will summon the militia, and they will run you off with bayonets, if need be."

"You do not understand our presence here, Murdock. We have come to talk to you, not to make trouble. We simply wish to make our point, and when we have made it and you have understood us fully, we will leave. No force is necessary to move us."

"All right then, what is your point? Make it, and be quick about it. I will not tolerate a herd of animals tracking across my land."

"Animals?" Lawrence Ready, throwing off his wife's restraining hand, shouted out. "If we are animals in your eyes, then it is because that is the way you have treated us. Like unwanted dogs."

"Hear, hear." Others joined in.

Brendan's hand shot up for quiet. "We are not here for name-calling, Murdock. We are here to tell you quite simply that until you return to cottage and farm those you have turned out, no one in Prince County will work for you. Your fields will turn to weed, and the spliced wood of your ships will warp and bend in the silence of your boatyard."

"Are you threatening me, McMahon? You and this seedy lot of unwashed rabble? Did you think for one minute I would listen to this insane threat of yours? Leave my land. Gentlemen, come forward, please."

Murdock snapped his fingers, and two burly and glowering men stepped from the house. They held rifles almost tenderly in the crook of their arms. They did not speak, and they barely moved. They were strangers to Brendan. From England, he thought, no doubt specially commissioned by Murdock for the express purpose of protecting him and his property.

"Tell your lackeys to put their rifles away, Murdock. You'll have no need of them. But do not be too quick to dismiss our demands. If you look closely, you will see that many of our members are still working but have bravely made this sacrifice to stand with us."

"I see them. And I praise their bravery but abhor their stupidity. The ledger will be well read this night, I assure you."

The word was like a thunderclap to Daniel, who had been momentarily transfixed by the scene being played out before him. He snapped out of his reverie and crawled through the high grass, emerging finally on the other side of the house. He lay for a few moments, his heart pounding and throbbing in his ears, and then, with a deep breath, he rose from the grass and raced for the rear of the house. Once at the back door, he pressed against the clapboards, listening for any interior sound. He could hear only the agitated murmuring of the crowd at the front of the house. He would have to act quickly. He turned the doorknob, ducked into the scullery, and crept across the wide wooden floors. The long oak table was bare except for a vase of lilies at its center. There were two stairways. One was twisted and winding in a snakelike design, and it was directly off the kitchen. He decided to take that instead of the more formal one that led gracefully from the upper chambers to the French glass-front portico door.

His wiry, long-legged body wound around the stairway until he was on the second floor. He walked quickly along the passageway until he came to the room he assumed must be Murdock's. Although it held a large four-poster brass bed and a large fireplace, the room was clearly dominated by the tall, sturdy desk set close to the windows.

He had to hurry now. The desk held papers and documents; one of the lower drawers was open, and a long, pointed quill lay across an official-looking document as though dropped there hurriedly.

It was a strange feeling being in someone else's room, and the room of so powerful and public a figure at that. He lifted the papers, not quite certain what he was looking for. He did not know exactly what the ledger looked like, although on those occasions when the family visited Digger Shanley in Charlottetown, he did see the important books that Digger brought out to show his mother and father and that he always referred to as his money books.

The shouts from below were fiercer now, and he sidled over to the window just as he heard Murdock say, "It is on the desk in my room. You, fetch it and bring it to me."

Daniel's heart missed a complete beat, and then it raced wildly. He heard a door slam shut below, and he felt nailed to his place by the window, as though his bare feet were stuck to the floor. He would be caught, collared by this man whose boots already thumped on the staiarway. Finally, with a great and sudden surge of energy, he sprang to the bed and slid under it, the long, trailing blanket obscuring him.

The boots thundered into the room, and Daniel's heart wanted to explode in his ears. His throat closed on him, and breathing became difficult. He heard the rustle of papers, a short, profane statement, "All right, guv, I'll find your papers. Bloody book. God damn my eyes, where are—Ah, this must be it." Then more rustling of papers and the boots thumping out of the room, down the corridor and down the stairs to the first floor. Daniel waited for the door to slam, and when it did, he rolled out from under the bed, straightened, went directly to the desk, and opened the deep drawers on the sides. They were full of papers and letters, but nothing that could pass as a ledger. Daniel was terrified now. What if the man had taken the wrong paper? He would return in moments. Fear crept up his spine. He must leave. He could not stay here. He would be found out. Oh, God, why had he come? Yes, why? He could have been back on his Cape, sitting on a hill and watching the endless waves breaking on the shore. He would go at once. He closed the drawers carefully, leaving only the open one as he had found it. He turned and was about to go when he caught himself. No. He was doing this for them, all of them down there who shouted in frustration and anger at this terrible injustice. He would not leave. He would do what he had set out to do. He would not go without the ledger. He went back to the desk and rolled back the top. All the drawers were compartment-sized receptacles for the storing of notes and small items. But in the center, formidable-looking, was one large one. He pulled it open slowly, and there, resting by itself, was a thick black book. He did not have to look any farther. Daniel reached in, took the book, closed the drawer, rolled the top down, and tiptoed out of the room and down the back stairs. He stopped momentarily to look at the pages. The names of neighbors and family friends shouted at him in black script from the book. The corners of his mouth broke into a smile, then froze as he heard the thump of boots again. This time they approached the staircase he now occupied. He turned to go back up, but as he did, he heard a voice boom out, "Not the back stairs, you ox, take the front ones. When will you ever have another chance?"

"Yeah," another voice grunted in response. "I've been takin' the back stairs to everythin' all my life." The thumping changed direction, and Daniel raced down, across the wide floorboards, and out the rear door. He did not stop running until he was deep in the woods. When he halted, he settled heavily on a fallen log, breathing in choking gasps. He'd done it. He'd actually done it. There it was, lying on his lap, Jarrod Murdock's sacred ledger. "Father will be so proud of me," he said aloud, smiling as he turned the pages and saw names and debts and payments. Then, abruptly, he closed the book and cocked his head. A sound came softly but unmistakably from the riverbank. He listened again, straining his ears. A blue heron fluttered from a tall tree, its neck outstretched and its beak poised as, legs trailing, it glided off to the reedy marshes in search of fish. He returned to the ledger. Again the sound came. This time he followed it.

At the forest opening he paused for a moment until the irregular sounds of weeping led him to the river. Lying with her head in her hands, her shoulders trembling, was a girl. She was alone on the soft moss of the embankment. Her sobbing was so pathetic it moved Daniel to a sudden sadness. He was about to speak when he realized he was carrying the ledger in his hands. He retreated a few steps, looked about, and saw another log. He rolled it over, secured the ledger in the yellowed grass, and rolled the log back over it. Then he returned to the sobbing girl.

With a shy hesitancy he spoke gently to her. "Excuse me, miss, may I help?"

At first she stopped crying, and then she sat up, her face stained with tears and dirt. "Who are you? What are you doing at Port Loyal? How dare you?"

Daniel's face reddened with embarrassment. She was a pretty young thing, he thought, but terribly rude. Her sudden attack made him feel foolish, and he was immediately sorry he had even spoken to her. "I—I—I'm sorry, miss, I thought you were in need of help, but I can see I was wrong," he added sharply. She wiped the tears away, and with them the shock of being discovered by a stranger, especially a boy her own age.

Daniel turned to leave, angry now because he would have to come back for the ledger. "Wait, please don't go. I'm sorry. You just startled me. I was ashamed." She had seen the look of rejection on his face. Daniel softened to her voice, more like a bird's song, he thought. Blond curls fell to her shoulders. She was wearing a white dress and, around her neck, a gold locket on a chain. He had never seen anyone so beautiful. He could not explain the strange weakness he felt in his legs or the catch that he heard in his voice.

"I was on my way to the river and I heard the sound of weeping and a crane flew out of a tree and I was on my way to the river and a blue crane—" He clamped his mouth shut. He wanted to swallow his tongue. Why was he talking such rubbish?

She rose from the moss and smoothed out her dress with long, slender fingers. Her nose was tipped to the sun, and he could see a sprinkling of freckles on it. She pulled herself up the path as he stood awkwardly, deciding what to do with his hands. Finally, it struck him that he should make some attempt to help her. She clasped his hand and joined him on the spongy green banking.

Her head lowered at first, then slowly raised as the sun shone full and bright on her wheat-colored hair. Daniel pulled his hand away. His face was hot, and he knew it was the same color as the wild red berries that grew along the marsh.

"Do you live hereabouts?" she asked, her eyes narrowed against the sun.

He had sat in the one-room schoolhouse occasionally, looking over at a girl who held her slate coquettishly in her hands, her bare arms soft and downy in the sunlight, and wondered why he was so attentive to her movements. But just as quickly he would turn his attention back to Mr. Prendergast, the giant of a man who taught the entire township of Tignish. Here was no Big Tom Prendergast to capture his attention; there was only this mysterious feeling that led him into a dreamy trance at the sight and sound of her.

"No," he answered quickly, aware of his long silence. "No, I live up cape, Tignish." Why did he blurt out the truth so freely? Why did she twist his tongue like the taffy at the Summerside Fair?

"Oh." She placed a delicate hand to her mouth, and her blue eyes turned dark, losing the sparkle the sun had given them.

"What is it? Did I say something wrong?" He stepped back and shoved his awkward hands into his back pockets.

"Are you with them?" She nodded in the direction of the house.

"Well, yes, er, no. Sort of, I fathom. Oh, I don't know. I trailed along after them. I was curious." He almost told her that he had entered the house and stole the ledger, but he stopped short of that bit of truth.

"They came to make trouble for my father," she continued, her eyes sad again. "That is why I was crying. My father does not have many friends, and I feel sad for him."

"Jarrod Murdock is your father?" It seemed impossible that this soft, delicate wren of a creature could have such a hawk for a father.

"Yes, he is my father. I am his daughter, and I'm proud of it." She thrust out her jaw defiantly. It was not the defiant chin he noticed, however, but the soft, curved line of her ivory neck. He would never in his life meet such a beautiful girl again. Of that he was certain. But of his emotions and this inner warmth accompanied by a strange fear he was *not* certain. Lately he had felt a difference creep over him. Always one who was happiest alone, he found himself of late even more the citizen of a private world. Now, here in this dappled place, he felt as private as he had ever felt walking the deserted beach or lying in the tall sharp grasses of the windy cape. Yet in this sun-splashed world he was not alone. He was with Jarrod Murdock's daughter, and he felt as though he had always been with her, sharing the privacy of this silent world.

"Please, don't be angry with me. Your father and my father have problems, but they are not our problems surely." He smiled for the first time, and the sharpness of her chin softened, the sparkle returning to her eyes.

"I am Margaret, but you may call me Peg. What is your name?"

"Daniel. Daniel McMahon. My father is in the Assembly with your father."

"Yes, I have heard the name. Look, Daniel, let us be friends, and we will begin our friendship by never mentioning our fathers."

"Shall we shake hands on that, Peg?" Their hands clasped warmly and firmly, and Daniel McMahon experienced a happiness he never knew was possible.

They sat for more than an hour on the edge of the mossy banking, their low voices mingling with the splash of fish and the screech of circling cranes. They spoke of school, and confided their secret goals. Daniel told her how for long hours he would sit on the cape, writing poems about nature. Their talk was easy and spontaneous, and then, suddenly, the easy afternoon calm was broken by a thunderous voice on the other side of the woods. "Margaret, Margaret, are you there?" It boomed forth like the first rumblings of a summer storm.

"It is Father. I must go, Daniel. He would be furious if he found me here talking to you—a McMahon. Will I see you again? We can talk. It was so enjoyable. May we?" she urged.

"Of course. I will be back, Peg."

Then she was off down the path, her long white dress gradually disappearing into the trees. Daniel stood for a long time alone, his heart heavy with melancholy. He wanted to see her again. And he would, he vowed.

He then retraced his steps and retrieved the ledger. Hugging it to his chest, he decided not to tell his father he had stolen it. He would keep the secret of its possession to himself. After all, it was enough that Murdock did not have the ledger. He certainly would never tell Peg about it. She would be angry and consider him nothing more than a common thief, and he knew that destiny had brought them together this day and that nothing on earth would ever separate them again.

He secured the ledger under his arm and started off along the river, across a potato field, and down to the shore. He would still be home before the column of marchers returned to the farm. At the shore he looked back once, his entire being inexplicably alive.

Jarrod Murdock had not slept well, if he truly had slept at all. As far as he was concerned, there had been a death in the family. His ledger was missing. He turned the house inside out. He questioned his hired thugs, but all they could offer were blinking eyes and a sing-song Liverpool accent: "Never saw no bloody ledger, guv. Swear it, I do. Aye, swear it, no bloody book touched these 'ands, guv."

Mrs. Dawson, reduced to tears, sat trembling on a milking stool in the scullery with Murdock's wild eyes flaming at her, his breath hot in her face.

"God damn your kind, woman. Why did you leave this house when that mob descended yesterday? Why?"

"I went for berries, sir, wild blueberries they were. I was to fix them as a surprise for your dessert, sir."

"I'll surprise you, damn you. You will be looking elsewhere for work before this day is over." He paced the small room impatiently.

Even Margaret was not immune to the thickly arched eyebrows and stiff pointed finger.

"I was afraid and sad, Father. I was sad for you, and I went to hide near the river to be by myself."

"Sad for me? Where do you get ideas like that? You sound like your mother, always pining away. Don't be sad for me, Margaret; be angry with *them*. If they had their way, they would take everything I have worked for. I swear that one of them entered this house and stole my ledger. Do they think for one minute that they can force my hand? If they want war, then I shall give them one. I'm leaving now, and I order you to stay in this house. Do you understand me, Margaret? My Little Peg," he added with an attempt at tenderness when he saw her brown eyes cloud in fear.

"Yes, Father, I understand."

"Good. I will be back in time for an evening walk."

His boots thudded ponderously across the floor, and he was gone out the front door and to a waiting horse, the reins held by one of the two Liverpool men. "Come," he said grimly, "we shall ride hard. I have things to do this day."

The McMahon farm was a blur of activity. It was evident that the march to Murdock's had tied the knot of camaraderie even tighter.

"A good loyal friend and Irishman—an Aran Island man—once told me no man should starve if God was good enough to plop him on a croft by the sea. It was a good lesson. We will live on fish and cabbage until Jarrod Murdock gives in or—" Brendan looked at Reilly and Dalton and shook his head solemnly, as fantasy reluctantly conceded to truth.

"Or *what*, McMahon?"

"Or he will *not* give in, and he will send to England for men to work his fields."

"But would they come if they knew there could be trouble?"

"That kind of hooligan would be ready for any sort of trouble, you can bet your lobster traps on that, Reilly."

"We have the militia; that is why they are here, to defend the islanders."

"Have you lost your senses, Reilly?" Dalton's red face glowered. "Where did ye ever see an army take sides with the likes of us?"

"Their captain is English," Brendan asserted. "I expect he is a good soldier, but I am not certain I trust him. Of course, I don't think he trusts me either. I believe he thinks I helped Dennis Hurley escape, and we know that certainly isn't true." Brendan chuckled, his blue eyes glistening, and they chuckled with him.

"Who knows?" Dalton added grimly. "Maybe Dennis was luckier than any of us. I hear tell the Micmacs helped build him a good solid cabin over on Lennox Island and he's settled in like an Indian."

"He's still a wanted man. Still a criminal on the run. Don't you ever forget that, Mick Dalton. No. We do not look for violence, but we will fight here and in the Assembly for what is our right. Mark me. We will do what we must to save our land."

The day had been mild, but now it seemed even milder, with almost a sudden balm soothing the water. Simultaneously the men held their heads high, meditatively scanning the sky. Shadows stretched like long black fingers across the tops of the waves. The ocean turned strangely calm. The water was slick, as though oozing with kerosene, and a giant hand reached up and eclipsed the sun, only to release it later.

"The day has changed," Dalton said, sniffing the salt air.

"Aye, it doesn't look good. Come let's get the women and children burrowed in their lean-tos, there's a storm blacking up out there. Look at that barquentine. There's a keen captain for you, putting out to sea. He'll be better off out there if a gale blows around the North Cape. I've seen a ship or two smashed up on those rocks."

The sun still shone, but its brilliance was now smudged with shadows into a twilight copper. Indeed, it was more the color of dusk than of midmorning.

"It's too damn quiet. Let's get back to the house." Brendan's voice had an edge to it. "I have a feeling we may be in for a little more than a summer squall."

The sun continued to shine, but drops of rain as large as duck eggs fell heavily along the beach. As they mounted the cape, the sun was snuffed out by the squeeze of a giant black cloud, and the wind picked up, slashing rain pellets through the sharp rubbery grass. By the time they reached the house the seas were rocking and a gale force wind wound around the corner of the North Cape and howled wolflike through the pounding surf.

"Hurry and get inside, Brendan. You'll be blown away." Mary ushered them into the kitchen, where the fireplace pot bubbled on a low flame.

"God, woman, it's as hot as hell itself in here. Were you expecting a snowstorm?" Brendan shook his head at his wife in mock disgust as the others laughed.

"Oh, be gone with your blatherin'. Sure you make more noise than a henhouse."

"Oh, I do now. Well, I'll show you, Mary McMahon." He made a pretense of diving for her, and the kitchen exploded in laughter just as Peter, looking extremely upset, pushed his way into the room.

"Father, three riders are approaching, and they are traveling at a gallop. I think one is Jarrod Murdock."

"Murdock? This is a surprise visit, is it not?"

Brendan stepped quickly through the narrow passage past the parlor, which was crowded with evicted farmers and homeless immigrants all sheltering from the storm. The word spread quickly, and the hush that fell over the house was rivaled only by the strange calm that swept in from the sea and hovered over the silent land.

Murdock reined up below the porch but made no move to dismount. The rain fell heavily, and the sky had turned crow black.

"What brings you out on a day like this, Murdock?" Brendan was guarded but hopeful that yesterday's talk had pierced his thick, stubborn skull.

"You know why I'm here, McMahon." The scowl was as black as the sky, and the voice truculent and full of hate.

Brendan's eyes narrowed as he came to the top step. "No, Murdock, I do not. Speak your piece."

"I repeat, you know why I am here. I want it back."

"You want it back? You want what back?" Brendan turned to the quiet group that had followed him outside and shrugged, a puzzled look on his face.

"I am no fool, McMahon. Do not treat me lightly. I will destroy all of you." He shifted in his saddle and glanced at his two riders, who cradled their rifles across their laps.

"Murdock, you must have been struck by the light of a full moon. You are talking in riddles. Speak up! What is it you want from humble farming folk who have so little to offer? Especially to a man of your means."

Yesterday they had been on Murdock's land, and he had held the high ground; but now it was McMahon land, and Brendan straddled the top step defiantly.

"Damn you, McMahon, I want my ledger back. That is personal property, and you are thieves, all of you. I will take it by force if need be."

Brendan conceded the top step in anger.

"We know nothing of your bloody ledger, Murdock, although I doubt there is a man or woman among us who will shed a tear for its loss. But I will tell you straight. Never again cross my field talking of violence or we will return your violence a hundredfold. Mark me. And mark me well."

The words were hissed through tightly clenched teeth, and Brendan's blue eyes sparked with flame. The onlookers waited for the McMahon temper to erupt and for Brendan to tear the thick-bodied Murdock from his saddle. But as Murdock glared back, the sky overturned and poured itself free in a wild wind sweep of rain that slapped and buffeted fiercely. The frightened horses reared from the sudden, violent attack as the snapping crackle of blinding yellow streaks of lightning that danced in frenetic movement across the open meadow were followed by the booming distant thunder.

"Come inside and talk, out of this weather, Murdock, before you're blown off your horse," Brendan shouted above the din of the storm.

"I wouldn't take refuge under your roof if I were dying of exposure, McMahon." The rain swished and swirled, turning the chestnut rump of Murdock's horse in a half circle.

"You're a bloody stubborn man, Murdock."

"I'll be back, McMahon, and the next time I'll have Captain Eliot and the militia." A gold ribbon of lightning unwound in snapping staccato streamers of flashing sparks, and a new and more thunderous boom resounded, terrifying the horses to impetuous flight across the dooryard. After reining in and halting his formidable beast, Murdock rose to full height in the saddle, one hand holding firmly to the reins, the other raised in defiance to the McMahon. "I will be back," he roared through the gusting, pelting hail of rain. "I will be back."

Brendan watched him gallop after the fleeing horses of his hired men as the thunder and lightning boomed and flashed all around them.

"He looked like a man gone mad," Reilly mumbled as Brendan ducked back onto the porch, his black, curly hair spiky and wild from rain and wind .

"What did he mean about the ledger?"

"It's gone, and he blames us. Jarrod Murdock lives for that book, and everybody knows it. Anybody who harbors ill feeling for Murdock could have stolen it. And there are plenty who hate him."

The wind picked up and tore in a banshee shriek across the strait, ripping through the marsh grass like an invisible scythe and banged and thumped against the wooden house.

The porch, the parlor, the kitchen all were buzzing with Murdock's unexpected visit. Mary stood poised with a tin of hot tea to her lips, the windows rattling behind her.

"What did he want?" Peter asked his father. "Is he willing to bargain?"

"No. He is not. He is a very stubborn man. He thinks we stole his bloody ledger. How in God's name does he figure that?"

Daniel, sitting in the corner of the crowded kitchen, felt his face flame with guilt.

"What would anyone want with his ledger?" Peter questioned.

"Well," Brendan answered, taking a cup of tea from Mary, "it's no secret that Murdock regards that book as most of us regard the Holy Bible. And there are entries made that hold many a farmer in debt. He may have trouble collecting his debts now. Surely he does not have every one memorized. Once he misquotes a figure to a farmer, the farmer will know Murdock's at a disadvantage."

"And then what, Father?" Peter was growing up, and Brendan was happy to see him interested in the problems of the adult world.

"Then, if Murdock is wrong, because each farmer will know to the penny what he owes, that man can argue that the debt is way off and Murdock had best settle for such-and-such or go to a court of law."

"Is he very upset, Father?" Daniel asked solemnly from his corner hideaway.

"I would say he is fit to be tied, Daniel."

"Well, he deserves the misery he is suffering, the way he has treated these people." Mary was adamant, and her high cheekbones indented with anger as she inhaled quickly. Mary was tired, and her temper was quick. Her house was not her own anymore. At first she had been happy to welcome her neighbors, and then the new immigrants, but as day wore into day and her kitchen was still overrun, the fields overloaded, she felt the world of her family, the world of privacy, slipping away. And now this miserable storm had driven them all inside.

Brendan could read the signs of fatigue and anger in the black circles under her eyes, but he was so caught up in this turmoil with Murdock that he did not read the proper message in those circles.

Night fell, and outside, the wind shrieked like some animal gone wild. The rain cut and slashed in a stinging attack that penetrated the cracks and roof lines of the house.

"Jesus, Mary, and Joseph," Mary cursed from her bed, "will that bloody rain never cease?"

Brendan, lying beside her in the brass bed, his naked chest still heaving in frustration at Murdock's visit, barely heard her cursing as he pondered the meaning of the stolen ledger. He cared nothing for Murdock's loss, but it was undeniably a stroke of good fortune for the tenant farmers. It was something they could fight him with. They would make him prove every shilling owed. Brendan's mind raced along with his heart. He hated Murdock. Nothing would please him more than to break Murdock in half, but that was not the way to win this war.

"I'm speaking to you. Have you lost your hearing, for the love of God?" Mary squirmed into her pillow as a new and more violent wind shook the crossed oak rafters of the house.

"What? What are you saying to me?" He sat up and rested on his elbow. "What's wrong with you, Mary? I noticed your angry face downstairs. What is it? Have I done something?" He reached out and touched her shoulder, and she tensed at his touch. "What is it, woman? What's buzzing around in your bloody bonnet?"

She bolted up in the bed, her eyes fiery in the darkness. "I will tell you what's buzzing around in my bloody bonnet," she repeated with crisp emphasis. "I want my house to be the home it used to be before you went sailing off on your bloody errand of mercy."

"Oh, so that's it. Have you no charity in your soul, woman?"

He could feel her glaring eyes angry and wide, and when she answered, her words were bitter but well measured. "I can share anything I have to with my neighbors and countrymen. I can and I do while you walk among them like some reigning monarch and they do all but fall at your feet. Well, listen to me, Brendan McMahon, this island has no kings."

"And no queens," he rasped back.

"Aye. And no bloody queens either. You are right about that. I work hard as any woman on this stretch of Godforsaken earth. I bow to none. Charity! Charity can go to blazes. I do what I have to, but I do not have to like it."

"Maybe you should have stayed in Massachusetts and married your mill owner friend. I'm sure you would have fit in just fine with all those pale Yankee women. That is, if your Channing Evans would have married an Irish farm girl."

His words cut deep, and her voice rose sharply. "Channing Evans happened years ago. Are you so sick with jealousy that you cannot forget that part of my life?"

"I can forget, but I cannot but notice how you treat the other women. You cook and you feed, but your heart is not in it. Where is your heart, Mary? Is it with us?"

"My heart is with my family, Brendan McMahon, though I would rather live in Boston or even Charlottetown than on a farm that sits between two seas. Make no mistake about that."

He sighed deeply. "Well, I am sorry, Mary Roark, but this is the only home I can give you and the only life I can offer. Take it, or you can bloody well leave it."

He was shouting now, and James, asleep in the trundle bed under the wet and creaking eaves, sat up, whimpering, "Is something wrong, Mother?"

"No, my son, go back to sleep, your father has had a bad dream."

"Goodnight, Mother."

Brendan threw off the sheets and dressed quickly.

Mary lay back against the pillow, saying nothing. She wanted to say how silly it all was, how tired she felt, how she just wanted to be alone with her family, and was that so much to ask? She wanted to ask him to hold her and to be gentle and soothing and affectionate. But her pride, her thick Irish pride, prompted only silence, and he left the room, bumping into a bureau and cursing loudly.

"Please, Father, do not curse. It is a sin."

Brendan reddened at the sound of his son's admonition, and he stammered his apologies, shutting the door softly behind him.

Throughout the night the storm swelled and rushed. The wind gathered, throwing itself full force against the house, and at first Brendan, lying stiff and restless in the attic room and still seething in his anger, thought the continual thumping was the great wind itself until he rose, stepped awkwardly around the sleeping bodies, and stumbled down the stairs in the direction of the sound.

Pulling open the door to the side porch and bracing himself at the same time against the wind, he peered around and made out the huddled figure of a dripping Patenaude.

"Patenaude, what in blazes are you doing out in weather like this?" The gray beginnings of dawn strained on the rain-streaked horizon.

"Brendan, there is much trouble. A ship makes for our beach. I fear many sailors are already lost. It gets so close only to be blown back out. Strong arms and backs are needed. Come."

Brendan pulled the waterlogged Micmac inside and began rousing the others, whispering softly to them not to disturb the women and children. Upstairs he peered into the tranquil faces of his sons and woke only Peter. Daniel slept on his back, a thin blanket covering him.

His face was soft, pink-cheeked, and he slept so peacefully he seemed to be in a world of pure and gentle thoughts.

James, the youngest, lay with his round ball of a little boy's body curled fetally, rosary beads twisted around his fingers like twine. Our priest to be surely, Brendan thought. He straightened and turned to see Mary sitting up in the bed, her chemise loose around her full breasts. He felt a sudden rush of blood shoot to his heart and the warm desire to take her in his arms; instead he nodded and said, "There's a ship in trouble off our shore. We will do what we can. I'm taking Peter."

She sat up, rigid now, her eyes sharp and accusing. Her black hair, streaked in places with gray, fell in a long fan over her bare shoulders. "Leave my son here. His place is with his mother, not on one of your mad adventures."

"He comes with me. He is my son, too, and his place is with the men of this county. No harm will come to him. He is a man now and capable of performing the duties of a man. That will be the end of it. No more talk. There has been too much talk this night."

"I am ready, Father." Peter stood framed in the doorway. His shoulders were wide, and his body was long like his father's, but not yet filled out. His face was tight and grim, especially around the mouth. He had heard the sharpness in their voices, and it troubled him. They were a close family, and any dispute upset all of them.

"Aye, we must go." Brendan turned and brushed past his son. "Hurry now, say good-bye to your mother."

Mary brought the covers modestly to her shoulders as Peter bent and kissed her forehead. "Do not be angry, Mother. I am a man now, and there are things a man must do."

"Yes, I know." She sighed. "I have seen too many men do things they must do only because they *are* men. It will never be any different. God go with you, my son. Take good care of your father." She smiled and hugged him with one bare arm extended as the other hand gripped the blanket firmly.

When he was gone, she went to the window and looked out on the hellish, blowing, rain-swept morning. The rain was like nails pounding against the glass, and only when a gust blew the wetness in a great gray sheet, clearing her view for a few moments, could she see the black, huddling figures of Brendan, Peter, and the others against the gray horizon. They sloshed through the running clay, around puddles and ditches of blood red water that were like rivers fingering throughout the fields.

Beyond the beach she could see the black hulk of a ship tossing like a bobbin in the gale-driven waves. She left the window and dressed quickly, fear and anxiety choking her. "Please God protect my husband and my son. Forgive me for my temper and my tongue."

The barque, its name indiscernible behind the thick curtain of rain, rose and then fell below a giant wave two hundred yards from shore only to appear again, lifted, it seemed, by an unseen hand below the boiling surface.

The wind continued its insane shriek, like the ancient sirens of a myth, as Brendan shouted above its whine, "They are going to have to get a line to us so we can secure it and try to pull her in."

"But how can we get close enough to yell to them? They will never hear us over this wind." Patenaude even then was cupping his hands over his mouth to create a horn.

"We have to keep them away from the chain of rocks. It's a miracle they haven't hit yet. Can you make out anyone on deck?"

Reilly screamed back, "Aye, I have owl eyes. I can see two figures near the mizzen. There, see, no, it's gone below the wave now. Wait. Ah, there now. They see us."

"Aye," Brendan noted, "they're waving. There are two of them anyway. Patenaude, you say some have already drowned?"

"Yes, Brendan, they tried to swim for shore, but they did not get far. They were swept out to sea. We saw them from the hill."

"All right, follow me. Reilly, Dalton, Ready, come. Patenaude, you stay on the beach until we wave you over. Too many on the rocks would be dangerous."

"Father, I want to come, too." Peter stepped forward, his sweater soaked through and already weighing him down.

"No, Peter, you stay with the others. There will be plenty to do once we get a line."

The boy stepped back and turned his eyes to the sea, trying to hide his disappointment.

Brendan and the others slogged along the muddy beach, which was strewn with dead fish and the long black rubbery stalks of seaweed. Even the jagged, usually clear rocks held a slimy surface of Irish moss and weed. The men, crouched Indian-fashion, slowly made their way out to the point. They were now within shouting distance and could make out the name of the ship—*O Diabo*, LISBOA. One man was lashed to the mast, while two others held onto the windlass.

Brendan stood, feet planted firmly between the crevices of rock, as the waves smashed and rolled against the jetties.

"Throw us a line," he shouted. "Throw a line." He stretched his hands out to signify rope, afraid they would not understand. At first they remained frozen in position as another wave roared and smashed into the ship. She rose on the tide and was once again brought in closer to shore. Brendan could make out the dark skins and frightened eyes of the two sailors, and he motioned for them to hurry. One of them nodded and relinquished his place at the windlass to go aft. He reached for a line of coiled thick hemp, stretched it out, tied a weight to the end. Then he curled it in a wide arc above his head and hurled it in the direction of the jetty. It fell short by several yards and then the ship lifted again as the Portuguese seaman clung to the railing to avoid being dumped over the side.

Brendan wasted no time as he tied a line around his waist, handed the end to Dalton, and plunged into the seething surf. He stroked against the mountainous waves; his first attempts were futile, and he was driven back against the rocks. But as the tide slipped past, the sea calmed long enough for him to grab the line. His arms were like lead weights as he began the swim back to the rocks. Just then another wave mounted and wrapped itself around him, smashing him head over heels below the surface.

Peter, having watched from the shore, was already racing across the dangerous slime-backed rocks, and when Brendan was engulfed in the wave, he dived straight into the thundering surf and came up by his father's side. Brendan's body was entangled in the rope, and his eyes were fixed strangely in his head. He had swallowed a good measure of water and was heaving it up as he began to sink again beneath the waves. Peter cradled his father's head in the crook of his arm and managed to gain the rocks before a new watery onslaught made its surge.

Hands reached and pulled both father and son to safety. Peter lay there gulping for breath, while Brendan choked and gagged and slowly gained his strength. Dalton, meanwhile, summoned the others to begin hauling the barque ashore. They jumped down into the sand, guiding her away from the treacherous rocks, and began their tug-of-war with the ocean.

O Diabo steadily gave under the strength of the islanders, and the momentum of their cadence was slowly bringing her to when suddenly a black, ugly hill of water began to pitch, rise, and roll far out in the Strait. It rose to an incredible height and folded over the ship like a watery shroud, totally eclipsing the helpless craft. The islanders watched the wave fall and crack against the ship and then sweep parallel to the beach. When it passed and the barque was visible again, the two sailors were gone. One of them, driven in by the tide, washed up at their feet. The other sailor was nowhere to be seen. Ready lifted the man from the waves and carried him to the shelter of the cape, but even as he placed him under the sandy canopy of the dune, he knew the sailor was dead.

When the islanders had finally succeeded in bringing *O Diabo* to shore, they lashed her down and sat back for a moment's rest, studying the rigging, the black wooden hull, and the tall, sturdy mast. Then they rose and climbed over the sides.

Reilly was the first on board, and those behind him heard his startled words: "Jesus, Mary, and Joseph."

"What is it, Reilly?" Dalton shouted as he joined his friend.

"Oh, Christ, look at that. This is the devil's own ship, make no mistake about that." There before them was a man tied to the main mast, his bare chest rutted and torn in deep red welts, the victim of an intense and cruel whipping. The man's once ebony face was twisted in pain and now gray in death.

Patenaude cut him down as the others inspected the vessel. "They all have been victims of the sea," Brendan reported simply.

Peter gazed at the whipped sailor, lying lifeless on the wooden deck thousands of miles from home and family, and then up into his father's eyes. There was no need for either of them to say anything.

The rain continued its steady beat against their oilskins and the wind howled, but they went grimly about the task of burying the dead on the bluff overlooking the brutal sea.

Standing around the wood stove, drying off and drinking piping hot mugs of tea, the islanders recounted again and again the story of Brendan's rescue by his undaunted son.

"The McMahon is losing his grip. He's not the strong man he thought he was." Dalton slashed away with his sharp tongue.

"Aye," Reilly joined in quickly. "All it takes is one little wave to topple the man. Well, Mary, you can count your blessings, you have a strong son to aid you as you get along in life."

They all roared and thumped Peter's thin back while he, flushed from this new and sudden adulation, kept looking to his father for approval. Brendan, as proud as any man could be, smiled and roared his respect for a son grown to manhood.

Not to be outdone by the quick verbal shots of his neighbors, Brendan announced that while the rest of them stood on the rocks, struck dumb with ignorance and cowardice, another equally strong McMahon dived into the waves to rescue his drowning father. Brendan's laughter could be heard above the wind that seemed finally to be blowing itself out.

"Oh, the devil you say."

"Sure, it wasn't that way at all, at all."

But that is how the story was told and retold that day and in future years.

As the day wound down, it fell to Brendan to make the announcement that had at its core the disposition of the ship that had been presented to them only half a day before.

"Come, everyone, we are going down to the ship. Dress warmly, you young ones, there is still a rain." He rifled through the cabinet in the parlor room and brought forth a large stone jug. "I think this is appropriate for this day."

Then everyone followed the two McMahons, son and father, down to the beach.

Mary, thankful to God to have them back, walked with the others, while Isabella, who had arrived soon after the storm abated, held firmly to Abigail's hand. James and Daniel joined the other young people in splashing through the many small rivers that flooded beach and field. Gabriella, her skirt billowing, walked with Cathleen and Sean.

In front of the beached barque, her tattered sails thumping and clapping in the wind, Brendan broke out the poteen, but before he passed it around, he declared, "We take possession of this unfortunate vessel with sincere and respectful memory of her crew. We claim her as salvage, but first we will free her from the evil name that brought her so much ill fate and rename her the *Saint Peter* in memory of the first bishop of Christ and the young man who showed so much courage this day. I salute my brave son Peter. *Sláinte*." And with those few words Brendan drew a long, hard draft on the jug and passed it along. Out on the Strait there was a calm ripple to the waves and clouds raced across the sky, which was finally turning from gray to blue.

"With new timber and a few days' labor she will be able to take to the seas again," Dalton said.

"Aye," they agreed.

"But then what?" Reilly asked. "What do we do with her?"

"Do with her?" Angus MacHattie, newly arrived on the scene, glowered at Reilly. "The trouble with you Irish is you know nothing about business. The Lord God sails into your arms on a Portuguese barque, making a gift of it to you, and you ask, 'What do we do with her?' Damn it, man, you scavengers who brought her in have a share in her. Sail her to Europe. Make her work for you." He spit in the red muck in disgust. "Irish! Bah!"

Brendan laughed, but he knew the crafty Scotsman was giving them good counsel. "Angus is right. Yesterday some of you wondered if you would ever farm again. Well, just possibly you may not. Some of you will be sailors, and I have a feeling the *Saint Peter* may just be the beginning for many of us. Join hands, lads, God has been good to us this day."

"Hip, hip, hooray."

"Hip, hip, hooray."

"Hip, hip, hooray," they shouted jubilantly.

The fury of the storm that had brought the good fortune of an abandoned, albeit ill-fated ship to the red shores of Tignish was not fully realized until three days later, when the restless and battered sea spit up its ravaged prey on the breakwater off Malpeque Bay.

Two fully loaded barquentines, their holds bulging with Liverpool-bound timber from the forests of Prince Edward Island, were tossed like sticks against the treacherous rocks and smashed to pieces, their remnants blown seaward by the anger and passion of the devil winds. Many islanders were lost in the erupting and volcanic surf.

Jarrod Murdock was the owner of both vessels. When word reached him, he was penning a letter to his son in West Devon, announcing his need of a work force of farmers: "good strong men for good hard work—a just wage for honest labor and a solid roof overhead." He dismissed the messenger, who stood in fear before him, and stalked to the window, to glare at the ocean. Somewhere out there floated thousands of pounds sterling of Murdock property. And below the house, two more half-constructed craft, victims also of the storm, were being hoisted for repair before the work of building them could continue.

The day was dark, hanging with the gloom of low gray clouds. He reached for the letter and tore it into little pieces with short, rapid movements. What with this latest financial setback, he could not afford a new work force, part of whose compensation would be a colonization and transportation wage. No, he must tighten the purse strings instead of loosening them.

"God damn them. Those miserable Irish bastards. They've left my fields to dust, they've stolen my ledger, and now I have *this* burden thrust at me." He smashed his right fist into the cupped palm of his left hand, the sick slapping sound of flesh against flesh reverberating in the still room. He knew he would have to swallow his pride and talk to McMahon. But McMahon would not have it all. There must be a deal, their jobs and cottages in return for his ledger. He must have the ledger, and then those bastards would pay every shilling owed.

Brendan McMahon approached the wide porch that wound itself in summer shade around the entire house at Port Loyal.

He had come alone as requested. Murdock had been definite about that. And the McMahon, for a brief moment, had been tempted to respond by summoning the arrogant Murdock to *him*. But he thought better of it. Too many things were going well. The ship, the *Saint Peter*, was already under steady and enthusiastic repair. His son Peter had emerged as a respected islander among his peers, and even Mary, mercurial as usual, had given him the favors that only she could give.

So it was a buoyant McMahon who faced the scowling black-frocked Murdock.

Murdock did not invite him inside, nor did he offer him drink to slake his thirst after the dusty ride, even though both of these courtesies were island tradition.

Murdock stood belligerently, feet apart as though he were straddling a ditch. His heavy eyebrows rose like black brushes, and his firm jaw jutted out, his lips clamped tightly together in a hard, straight line. His mouth scarcely moved when he spoke. "You know why I sent for you, McMahon?"

"You did not send for *me*, Murdock. *I* chose to come," Brendan countered as he sat on the white railing. "Get on with it. I am a busy man these days. All of us up west are busy." He smiled.

The black brushes arched as though Murdock were about to ask how croftless farmers could be busy at anything these days. Instead, he made his point, firmly and sharply. "Your farmers can come back to work. This nonsense is helping neither them nor me."

"First off, they are not *my* farmers, as you put it. The people up west are free. And second, I am not sure how many families I can guarantee will want to come back."

"Do not waste my time with foolish banter, McMahon. What is it you want?"

It was an enviable position, Brendan thought, because that was just the point: He did not want anything. His heart soared with a new and brighter confidence than he had known in months. The sick and dying Irish, the strained relations at home, and his feelings of failure in the Assembly suddenly drifted away with the soft summer breeze that ruffled through the surrounding birch.

"You see, Murdock, many of us have other interests these days." McMahon's voice had a playful lilt to it. "So I am not sure how many farmers want to come back and work your fields."

"Interests? What other interests could immigrant farmers have except the potato and the turnip?"

"Look, Murdock, in your message you said you wanted to make

a deal. I see no need for deals, but what did you have in mind? I owe it to them"—and he nodded west—"to report all that has taken place here."

"McMahon, I want my ledger back. It's no secret that it contains all the records of my business dealings. I was stupid." Murdock looked down, thought a moment, then rephrased it. "I was careless. I will never be as careless again. But I am prepared to grant all those who left me without good notice a roof and land to work. What more do they want?"

"Some may want just that, Murdock, to be sure. As for your ledger, may God strike me dead, I do not know where it is any more than you do."

"God damn it, McMahon. I know one of your number stole it from my house the day you tracked in here like a pack of wild dogs." Again his mouth barely opened as his words rushed in a viper's hiss.

"Be careful, Murdock. We do not need you; you need us. It will serve you better to remember that. You and your dying farms. I will tell them throughout the county they can come back. The wages and the conditions will remain the same, but I expect they will be paid for the indecent hardship you have put them through."

"What? Pay them for not working? Damn it, McMahon, you must be crazy. That is the most absurd idea I've ever heard."

"Look, Murdock, you're the one who sent them packing, never giving them a chance to show what they could do. You drove them off. Now you can pay for it. Take it or leave it. We will not starve *now.*" The "now" had an ominous ring to it, and Murdock suffered over its meaning; but he kept the question deep and silently burning inside. He had to have the farmers back; even now the fields were fallow and choked with weeds and growth. It would require long hours to prepare for August harvest.

"Very well, McMahon, very well. Fate has dealt me a severe blow, but I shall have the upper hand again. Fate might visit you the next time. And when that happens, I will be there to collect. Send them back. The conditions will be worked out here at Port Loyal. But I do not want them on my immediate property. They can gather at the boatyard on the river. That is all I have to say in the matter. And I assure you I will not rest until I find that ledger." He turned on his heel and disappeared into the cool darkness of the shaded house.

It had worked out well. Most of the homeless were farm people with earth and root pumping through their blood. And only a handful had a desire to be seafaring men. But, oh, those who did! Couldn't they see the rewards of setting sail for England and the American States with a full belly of cargo waiting to be dumped on foreign wharves?

Aye, there was new air, fresh and clean, blowing through Canada, and the thought of Digger Shanley, a shrewd businessman who would see a rare opportunity in working with his own, urged Brendan through the birch grove and homeward.

CHAPTER XXV

SNOWS DRIFTED AND blew over the island in icy, crystal gusts, closing the road to Summerside and disappointing Mary. She peered from the window of her bedroom and saw only the blur of blowing white fur across the bay. "He won't be coming today. Not even the iceboats would dare passage from Nova Scotia," Mary said, more to herself than to Cathleen, who was dusting the oak banister of the staircase.

"Did you say something, Mary?"

Mary let the curtain fall into place and came out onto the top step. "No, I was just talking to myself. I was just saying, 'I do not think Peter will be joining us for Christmas Eve.' The snow must surely have shut down the ferry from the mainland. And this such a special Christmas, the last we shall probably spend together."

"Oh, now, you're sounding like the melancholy Irish, Mary," Cathleen said chidingly, and looked down at her sister-in-law. Mary's raven hair still shone in the afternoon light, but there was more gray these past years, even though life had become so much easier since they had left Tignish and the old Wallace farm. Gabriella and Edward and the six-year-old Kate lived there now.

"It's this house. It's big and sprawling. I never should have allowed Brendan to build it. It will be drafty and empty in a few years, and we will be getting lost in it."

"You know you love this house, Mary McMahon. You're just upset because you see your family going off in different directions."

"And where is my family going to all of a sudden?" Brendan appeared below, stamping snow from his boots, his black greatcoat holding epaulets of snow and his ruddy face redder still from the wintry blasts of his walk back from the deserted harbor.

"Oh, every which way. I know I sound ungrateful, Brendan," Mary said as she descended the stairs, Cathleen dusting silently behind her, "but this will be such a sad Christmas Eve. Peter not joining us and James returning to the seminary in the New Year and Gabriella caught up in Tignish under a blizzard. Where's Daniel? Is he with you?" She joined him on the landing and helped him off with his coat. "You look handsome in your frock, Mr. McMahon."

When he leaned down and kissed her, her blue eyes still held a youthful sparkle. "Did I hear you berating Brendan's barque?" he roared, holding her tightly. "Merry Christmas, my lovely Mary."

In the half dozen years since the *St. Peter* was christened in the frothing, foaming surf of Tignish, Brendan, in partnership with Digger Shanley, had added two more barquentines to the Tignish Cooperative, formed with shareholders Dalton, Reilly, Ready, and any of those original farmers who chose sea instead of soil.

As with all growth, there came change. The move to Summerside, ambiguous as it was for the McMahons, sadly bidding goodbye to the farm, the cherished fields, the windswept strait, and the neighboring Profitt capes, and yet happily greeting the new house that Brendan had built—"like a ship," he said more than once—was a necessary one. Summerside, not as teeming as Charlottetown, was nevertheless bursting with commercial potential in an age of sea travel. Prince Edward Island ships were no longer a rarity in foreign ports.

"Brendan's barque," he said in the old brogue, "bad cess to the jealous bastards."

"Now, Brendan, it is Christmas Eve, and not a time for cursing. There are always those who will be envious. We have worked hard for this lovely home. I'm just melancholic, Cathleen is right."

"Hello up there. How is my sister on this eve of Christ's birth? Where is that nephew of mine, Cathleen? He is a fine lad but a wild one, always about."

"No wilder than his uncle," she replied, chuckling. "He's off with Liam. They took a stroll to the grange. Liam is getting a crew together for the New Year."

"Oh, they'll be sitting around fires for weeks if this weather doesn't change. The almanac says we are in for a bad spell."

Mary hung the wet coat up to dry by the fireplace and cleared her throat several times, but she did not speak.

"Well, what is it, woman? I know that sound means you have something to say." He stood on the great hooked rug that hugged the oak inlay of the polished and gleaming floor. His large hands rested on his hips. "Well," he repeated, "what does Mary Roark McMahon have on that pretty mind of hers?"

"Well, well, it's—it's really Cathleen who has something to say, Brendan. Cathleen, are you listening to this?"

"Yes, Mary, I am." Cathleen joined them in the parlor, the feather duster moving nervously in her fingers, signs of a blush coloring her oval face.

"Well, do we have a band of tinkers stealing tongues? Say it, Cathleen. Say what's on your mind. We have never been known to move from one foot to the other in this family."

"Liam has asked me to marry him, Brendan." She looked at him directly as a pile of snow shifted on the roof and then slid swiftly to the ground with a startling thud.

"Well," he said finally, "I thought that was the new husband falling off the roof."

"Oh, Brendan, I am so happy you approve." Cathleen came into his outstretched arms as tears spilled happily from her soft eyes.

"Approve? Who am I to approve or disapprove? But I do say Liam Malley is a fine, rugged Irishman even if he is County Clare. And God knows you deserve every bit of happiness you get. You are happy, are you not?"

"Oh yes, Brendan. I never ever thought I could be so happy again. Liam is such a wonderful man, and Sean looks up to him so."

"Liam has been a savior to all of us on the island. He has made an excellent sailor out of Peter and—"

Mary cocked her head in that familiar fashion of hers. "What is it, Brendan? What has startled you?"

He left them in the parlor, studying his departure with puzzled frowns as his voice trailed off. "I almost forgot." He opened the front door. The glass fan front was iced with snow, and it was not until the great door, with its snow-dusted brass knocker and speckled holly wreath, had swung all the way open that the snowman hunched against the blizzard turned and revealed the smile of Peter McMahon.

"Well, Father, did you forget me, or am I to be another Christmas ornament?"

"Come in here with you now, my boy. Your father is getting stupid in his old age. I got involved with those two women and forgot you were out there." His rough hands pulled the young man into the warmth of the foyer. "Here he is, Mary, your oldest boy back from the wilds of Nova Scotia."

Mary ran to her son and embraced him, snow and all, as he dripped all over her shirtwaist.

"Sure I met him down by the harbor, trudging through the drifts."

"How did you come to us this day, Peter? There was no ferry." She beamed with joy.

"I came from Cape Traverse to Tormentine, Mother, and you will be proud to know that I paid only half fare because I volunteered to pull Her Majesty's mail when we reached the mainland. But there is much snow down, and the harness was wet. I was happy to see that chore done. And what do you think of your son and his frugal ways, Mother? Have you not taught me well, eh?"

"Taught him too well, I'd say." Brendan smiled. "The next we know he'll be taking a wife with economy like that on his mind."

"Ach, the devil breathe fire on you," Mary said fiercely, "my son will not be rushing into marriage, sacrament though it is, bless us."

They all returned to the warmth of the parlor as Brendan urged Peter to tell the story of his first journey on behalf of the Tignish Cooperative.

"Well, go on lad, tell your mother and your aunt about your success. It was a good trip he had. Go on, tell it, Peter."

"Give the lad a chance to let his feet thaw out a bit, Brendan; sure he must be exhausted and cold. Cathleen, would you put the pot on for tea? Oh, bless you. Go on now, Peter. We are all ears to find out about your success."

"Well, of course, it was no great success; but I have seven signed contracts with trading posts from Halifax to Cape Breton. Furs and fox and timber, and we do not go in ballast. We go with potato and turnip. We make out both going and coming. Liverpool is crying for Nova Scotia fur and wool and timber. Yes"—he stopped to catch his breath and smile awkwardly—"I guess it was a great trip after all." At that the three of them howled, and Peter joined in.

"Well, I am proud of my son. Proud indeed. And now Cathleen has news for you, Peter. Go on, Cathleen. Is everyone shy in this house?" Mary prodded.

"Only I," Brendan put in, happy and proud, too.

"Sure you have never been shy in your life, Brendan McMahon."

"Now go on and let Peter be the first of the children to know. It's fitting since our dear Gabriella cannot be with us because of the storm."

Cathleen, her face more radiant than any of them had ever seen, went to Peter and put her hands on his shoulders. "Liam Malley has asked me to be his wife, Peter. Are you happy for your old battleax of an aunt?"

"Old battle—. Why, don't you ever say that about yourself; you are the finest aunt anyone ever had. And Liam Malley is a very lucky man. A very lucky man, indeed. Is he not, Mother?"

Cathleen stood back and looked at each one of them, the spilling tears salting the corners of her mouth. "I am such a fortunate woman. God has been good to me, giving me such a family. He has indeed given me a new life. I just want you to know I love you." And then she could not continue and raced from the room.

They sat for a moment deep in their thoughts, Mary smoothing the folds of her full black skirt, Peter shy at this entrance into the world of his parents, and Brendan, big-boned and square-jawed, finding it a little difficult to swallow for a moment. "Tell us more about your trip, Peter McMahon. Tell us the terms of the contracts," he said, finally, breaking the silence.

"Well, Father, I did as you instructed. I stayed away from the more successful merchants because, as you suggested, they are probably booked up with larger shipping companies. I chose carefully among the smaller firms. And they were very open and friendly. Some have been wanting to sell to foreign ports, but they were afraid they couldn't afford the fee. I explained that our fee would be two percent of each consignment, and they were amazed. The big shipping companies are charging eighteen percent! Can you imagine, Mother, eighteen percent!"

Mary smiled approvingly when he continued, his big eyes blue and flashing as the excitement of his story mounted. "I was honest, Father. I told them we were a small company. To each I mentioned Mr. Shanley."

"Did they know him? Did they know Digger?" Brendan leaned his large frame against the hard pine mantel.

"Most did, Father. Mr. Shanley has a very fine reputation as a good businessman and an honest one."

"Aye. He has given the Irish a good name in Canada, Mary. Digger is one of a kind, God bless him. So you had no problems then. Fine, lad. And what of the shipping dates?" Brendan had worried over this part of it because he knew he would meet with opposition from his wife. But she had to be told, and this was as good a time as any. He waited for his son's answer, knowing the storm inside the house would far outdo the one that blew and drifted without.

"Yes, Father. That, too, met with their approval, although they were surprised at first that we would dare a crossing in winter. But they were anxious to get to the English markets. They said if we had the courage to cross, they would have the courage to ship with us."

Mary sat up, rigid now, her firm jaw raised in a question and the delft blue of her eyes penetrating. "What is this crossing in winter? What are you both saying? What madness has brought this about?" She looked from one to the other, shadows of black forming over the blue.

Brendan made a mock effort at warming his hands over the crackling fruitwood fire. "It will be all right. There is no danger," he said to the flames that licked and spit at the wood.

"No danger? No danger sailing a ship through winter waters? Are you both insane? It is not as though you are natural sailors. You are both of the soil, not the sea. No, I will not permit my son to set sail until the waters are calm."

Brendan turned to gaze into those piercing, fiery eyes. "Are the seas ever calm? Did you not come to Boston from Galway in June, and did you not run into mountainous seas? Did we not salvage the *Saint Peter* from a *summer* storm? Do not tell me you will not permit my son to sail in winter. We have built up this business in a few short years, but our business has been limited. Now we are competing with Jarrod Murdock and the other islanders who have already discovered a whole world of commerce out there." He raised his mighty hand and pointed in the direction of the snow-blown harbor.

She held his gaze. "When we had nothing. we were a tight, little family, and now we are scattering like wild birds to the corners of the globe. Do you honestly believe that our son is sailor enough to guide a ship through dangerous waters." She emphasized "our" as Brendan winced at the intended sarcasm. Her tongue could be a formidable weapon when anger stirred her.

"Listen to me, Mary, we have been over this before. Liam is still the master of the *St. Peter*. And no finer captain ever stood on the deck of a ship."

"Oh, I know that only too well. And now he will be going off, leaving a wife and stepson behind. Is there no end to good-byes? And what if this voyage proves successful? Will you not cram the two other ships full of goods and follow the *Saint. Peter*?"

"Of course we will. And *our son* will be captain of one of them, and if we can ever wake Daniel from his daydreams, we will make a sailing man of him, too. Look, Mary, the past years have been good to us. We have worked and we have prospered. You live in the finest home in Summerside, and you want for nothing. Is there no pleasing you, woman?"

"I want a family that used to be close; *that* pleases me."

"Mary, you are the last person to talk of families traveling to opposite ends of the globe. What did you do but leave your family in Oranmore never to see them again?"

"I left to make a better life for myself, so that there would never be reason for separation again. How dare you use that as an argument against me? What was I to do? Stay in Ireland and starve? I wanted more out of life than an early grave. And I want more out of life than an early grave for my son—a watery one, I might add. You talk of Daniel. Next, you will put Abigail on board to cook the meals."

"Ach, woman, you are impossible. A man must do what a man must do!"

"Yes, and a woman must remain at home and wait in silence for him to do it."

"Yes. Yes, damn it, you have that part of it right." He slammed his first on the mantel.

Peter went to put his arm around his mother's shoulders. "Mother, you are right and Father is right. We are a family. And we are a family on the move. We are building something for all of us. And we are not foolhardy. We are not putting out to sea if the weather is bad. We will wait for fair skies, but then we shall be off. Please, Mother, trust me, I am your son. Have you ever known me to be wild and irresponsible?"

She was silent for a moment.

"Well, have you? Have you, Mother?"

"No. No, I have never known you to be irresponsible, my son. You are a fine son."

"Good then. Come, it's Christmas Eve. Let's make it the best we've ever had. Please don't argue on this night. Father?"

"The lad is right, Mary. It is Christmas Eve. What do you say to that?"

"I say simply that I love my children, and I pray God will always protect them."

"And what about your husband, Mary Roark? Do you not love him, eh?" He held out his arms, but she did not go to him. Instead, she extended her arms and waited for him to come to her. And when he did, he said, "Jesus, woman, but you are a proud one."

Throughout the house wafted the tantalizing aroma of roast goose and bubbling brown gravy, which Cathleen now laid out on the table, already heaped with potatoes, turnips, nutmeg, molasses cakes and blueberry pies and home-baked cookies, and breads, both soda and white.

Gabriella and Edward had finally made their way through the storm and at that moment sat thawing out in front of the fire, while

Abigail, eighteen and newly engaged to Stephen Foley, a Summerside merchant of dark good looks, stood beside her intended, listening to her sister tell of their perilous journey.

"Edward said it would make a wonderful story like one of those Sir Walter Scott adventures. I told him to write it and he would be famous and we would go to London."

"I'm afraid I am just a newspaper writer. But maybe it will be something for me to do in my retirement."

"Retirement? Did you ever hear the like of it? He looks more like a boy every day." Gabriella looked at her handsome young husband with pride. "We finally stopped at Peter Gallant's—he's the printer for the *Sentinel*—and Peter gave us hot buttered rum to thaw us out for the rest of the trip. I suspect it went right to my head. You know, Father, I've often wondered how you could ever drink that poteen of yours." She looked over to Brendan, who sat contentedly beside Mary on the long brocade couch.

The easy intimate chatter crackled and sparked along with the fire. Liam and Sean sat near each other as though they had always been father and son, while James smiled at his storytelling sister, his face glowing with a deep love for this moment of sharing.

The only shadow to cross the room was Daniel's absence, which prompted Mary to look around expectantly at every sound.

Midway through dinner as she served more goose and the talk moved from the coming marriage of Liam and Cathleen to the always volatile subject of confederation, a door opened and closed in the rear of the house. Mary, still half-listening for any sign of Daniel, gave the meat tray over to Cathleen and left the dining room as though in search of something in the kitchen. Brendan was holding forth on the selfishness of those island merchants who were fighting confederation because they would be personally hurt by joining the rest of Canada under a united charter. "They care nothing for the growth of this country, only the growth of their personal fortunes."

Mary had heard it all before, and she closed the door on it. It was Christmas Eve, and she only wanted her flock together, all of them, with no stray sheep wandering the drifted, snow-packed lanes of the town.

"You are late, Daniel. We waited as long as we could. The others were hungry. I had to serve the meal."

His face was raw, and he blew on his hands after peeling off his icy mittens. "Oh, I am sorry, Mother. I lost track of time. You should not have waited for me. I had things to do."

"Where have you been, Daniel? We will be attending midnight mass as a family. Father Gautier has come to Summerside to say Christmas mass at Saint Gregory's. Surely you will come with us—as a family," she repeated for emphasis.

"I do not wish to go to mass, Mother. I do not wish to take part. If you will excuse me, I just want to go to my room."

"I will not excuse you. You will join your family, and you will come to the table this minute. Do you understand? All your brothers and sisters are here."

"I'm happy for you, Mother, it will make a happy Christmas for you and Father, but do not force me to go to church. I simply don't believe any of it. It's fine for James; he wants to be a priest, and that is wonderful. James is a good person. He may even be a saint someday, but I am not James. I am not any of you. So please, Mother, just tell them I took a chill and went to my bed."

"No, I will not. You will come to the table immediately."

Daniel hung his frozen coat on a hook and simply walked off. He had no intention of arguing with his mother. His mind had been made up for a long time now, and he was not going to sit through a service that meant nothing to him. He would not be a hypocrite for any of them. They were the hypocrites, the Protestants and the Catholics alike, with their talk of charity and Christianity.

"Daniel, come back here! Daniel, do not turn your back on your mother. Do you hear?"

But he did turn his back as he ascended the stairs to his room.

She stood there until she heard the bolt of his door click and lock. Snow slid from the roof, and a new wind rattled the large kitchen window.

There was nothing she could do now. She would wait until after mass and discuss it with Brendan when they returned. She shut the door and quietly joined the others just as Edward Ahearn was announcing proudly that he had decided to run for a seat in the Assembly. Brendan was pounding him on the back in congratulation, but Mary was too distracted to take it all in.

Daniel's eyes penetrated the darkness as he visualized the lovely Margaret, his Peg, before him.

In the six years since the day he came upon her by the river bank, they had met whenever they could, on windy capes, in darkened stables, or beneath the waving lush grasses that separated highroad from shoreline.

Many times it was difficult for Daniel to keep their appointment because there were others in his family with whom he had to contend, while Margaret had only old Mrs. MacKenzie, the somber Scots woman who cared for Peg and Port Loyal when Jarrod Murdock was off to the Assembly in Charlottetown or in Devon on shipping business. There were times when Peg wished Mrs. Dawson had not been dispatched so cruelly by an angry Murdock. But keep the appointment he did, even at the risk of discovery. One such day the past summer Daniel's chore was to tend the lobster traps, tagging them and protecting them from marauders, either other fishermen or scavenger fish.

He beached his rowboat along a spit of land washed clean by the sparkling surf and walked cautiously along the sand until he came to an island of sea-sprayed rocks. Then he jumped from one to the other until he was on the far side of the jetty, where she lay, waiting for him.

"I thought you would never come to me, my beloved Daniel."

"I couldn't get away sooner, my lovely Peg. I have the feeling I am always being watched." He knelt beside her, as the retreating tide bubbled and foamed, leaving dark puddles in the wrinkled sand. She lifted her head, and he took her face tenderly in his hands. A gentle summer breeze brushed Daniel's hair, tossing it in the sun. They trembled, each to the other's touch, as their lips met, softly at first but then with a growing intensity that neither seemed willing or able to control.

"Oh, Daniel, when do we dare tell them of our love? When may we be together without fear of being found out?"

He brought her body closer to him.

"I want to love you so, my Peg."

"I know you do, Daniel, but we must wait until we are married."

"They will never let us marry, you know that. It's bad enough, surely, that our fathers hate each other, but it's also the religion. You are the black Protestant, and I am the papist. Oh, damn their religion. What kind of religion keeps a man and a woman from marrying?"

"I know," she said almost painfully. "I know."

He kissed her again, and their mouths opened wider as their tongues touched and their bodies tingled with joy and excitement.

Dressed in a long white linen frock, her oval face framed by a matching linen bonnet, she was to Daniel the most delicately fragile and beautiful creature he had ever beheld, and her beauty brought a surge of desire within him. He loosened the bows of her bonnet and removed it, allowing her hair to swing free. His hands found her rounded breasts.

"Oh, Daniel, we must wait."

"No, Peg, we must wait no longer." His breath came heavily as his hands began to undress her. She did not struggle, and in moments the years of frustration and desire were gone as their young, tight bodies found each other in both pain and ecstasy.

They lay in the shadows of the rocks until the sun turned cold and they knew they must leave each other again.

"You are not sorry to have loved me, are you, my lovely Peg?"

"No, because as far as I am concerned you are my husband, Daniel McMahon. We were married this very day."

"My wife, my darling wife," he breathed as he smoothed the hair from her foreheaad.

They soon parted with the plan to meet the following week in the same place.

But he hadn't seen her again until this very day as he tramped the snow-swept back roads of Summerside in one of those black, meditative moods that led him nowhere and gained him nothing except the reputation of somehow having turned strange in the past months.

There were some who knew, of course, that the old Scots woman had seen them on the beach that day and reported it to Jarrod Murdock upon his return from Charlottetown. From that moment on Margaret was never left alone, and a startled, if not astonished, Brendan

McMahon had been notified that if his son ever trespassed on Port Loyal again, he would have his head blown from his body.

Once the truth of their relationship was known, and Brendan McMahon could finally judge it with some degree of objectivity, he prohibited Daniel from ever seeing her again.

"A Protestant would be bad enough, but Jarrod Murdock's daughter? Have you no shame?"

"And are you not ashamed, Father? You, who've always said we all were islanders together, no matter where we came from?"

"We have good friends among Protestants, and we always will. But when it comes time to marry, you will marry a good Irish Catholic girl. Remember that, Daniel McMahon. As long as you live under my roof you will do as I say."

"Oh, Irish Catholic? I cannot even choose a French girl if I like? And must this wife of mine be a Galway peasant girl like my own mother?" Daniel was sorry as soon as he uttered the words. Frustration had robbed him of control and common sense.

Brendan did not hesitate to uncoil a right fist that broke Daniel's nose and covered his face in a scarlet mask.

Mary walked into the room just in time to hear the sick, snapping sound of fist on bone. "Stop it, you thick beast. Stop beating my son," she screamed, and thought for a moment she might faint.

"Aye, your son? Then your son he can be. Wash his bloody face for him and ask him what he thinks of his own mother. Peasant girl, indeed," he spit it out, and pounded out of the house. He did not return for three days, and when Mary asked him where he had been, he grumbled something about the *Saint Peter*.

It was all so vivid, even after all the months of loneliness. Daniel had written hundreds of lines of poetry to Margaret but had never delivered any of them. Even now they were resting between the pages of Murdock's ledger, kept these past years in a variety of secret places. The ledger had given him a feeling of power because only he, Daniel McMahon, knew where it was. Its disappearance had caused Murdock much turmoil and many thousands of pounds sterling when the king's magistrate in Charlottetown had found in the case brought to the bench by Brendan McMahon that all debts had to be settled at half the debtor's claim. It was the first victory the common farmer had ever experienced over an affluent landowner.

Brendan's competence and popularity had been assured after that victory, and his name rang along the highroads of Prince County, out to the hulking shoulders of the capes and to the raging Strait. No other immigrant islander had ever known such success, and all because of the quiet initiative of the darkly brooding Daniel McMahon, who had wanted to please his father but who now could never tell him.

It flashed through his mind as he lay in the silence of the house, empty now that they had gone to their meaningless service. What kind of God was He if He denied two people the chance to marry? No one would ever keep them apart. Only a few hours before, he had seen her. After all the months of separation he had been with her again.

In front of the livery stable in Summerside a horse had thrown a shoe and several people milled about the sleigh as an old woman shuffled through the crowd in search of the blacksmith. Daniel, out of curiosity, glanced at the occupant of the sleigh, and his heart went weak. Wrapped under a thick fur rug was Margaret Murdock.

"Peg," he whispered up from the side of the sleigh as the snow blew in dizzying flurries about them. "Peg, it is I Daniel."

Her eyelids fluttered, catching the flakes, and her hand, hidden before, appeared from the covers. "Oh, Daniel, Daniel, I have missed you. My father will not allow me out anywhere without her." She gestured at the retreating figure of Mrs. MacKenzie.

"When may I see you? How, where, my beloved Peg?"

"Father leaves the day after the New Year for Charlottetown. I will try to meet you at the river where we first met. Mrs. MacKenzie takes meals to her husband at the saw pit in the shipyard during the noon hour. She does not return sometimes until two o'clock. I have been ordered to stay in my room while she is away. But go now. She will be back with the smith. My heart is heavy without you."

He bundled himself off in the gray afternoon, his heart singing for the first time in months. But he did not go home, even though it was Christmas Eve and he knew the family would be expecting him. He went instead to the white clapboard church with the black trim. Saint Gregory's, built by the hands of the faithful, his father and brothers and himself among them, was vacant and drafty. The floorboards creaked under his feet. He knelt in the cold shadows of the rear pew. *Benedicat vos, omnipotens Deus, Pater, et Filius, et Spiritus Sanctus*, the Latin phrases, written on wooden tablets that hung from the lime slate walls, were as dead to Daniel as the chapel in which he knelt.

He spoke directly to the altar. "I believe in a God who loves all people. I cannot believe in a God whose language is not understood and who separates people by their religious beliefs. I will always love a God who loves and protects me and understands the misery that invades me.

"Dear God, if you are here, or wherever you are, I beg you and I plead with you to bring Peg and me together. I cannot and I will not live without her. I have suffered all these months. I have suffered because the good people of this island, your good people, would separate a man and woman because they go to different churches. My prayer is simple. I ask for your help. I ask for God's help, not the help of some priest or minister."

He wanted to sob his lungs out, but he withstood the temptation, keeping the ache deep inside, the way he had always kept so many things. He knew he was different. He always had been, but it had never really mattered because he kept so much to himself. Then, after meeting Peg, he had crawled deeper into himself, thinking only of her, of them together. He would suffer through the holidays until the New Year, and then they would meet to plan a strategy that would bring them together once and for all.

He gazed at the crude carvings of the stations of the cross that hung in thirteen scenes about the chapel walls. The snow blew fiercely against the stained-glass windows and the windblown bell in the peaked tower hit slightly against the belfry in a low, irregular clang. He did not know how long he knelt in the chapel, but when he rose, it was dark and he stumbled to the wide doors. He did not cross himself on leaving, nor did he utter a departing prayer.

Daniel made brief appearances about the house during the days that followed. He and his father held courteous, if banal, conversations, both somewhat distant and formal. It was as though they both knew that the next confrontation would be their last, and although it would surely come, they both made an effort to hold back the inevitable.

He spoke with his sisters and played happily with Kate. He shook Peter's hand firmly and with obvious sincerity when Peter left for Charlottetown after Christmas.

Along with the happiness of the holidays came Mary's realization that James would be returning to his seminary at Saint Andrews and would not be back until summer. There was, of course, a happiness in having a priest someday grace the family. It was a gift from God for any Irish mother, and although James had years of study ahead, he seemed destined for his vocation. In view of Daniel's stand against the church, it was as though God had given His rewards as well as His crosses. One must, therefore, be grateful.

The day after New Year's, Brendan left in the early-morning snow for the Charlottetown Assembly with the promise of returning at week's end. James was to travel as far as the capital with his father and then on to Saint Andrews by coach.

The snow, which had let up the last few days, was growing again in intensity. It shifted in the wind and blew in white, dusty sheets against the sleigh. The horses dug deep for a foothold, their great open mouths exhaling steamy clouds of furious smoke.

"Maybe you should wait until the snow ceases, Brendan," Mary shouted above the wind from the porch.

"No, the sooner we leave, the sooner we will get there. I will return on Friday." He slapped the reins against the broad white backs of the horses. James raised a gloved hand, and the sleigh lurched forward into the blizzard. Mary brushed her tears away as Daniel watched from his room. Then he quickly dressed and briskly descended to the back entry, where he threw on his long beaver coat, strapped his snowshoes to his back, and slipped quietly out of the house.

Mary, returning to the kitchen, heard the door close and went curiously to the window in time to see him huddling off into the descending snow. "Blessed Virgin Mary, protect my suffering son." She knew, as though it had been told to her, that he was off to see Margaret Murdock.

It was too late to stop him even if she could have. She should have done something a long time before about this private son of hers. The years had been filled with the work of making a home for the family, a future for them, a better life, yet she felt that family slipping from her grasp at this moment. "Oh, dearest Savior, protect my Daniel this day and forever," she said to his fading back.

The skies overturned now, emptying a never-ending avalanche of snow that mounted and drifted through the steel gray morning. It was not a pretty snow, not a feather duster of white, but a battering, brutal attack of frozen crystals that shattered and cracked against the trees and bush and chimney.

Mary busied herself in the empty kitchen. Gabriella and Edward and her lovely elfin granddaughter, Kate, were already resuming their lives in Tignish. Abigail was at work in the Summerside office of the Tignish Cooperative, so when Mary heard the distant tinkle of sleigh bells, she welcomed them, no matter who it was arriving down the lane.

She peered out the window to see two white figures, like frozen polar bears, emerge from the sleigh and elbow their way through the gusting snow to the front porch.

Mary flung the door open, allowing them to enter.

"Jesus, I have never seen a storm like this one."

"My God. Brendan, and my James. What happened? Was it that bad?"

"That bad? Every man and boy in Summerside is at work clearing the lanes to town. Let us catch our breath and drink some hot broth to thaw our frozen bellies, and then we will join them. Charlottetown will have to wait. There will be no Assembly this week, you can mark me on that."

Mary brought two steaming cups of soup, and they drank it gratefully as the snow fell in puddles about their sodden boots.

"I suppose Daniel McMahon is already out clearing the lanes with the rest of the good citizens." He said it with an acerbic edge to his voice because he was never really sure what his second son might be up to these days.

Mary hesitated at first, but as she saw the day turning black under a new attack of ice and snow, she felt a shuddering and stabbing pain of fear. If Brendan could not get through, how then could Daniel?

"Brendan, I am in fear for Daniel. He left directly after you, and I have the worst feeling that he has gone to see that girl."

"That girl? You don't mean the Murdock girl? Surely he knows our feelings on that subject. He knows he would not be able to set foot inside this house if he were ever seen with her again. Surely, Mary Roark, he knows that. We have made our point clear on that matter. Have we not, woman?" His voice shook as the wind banged and battered the house. "Answer me, Mary, have we not been clear on that matter?"

"Be easy, Father. Don't lose your temper." James tried to soothe the man whose fury he had seen many times, but never directed at him.

The McMahon responded to the soft voice. "Aye, I'm all right, James. I'm all right. I just want to be certain your mother agrees that Daniel knows our position on that matter."

"I am sure he knows *your* position, Brendan. Was I not present the day you struck him such a fierce blow?"

"Oh, it is only my position, is it? Are you such a woman of the world that you would allow a son of ours to make a fool of himself over a Protestant girl?"

"I am not arguing with you. I'm as much to blame as anyone. When did we even discuss it with him?"

"And when did he ever *offer* to discuss it? Aye," he said, nodding in agreement, "that is exactly where he has gone. He thinks that Murdock has gone off to Charlottetown to the Assembly—like his own father," he added woodenly.

"Come, James," Brendan said, "we must go after him. He could not have got far in this weather. If he goes near Port Loyal, Murdock will blow his head off. He has vowed that to me."

"What will you do when you find him?" Mary's concern was twofold. There was fear of Murdock's fury as well as her own husband's.

He stopped for a moment, pulling on his thick woolen mittens, and looked at her numbly. Then he lowered his head in long thought before answering. "I don't know, Mary, I do not know."

In minutes the snow had swallowed them as the sleigh pointed for the highroad to Port Loyal. The whole world, it seemed, was iced marble. A dozen or so men headed south on the road to town, shovels on their shoulders, but as the two giant horses warred northward, there was no human life to be seen.

James sat back under the thick black rug, only his round pink face open to the wind and snow, as he whispered prayer after prayer that his father would be forgiving and that somehow all this, so much of which he did not understand, would be settled.

They had been traveling for almost an hour before Brendan spoke, and when he did, his voice, generally strong and determined, seemed uneven and hesitant. "Say your prayers, James, as I am sure you are, that I do the right thing. Daniel was always such a quiet one. It was hard to fathom just what was on his mind. Do you know what I mean, lad?"

James's face, numb from the biting frost, barely moved when he spoke. "I never played much with Daniel, Father—he always seemed to be off somewhere—but I love him. He is my brother."

The McMahon's mouth quivered. The boy beside him, who would some day be a priest, had given him the answer he so desperately needed. Daniel McMahon was James's brother, and James loved him. Daniel McMahon was Brendan's son.

They came to a grove of willows, and he was struck by their suppleness and by the realization that despite their bending under the force of island storms, they, nonetheless, retained a certain grace and quiet majesty, so unlike the oak, which battled every onslaught of weather with such stubborn and blind fury. There was a place for the willow in this world, he thought, a very respected place.

Out along the vast snowfields below Port Loyal, the idle boatyard lay covered. The saw pits and the workhouse were lifeless save for the chimney smoke that trailed along with the icy blasts of wind. Masts, like white totems, and the sway-backed barquentine hulls huddled like beached white whales. The Murdock boatyard for all its commercial success was helpless under the stampeding fury of nature.

"Look, Father, down there along the river. A figure on snowshoes."

"Aye, good lad. Daniel it is. I would know that long step of his anywhere."

Brendan snapped the whip lightly and guided the sleigh expertly down a side lane, being careful to stay out of the mounting fields of snow.

"Here, we must stop. We will not be able to get through. We go on foot."

They jumped from the sleigh, stumbling at first in the deep snow, and began to trudge across the field. At the lip of a hill Brendan called out, "Daniel. Daniel," His words rang across the white fields and along the frozen river.

Daniel looked up and saw the black, powerful figure of his father, and he stopped momentarily, fear stricken. His father had followed him in a blinding storm to stop him from seeing her. Murdock, too, was no doubt at Port Loyal with a shotgun, and Peg, his Peg, was locked in her room. "Oh, Christ, what are they doing to us?" he sobbed. "We haven't hurt anyone. Who are they to keep us apart?"

"Dan . . . iel. Wait. Dan . . . i . . . e . . . l. Wait for your fa . . . ther." The words tumbled across the fields in a frozen echo that drove nails into Daniel's heart. He looked in the direction of the hill. His father was plowing through the snow toward him.

"Oh, Jesus, leave me alone. Leave me alone," he screamed at the approaching figure.

Halfway down the hill Brendan stopped, and almost more to himself than to his anguished son, he said, "No, lad, be easy now. Everything will be all right."

But the words did not reach Daniel because he had already turned in the direction of the river. His eyes darted left to right in frenzy. He would cross the frozen river below the boatyard, and once on the other side he would cross again to their first meeting place. Maybe she would be there. Maybe she had been able to slip away from the house. If only he could see her for a moment, just to hold her and tell her how much he loved her. It would be worth anything that came afterward.

He set out across the river. The travel was easier and quicker underfoot, but he was tired. He would rest on the other side.

His father's voice boomed somewhere behind him as he continued across. Then suddenly he heard a frightening sound. There was a sharp, penetrating crack from below the thick layers of snow. The river was solid, for sure, in this weather and at this time of year. He stopped to catch his breath and survey the terrain. He was in the middle now, so going ahead was just as long or short as turning back. He continued cautiously. When it was solid underfoot once again, he headed for the island of pine, which, he knew, was close to the other shore.

Again he heard that awful crack, more pronounced this time and more prolonged. The snow turned to slush under his feet, and suddenly water appeared over the slush and snow. Terror gripped him. He could not go back, because somewhere under the snow back there was the first crack. He could not stay where he was because water already lapped over his snowshoes. He turned once to see his father on the shoreline with his hands outstretched, and he went on. The horrifying snapping and cracking continued, and this time there was no stepping back because all too quickly the ice and snow disappeared beneath him and black, bubbling water rose to meet him. One moment it was up to his hips, and the next he was below the surface.

Brendan and James watched in horror from the shore. And then Brendan began to run across the frozen river, followed by James, who screamed after him, "Father, Father, do not go on. You will be lost, too. Oh, Father, please, please." The boy sobbed and screamed and choked in uncontrollable sorrow at what he knew already to be true. His brother Daniel was gone.

Brendan, also realizing it as the cracking ice snapped beneath his boots, knelt in the snow, rocking with unrestrained grief, his great mittened hands pressing against his head as he sobbed.

It was not until the spring thaw that Daniel McMahon's body washed up on the shores of Port Loyal. Mercifully Peg was not there. A few weeks after the tragedy she had been sent off to school in West Devon.

CHAPTER XXVI

SPRING BROKE QUICKLY from the icy clutches of the snow-packed winter, and within days, it seemed to the islanders, the worst winter in memory thawed, and melted ice ran in bubbling rivers and streams along the red ditches below the highroad.

With the thaw came the scent of moist earth cut from the lingering gauze of April. Another winter, violent in its raging attack as this one had been, was slipping away under the apple sun of spring.

For Brendan and Mary and the remaining children, however, the winter's violence had not been the storm-driven snows but the personal violence of a tragedy that stole from them a son and a brother.

Brendan's behavior had been unexpected and uncharacteristic, and Edward Ahearn reflected on it as his square rig drawn by a sickly and spotted dray horse, slogged through the red, wheel-furrowed streets of Charlottetown. Edward, oblivious of fashion, wore a mud-spattered black frock coat and a string tie of unequal lengths; hatless, his black hair blew like a mop in the morning sunlight.

He had known Brendan McMahon as friend and father-in-law, and always he envied this man of the quick fists and great strength. But these days Brendan spoke little and acted less. He sat for long hours in front of the fire, mumbling only when someone's insistent question finally penetrated the wall of his stoicism. When Edward brought up confederation, the subject did not bring fire to Brendan's eyes; he would listen to the cerebral rhetoric of his son-in-law and then return his gaze to the sparking wood.

If anything commanded his attention, it was the shipping business. With Peter off to Liverpool and Liam down the Maine coast, the Tignish Cooperative was gaining a reputation.

In all the years that Edward had been the editor of the *Sentinel* he knew he could rely on the booming voice of Brendan McMahon to reiterate that paper's sentiments on confederation. But in the three months since Daniel's drowning, Brendan had grown silent on all matters but business.

If only Brendan would reach for a keg of poteen and drink himself into oblivion and tear up a Summerside saloon with his bare hands, if only he would grieve openly, possibly all the hurt and doubt and guilt, yes, especially the guilt, would gush forth in a torrential pouring out of the soul until nothing was left but the eternal emptiness.

But he did none of these. He simply buried himself for long hours in the business of making money. His heart seemed somehow replaced by a stone. Even Kate, whom he had bounced proudly on his knee on so many occasions, now seemed to mean nothing to him.

It was Kate, though, with a child's softness and naïveté, who soothed the hurt in Mary McMahon's heart. The two were almost more like mother and daughter, the lonely child staying for days at a time at the Summerside home of her grandparents. It was a relationship Gabriella encouraged, hoping that in some way the child would help fill the void left by Daniel's death.

It all had been so sorrowful and so unnecessary. Two warring institutions devoted to the love of God had brought only death and misery. And the two enemies, Murdock and McMahon, were embittered even more by a situation which could only become worse. But if Brendan had any desire to tear Murdock apart, he would have to begin by tearing himself apart because he was as much to blame for Daniel's death as Murdock.

So Brendan McMahon lived with his guilt and hid it behind an unnatural bid for financial success. He became quickly and almost overnight a man consumed with commercial power.

Edward Ahearn had lost a valuable ally, but more important, he had lost the intimacy of a relationship he considered like that between father and son. He prayed that this man who possessed so much love of soil, love of family, and love of the island would not become a very copy of his bitterest enemy, Jarrod Murdock.

Knowing that he could not count on Brendan, Edward, heavy of heart but no less committed to his quest for election, tramped up and down the dusty highroads, walked across countless pastures, rode his doughty horse to a lathered sweat, and touched the hands of virtually every man, woman and child in Prince County. He explained, clearly and simply, what they could expect of him, and he asked for their support. In the end, they did not disappoint him.

A new mood was stirring along the roads and waterways, along the cobbled streets of Summerside and Charlottetown, on the bustling docks and on the farms. It was not just the election of Edward Ahearn —although his constituency saw in him a man of extraordinary talent and energy—but the time. The time was right for growth and political zeal. The tiny island fairly burst its seams with activity. Shipbuilding was at the apex of its growth. From Fortune Bay, New Glasgow, Saint Peters, Rustico, Port Loyal, where Murdock's empire grew, to Summerside, where the McMahons were gradually building a fleet that would roam the ocean corridors of the world, there was vitality and vigor in the air.

Because there were vast regions of forest, and forest meant timber, and timber meant sturdy sailing craft, the islanders were establishing a fine reputation for their registered vessels.

Prince Edward Island, the smallest of the potentially confederated provinces, boasted a fleet of 254 vessels and more than thirty-two tons. The exhilarating air of pride matched the islanders' independence, and love of their home was generating a begrudging admiration among the other provinces.

Brendan McMahon was an integral part of the growth, but there was little joy in the brooding Byron of a man. His strong body seemed a shade stooped, as though there were nothing for which to hold his head high. His shiny black hair was interspersed now with dustings of gray.

He *was*, in his own melancholy way, happy for Edward because he knew Edward to be a good man, Edward would be good for the Assembly as well as for the entire island.

But the flame that before Daniel's death had burned brightly for confederation was snuffed out and cold within him. On long winter nights, when the blowing snows brought back the memory of tracking Daniel to Port Loyal, he would go to his dead son's room and sit on the bed, his head in his hands. How he had failed this son of his, this son now gone from him.

The years when they should have been closer, Brendan had been breaking his back over a plow from the crack of dawn until the black of night. Daniel, never quick to discuss anything with his father, had lived his few years in mystery.

On one cold and snow-driven afternoon, Brendan huddled by the window of Daniel's room that looked far out over the harbor. The wind banged against the house, and cold air rushed in at his feet. Strange, he thought, a new house, solid in structure, yet with cold air blowing in. He stooped down and felt with his hand along the wall, lingering at the point where the floor met the mop board. He felt farther, and as he did, the pressure of his hand caused a board to tilt up. One long piece of flooring came away, and then two more. He brushed the curtains back from the window, allowing the waning afternoon light to enter. When he bent to inspect the gap left by the loose boards, his eyes fell on a large book, much like one of the ledgers he used for his shipping and business log. He lifted it from its wooden coffin beneath the floorboards, and it seemed as if a hammer had slammed into his chest. "Jarrod Murdock's Port Loyal ledger," he whispered, "my own dear Daniel was the one who stole Murdock's bloody ledger." He clutched the book to his breast, and his body shook with sobs so deep he began to choke. But he paid no heed to the choking as he held the ledger tightly with affection, as though he were holding his own dead son in his arms. It was as though an impregnable wall had finally given way and the stored-up waters of a hidden well had gushed forth.

Mary, alone in the kitchen, heard the wailing and rushed upstairs. When she opened the door, she saw her husband kneeling on the floor, rocking back and forth, repeating their son's name over and over.

"Oh, Brendan, oh, my dear husband, how you hurt so. How we all do." She went to him and took his head in her hands and brought it close to her bosom, and he sobbed into her breast like a little child who was lost and then found but was still full of fear and loneliness.

She held him, soothing him, until the light disappeared from the room and a chill crept along the floor. "There now, you will be better for having cried it out, my dearest. You have held your grief inside too long. God is good. You will be your old self again. I am sure of it."

Finally, he stood on weak legs, his ribs aching from the strain of his sobs.

He held the ledger up to her. "Jar . . . Murd—Murdock's ledger, Daniel was the one. He was as much like us . . . like us, Mar—Mary, as any of our children."

Her eyes opened wide, and her hand trembled at her breast. At first she could not speak, but at the realization of what he was saying she cried out in a shaking voice, "Oh, Brendan, he was so deep. He was so much like his own father. So much like you, Brendan." She wiped the tears away and guided him to the door. "Come, my darling, it is cold in this room. Let us go downstairs and sit by the fire."

He followed her out of the room and shut the door softly behind him.

The next morning he left the house early, carrying a lantern in his right hand and the ledger tucked under his left arm.

The snow had ceased, and in its crystal wake the layers of crust cracked under the crunch of his heavy boots. He approached the quays and walked down the empty pier to where the *Saint Peter* was moored and pulling insistently against her ropes. The crew that stayed aboard was still asleep and warm in the belly of the ship. He walked past and lowered himself to the snow-covered rocks along the shore. He stood for a moment and looked up at the silent graveyard, and then he opened the ledger. He had discovered the poems and letters written to "My Peg," but out of respect for his son's privacy, he had not read them. He ripped a page from the ledger and doused it with oil from the lantern. He placed the ledger and the letters in the snow, scratched a match across his fingernail, and ignited the page. He then poured the remaining oil on the ledger and the letters and poems. White smoke curled up from the snow and rose to meet the early-morning clouds. Flames engulfed the paper, and in a few short moments only ashes remained in the black soot of snow that melted at his feet. He looked down at the small conflagration, kicked the remaining ashes into the frozen waters of the harbor, raised his head high in the direction of the hill again, crossed himself, and turned toward home and Mary.

CHAPTER XXVII

THE FOURTEENTH DAY of July, 1866, was dry and hot. The sun had blazed over Charlottetown for nine days, turning the lush grass of its parks and meadows into a streaked yellow straw. But hot and humid as it was, the market district swelled with Saturday morning shoppers, while along the shores of the Hillsborough River men and women, parents and children, flutterered and kicked their naked legs in the refreshing silver sprays of water.

Charlottetown itself was sparkling gold these days and not only because of continued sunshine. Just two years before, a conference that would have far-reaching effects not just for islanders but for all of Canada had been held right there in Charlottetown.

At Province House delegations from Upper and Lower Canada had been present, along with leaders from the Maritimes. Their meeting had brought the slow but persistent flame of an idea to a bright and flickering awareness: confederation. It burned in the hearts and glowed in the faces of many of those assembled, particularly Edward Ahearn.

To be sure, Jarrod Murdock and his forces had cast great, spidery shadows over the meeting, and when the delegates finally convened, Prince Edward Island had still not acted to join a confederated Canada.

For some, it was a disheartening defeat, but for Edward and Brendan, who joined some of the other delegates later at the White Swan, there was still a feeling of optimism in the air.

"We are gaining on them, eh?" Edward, smiling in the direction of his father-in-law, held his rum high and then swallowed it.

"Aye." Brendan smiled back over the bobbing heads at the bar.

"Who is this Murdock who sits like a mute Buddha but seems to dominate your chambers, Mr. McMahon? He is, it seems to me, the one stumbling block to an entire and completely confederated Canada." The man speaking was tall and trim, with a bushy white mustache. His eyes were set deep in his head, and he nodded when he spoke. His English was precise and well thought out, but it carried with it thick traces of Quebec French.

"Ah, Mr. Thibeau, that of course is our island's story. Mr. Murdock and I have been at opposite ends of the conference table for too many years now. I might say that I admire him as an adversary and thus present myself as a statesman who can go beyond the realm of personalities."

The French delegate's head nodded slowly. "Yes?" The word carried with it the unsaid words *But you cannot?*

Brendan smiled and sipped his rum. "But I am a simple man, not a statesman. I have no use for Murdock or his ilk. There are many men in this room who do not share my views, but they are good men, men who have sweated for what they have and who have in turn given much to this island and its people. Murdock, although he too has sweated and worked just as hard as the rest of us, has kept and never given. He is a businessman for whom business means acquisition. People like Murdock are selfish, and mark me, someday they will choke on their own greed."

"Well, my friend, you speak with much eloquence and just a *little* emotion." Thibeau's head bobbed.

"I learned a few eloquent words from a great man many years ago."

The bar had become more crowded as delegates from New Brunswick and Ontario, Quebec and Nova Scotia laughed and traded stories like old sea captains. A bond was being formed, and Brendan and Edward could feel it as though it were tightening its grip around them like an affectionate embrace.

Yes, Charlottetown had a proud image these days, and on this Saturday the old town glowed and beamed. Mary and Brendan had arrived the day before and taken rooms in Great George Street. Edward and Gabriella had decided not to make the journey. Edward was working on a report for the Assembly and a three-part editorial for the *Sentinel*, and Gabriella, who loved the farm and the sea, was happier roaming the rugged capes. But because she knew it would please her mother and father, she had allowed Kate to join them.

It was a special occasion, one that was not always well attended. But because of this new feeling of pride, the city councillors, assemblymen, clerks, prominent Charlottetown citizens and their guests, were invited to the Annual Promenade and Reception given by the Community for a United Charlottetown.

The city shook with merriment in spite of the heat. Jugglers and street peddlers, mimes, clowns, and little groups of musicians thrilled the delighted visitors and, more than anyone else, the dark-haired lovely Kate. Her blue eyes widened at the blocks of buildings that rose three floors to the sky. And the market! The smell of spices and limes filled her with dreams of distant places, vast cities and seaports and exotic people.

"Well, Kate, are you enjoying your visit? What do you like best?"

"Oh, Grandfather, it is all so filled with color, and everything is so bright, and everyone seems so happy."

"And are you happy?" Mary squeezed her granddaughter's hand.

"Oh, I have never been so happy in my life."

"The city is so alive. I love being here myself." Mary smiled.

They were walking past Government House. Small boats with limp sails sat on the still and shimmering waters.

"You always did love city life, Mary Roark. For myself, I enjoy the long stretches of quiet beach on the North Cape."

"Oh, Brendan, be gone off with you. I am more than content with our lovely home in Summerside, and Summerside is exciting these days, too." She looked down at the vibrant child. "You see, dear Kate, your grandpa thinks I'm going to raise my skirts and run away to Paris."

"Or Boston," he said, but quickly smiled and hugged her. There was no sarcasm in his voice now when he referred to Mary's past adventures.

"What was Boston like, Grandmother?"

"Go on, tell her those stories she loves to hear. I'll not be pouting about them. There, sit over there, you two, look out at the harbor, and talk about faraway places. I'll be back in a while, and then we will go to our rooms and freshen up for the ball."

"And where might you be off to if I may ask, and as if I didn't know?"

"I'll be dropping in to see some friends. Don't worry about me. I can take care of myself in the big city."

They watched him stride up the hill.

"I love Grandfather so much, and I love you so much, Grandmother."

"Oh, my little doll, you are such a joy to us both."

"Do you love Grandfather very much?"

Mary was quiet for a moment and then said, almost in a whisper, "It seems I have loved him all my life. It goes back to when we were not much older than you and we would pass each other on the muddy lanes of Galway, or I would catch him looking at me as I sat on the stone quays of the harbor. It seems I did that a lot in those days. I was always looking out to sea, wondering what was on the other side and what kind of life I could find there for myself."

"I do that many times. I sit on the tiptop of the capes and dangle my feet out over the beach and look far out over the water and dream." She looked up into Mary's face. "Do you think we are very much alike, Grandmother? My mother says we are. She says she is like Grandfather and I am like you. Do you think that is true?"

"Oh, in a way it is. I suppose I will always wonder what life in Boston or Evansborough would have been like. But I believe it all would have turned out much the way that it has, and it has turned out well. Your grandfather is now a wealthy and powerful man, who uses his money and power for the good of others as well as for his own family. I am proud to be his wife."

"He is proud to be your husband, too. He told me once that everything you both had was because of you, because you were the one to stand up to the Assembly for your rights. I hope I can always be like you, Grandmother."

Mary's eyes glistened. "Well, aren't you the one to go blatherin'
on? Come here to me, I'll tell you all about the States." The twelve-
year-old settled next to her grandmother, and Mary continued the story
that began more than thirty-five years before on a crowded dock in
Boston.

Jarrod Murdock walked into the cool late-afternoon shadows of the
Regent Hotel. A thin, rather wan young woman was by his side, and
the hotel attendant immediately signaled for a boy to take their carpet-
bags.

"Good afternoon, Mr. Murdock. It is a pleasure to serve you, sir.
Are you here for tonight's promenade, sir?" The clerk was overdressed
in a heavy frock coat and a starched collar that seemed to be slowly
choking him to death as he tried discreetly to loosen it.

"I don't see that that's any of your business, young man."

"Oh, no, of course, sir. I am sorry. It is so warm. Forgive me, Mr.
Murdock . . . and Mrs. Murdock."

"The woman is not Mrs. Murdock."

The clerk's eyes opened wider at the obvious brazenness of the
man.

"Sir?" he asked in spite of himself.

"You ignoramus, she is my daughter. We will want two rooms on
the river side. Be quick about it. We have traveled through the most
intense heat of the day. We will require tubs immediately." Murdock
checked the room numbers on the keys, and satisfied the rooms were
adjoining, he said, "Come, my dear. I want you to have a rest now."

They could hear first strains of violin music even before they entered Charlottetown House. The night was crisp and clean, and a
hint of salt was in the air.

The music grew louder as they ascended the wide staircase to the
music chamber.

Mary looked proudly at her tall strong-featured husband, whose
black suit fitted tightly around his wide shoulders and down the broad
back.

"You look handsome, Brendan McMahon. You are the handsomest
man here tonight."

"And you are the most beautiful woman on the island." He grinned
at her.

"Only the island? What happened to your powers of exaggeration?"
She feigned hurt in the slight droop of her mouth.

"All the world is an island, the poet wrote."

"Oh, Brendan McMahon, you have more high talk than a chamber
of barristers."

He chuckled boisterously, turning several heads in the line in front
of them. Then he clamped his lips shut in a more than obvious attempt
at decorum.

The room was decorated wtih festive paper streamers. Silver-haired women in long taffeta gowns walked about, offering trays of delicacies for selection and approval, while waltzing couples glided with a grace and elegance reminiscent of Viennese ballrooms and European quadrilles.

While the musicians took their recess, the gentlemen smoked on the veranda, the curling smoke mingling with the aroma of full-blooming flowers and the omnipresent scent of the sea. Byron Jelfe sidled over to Brendan and shook his hand vigorously. "So good to see you, McMahon. It seems everyone is here this year. I think we are entering a new time in our history. Pages are being turned, and the story is becoming more optimistic, wouldn't you say?"

"Well, I don't think I could say it quite as well, but yes, I do feel a change in the air. Even in the numbers that have turned out tonight, I think there is an indication, and a solid one, that the island is emerging as a unified whole. It is very encouraging. How are you enjoying yourself?"

"I am having a wonderful time. My wife and I have not stopped dancing since we arrived. In fact, I left her chatting with Mrs. McMahon and the ladies while I came out for a breath. Well, I hear the orchestra beginning. I have no intention of missing a dance. By the way, where are you staying?"

"We took rooms in Great George Street, at the Regent Hotel. We have our granddaughter with us."

"Oh, you're at the Regent, McMahon. We are at the Crown." Jelfe and Brendan turned to the voice behind them. It belonged to Stephen Ordway, an amusing man who was from Hunters River but spent much of his time as a ships broker in Charlottetown.

"Ah, Mr. Ordway, good to see you, sir."

"Mr. Jelfe, Mr. McMahon. I didn't recognize you at first. I've been having trouble with my eyes, I need new spectacles. But I must say, gentlemen, I have never seen either of you looking better." He let his remark sink in, and then he tilted his bald head back and roared with approval at his own humor.

Both Jelfe and McMahon laughed in spite of themselves because the man was so engaging and well liked by all. Then they both excused themselves to rejoin their wives, who seemed to be whispering together in a corner of the foyer.

"Why is everyone so conspiratorial?" Jelfe asked his lovely wife.

"Yes, what is it?" Brendan questioned Mary, who only turned away.

"Mary, for God's sake, you're crying. What is it? You were so happy . . . what, in God's name?" He held her shoulders, turning her around slowly to face him.

"Oh, Brendan, it's just the reminder. Jarrod Murdock is here, and he has—he has his daughter with him. Margaret."

"Margaret?" Brendan's jaw dropped, and his mouth flew open. "I thought she was in England, in some school or institution. I don't wish to see her, Mary. I'm sorry, but I have no stomach for any of it."

"I agree, my husband. Let us leave quietly."

They descended the stairs, and the music began to fade as they headed back to the Regent.

"I was beginning to miss Kate anyway," he said simply, and locked his hand in hers.

The dancing continued in the music chamber as Murdock, poker-stiff and awkward, all but pushed his little Peg around the floor, completely oblivious to the clumsiness that forced couples to sidestep him rather than be jostled.

Margaret was a pitifully thin little creature. Her eyes were gray coals, and all the flame seemed to have disappeared from her cheeks. She smiled thinly at her father and treated him with every courtesy, even listening to his grumbling and begrudging diaglogues with other members of the Assembly.

"It is good to see you here tonight, Jarrod, especially with your lovely companion." Stephen Ordway was such a gracious and well-meaning man that over the years even Jarrod Murdock had enjoyed a drink or two with him.

"Where are you lodging tonight, Miss Murdock?"

"Father and I are at the Regent Hotel, Mr. Ordway."

"Oh, oh, the Regent, is it? Jarrod, your lovely daughter tells me you're at the Regent."

"Yes. Although I'm not certain I like the service. But it is quiet. No riffraff."

"I hope it's quiet tonight." Ordway smiled and winked at Murdock's fawning entourage.

"It will be. That's what I am paying good money for."

"Well, you just behave yourself. No bickering or shouting in the corridors. It isn't the Assembly, you know, and there are times when a truce should be recognized."

"A truce? Shouting? What in damnation are you talking about, Stephen?"

"Why, Brendan McMahon. He is staying at the Regent, too. I hope you are not on the same floor. How would that be, fellows? They might have to call in the militia."

Murdock's eyes grew wide. His turned-down mouth clamped tight, then opened. "Don't ever mention the name McMahon in front of my daughter, you idiot, or in front of me. I thought I was paying good money to be free of riffraff."

"Oh, really, Jarrod, I meant no harm, just an old man making a bad joke. Please forgive me, Miss Murdock, sometimes I become a little silly. I've had three glasses of port."

Margaret, embarrassed for the old man, shook her head, "It is nothing, sir. Really it is nothing."

"It is more than nothing." Murdock flared up again. "Come. The evening is over." He took Margaret by the arm and guided her out of the hall without so much as a good evening.

At the Regent Murdock thumped on the counter, demanding attention.

When the harried clerk arrived, he was still trying to fasten his starched collar, but in his nervousness he could not find the collar button.

"Mr. Murdock, what is wrong, sir. How may we serve you?"

"You may serve me by sending a valet to rooms two-oh-one and two-oh-three to pack all our belongings. Then you may have the cases transferred at once to the Crown in Pownal Street."

"But, sir, you are already paid up for tonight's lodgings and you have used your rooms."

"Listen, you babbling town idiot, you can keep the bloody money. You can rent the rooms again. That's what a good businessman would do, but there are not many of those on this island, I have observed." He threw the keys on the oak counter and wheeled around just as Brendan, Mary, and Kate appeared in the doorway. He almost knocked them over in his haste to get out. "Come, Margaret, now."

If it had not been for the sight of the pale girl and the sad memories she summoned in Brendan, he would have gone after Murdock and broken his neck once and for all. But as the girl lifted her eyes he saw in them only softness, love, and a quiet acceptance. Brendan lowered his head, and when he looked up again, father and daughter were gone.

The heat of the summer night kept Brendan tossing and turning, and the sound of late-night revelers carried up and down the street until finally, exhausted and with the night beginning to gather stillness around him, he fell into an almost unconscious state. He lay there motionless, numbed, but somewhere in the back of his mind he could hear a voice, at first distant, and then closer, and finally more demanding as it penetrated his brain.

"Fire. Fire," shrieked the voice. It was the town crier, and his insistent shouting brought Brendan tumbling from his bed and to the window, shouting into the night, "Where? Where, crier?"

"Corner of King and Pownal streets. Corner of King and Pownal streets," the crier repeated as he raced through the dark.

"What is it, Brendan?" Mary sat up in the bed.

"A fire. I had best go join the bucket brigade. This is not a good night for a fire, Mary, if any night is, God forbid. It is terribly dry." He threw on the trousers to his good suit and his white dress shirt, then tugged on his boots.

"For God's sake, be careful," she warned.

"Oh, surely what is there to worry about? I'll return in no time."

He slipped out the door. Already other volunteers were gathering in the corridors, hurrying down the stairs and out through the main entrance.

When Brendan reached the street, he stopped dead in his tracks and whispered, "Sweet Mary, Mother of God, save us." The entire sky was alight with flames and dense with smoke.

A house and two outbuildings on the corner of King and Pownal were already smoking shells, and the flames were spreading quickly up the street. The fire brigade had still not arrived, so volunteers formed lines, and passed buckets.

Brendan was close enough to feel the heat singe his hair, but with sweat pouring out of him and his white shirt a soaked gray rag, he continued to pass the buckets.

The line of volunteers now extended all the way to the river, and the sloshing buckets were passed almost a full mile to the heart of the fire.

The wind, which was light and airy, blew west by south, driving the flames in a westerly direction to the south side of Dorchester Street, on the corner of which stood Digger Shanley's original shop.

Digger awoke to the ripping whoosh of flame and ran to his bedroom window, only to be met by the melting heat of the driven flame. The fire smashed through his window, and he knew that he would have to jump for his life.

The fire engine finally arrived on Pownal Street, and the hand pumps that were fed by the bucket brigades began their monumental task of trying to engage the spreading flames in a war that was already lost. The most the citizens could do was to continue to pass the buckets and hope that those who had been inside the flaming buildings had, indeed, escaped.

Brendan continued to pass the buckets and pick up the slack when someone else slumped over with heat or exhaustion. He worked his way up and down the frenetic line of volunteers until he was directly in front of the Crown Hotel. And then, as though someone had told him to, he looked up at the third floor, where the flames licked with greedy and insatiate tongues at the wood, and saw two figures in a window. In the illumination it was not difficult to distinguish Jarrod Murdock and Margaret.

Murdock was attempting to push the girl through the broken window, but she seemed to be fighting him. The more he pushed, the more she smashed and beat on him until finally she slipped by him and Brendan lost sight of her in the smoke.

Now others on the street were looking up, and what they saw was Jarrod Murdock standing in the open window, poised as though ready for a flight into the smoky night. But just then a new wind drove the flames into his face, and his night gown ignited like a Roman candle.

The onlookers watched helplessly in horror as the man became a human torch, and only then did his flaming body hurtle to the earth below. Brendan McMahon knew that Murdock was dead.

Still they passed the buckets, and still one wooden building collapsed and fell with a crash into the next, sending flaming debris sparking in the night.

"It's getting away from us," said one weary, soot-stained volunteer with a sigh.

"Forget bloody Pownal Street," someone commanded. "Turn the engine, shift the line. It's tearing through Great George and Water."

Brendan turned in horror to see flames ripping along Great George Street.

"Jesus, Mary, and Joseph." Brendan's voice erupted from his soaked chest. "Mary and Kate."

He raced past the Crown and sidestepped two men who were dragging the smoking, blackened body of Jarrod Murdock into a doorway on the other side of the street. He could see that Murdock had no hair and that his face was like candle wax.

Brendan raced down an alley while the fire raged to his left and threw up an elbow just in time to ward off a piece of flaming timber that struck him fiercely, gashing his arm. The heat was intense now, and he began to choke on the billowing clouds of smoke.

Two buildings, their upstairs porches tilting, leaned into each other as he dived for cover into a sand pit. They slowly broke open, their timber disintegrating and spilling into the alley behind him.

McMahon caught his breath and rolled out of the sand. He rose to his knees and pushed off down the alley. He was in Great George Street now, and the fire was in front of him as though it had leaped over buildings to beat him to his objective. Flames danced from the windows of the Regent. He thought he was about to faint. They were in there. They were beneath that blazing canopy. The great glass panel on the front entrance door was smashed, and the gaping hole revealed the smoke-filled lobby, in darkness save for snakelike flames that writhed and wriggled along the staircase.

He kicked the door in and was immediately overwhelmed by heat and smoke. He could not find the staircase, and he dared not open his mouth to shout lest he swallow too much smoke.

Sobs of frustration crushed his stomach, his chest, and his throat, and he backed out into the street, the tears burning and blinding him. He stood for a moment watching the advancing battalion of orange flame, and then he pitched forward onto his face.

The gray haze of early morning brought with it the pungent smell of ash. Smoke trailed into smudged clouds. The ceiling of the city was dirty gray as though the pink dawn were far above it. People walked without purpose, kicking over the smoking blistered timbers almost reluctantly, as though in fear that a blackened body might be lying beneath.

Those who had manned the brigade of wooden buckets lay on the soft morning dew of the grass, their hands swollen and their eyes shot through with blood and smoke.

Brendan awoke to find a young girl with black satin curls bathing his face with a wet cloth. He tried to sit up, but a deep and insistent hacking cough drove him back down on the cushion of wet grass.

"Please, Brendan, lie there and rest. Let Kate take care of her grandfather." Mary came into view as she knelt beside Kate and bent down to kiss her husband softly on the cheek.

"How—how did I get here? And you? Oh, God, I thought you both were gone." Again the choking cough grabbed at his throat.

"Shhh." Mary put her fingers to his lips. "Be still. Do you Irish never know when to be quiet? The fire brigade found you and brought you to the park. We were already here, thank God, and we saw them carrying you in. I thought you were dead or dying."

"Oh, Grandfather, we worried so. The good man at the hotel, the funny, nervous little man with the tight starched collar, saved all of us by banging on the doors."

"I never saw such a change in a man." Mary smiled. He seemed such a mousy little soul. But when he pounded on the doors, he *commanded* everyone to leave the hotel. He should be commended. He saved many lives, and not one person in the Regent was injured."

Brendan nodded and breathed slowly and deeply. There was a slight whistling sound, but already he felt his breathing become more regular.

"Are there many injured?" he asked with slow deliberation.

"The rumors are just filtering through now. People in the crowd have said that Jarrod Murdock and his daughter were killed. I don't know if that is true, though."

Brendan spoke again. "It is true, Mary. I saw him die. I was not sure about the girl."

"Those who said it swear it is true. Strange—isn't it?—that he should come to such an end."

"There would be those who would not think it strange at all, Mary."

"Aye, I suppose."

He sat up on his elbow and felt stronger. "Thank you, Kate. What would we do without our young beauty?"

She leaned over and hugged him then, sobs shaking her young body. "We—we were so—so worried about you, Grandfather."

"Well then, it was worth it to know that." He gave her that perennial grin that always made him appear much younger than his years.

The militia, bone-weary, stumbled into the park in twos and threes and threw themselves on the grass.

The mayor and several Assembly members went over to speak with the captain, and it was obvious that his report was terribly upsetting.

"What are they saying, Mary? Can you make it out?"

"No. I cannot, but the mayor seems disturbed."

"Well, go then, woman, ask him, for heaven's sake."

"It did not take you long to become your old self again. You recover quickly, Brendan McMahon."

She walked over to the knot of officials and dutifully stood several feet away but within their gaze.

Finally, the mayor broke away and came up to her. "How is your husband, Mrs. McMahon?"

"He's coming along fine, Your Honor. Ah, is there some disturbing news, sir?"

"I am afraid there is, Mrs. McMahon. There have been several fatalities, Jarrod Murdock for one, and his daughter. She was found inside the hotel. Strange, she could have jumped as her father did. She must have become confused. Then our dear friend Stephen Ordway.

His sight was poor. He must have been blinded by the smoke. It seems he fell over the railings. A mother and father and three children, Scottish people, immigrants newly arrived—very tragic. And a personal loss for you and your husband, I am sorry to say. Digger Shanley fell to his death from the window of his room over the store."

"Holy Mother of God, have mercy on him—on all of them." Her eyes filled at the thought of their dear Digger, the kindest creature God ever put on the earth. "He is with Una now," she said softly, and she returned to tell Brendan what she dreaded to tell him.

Three days later they left Charlottetown for home. They had come to celebrate, and instead, they had stood by to see Digger Shanley placed in the grave.

They left the charred remains of a city that had pulsated with excitement only a few days before, and as the coach took them past the Hillsborough River, not one of them looked back up the hill at the black and blistered town.

PART FOUR

THE STATES

1873–1874

CHAPTER XXVIII

THE YEARS PASSED, and Kate went on to Prince of Wales College. Her beauty and intelligence were a constant surprise and delight to the entire family. She was a special prize, and they would have liked nothing more than to keep her close to them always. But, as they all knew and feared, she was too spunky, too unsettled, and too curious about the world to settle for a quiet life on the island.

No one knew this better than Mary, who had, so long ago, had similar dreams of her own. Several times, Kate had mentioned to her mother and grandmother that, after finishing her education, she hoped to be able to travel. At first she was somewhat tentative in presenting her plan, knowing how painful her departure would be. As time went on, however, her voice became stronger, and finally—all too soon, it seemed—the day they had dreaded was upon them.

For Kate it was a time of excitement, trepidation, to be sure, but mainly intense excitement. For Gabriella it brought sadness; for Edward, a mixture of understanding and loneliness; and of course, for Mary and Brendan, a reminder of another day years before on the rain-wet quays of Galway City.

Kate had taught for a year at the Pleasant View Schoolhouse, and she had given to her teaching all the industry and diligence she could muster. But too many days her indigo eyes peered across the red clay of the highroad and past the potato fields to the Strait. It was that inviting, rolling water with its ships and commerce that called her, beckoned her, urged her to leave the country schoolhouse and take a chance with destiny. After all, she had taken her degree in foreign languages, and here she was teaching sums and reading. Only when she was teaching geography did her heart skip a beat or her pulse quicken. There were so many exotic places to visit—Venice with its music and its secret canals, Switzerland of the snow-capped chalets and mountains, even Paris, where she could dance all night and show off her fluent French. And there was Boston.

Boston held a peculiar fascination for her, probably because ever since she could remember her grandmother had told her stories of the excitement of city life. Of course, her own mother had often argued with Grandmother about "that silly city talk. You will have the girl believing all sorts of silly things. You mark my words, Mother, if you keep talking the way you do, one of these days Kate will be striking out on her own, and we will never see her again. And no one will be lonelier than you."

It was true, of course. Mary could not deny it, and when Kate told first her mother and father and then her grandparents that she had secured a teaching position in the States, Gabriella naturally pointed the accusing finger at Mary.

"Did I not tell you time and again that you would put ideas into her head? Now you have gone and done it, Mother. Well, you will be the biggest loser. You won't have her to come visit and chat over a cup of tea. And I won't have her coming by the farm to tell me about the schoolhouse and the students."

Mary's heart was indeed heavy, but hadn't she herself left her parents and her native country? Surely she would be a hypocrite if she attempted to dissuade her granddaughter from doing the same.

"Maybe you are right, Gabriella. I do not wish to argue over it. But the child is twenty-three years of age. She is a woman, and she is highly educated. She finds the island too small, too narrow. I cannot blame her. Let her go. As lonely as we all will be, we cannot stand in her way."

So the day came, a day that found her alone in her room reading a breezy and supportive letter from her uncle, Father James, who was himself a teacher at a seminary in Montreal—"and at times a very restless one, I might add. But go, Kate. By all means, go to Boston, and if you do not like it, you can always return. Tell my father to give you enough money for passage back. Now I must run and give a lecture. God's blessings on you."

Edward, because he was the least demonstrative of them all, had been chosen to accompany her to the packet ship in Charlottetown. Leaving her to board by herself while he went about his business, he kissed her cheek, wished her luck, and excused himself. He then climbed a hill that hung out over the Hillsborough River and sat under a tree, sobbing quietly as he watched the *Down East* disappear around a bend.

Kate Ahearn watched from the main deck as Charlottetown and the island slipped quietly past. Boston was out there waiting, and she was anxious for the challenge.

Miss Estelle Kent's Finishing School for Girls of Fine Boston Families lay in the dappled September sunlight.

Kate stood before its imposing brick archway and wrought-iron gates. Horse-drawn carriages clopped rhythmically along Boylston Street in Boston's Copley Square. Excitement tingled within her. The city was pumping in her blood. There was activity everywhere, and her eyes traveled up to the golden dome of the State House.

Oh, Boston! She had dreamed of coming here so often. Wouldn't

Grandmother love it? She felt a sudden flash of loneliness but shook it from her mind and continued the sweeping survey of the square and the brick-fronted bow-windowed town houses.

"Well, are you going to stand there all day or are you going in? The pavement is for walking, not gaping."

Tall and erect, with a severe chignon of graying hair, Miss Kent, by her strict and rigid stature, commanded instant respect. "You are too old to be a student, and by your luggage and the fascination you assume for our architecture, you must be my French teacher, Miss Catherine Ahearn."

Kate stooped and reached for her luggage while stammering her affirmation, and as she did so, she tripped over her long skirt and toppled unceremoniously to the brick walk. Then, struggling in a rush of skirts and petticoats, she righted herself and, with fiery cheeks, stuttered a distraught apology, "Miss Kent? I—I am so—so embarrassed. Please, Ma'am, for—forgive me."

Estelle Kent narrowed her eyes at this girl, barely older than the pupils she would teach, and wondered if her old friend at Prince of Wales, Mr. Danton, had not been too extravagant in praise of his former student.

"Well, come along then, pick up your things, and watch what you are doing this time." Miss Kent opened the door to the sound of giggilng as several young ladies scurried across the foyer and up the mahogany staircase. "Ladies, stop there, this instant." Five young women stopped and turned. "What is it you find so humorous?" No one spoke.

"Alicia, possibly you can explain this display of jocularity. Well?"

"Please, Ma'am, it was so funny. She was all tangled up in her skirts." The others suppressed giggles behind their hands.

"That will be enough. You were not even supposed to be on the first floor. This is study time. Now go back to your rooms at once."

The five, their long skirts ruffling, raced up the winding staircase and were gone.

Miss Kent watched after them for lingering minutes, and when there was silence overhead, she turned to her new teacher and asked briskly, "Have you had luncheon?"

"Ah no, Ma'am, but that is fine. I am not hungry. Really."

"While you are under this roof, you will take three meals a day. If I have to ship you back down East, I do not intend it to be in a box. Now come to the dining room. Leave your bags right where they are. Someone will take them to your room, which is the first door on your right off the staircase."

"Oh, Miss Kent, that is thoughtful of you, but I can surely take my own bags up."

"My dear *young* woman—and by the way, are you actually twenty-three years of age?"

"Why, yes, Ma'am. Why would I lie?"

"Oh, no one is accusing you of lying, for heaven's sake. You just do not seem very much older than the girls you will be instructing. But as I was about to say, I have no intention of being thoughful. It simply is part of my philosophy—you are a teacher, an educated person; you are not a servant. The students will respect you for your knowledge and the knowledge you impart to them. Is that clear?"

"Yes, Ma'am."

"Come then, follow me to the dining room."

The dark mahogany doors swung open into a room of elegant proportions, its far wall dominated by a large and exquisitely detailed French tapestry depicting a fox on the run and red-tunicked hunters and horsemen, bugles held lightly to their lips, while maidens held their hands breathlessly over their bosoms in timeless anticipation.

Miss Kent motioned for the young teacher to sit, and Kate obeyed.

"I shall return directly. I must inform Cook that she is to have a place set for you." The headmistress started toward the kitchen as Kate mumbled something inaudible.

"I beg your pardon, Miss Ahearn, were you addressing me behind my back?" She returned to within a few feet of Kate and glared at her. "Do you have something to say to me?"

Kate swallowed hard for fear of further offending this stern taskmaster of a headmistress.

"I am waiting, Miss Ahearn."

"Forgive me, Ma'am, I was just commenting to myself on the tapestry."

"Well, what do you have to say about the tapestry?"

"I just—I just said, oh, it just reminded me of something, that's all, really."

"Well, speak up, what did it remind you of?" The woman pressed her inquisition to the point where Kate wanted to jump from the chair and run out into Copley Square and down to Rowe's Wharf for a packet ship back to Charlottetown. Instead, she said quietly, "'For ever wilt thou love, and she be fair!'" Then she lowered her head humbly.

Miss Kent's expression softened, and she sat next to Kate at the table, "Keats. 'Ode on a Grecian Urn.' Well, my young teacher, it seems you have been exposed to a proper education in the wilds of Canada after all. There are only a few of us who would have noticed the connection between the tapestry and Keats. What is it you see in both?"

Kate lifted her head, and for the first time since her clumsy arrival, she felt her confidence returning. "Well, the perfection and timelessness of art as a contrast with the living world of change. In both scenes desires never cease, but possession is never possible."

Miss Kent smiled, and Kate was surprised that it was such a pleasant smile. "Yes, yes." She nodded. "Ah well, I will inform Bridget that we have a very hungry scholar to feed. If you will excuse me, my dear."

Kate's first weekend in Boston was spent in a whirlwind of sightseeing with Miss Kent. The Common reminded her of the Charlottetown parks, but there was more of a rhythm, a purpose, almost like a dance, to the promenading couples who strolled the walkways and paths in their fine clothes.

There was Faneuil Hall and the Moses Pierce House, a three-story brick dwelling, separated from the Paul Revere House by a walled garden. "Frankly I like it better than the Revere House," Miss Kent told her in confidence.

They stopped in at the Old Corner Book Store at Washington and School streets. The shop was crowded with top-hatted men and a few serious-looking women. "Look over there, Miss Ahearn, you see that man holding court?" At the south end of the cramped, book-scented shop a tall, gaunt man was pointing to a passage in a book as he seemed almost to be lecturing to the group.

"That is Mr. Longfellow."

Kate gasped, "Henry Wadsworth Longfellow? Oh, Miss Kent, all of this is so unbelievable. I know almost every stanza of 'Evangeline.' Many of my friends were descendants of the Acadians who were robbed of their land and sent into exile."

They continued on to the great gray obelisk of the Bunker Hill Monument, across the footbridge spanning the sun-smudged surface of the Charles River, past the Boston Athenaeum, and finally back to the school for afternoon tea and preparation for the beginning of the new school term the following morning. Kate, of course, in anticipation of her new teaching assignment, slept badly and then had to drag herself from bed after having finally fallen off in the early hours just before dawn.

At breakfast she was introduced to the six other women on the staff. Conversation was limited but by no means unfriendly until they all rose resolutely to face the new term. Kate had been tempted to take her plate, knife, fork, and coffee cup to the kitchen when she remembered Miss Kent's philosophy. Turning from the table, she caught sight of a large, open-faced woman with a blunt nose standing in the kitchen doorway, apparently staring at her, and Kate felt herself beginning to blush.

The woman motioned her over. "Good morning to you. Miss Ahearn, is it? Sure that's a fine Irish name. They tell me you're from Canada. And where are your people from in the old country, might I ask?"

Kate smiled. "County Galway, and proud of it," she said, cocking her head in the same manner as her grandmother.

"Ah, sure you have it written all over your pretty face. I'm from Galway meself, gone all these years from me home. But I am content here. Miss Kent is a good woman. Do as she wants, and you'll get along fine. She pretends to be a cold fish, but ah, it's all an act. So it's a teacher ye are. Well, I'm proud of ye, lass. Now be off to your classroom, and show them what scholars we Irish are. Good luck. Oh, my name is Bridget Burke, and my kitchen is always open to ye." With that she ducked back inside, her face beaming with deep pride.

Kate hurried now along the corridor, her heart pounding with anxiety. Could she hold their interest? Was she bright enough to teach these daughters of wealthy parents? Would they be too sophisticated for her? She stopped before the heavy oak door to gain her composure, and she could hear giggling and unbridled laughter from the classroom. She summoned up all the strength of the McMahons and the Ahearns and stepped into the room.

A honey-haired girl, pale but pretty, was pantomiming a person falling all over herself, and the others accompanied her efforts with gales of laughter. Kate recognzed the girl as the one Miss Kent had called Alicia.

She cleared her throat, and they all turned in her direction. "Good morning, ladies. You may take your seats." They looked at her and then at each other and, somewhat self-consciously, continued to giggle. Suddenly there was a knock on the door, and Kate turned to find Miss Franklin, the mathematics teacher, standing in the doorway. "*My* students are attempting to do their numbers. Their success or failure will depend on whether you can control these chattering magpies. Thank you." And she turned on her heel and was gone.

Kate's Irish temper began to surface. She looked at her students with a cold, unblinking stare. Her voice was a monotone of chilled steel. "Sit. Now," was all she said, and she cut each one of them in half with her eyes. Only when she could hear her own heart pounding with anger and purpose did she continue, so quietly they had to strain to hear her. "I am Miss Ahearn, and I shall be teaching you French, Latin, and English. I trust we shall have a successful year."

They stared at her rather homespun appearance, the satin black hair pinned severely back off her forehead and held in place by somber black combs. Her accent now amused them, and they looked in the direction of Alicia Evans to break the tension once again.

Alicia did not disappoint them. She raised her hand, and Kate nodded. "Yes, Miss?"

"Excuse me, Miss Ahearn, but what foreign country are you from?" The slightest smirk was in her voice and in her face.

"Foreign country?" Kate let her guard down. "I am from Canada. I would hardly refer to Canada as a foreign country. We are your northern neighbors, Miss, eh. It is a confederated country, united like your own. My own province attained confederation in 1873." She said it with pride, remembering her dear father and the joy he and Grandfather McMahon had experienced through that entire week of celebration.

"Anything north of Cape Ann is considered foreign to us, Miss Ahearn, eh." The giggling began again.

Kate stood quietly, working her own form of intimidation with the ice of her eyes.

"Well," she said finally, "it seems I shall be teaching you geography as well as your other studies. And may I add, Miss, that imitation, they say, is the highest form of flattery, eh? Let us hope your French will be spoken with equal facility. Now, shall we open our texts and begin to work?"

As the term progressed, Kate's fair but firm rule was the talk of the school and the envy of the other teachers. Miss Franklin, lost in her insensitive world of numbers, commanded silence but not respect. The girls, after all, were the products of the New England rich whose parents traveled a great deal, leaving many of them in need of someone other than their peers to confide in.

Penelope Fairchild was one of those, and although she was a cousin of Alicia Evans, and Alicia had still not warmed to Kate Ahearn, Penelope nonetheless came to Kate on many occasions to discuss her school problems, none of which was very serious to the world at large, but all of which were certainly important to her.

Little by little the girls gained confidence in Miss Ahearn, and their attitude did not go unnoticed by Estelle Kent, who stopped Kate on the stairway one morning two weeks before Christmas recess. "Catherine, I am just in the process of posting a letter to your former professor Mr. Danton. I took the liberty of saying how fortunate it was for us that you had asked him if he knew of any teaching opportunities in Boston."

"Oh, how kind of you to say that, Miss Kent. He thinks so highly of you, I know. And thank you for telling me. It will make Christmas away from home much more bearable."

"Oh, and about Christmas, Catherine. I received a note from a Harvard friend whose sister attends our school. You have Miss Charity Hazleton in class, I believe."

"Why, yes, yes, I do. Is there anything wrong?"

"No, of course not. Her brother is in his last year at Harvard, and he seems to be in danger of failing his French and Latin. The poor boy is very upset. He will pay handsomely for a tutor, and I immediately thought of you. The extra money could help with Christmas and clothes. I know how much you love clothes, Catherine. Are you interested?"

"Oh, yes. Very much so. I have my Christmas savings practically spent. Oh, I think it would be a grand opportunity. When do I begin?"

"I shall be in touch with him. I shall tell him to come by here at his convenience. I do not want you going over to Harvard. Some of those ruffians do not know how to treat a lovely young woman. Besides, there would be no chaperone." That conversation, hurried yet complimentary and warming for Kate, had taken place on a Thursday. On Sunday afternoon, just after returning from mass, Kate was told that Miss Kent was waiting to see her in the formal parlor.

Kate could not for the life of her think why she was being summoned until she walked into the spacious room and saw a young man seated on the edge of a silk brocaded chair.

"Oh, Miss Ahearn, this is Mr. Peter Hazleton, the young man of whom I spoke."

Kate inwardly chided herself for the blush she felt in her cheekbones. Surely, over the past few days, she had not given much thought to the young man she would tutor, but this young man, tall and straight

and muscular, of such yellow hair and a clear, smiling face, with sparkling eyes greener than she had ever seen, took her by surprise.

"How do you do, Miss Ahearn? Thank you for allowing me to drop
by on a Sunday, but I am desperate." He bowed slightly, and his smile
filled and warmed the entire room.

"You do not seem that desperate, Mr. Hazleton," Miss Kent offered
somewhat bemusedly.

"Well, I wasn't. I mean, I wasn't aware of my desperate straits
until just moments ago. What I mean is, oh, well, I do need help. I do
hope you can help me, Miss Ahearn."

"*C'est possible*, Mr. Hazleton."

Their eyes held for a moment, and Miss Kent prudently decided
she had to organize the girls for the upcoming Decoration Night festivities. "Well, if you will excuse me, I have some items that need my
attention."

"Huh? Oh, yes. Yes, of course, Miss Kent. Ah, thank you."

"Do not dally too long, Miss Ahearn. This is a busy week for all
of us."

"Yes, Ma'am. I mean, no Ma'am."

They watched her go out and leave the double doors open behind
her.

"Well?"

"Well?"

They overrode each other's words.

"When do—"

"When do—" They broke into laughter.

Peter put a finger to his lips. "When do you think we can begin
the lessons, Miss Ahearn?"

"I am free after dinner any night from seven to nine—that is,
except this Wednesday. Wednesday is Decoration Night, and the parents come and trim the holly bush and partake of punch with us."

"Well, tomorrow night then? At seven. Here in the parlor? I'll
bring my books? Is that fine with you, Miss Ahearn?"

"I think that would be fine, Mr. Hazleton. Until tomorrow night
then." He bowed again, but even less than before, so intent was he on
looking at her. He backed out and bumped into a poinsettia plant set
on a table near the double doors. He grabbed frantically for the plant,
securing it as it teetered on the table. "Huh, well, yes. Tomorrow then."

When he had left, it was her turn to giggle at awkward and embarrassing entrances and exits.

He arrived before seven on Monday and Tuesday evenings, and she
was surprised by his facility with French and Latin. His only problem
was one of concentration. He seemed to have no incentive to learn. At
least that had been his problem before he met the lovely Kate. Now
he wanted to do well. He wanted, indeed, to impress his teacher.

On Wednesday Miss Kent's School was bedecked and festooned
with greenery. The foyer held holly wreaths, and the fan window over

the main entrance was frosted from the cold. The brass knocker was now dusted with a light helping of snow, and outside, as the guests arrived, their coats powdered white, delicate flakes flew about the gaslights.

The girls stood shyly with their parents or, sometimes, self-consciously alone. Kate, effervescent and happy, moved among them with a tray of apple punch in sparkling cut-glass goblets, her fresh and youthful beauty causing many a father's head to turn.

One man who sipped courteously from the glass she served was not a father, but a grandfather. His white hair was as soft as the snow, and his hawklike face was tight-skinned. He was tall, straight, and lithe and except for his white hair would have appeared to be a much younger man.

As he watched her moving about the room, he had the strange feeling that they had met before. But of course, he had never seen her. He knew that. Age was playing tricks on him. Still, he sidled over to Miss Kent and excused himself by saying, "You have a new teacher, I see, Miss Kent, and what is her name?"

"Oh, she has turned out so well. Her name is Catherine Ahearn, Mr. Evans."

"Seems to have a lot of spirit, Miss Kent."

"She does, and the girls respond very well to her. Your granddaughter has her for her language classes."

"Interesting. I must ask Alicia what she thinks of your Miss Ahearn."

"Yes, do that, Mr. Evans."

He threaded his way back to where his granddaughter sat by the fire with her grandmother, who was saying, "Really, Alicia, you know your parents would like to be home for Christmas, but your father had business in London. Certainly you wouldn't expect your grandfather to go off in the dead of winter at his age."

"Well, I daresay if I had to go to London, I could easily make the trip. My age? That is an insult, Prudence, and one directed as much to yourself as to me." He did not smile, and Alicia felt the tension. Prudence Evans turned resolutely into the fire. It was just one more occasion on which she had said the wrong thing.

"Why did *Mother* have to go? Is she on business also?"

"That will be enough, Alicia. I should think you would be appreciative that your decrepit old grandparents would even dare come out on a ghastly night like this." He directed his sharp-tongued remarks to his wife's back. But of course, she said nothing.

"Tell me, Alicia, who is this new instructor, this Miss Ahearn? I understand she is one of your teachers."

Alicia turned her pale face toward her grandfather and muttered, "I hate her."

"Goodness." Prudence turned from the fire to face her granddaughter. "Those are very harsh words, my dear, really."

"I don't care, Grandmother. She makes me sick. All the girls think she's so wonderful. But she doesn't fool me, the foreigner."

"Foreigner?" Evans asked. "She doesn't look foreign. Where's she from?"

"Oh, somewhere in the middle of the woods in Canada."

Evans was about to sip from his glass when his hand began to tremble, and he spilled the punch onto his wife's shoulder.

"For heaven's sake, Channing, do be more careful. What is wrong with you? You look as though you'd seen a ghost."

Absently he placed the glass on the table beside him and walked back through the milling girls and their relatives. From the foyer he looked across to the open and spacious parlor. He leaned against the double doors, nodding to those who passed, and then he slowly walked into the room and sat rigidly on the silk cushion of a love seat and looked slowly in the direction of Catherine Ahearn. He had been right after all. It was Mary Roark, as she'd looked almost forty years ago. She had those same flame-lighted high cheekbones, the bird-soft raven hair, the jaunty walk, the cock of the head, and the round, full breasts and narrow waist. Mary Roark was the most beautiful and desirable woman he had ever seen. She was the only woman he had ever really wanted. He would never forget seeing Mary and that McMahon bastard heading north to Canada, out of his life. Oh, he'd made inquiries, but when the man named Douglas never contacted him, he'd married Prudence Fairchild for better or for worse and concentrated on making as much money as possible. His life had been convenient, if not altogether dull. He could not believe he was reliving it after all these years. And this girl-woman, who was she? Was she Mary Roark's granddaughter, or was she a sister's or brother's relative? The more he studied her, common sense and intuition told him she had to be a granddaughter.

Now she came his way, offering the tray again. "I believe you already had some punch, sir, but since it is all gone, you must have enjoyed it. Please have another."

He looked into her eyes, the color of deep and secret lakes, and his poise seemed to desert him.

"Is there something wrong, sir? Are you unwell?" She cocked her head in that way so familiar to him even after all these years. Her voice expressed sincere interest, but he pushed her solicitude aside. "Nothing, it is nothing, my dear, take care of your other guests."

"Why, yes, sir, if you like."

She straightened and was about to leave when he said, "I wonder, my dear, if I may speak with you sometime? It, ah, concerns my granddaughter."

"Why, surely, sir, and who might your granddaughter be?"

"Alicia. Alicia Evans."

"Oh, I see. Yes. Possibly that would be a good idea. I am sure Miss Kent will make the proper arrangements. Now I must be about my duties."

He watched her move back across the foyer and into the reception room. All the desire and passion he had buried inside for so long came rushing at him. This beautiful young woman had stripped away the years and brought forth the memory of Mary Roark.

At the end of the week Peter arrived again, ruddy-cheeked, with his gold hair plastered across his forehead from a wet snow but armed with his books and his perpetual smile.

Kate showed him into the parlor, leaving the double doors open as Miss Kent required when a man was visiting.

"Now, Mr. Hazleton, shall we begin with Latin or French?"

"Oh, it makes little difference, Miss Ahearn, I am equally prepared in both." He took his seat beside her at the writing table. She spread her texts out on the green hand-tooled leather table top, smoothed the pages of her Caesar's *Gallic Wars*, and said, "All right, Mr. Hazleton, turn to your *Commentaries*, page one hundred thirty-six *Tertius Liber*. Read the Latin first, and then translate after several words so you will keep the continuity of thought. It will help you in context. Ready now, shall we proceed?"

"Yes, Miss Ahearn." The green eyes sparkled.

"*Quinque bella gesta adversus varias gentes Galliae describuntur hoc libro.*" He looked up at her, and she nodded encouragement as he translated: " 'Five wars carried on against various nations of Gaul were described,' I mean, '*are* described in this book.' "

"Good. Continue, please."

"*Primum adversus Veragros et Sedunos quod gestumfuit ipso quidem absente*, 'the first against the Veragri and Seduni, which was carried on, himself indeed absent or being absent.' There, how do you think I am progressing, Miss Ahearn?"

She smiled. "You are doing extremely well, Mr. Hazleton. I just cannot see why you need a tutor."

"Oh, but I did. I mean I do. I had no incentive, but now I have great determination to do well. Here, let me continue. *Sed auspicus à Galbâ legato*, but under his auspices'—'under' is understood in that situation— 'by Galba, his lieutenant'—'his' is implied." He continued on as the fruitwood cracked and sparked in the fireplace and December marched like Caesar's legions, not across Gaul but certainly across Copley Square.

"All right, Mr. Hazleton, that will do now. Open your French text to page one hundred ninety-two. Today we will discuss the verb *faire* causatively."

"Now we mentioned this verb last time, but just let me repeat: This verb plus an infinitive corresponds to a great variety of expressions in English which may be explained by the meaning '*cause to do or be done.*' Do you understand that concept?"

"Yes, I think so."

"Fine. Now I shall give you the English, and you translate into French:

" 'I have made the children write.' "

"Oh, let me see, '*J'ai fait écrire les enfants.*' "

" 'He will make them listen.' "

" '*Il les fera écouter.*' "

" 'The dress she got made for herself.' "

" '*La robe qu'elle s'est fait faire.*' "

"All right now, let us look at the following concept: A governed substantive follows the infinitive, but a governed conjunctive personal pronoun goes with *faire*. Continue: 'Have the servant come'—that is, get the servant to—"

" '*Faites venir la domestique.*' "

" 'Have her come.' "

" '*Faites-la venir.*' "

"Hmmm. Very good, Mr. Hazleton. Very good. Now for next time, work on the rule that states: If the infinitive with *faire* has a direct object, its personal object must be indirect, for example, *Je fis lire mon fils*, 'I made my son read.' Any questions?"

"Yes, I have a question, Miss Ahearn. Please do not think me bold, but is your accent Canadian?"

"Why, yes, it is, Mr. Hazleton." She reddened defensively. This city continually surprised her by its parochial attitudes.

"May I ask what part of Canada?" he continued politely.

"I am sure you've never heard of it, Mr. Hazleton." Her answer was clipped and terse, and she gathered up her texts to signal the end of the lesson.

"Maybe I have," he pressed on. His smile was wide and appealing.

"Very well, if you must know, and I am sure you are like most others who have never heard of it, Prince Edward Island." She said it sharply, and his smile faded, but only for seconds. It returned when he said rather matter-of-factly, "Oh, Charlottetown?"

Her mouth opened in surprise. "You know Charlottetown?" She almost screamed it in disbelief. "You have heard of the island?"

"Heard of it." He chuckled good-naturedly. "I've been there."

She could not hold back her excitement, and as she leaned forward, she knocked her texts onto the Brussels rug.

He leaned over to retrieve them for her just as she did, and her silken hair touched his cheek. Its suggestion of soft, yet mysterious sensuality excited him. He handed her the books. The intimacy of the moment was not lost on Kate, either. Then sudden tears sprang to her eyes.

"Oh, Miss Ahearn, forgive me, it was an accident. I would never be so brash and offensive."

"I am sure you would not, Mr. Hazleton. You are a perfect gentleman. It was just so strange to hear the name Charlottetown from a— a stranger. It gave me such a sensation. Well, I must not hold you up, Mr. Hazleton. You have a windy, snowy journey back across the Charles to Cambridge."

"But are you from Charlottetown, Miss Ahearn?"

"No." She brushed a tear from her eye. "I am from Tignish. Surely you have never heard of Tignish."

"But surely I have. It's on the North Cape."

She was struck dumb. His laughter filled the room. "You see, my father is in the shipping business, and I have sailed to Canada many times. Why, I probably passed you on the street or in the market district. But then"—he knew he was taking a bold step—"I am sure I would have remembered you had I ever seen you."

This time she did not blush but merely smiled.

He was happy that he had taken the chance because it gave him the courage to take a second, even bolder step. "I wonder, Miss Ahearn, if I may ask you to join me for tea. It's just around the corner, and we could talk about Canada and your Prince Edward Island. It's such a lovely little tearoom, the Blue Ship, and they have the most delicious pastries, and I had barely any dinner and—well?"

"I would love to have tea with you, Mr. Hazleton. Just let me tell Miss Kent I will be going out for a while."

Copley Square was a swirl of flakes. The gaslights blinked pale yellow eyes in the blowing white night. A few horse-drawn carriages huddled off to the stables like hunched black husks, and pedestrians slid and frolicked or hurried off into the gathering darkness to sit before cozy fireplaces.

Snowflakes clung to Kate's bonnet and eyelashes and to Peter's hatless head. They passed the Boston Society of Natural History, a silent tie to the past with its great Grecian portico and pillary, and crossed over to Newbury Street. Just east of Copley Square, between the Emmanuel Church and a tobacconist, was the Blue Ship tearooms. A doughty sign depicting a sharply defined brigantine now blew like a windy mast in the December gusts.

Inside, they were struck by the sudden warmth of a large walk-in fireplace, where pots of water bubbled and boiled. Several tables were already occupied, but they caught sight of one in the far corner adjacent to the wide hearth.

The sizzling sound of beef turning on a spit caught Peter's attention as he hung his coat on a bamboo clotheshorse.

"I am famished. Would you join me in a steak and kidney pie, Miss Ahearn?"

"Oh, no, really, I had a most sufficient dinner. Miss Kent insists we have all our meals at school. She believes the atmosphere should be one of family."

"Is it?"

"Yes, mostly. Everyone is very pleasant—with one or two exceptions." And she thought of the horse-faced Miss Franklin, who only grunted in answer to Kate's salutations.

"Do you have a large family, Miss Ahearn?"

"Not really. I am the only child, but I have cousins and grandparents and Mama and Papa."

"I imagine they miss you dearly."

"Yes, I suppose they do. Mama especially. Papa is very busy with his newspaper and the Assembly."

"Your father is in politics then?"

"Yes. Very much so. Mama thinks he works too hard at it."

"Are you lonely for home, Miss Ahearn?"

"Only when I am reminded of it. Of being lonely, I mean."

"Oh, damn, how stupid of me to bring it up. Here, let's talk about something else. You see that clotheshorse. I'll wager that came from Singapore."

"But how do you know that, Mr. Hazleton?"

"Because I have seen many like it in my travels."

"When do you have time for such travels with Harvard College and your studies?"

"Oh, my father has employed me on his ships ever since I was quite a little lad. He pays me the fair wage just like any ordinary seaman, and every summer I'm off somewhere for three or four months."

"You must be very worldly then, Mr. Hazleton, for your years."

"I do not know what you mean exactly, Miss Ahearn."

"Well, most young men your age have surely not seen as much of the world as you."

She knew she had offended him with her brashness, and she was sincerely sorry, for he seemed such a sensitive and kind young man. Attempting to move the conversation to a less personal topic, she asked, "What is your favorite place in the world? Other than Prince Edward Island, that is?"

He smiled, and she was happy he was not the petulant or moody kind who bore grudges.

"I should say the island will always be special and even more so now. But the place—oh, here is our waitress. Are you sure you will have no dinner?"

"Yes. Surely, indeed. Just tea, thank you, and I think I shall have one buttered scone."

"Fine. Then I shall not eat alone. I will have the steak and kidney pie, and I, too, shall have tea. Thank you."

The waitress curtsied and bustled off to the kitchen.

"Now where was I? Oh, yes, my favorite place. Let me see, probably a little island—you see, I do love islands—a little island no one ever heard of, Place of the Night Star it is called, deep in the South Pacific. We swam in warm waters that were shimmering gold from an enormous moon."

Kate's pulse quickened. She had such a temptation to ask with whom he swam.

"Yes. That is the most enchanting lagoon in the world." He remembered all too vividly swimimng naked with the native girls. He once told someone that it was like being in one of those frescoes of pagan Rome he had studied in Professor Dornier's history of art class. "Except"—he had laughed—"I didn't think I was in hell; I thought I was in heaven."

He lingered over the memory. "Yes, most enchanting."

"Ah, and what do you plan to do upon graduation, Mr. Hazleton?"

"Well, Father has me in mind for an eventual full partnership in the business, but he insists I get a good, long voyage under my belt first, probably to China. So I will do that upon graduation, and then it's back to Boston, where I will settle down and become a Beacon Hill man of commerce and a charter member of the Somerset Club."

"Your father has your life fairly well thought out."

"Oh, yes, as his father before him, and grandfather, and so on back down the line."

The waitress arrived, curtsied again, and served the piping hot pie and scone. She poured the tea and bustled off.

They ate for several minutes in silence, save for the crackling firewood and the muffled conversations of other late-evening diners.

"I expect I should be returning, Mr. Hazleton, and you, poor soul, you must trek all the way back to Cambridge in this dreadful weather."

"I do not find the weather dreadful at all, Miss Ahearn. It is a most romantic night. I shall fly back to Adams House like Icarus and with no danger of my wings melting. Shall we go?" He left some silver on the table and helped her on with her heavy fur.

"My, but that is the heaviest and no doubt the warmest coat I have ever held. What kind of fur is it?"

"Fox. My grandfather trapped it, and my grandmother had it fashioned for me by the Indians." She smiled. Two such different worlds, she thought. But how charming and interesting was his.

A week after Christmas holidays Mr. Channing Evans came to Miss Kent's School by an appointment previously made. Miss Kent showed him into the parlor, where Kate was waiting, and then quickly excused herself, closing the double doors behind her.

Evans smiled. "Well, I seem to have reached that grand old time in my life where I am either trusted or considered harmless behind closed doors with a beautiful woman. Come sit here on the love seat, my dear, and we shall talk."

"Yes, sir, of course. I am happy you came because I do not enjoy the hostility that seems to exist between Alicia and me."

"Alicia?" he asked with a wrinkled frown, the result of too many sun-filled summers on Rockport's Cape Ann.

"Why, yes, sir. Is she not the reason for your visit?"

"Oh, of course, of course, my dear. I am here as the surrogate father. My son has been in London for several months on business." He crossed his legs casually, exposing black, richly textured leather boots.

"Now Alicia is a very strong-willed girl. She can be spoiled at times, and she enjoys an audience. Strange, she is so unlike her brother at Harvard. Patch is a serious student and not at all demonstrative. I like a serious young man, do you not, Miss Ahearn?"

"Uh, yes. I suppose. But Alicia, she—"

"Oh, yes, back to Alicia. She is sixteen and lovely in a frail sort of way. I suspect this hostility is just a phase young women go through, not quite women, yet not quite little girls anymore. Don't you think?"

"I really do not know, sir. I just know that I try to be fair with her, but she does not respond to that approach. I am quite nonplussed."

"Oh, do not be, my dear. You must be firm with her."

Kate turned to him as he sat, relaxed and comfortable, on the love seat. He seemed in no hurry to leave, yet he showed no deep interest in his grandchild. He was a handsome man in that Yankee fashion she saw so often on the streets of Boston. So like those wealthy barristers and brokers she noticed entering the fine gentlemen's clubs on Beacon Hill and Joy Street. They all had that lean Spartan look; patrician profiles, long, bony fingers, and tightly tailored suits of good tweed or the black frock-coated outfits of the somber world of business. They were polished, poised, well mannered, and insincere. She hoped Peter was not this type.

She did not try to avoid his gaze, but rather, she looked directly at him. He was here for another reason, she was certain, but he seemed unwilling to mention it. She would wait, then "let him play his hand." That's what her grandfather would have said.

"You think being firm is the answer then?"

"By all means. By all means."

"You do not think there is a possibility she is simply lonely for her parents and looking for any attention she can get?"

"Ha." He chuckled, a nasal Yankee laugh. "Ha. That is good. Quite good. Oh, how wonderful to be young and idealistic, or do they go hand in hand? Where did you learn that liberal approach to the classroom?"

"It is just a theory of mine."

"Something you learned in normal school, I suspect."

"Not normal school, Mr. Evans. University."

"Oh, a proper liberal education, then. Good. Tell me what university, my dear."

"Prince of Wales, sir."

"Prince of Wales? Is that in the East? But surely it could not be. I am sure I would have heard of it."

What was the purpose of this strange line of questioning? Kate simply could not fathom it.

"Down East, Mr. Evans."

"Down East? Maine?"

"No. Much farther down East. Canada. Prince Edward Island."

The brown eyes moved slightly. There was the suggestion of a frown. He was certain now. Prince Edward Island. That had been McMahon's destination when he took Mary Roark away from Evansborough. Prince Edward Island, some deserted rock in the middle of an ocean somewhere, some wind-swept, barren backwoods island with no future, no culture, when Mary Roark could have had so much had she stayed.

"Your people, do they go back a long way on this splendid island of yours?"

"No, and certainly not as far back as the pilgrims in this country. My grandparents came to Canada from Ireland."

"Oh, Ireland. Yes, we have many Irish immigrants living in Boston. They are fine, hard-working people. What section of Ireland did your grandparents come from?"

"From County Galway. My grandparents have told me stories

about their younger days; but they are Canadians now, and they do like to dwell on the past."

He leaned closer. His eyes were two brown stones fixed and un-blinking. "Your grandparents? Are they still alive?"

"Oh yes, very much so. My grandfather is a very successful busi-nessman and a member of the island Assembly and my grandmother—"

"Yes, your grandmother?" He shot the question at her, and the brown eyes jumped in his head.

"What? What about my grandmother?"

He braced himself. It was unlike him to show his emotions so openly. Smiling, he said more slowly, "Your were speaking about your grandmother. You seem so affectionate when mentioning your grand-parents."

"Oh, well, my grandmother is still very beautiful and so full of the zest of living. She loves the cities and fine clothes. I suppose in a way she is the reason I am here in Boston. She was here many years ago, and she told me what I could expect."

"And what was that, my dear?"

"The fine houses and clothes and the excitement of a large city."

"Are your grandparents named Ahearn also?"

"Oh, no. They are McMahons. Galway McMahons, and proud of it."

The puzzle was complete; the last piece fitted squarely where it belonged. His pulse quickened, but this time he betrayed none of his emotion.

"Well, it has been delightful chatting with you, and I shall be cer-tain to speak to Alicia about coming to you so you both might straighten out your differences of opinion."

"But I do not have any differences of opinion with Alicia, Mr. Evans."

"There, there"—he patted her folded hands as they rested on the lap of her pearl gray dress—"it will all sort itself out. Now I must be off to my club. I shall show myself out. Good day, Miss Ahearn."

She watched the rigidly straight figure as he passed under the bow window, heading in the direction of Arlington Street.

What a strange conversation, she thought. Nothing was any clearer than before he arrived.

CHAPTER XXIX

Winter, always harsh in New England, somehow managed to be pleasant, even though snow-filled. The snow served to highlight the Sunday afternoon sleigh rides that found Peter and Kate winding across the Back Bay, traversing the frozen Charles, and climbing the snow-packed lanes to Beacon Hill and Louisburg Square. There were stops for tea and pastry, romps on the Boston Common and then the great, sliding sleigh descent to Tremont Street below the golden dome of the State House.

Their relationship was warm and friendly, and on one gray, flurried Sunday, as he tucked the black bear rug around them both, he leaned toward her and gently kissed her cheek.

"Peter, you did not even ask permission. I should jump immediately from his sinful chariot and dash all the way back to Miss Kent and fall at her feet, saying how a Harvard man took advantage of me."

"Are you going to?" he asked in mock fear.

"No. Instead, I am going to kiss you in return." And she brushed her lips against his cheek.

His mint green eyes grew large, and then he jumped from the carriage and ran across the little park next to the Old Granary Burying Ground, screaming and scooping snow and tossing it in the air.

Kate, standing in the carriage with the reins in her hands, laughed and giggled in spite of herself and commanded, "Peter Hazleton, come back here this minute. The entire city is watching." And indeed it was. Puritan Boston glared down at him from the bow windows of its Bulfinch brick-fronted houses, now burnished orange in the late-afternoon light.

He returned to the carriage and climbed up beside her, looking like some primordial snow beast.

"Here, let me brush that off. Really, Peter, you will catch cold and miss your examinations, and all your work and study will be for naught."

"It would be worth it. Dear Kate, do you realize you kissed me back?"

She giggled. "It must be the day. It is a glorious day, is it not?"

"It certainly is. I shall always remember it, no matter what."

"Why do you say that, Peter, 'no matter what'?"

"Oh, nothing, I just think of this coming summer and graduation and six months at the mast. God knows where I will be, and I shall miss you so."

"Really, Peter, it is only February. Let's think of the present."

"If you say so, Kate. I have now put all demon thoughts of loneliness out of my head."

"Good. Now it is time I returned. I have study hours duty tonight."

Winter slipped idly by with sleigh rides out to Lexington and Concord, winding along the Concord River and into the wooded quiet to stop for tea and scones in a two-room inn that was a station on the Boston and Vermont Post Road, then back to Boston before the shroud of dusk descended.

Kate's heart was happy in the presence of Peter Hazleton. He was boyish and natural, not affected like some of his Harvard friends, who seemed, on occasion, to look down on her. With Peter there was continual enjoyment and a spontaneity that she had never before encountered. Yet, while she was comfortable with the smiling Peter, there was somehow something missing in their relationship, and it was, she felt as she lay thinking on many nights in the brass bed of her large and well-appointed bedroom, a feeling of permanence. She was, after all, the Canadian from somewhere up there in the tundra of the frozen north, or so she saw herself in the eyes of the Harvard crowd. She had not yet been introduced to Peter's parents, and it seemed she never would be, for there had not been any mention of such a meeting. So she put the thought out of her mind and determined to enjoy each day as it came.

Toward spring Peter was involved heavily in his studies, and the Sunday jaunts were reduced. Yet Kate looked upon this change of pace as a chance to resume her explorations of the many interesting and historic nooks and crannies hidden about the city.

So it was on a balmy Sunday afternoon in April that she accompanied cook Bridget Burke on a promenade about the less than elegant sections of Boston.

"Come see where the Irish live in this sprawling city, Miss Kate. It is not a pretty sight. There are many unfortunate souls who would have been better off had they stayed in Ireland." And Kate was duly depressed when she viewed the squalid tenements at the outskirts of the North End, the ragged clothing on gaunt children whose eyes seemed sunk into their skulls. This was a Boston far removed from the brick fronts and gleaming walnut doors and polished knockers. This was a different Boston from the green of Louisburg Square and Harvard Yard.

"Do not be alarmed, Miss Kate. Some of 'em are their own worst enemy. Far too many have the Irish curse of the bottle, God have mercy on them. But there are those who want to work and get ahead.

And so help me, they can do it if they want. Sure there is great opportunity for any man who wants to bend his back and save his money," Bridget lectured as they walked through the muddy, spring-thawing streets, tiptoeing across the long boards that served as footbridges over the muck.

Men and women hung out over their balconies, dreaming of clear lakes and fish-jumping streams, lush green hills, and vast verdant landscapes. Of course, the melancholy in their Celtic souls lied to them and obscured the memories of starvation.

Eventually the streets became wider and somewhat cleaner as they approached the far side of the North End.

"Where are you taking me, Miss Bridget? Is this a walking tour? Gracious, woman, I have study hour tonight. I shall fall asleep at my desk."

"Ach, and you with your farm background. I do declare you are becoming too much of a Boston lady. Sure you spend more time in the carriage than all those dowagers up on Beacon Hill."

Kate giggled her approval of this forthright woman. It was this kind of banter she had missed so much.

"I am taking ye to a political gatherin'. There is a young man makin' a step at political office. He's an Irishman and a Harvard College graduate, if ye can believe that now. I know his mother and father well. No harder-workin' people live in this city. Come now, step lively, it's just around the corner, but we'll have to sit down in the back. These menfolk think politics is no place for ladies. Sure when could an Irishman lace his boots without the help of a mother or wife?"

Francis Michael Joyce stood behind the wine-colored curtain that separated him from the crowd of five hundred raucous, Boston Irish. Their church responsibility was behind them, and the entire Sunday afternoon was spread out before them on long wooden tables.

They had come to hear *him*, to be sure, but the prospect of free ale and a collation of cold ham, tomatoes, and potato salad had been more than incentive enough to motivate their interest in the upcoming election for City Council.

Frank Joyce was alone except for his friend James Laughlin, who sat in a straight-backed chair, fidgeting and picking at his fingernails like some fastidious primping feline.

"Now you know what you are going to say?" Laughlin asked.

"Of course, I know what I am going to say. It's just how I should say it that bothers me."

Laughlin stood up and smoothed the sleeves of his suit coat. Its color was a conservative gray, the color of quiet opulence, but its texture was coarse, the material of so many imitations hanging from the racks at Oettinger's Tailor Shop on Canal Street.

"You say it directly. You show them that you are educated and several cuts above them. They are poor, hard-working souls who need one of their own to represent them in this Puritan bastion. Remember how you swayed them at Harvard. You, the son of County Clare immigrants, yet they voted you editor in chief of the *Advocate*. Quite an accomplishment for the son of immigrants. Now, judging by the noise out there, I think it's about time for me to introduce you."

"Damn it," Joyce swore, "I told McGillicuddy not to serve the ale until after I spoke. You're right. It's time. Go out and introduce me, Jimmy. Get their attention."

Frank Joyce wiped his hands against his pant legs. Why was he so nervous? God knows, if he could convince those Harvard Yankees to vote for him, he certainly should have no trouble with his own kind, even if they were day laborers.

Joyce was a strapping man, tall and straight, not thick-necked or stooped like so many of those to whom he would soon speak. His clothes were more Yankee in their conservatism and of a higher-grade material than those of his Harvard friend Laughlin. Frank's father, Christopher Joyce, had, like so many Irish, come to the shores of Massachusetts to escape famine and the prospect of a bleak existence in Ireland. He left with a wife and four children, one of whom died on board ship and another soon after arriving in East Boston.

Joyce, however, had with him on his arrival something that no other immigrant could boast. Sewed into the inside pocket of his baggy, greasy trousers was a hundred-pound note stolen from the cashbox of his landlord. He had walked into the lord's home to say his good-byes, and, finding the house empty, had begun a quick look around.

He surveyed each room, swearing to himself that in America he, too, would have a lovely and spacious home. When he came upon the room that served as an office and saw the open cashbox, he did not hesitate. He scooped up several pieces of silver and, without the slightest twinge of conscience, took the hundred-pound note and stuffed it into his pocket. Then he shoved his cap back on his head and left the premises.

Once on the highroad, he cut across the soggy bog to the squalid thatched cottage, where his wife and family were waiting in the dirty ox-drawn cart. In Galway City the hollow-bellied ox brought a price of fifty-three shillings. After one night in a dingy, urine-smelling room on the Galway quays, Christopher, his wife, Margaret, and the four children boarded an overloaded coffin ship for America.

The crossing was calm at first, and then a swift epidemic swept through the vessel, claiming the life of their four-year-old son and six other passengers.

They reached Boston with heavy hearts, but Christopher Joyce knew that he would not be landing on American shores a pauper, and throughout the long, sorrowful journey he would look off to the gray horizon and finger the crisp hundred-pound note sewn securely and secretly in his pants pocket. Christopher Joyce was no melancholic Irish poet. He was a realist who did not allow tradition or sentiment to interfere with his plans for success. Three years after arriving in Boston he became part owner of the Shamrock Pub; four years later he bought the remaining shares from P. T. Sullivan, who was fast succumbing to the lure of his own whiskey.

Francis Michael Joyce, the last child of the union, was born eight years after the Joyce family arrived in East Boston. He was an excellent student, and his father had great plans for him. "I'll see you mayor of Boston before they shovel the clay over me, boyo. Mark me."

Beyond the curtain they were cheering now, their clapping and stomping all but drowning out James Laughlin's introduction.

Frank Joyce, angered by this barbaric behavior, decided to wait no longer, and he parted the curtains and strode out onto the narrow stage.

Laughlin shrugged his bony shoulders, stepped aside, and descended three short steps to the hall, where he took a seat in the corner. His heart pounded. He hoped Frank would tell them all to shut their ale-guzzling mouths and listen. After all, this was his first public appearance since announcing his candidacy, and if he could not get past this crowd, then all their planning for the future would be wasted.

Joyce walked to the edge of the stage. "Good afternoon, my friends. I am honored that you would take leave of the warmth of your family circle to join me here today."

"Take leave? She bloody well threw me out on my arse." A keg-bellied, red-faced man roared in laughter as the others, holding their foaming glasses, saluted him in mock tribute.

"Ah, yes. Well, thank you for coming. If you will be seated, sir, I would like to tell you my reasons for seeking the high office of the Boston City Council."

"High office," another shouted, "sure it t'ain't the mayor's seat you're after. High office, is it?"

"Are ye exaggeratin' just a bit, Frankie boy?" still another jumped in to say.

Christopher Joyce fumed as he leaned against the door to the kitchen. A long apron covered his Sunday suit. He had wanted this day to be a success. He had hoped to see his Frank overwhelm these people with his golden rhetoric and his Harvard education. He envisioned his son rising up from the grass roots of the North End of Boston with thousands of Irish hanging to his coattails as he plowed through the rough seas of Brahmin dominance while taking the city in a tidal wave of power. Now all that was slipping from their hands. Jesus, Mary, and Saint Joseph, if Frank couldn't talk to a full hall of illiterate Irishmen, how in God's name would he ever succeed in politics? The Irish vote outnumbered the Yankees. It was through the ballot box that the Irish could rise above their poverty and unemployment. It was in City Hall where the patronage and the jobs were doled out. Christopher Joyce wanted that for his people, true, but his hopes for his son were not altogether altruistic. It was in City Hall that zoning laws were passed and licenses and permits could be funneled to the right people. And why not? he had argued with his son. Haven't the Yankees been taking care of their own for years?

But City Hall was a long way off. One had to win the skirmishes before winning the war and for the moment Frank Joyce was succumbing to defeat in his first skirmish.

"Gentlemen and ladies." Frank directed his remarks to the dozen or so women sitting tensely on the edge of their chairs.

When he mentioned the word *ladies*, the beery-eyed audience turned almost as one to the rear of the room.

"What the hell be *they* doin' here? Sure that's why we came, to get away from the apron strings for a few moments of peace."

"Aye. Aye, sure he's right. Sure we have little enough time to ourselves."

Kate felt her face burning, not so much from embarrassment, but at the obvious disregard for courtesy and good manners. Why, she had seen with her own eyes back on the island, men whose only education was the soil sit quietly listening to her father as he outlined his program for confederation or his plans for the export of potatoes and fish. Many of those who listened did not always agree, but they allowed her father to speak. Now here she was in civilized Boston, and this drunken rabble was acting like uncouth animals. God, she had known animals back on the farm to have more dignity.

"Come, Miss Kate." Bridget was nudging her arm. "Let's leave. Forgive me. This was a bad idea. Sure they wouldn't be wantin' us here."

Kate turned her blazing eyes on Bridget for a moment. "You can leave, Miss Bridget. I wish to hear what the young man has to say."

Bridget slouched back, holding firmly to her cloth bag as Kate narrowed her blue eyes and stared back at the men.

"Why don't you go to Saint Kevin's Church and light a candle for Jesus' sake and leave us to ourselves?" They roared their disapproval now, and a dozen flushed men stood up with their ales sloshing and spilling and waved their glasses in what they hoped was a menacing gesture toward the ladies.

Kate seethed. It was a disgrace. Her deep-rooted Irish temper flashed, and she jumped to her feet.

"Shame," she protested, "shame on all of you. Do you see yourselves as others see you? A bunch of beefy-faced drunks is what I see. You have a young man who humbles himself to come before you to speak, and you act like a pack of dogs. As for myself, I have no intention of leaving this hall until I have heard what Mr. Joyce has to say. So sit your unruly selves down, and give the man a chance."

They froze, stunned by her quick and stinging attack. Certainly they all had experienced the shrieks and moans of nagging wives, delivered in a litany of abuse and always on the same themes of liquor or money. But this well-dressed, well-spoken young woman, with the high cheekbones, the flashing blue eyes, and lovely raven silk hair, this woman so beautiful and articulate, took them by complete surprise, and they slowly took their seats. A tomblike silence fell over the room.

Christopher Joyce straightened from his position against the door. Laughlin half rose from his chair in an effort to get a better look at their unknown champion, and Frank Joyce took a deep breath and slowly exhaled it. The air was clear, the room hushed, and he knew he had best take advantage of his chance before he lost it.

He did not allude to Kate's policing of the hall but immediately began his speech, as though he had been engaging them thus for the better part of an hour.

"We need our own on the City Council, my friends. I know there are those of you here today who may say, 'Joyce is an upstart, a Harvard man whose parents are immigrants from County Clare. Who does he think he is anyway? If he wanted a college education, why didn't he go to the Jesuits, go to Boston College instead of hobnobbing with the Protestants in Harvard Yard?'" He had their attention now because all of it was exactly what they had been thinking and what they had been discussing over their free ales.

The hair at the nape of his neck tingled with excitement as his own emotionally charged words echoed in his ears.

"Well, I will tell you why. Because any Irishman—and I am an Irishman, let it be known—any Irishman who wishes to make a stand against Brahmin politics has to show them that he is not run-of-the-mill, not just another Jesuit-trained Irish papist. He must show them he is someone who can beat them at their own game. He went to Harvard, and he finished third in his class; he was in the clubs, and he was editor in chief of the *Advocate* and . . . and . . . and so much more." He hesitated for a moment but quickly regained his composure. They were listening to every word. "Do you know how the newspapers and the magazines depict us Irish? We are leprechauns and drunks, we are lazy and shiftless, and we fight at the drop of a shillelagh or a hawthorn stick. Is that the image you want your children to grow up with?"

"No. No, damn it," they shouted, and then, aware that they might be acting the stereotype, they sat back, embarrassed. "My father, who stands at the rear of this hall, my father made it possible for me to attend Harvard College. He worked long, hard hours for me because he knew he was sending a son of Erin to the very bastion of Yankee power. And he sent me not just for himself and for me, but for you and all Boston Irishmen. If *he* could do it and I could do it, you can do it. Remember, we are Americans—Irish-Americans—and we must stand together. If I have your backing, I cannot lose, and if I win, you cannot lose. We all are winners.

"Finally, remember that this is a special election to fill the vacant seat of a departed Council member. It's a fine opportunity for us because the Yankees will not be paying the kind of attention they do to regular elections."

He smiled for the first time, and laughter rippled up and down the rows.

"Remember, voting day is Tuesday, June twenty-sixth. I ask you for your help. A vote for Frank Joyce is a vote for all of us. Thank you for coming today. Now, McGillicuddy, break open that keg of ale."

They rose as one and cheered and clapped, but self-conscious now, they did not stamp their feet. Frank made his way through the crowd toward his father, and they shook his hand and thumped his broad back as he passed.

"We're with you, Frankie!"

"Count on your own, boyo!"

"Aye, you're as good as warmin' the Council chair."

"For a while there I thought you were a goner, Francis." His father shook his hand firmly. "We learned something today—never break out the ale until after the talk. That way you're sure of a captive audience."

Frank's eyes shone. He was happy for his father, who had broken his back for his family. But his eyes roamed to the last row where the older woman's broad back obscured the younger one.

"Thanks, Pa, I think we're on our way. Go mingle with your cronies. I want to speak to that young lady. She saved the day for us."

"Aye, that she did. But come back and mingle yourself. Give them the personal attention, and they won't forget you."

As Frank threaded his way through the garrulous and gesturing crowd, two old men stopped him to offer support and congratulations. He politely accepted their tributes and tried, diplomatically, to slip away, but one of the old gents had his hand locked in Frank's, and by the time he managed to extricate himself the young woman was nowhere to be seen.

He nudged his way to the door, smiling and shaking hands as he went. Once outside, he spotted her crossing to the opposite sidewalk.

"Miss! Miss! Please wait. I wish to speak to you."

Kate and Bridget turned and waited for him to cross. His smile was bright and wide, showing white, even teeth.

"Miss, ah?"

"Ahearn."

"Ah, Miss Ahearn. I wish to thank you for coming to my rescue. What would I have done without you? You have a fine daughter, Mrs. Ahearn." He bowed gracefully to Bridget.

"Oh, glory be to God, Mr. Joyce. I am only the cook at Miss Kent's School. Miss Ahearn is one of our *teachers*." Her voice rose proudly on the word *teacher*. "I know your parents from the Social Club."

"Oh, of course. Well, won't you both please come back and enjoy a repast?"

"Really, we must be off, Mr. Joyce," Kate refused politely.

"Oh, nonsense. I insist. I absolutely shall not take no for an answer." He guided her by the elbow, and before she realized it, she was recrossing the street, with Bridget bouncing along behind.

"My goodness Mr. Joyce, but you are persuasive. I am sure that attribute will be significant in your political career."

He laughed good-naturedly, but behind the easy banter he was thinking that he had never before seen such a strikingly beautiful woman.

Inside the hall the crowd parted as he ushered the ladies to the table. "Here, Pa, plates and silverware for our guests."

Joyce cocked an eye at the lovely Kate and nodded a welcome to Bridget. "How be you, Miss Burke? What do you think of my boy there?"

"He's a fine broth of a lad, he is. Sure the apple doesn't fall far from the tree."

A delighted Christopher Joyce filled her plate. "Sure you're a fine woman yourself, Miss Burke."

Many of the men in the crowd huddled in mumbling groups, occasionally glancing in the direction of the lovely Kate. They would not soon forget her, and neither would the effervescent, darkly handsome Frank Joyce. He could not keep his eyes from her, and Kate was very much aware of his preoccupation as she demurely sipped her tea.

James Laughlin, free now of a group that had buttonholed him, approached Kate and Frank. "Well, well, whom do we have here, Frank? Our angel of mercy, I'll wager."

"Yes, Jim, she certainly is. The campaign would have been over before it began had our Miss Ahearn not jumped into the arena. Jim Laughlin is my campaign manager, my conscience, my aide de camp and my alter ego. Jim, meet Miss Ahearn."

"How do you do, Miss Ahearn. A pleasure to meet you."

"It is very nice to meet you, Mr. Laughlin."

"Do I detect an accent of some type? Surely you are not from Ireland?"

Kate reddened defensively as she always did when her nationality was questioned.

"I am from Canada, Mr. Laughlin. My grandparents are from Ireland."

"Oh, Canada? So you are a two-boater, Miss Ahearn. Couldn't afford full passage to America! Well, no matter. You are away from the savages of the frozen north. You will be safe among us. I must be off, but let me take Frank for a moment—campaign business."

"Don't go away, Miss Ahearn. I'll return in a moment."

Kate watched them disappear into a back room, her cheeks scarlet from the sting of Laughlin's cutting remark. The arrogant weasel, she thought. But abruptly she returned her attention to Frank Joyce. He was different from Laughlin. He interested her. He was bright, handsome, gentlemanly, and exciting. It was so coincidental. She had lived with politics and politicians all her life, and here she was on a Sunday afternoon in Boston, attending a political gathering.

A few minutes later Frank emerged from the room alone. She was pleased that Laughlin was not with him. She had taken an instant dislike to the man. Such rudeness! Savages, indeed! The idea! If there were savages about, it was this unruly mob of ale-drinking, cigar-smoking ruffians.

"We just had to go over my schedule of speaking engagements. My next speech is Wednesday night at the Shamrock Club. I would be honored if you would attend, Miss Ahearn. Would it be possible? Really, please say it is."

"Well, I cannot say for sure, Mr. Joyce. There is a possibility. I tutor after dinner. I will have to consult my schedule."

"Oh, please try to be there. I need your support. You were such a help to me today."

"I shall do my best. Now it's time for us to start back. Thank you for your courtesy, Mr. Joyce. And good luck."

"Oh, please, allow me to escort you home. My carriage is out back."

"Oh, no. You mustn't, Mr. Joyce. You will disappoint your supporters. This is the most important part of your appearance, joining the others and sharing with them your aspirations for the future."

"How do you know such things, Miss Ahearn? You are quite remarkable."

"Because she is a *teacher*," Bridget piped in. "Now come, miss. I have dinner to prepare."

"Yes, yes. Good-bye, Mr. Joyce."

"Good-bye for now, Miss Ahearn, until Wednesday. Please try to come."

CHAPTER XXX

KATE'S DAYS WERE filled with teaching, and her girls were progressing splendidly. She had a solid block of followers in the school who flocked around her like Boston Common pigeons. Miss Kent was duly proud of her young teacher.

And Kate's nights, when she was not tutoring Peter, were filled with torchlight parades, surging crowds, cold ham suppers, and the canvassing of Boston's North End.

It was like leading two lives at once. She enjoyed the quiet scholarship with Peter and the solitary hours they spent journeying through the woods and farmlands north of Boston. But then there were the parades and speeches, the bustle and excitement of Frank Joyce's campaign.

If Kate Ahearn had been forced to decide of whom she was fonder, she would have been hard pressed, and so she simply continued to enjoy both relationships, until, that is one evening in the middle of June.

Miss Kent was herding all of the girls off to Rockport for a long weekend at the summer home of one of the trustees. Each year the house was made available for just such an outing, and everyone went along—teachers, custodial staff, cook, and the giddy, giggling girls. On this evening Kate was on her way to the train with the other teachers when Peter came racing up the street behind her.

"Why, Peter Hazleton, where's the fire?"

"Oh, Kate, I'm off to Rockport, too. A Harvard friend, Patch Evans, invited me for the weekend. We'll be seeing each other on the beach, I expect. Well, what do you say? Are you surprised? Are you happy to have me along?"

"Why, yes, of course, Peter. It should be so much fun. Will you be on the same train with us?"

"No. I have some business to attend to for Father. But I'll be there by dinner Saturday night. There's a delightful band concert at the beach pavilion. Do say you will attend it with me."

"I would love to, Peter. I will look for you after dinner, then, to-

morrow night at Pickard House off the road between Folly's Cove and
Andrews's Point."

"Why, you sound like a crusty old Yankee sea captain, Kate, and
this your first trip to Cape Ann," he teased.

Indeed, Cape Ann was a treat. All through the golden spring
morning Kate and the girls walked along the long stretch of beach as
sun puddles shone under their bare feet. They explored every inch of
beach, climbing the sea-washed boulders and peering far out to the
horizon. At mid-afternoon they picnicked.

At seven Peter arrived with his Harvard friend, Patch Evans,
whom Kate had met once before, when he came to visit his sister,
Alicia, at Miss Kent's. Alicia ambled out onto the wide porch to greet
her brother and his friend and then withdrew.

"How is she behaving these days?" Evans asked. He had the sharp
good looks and elegant build of his grandfather.

"It has been a struggle. The girl just does not like me, and you
can't force people to like you, no matter what."

"My grandfather told me to say hello and to invite you over after
the band concert. That is, if Peter will share you with us."

"Why, that would be delightful, would it not, Peter?"

"I suppose so," Peter answered with less than enthusiastic interest.

The moon was full and yellow as it played with the tips of the
waves. It would be a fine night for a walk along the beach and maybe
a midnight swim. Certainly Peter had not come all the way to Cape
Ann to sit on a wicker rocker, listening to Patch's grandfather talk
about the building of a textile dynasty.

Kate was content as she sat on the green velvet lawn in front of the
white pagodalike band shell, where brass and bugle and drum and
cymbal rose up in a blaring tribute to the newly arrived early-summer
crowd.

Peter was so handsome, she thought, in his summer whites and
light blue shawl-collared sweater, yet content as she was, her mind was
on other things. She looked past the bandstand into the twinkling night
and thought of Frank. One more week, and the election would be history. Oh, God, she prayed, help him win.

At that moment as she sat among the smart summer Rockport
crowd, she longed to be back in the thick of the battle in the teeming,
tenement district of the North End. There was something about being
among the Boston Irish that gave her a sense of herself. Here, among
these people who were always polite and courteous and discreet, there
was a certain shallowness that she could not quite fathom.

Finally, the bandmaster declared the evening over by tapping his
baton on his music stand; the blue-uniformed members struck up a
Prussian march, and the audience began slowly to disperse.

"Come, Grandfather is waiting. He is anxious to see you again,
Kate."

"All right, Patch. Shall we, Peter?"

"Yes, of course, Kate, but I had hoped we could walk along the
beach. Could we later, do you think?"

"I think that would be fine, Mr. Hazleton." She smiled, and he slipped his hand into hers.

Channing Evans was pacing the breezy porch that faced out to the sea as the three young people approached the house, their laughter floating in the night.

"Ah, here you are then. I thought you had deserted this ancient fossil, leaving him with his warm milk and biscuits."

He took Kate's hand as she reached the top step, and she smiled and curtsied. "How nice to see you again, Mr. Evans." She was so open and friendly, it was positively disarming, he thought.

"And a delight to see you again, my dear. Please sit here; this is the most comfortable chair of all. And you young rascals, frankly, I have no interest in you at all."

Patch laughed and led Peter into the house. "I'll prepare cold drinks, Grandfather."

"Good lad, Patch. Miss Ahearn and I shall sit and talk. I'm sorry my wife is not here, Miss Ahearn; she is up in Boston at some charity affair. Frankly I have little interest in social events these days. I think I am getting old. I prefer to sit and rock and listen to the sea rolling in on the shore."

"You are very poetic, sir, and that is noble and refreshing."

"Why refreshing, Miss Ahearn? Have you experienced no poetry since your arrival from Canada?"

"Oh, very little, sir, if you do not mind my saying."

"Not at all. You are just being honest."

"You see, it is the people. So many of them never take the time to enjoy the day or their families. Where I come from the family is very important. We are always clustered around, having tea and cakes and chatting like magpies."

Evans's eyes narrowed, and he looked off in the direction of the rolling surf as her words carried in the night. Strange how life is, he thought. Here, sitting beside him, was the granddaughter of the woman he had loved almost forty years before, a woman he could not have in spite of all his power and money. He had learned much over those years, he thought. How painful for all of us that wisdom comes too late, yet how fortunate that it does come to some of us before we die, so that we can mend our ways.

"Mr. Evans? Mr. Evans?"

"Uh? What did you say, my dear?"

"I was saying how sitting here with you is like talking to my grandfather. I hope you don't think me impertinent."

"Not at all, my dear. Won't you tell me more about your grandparents. They must be very proud to be able to claim such a lovely and intelligent young lady."

"Thank you, sir. Well, they are very healthy and active. Grandfather is still very strong, and Grandmother remains quite beautiful."

Mary's beauty was firmly embedded in Channing Evans's mind. He remembered holding her in his arms one snow-blown evening and thinking then that she was the most beautiful woman he had ever seen.

Of course, it was not to be. He was young and arrogant and, yes, greedy, like so many young businessmen. His textile dynasty came first, and the farm girl from Ireland came second. Yes, she had been better off with her Irishman. Evans saw that quite clearly now in the wholesome face of Mary's granddaughter.

"I enjoy hearing about close families. I think now that I should have been more like your grandparents, but for too many years I had only business on my mind. I had a lovely daughter to whom I should have been more devoted. She died of pneumonia when she was only eleven years old."

"Oh, I am so sorry, Mr. Evans. Indeed I am. God bless her and you."

Kate's hand reached out and patted his.

He nodded and smiled. "You are a very good person, Miss Ahearn, I can tell that. Maybe that is why Alicia and you do not get along. Possibly Alicia does not know how to respond to your sensitivity. I think Alicia and I will spend more time chatting over tea and cakes in the future. Yes," he said with more affirmation, "that is a vow I make at this moment, thanks to you and your grandmother."

"Well, are you two ready for us to join you with cold drinks, or are we intruding?" Patch Evans held the tray above his head in mock exaggeration of a waiter.

"Oh, all right, Patch, come join us if you must. I suppose Peter will be furiously jealous if I continue my disgracefully overt interest in Miss Ahearn."

They sat in contentment, the young men sharing stories of Harvard and Kate regaling them with the obstacles she had encountered as the only female in her class at Prince of Wales.

Finally, Channing Evans rose. "Well, I must be going off to my bed, but I am sure the night is still young for you three."

"Good night, Mr. Evans, thank you for inviting us." Kate curtsied, and Peter shook hands firmly.

"It was a pleasure. Thank you both for coming by."

He excused himself, and they stood quietly as he walked into the house.

"You know," Patch whispered, "I believe Grandfather is quite taken by you, Kate."

"Well, isn't everyone, Patch?" Peter said quite seriously.

Peter's long arms stroked through the moon-sparkled water. He could not believe that Kate had actually agreed to meet him for a swim. His heart thundered more from anticipation of her appearance than from the punishing exercise he was affording himself.

A silver streak of light illuminated the path from Pickard House to the shore, and he could see a silent figure picking her way among the rocks to the beach.

He treaded water silently in a slow, deliberate rhythm as her voice rose above the gentle lapping of the surf.

"Peter." At first the voice was a whisper, and then it grew more urgent. "Peter, Peter." He dived beneath the surface and came up nearer shore.

Kate stood in the glow of the moon with a long black gown covering her. Even her black satin head was covered by a hood.

"Kate, you came. You really did come after all. I thought you might think the water would be too cold."

"Too cold? My dear Mr. Hazleton, I have swum all my life in ponds and rivers and oceans that were absolutely frigid. If I said I would come, I would not go back on my word. But truthfully," she asked almost timidly, "is it cold?"

"No. It's marvelous. Come in."

She threw her head back, and her hair, free of pins, fell to her shoulders as she allowed her robe to drop softly to the sand. She stepped out of it and walked deliberately to the water's edge.

Her bathing gown revealed the roundness of her breasts just above the surface of the water, and her overhand stroke soon carried her out beyond him.

"Please be careful, Kate. How could I ever explain it if you drowned?"

She giggled and lay floating on her back, looking up at the cloudless sky.

"I've been swimming since I was a child."

He swam over to her. His heart pounded in his ears. He wanted to press her lovely body into his.

"Come on, Peter, I'll race you to that tiny island."

"All right, let's go."

Kate was indeed a strong swimmer, and it was only his male strength and pride that brought him out front by a few yards. They pulled themselves up on the island's grassy embrankment and stretched out side by side.

"You are a very good swimmer, Kate. I never saw any woman swim like you."

"I didn't think Cape Anne girls swam, Mr. Hazleton. I thought they just sat on the beach and watched the Harvard College boys do water tricks."

"Oh, say, Kate. Are you jealous of all the girls from Wellesley and Mount Holyoke Seminary? You shouldn't be, you know. You are more beautiful than any of them." His brain was pounding, and he reached out and swept her up in his arms. The kiss was long, and its passion brought him over on her as she lay in the grass. Their breathing was quick, and his hands slowly moved up to her breasts. She tensed momentarily, but he continued brushing and stroking until they turned hard and firm.

"Oh, Kate, I want you tonight. Let me have you."

Kate, mesmerized by the night and the romance of a midnight swim, was suddenly brought back to reality by his words.

"Peter, I am very fond of you, God knows. But this is not right.

Come, I'll race you back." She wriggled out of his arms and, without hesitation, dived into the black waters and stroked for shore. He stood paralyzed for a moment, then cursed quietly and rushed headlong into the water.

Kate stumbled out of the surf, and shivering as much from their intimacy as the Cape Ann waters, she ran for her gown. But it was not where she had left it. The moon was bright, affording more than adequate illumination, and the gown was nowhere to be found.

She was walking up and down the beach when Peter joined her. "What are you looking for with your lovely head practically in the sand, Kate?"

"My gown—I can't find my gown. I left it right here. Surely the night is not windy enough to have blown it away."

"Well, that is strange. But here, let me make you warm." He reached for her, but she slipped from his grasp.

"No, Peter, really, I must go. Besides, I am cold. Your Rockport water *is* much colder than ours. Good night." She gave him a quick kiss on the cheek and ran on up the beach.

Early Wednesday morning Miss Kent summoned Kate to her office. As Kate entered, the headmistress, with a firm chin and unsmiling eyes, stood up and produced the missing gown.

"Is this yours, Miss Ahearn?"

"Yes, ma'am, it is mine," Kate said weakly.

"You know where it was found?"

"No, ma'am, I do not."

"On the beach while you were having a midnight rendezvous. Scandalous, to say the least."

"But there was nothing wrong in meeting a young man for a swim, was there?"

"There was when one of our students viewed the sordid *tryst*, as we shall call it."

"What student, may I ask?"

"Never mind what student. It is sufficient to say the young woman was shocked by the behavior of one of her teachers."

Kate did not have to guess. She knew it had to have been Alicia Evans. Mr. Channing Evans had set himself a difficult task in solving the difficulties of that troubled child.

"Now I shall say it quite plainly, Miss Ahearn: If it happens again, anything at all, any action that besmirches the name of my school, you will be summarily dismissed." In spite of her chagrin, she added, "Even if you are the best and most popular teacher I have. Now get along about your business."

Although Kate would die before she ever consciously disappointed the headmistress who had been so kind to her, she nonetheless could not suppress the joy she felt that day for an entirely different reason. Just before her meeting with Miss Kent she had read a note that was sent to her by Frank Joyce in the early hours of the morning.

Dear Kate,

    We whipped the Yankees two to one.

                    Affectionately,

                    Francis Michael Joyce

                    City Council—Ward Ten

    Please come to the election party at campaign headquarters tonight. I will pick you up at seven. I will not take no for an answer.

    She read and reread the note all through the day, and then she read the results in the *Evening Transcript*. The editorial was devoted to Frank Joyce and "the mass of swaggering, brawling Irish who staggered to the polling places to vote for the man because he was Irish, not because he had any ability."

    Kate thrust the editorial at Frank as he escorted her down the stone steps while the girls giggled behind the bow windows.

    "Really, Kate, do not trouble yourself with that trash. The point is we won, and we won as a unit. We are becoming stronger each day, and mark me, someday the Paddys from the pigstys, will run the City of Boston. Stay with me, Kate, and you will be the first lady of this city."

    She looked into his deep blue eyes, a frown lining her forehead. "I do not understand. What are you saying, Frank?"

    "I am saying, Miss Ahearn, that you and I are going to be married."

    "Married. But what? I mean, good heavens, sir. I don't—I barely know you."

    "You will, my lovely Kate. You will. Now come, we must make time. I don't want to miss my own party."

    Kate Ahearn sat back and watched in stunned silence as he snapped his leather whip lightly against the swaying rump of the chestnut. The coach flew over the cobblestones with Frank singing his favorite song. "The Minstrel boy to the war is gone, in the ranks of death you'll find him."

    His sweet Irish tenor voice drifted over the streets causing pedestrians to stop and applaud. He doffed his bowler hat in their direction and continued singing.

    "You have a lovely tenor, Frank. I didn't know you could sing."

    "Oh, Kate, there are many things you don't know about me. But when we are married, you will realize what a grand and talented man I am."

    "Now, Frank, stop that marriage talk. I don't know what's got into you. Surely you haven't been drinking, have you?"

    "Now you sound like the Brahmins stereotyping the Irish. You know I don't touch liquor. It is debilitating, and I need my strength. I have too many things to do." He leaned over and kissed her on the cheek. "And one of them is marrying you."

    "Frank Joyce, you are impossible." But as she said it, already the thought of marrying Frank was beginning to settle on her consciousness.

The Shamrock Social Club was a square and plain building devoid of design or charm, but this night neither was necessary.

Frank Joyce beamed his way through a narrow corridor of cheering supporters, all clamoring for his attention. Kate tried to hang back, but Frank was having none of it. He took her hand and literally waltzed her to the stage as a five-piece band played "The Wild Colonial Boy."

He climbed onto the makeshift stage, pushed and lifted up by the rough, coarse hands of a dozen Irishmen.

"Frank Joyce. Frank Joyce. He's our choice. He's our choice," they screamed and cheered as the ale flowed and their ruddy cheeks grew ruddier.

Frank held center stage while his father, off to the side, beamed with pride.

Frank's mother, Margaret, sat shyly in the corner, a mere sparrow of a woman with long, coarse hands and a darting, beak-like nose. But when she smiled, as she frequently did, her sharp, birdlike features became almost attractive. The pride she felt in this handsome and dynamic son of hers burned like a bright flame that sparkled in her eyes. Her gaze, although centered on Frank, also took in the smiling and lovely Kate, of whom they had all heard such glowing reports. Her mother's instinct caught the gleam in Frank's eyes as he looked at Kate, and she did not have to be told that her son was in love.

Frank Joyce held up his hands in an effort to silence the crowd, and when the revelers' cheers reluctantly subsided, he spoke. "My good and dear old North Enders, we did it together. We did it because of you. Now you know what it is to be unified. As long as we are one, as long as we remain Irish and American, we can win any office in this great and mighty commonwealth. So help me God."

The applause washed over him in a great wave, and he stood in its midst, absorbing it until, flushed from the adulation, he jumped to the floor, taking Kate by the hand and threading their way through the shouting crowd, he guided her over to his mother. "Ma, this is Kate Ahearn. Kate, this is my sainted mother."

"Sainted mother! Oh, be gone with you, Francis Joyce. How do you do, Miss Ahearn. My son tells me you have been a great help in his campaign. Come sit beside me, and let the big man go off and shake hands. Go on, now, Francis, Miss Ahearn and I have some chatting to do."

Frank nodded approvingly and was soon swallowed up by the throngs of well-wishers still pouring through the doors from the street.

"Francis tells me you are from Canada. Do you miss your home, Miss Ahearn?" She answered her own question in that country fashion. "I suppose you do. And you are Irish? Well, of course, you are, with the name Ahearn. Oh, look, there I go. Francis always tells me that I never give anyone a chance to converse. Tell me about Canada, Miss Ahearn."

They sat chatting amiably, and even though the night was warm and the hall was jammed, the young woman and Frank Joyce's smiling mother enjoyed the friendship of a cup of steaming tea. For Kate it was

like sitting in the Summerside kitchen of her grandmother. The lilt of
the Gaelic rose and fell in the soft lyric she had known all her life.
She felt an uncontrollable warmth and a tingling of her blood as it ran
up her spine and down her elbows. For a few moments she was not
in a noisy, crowded hall in the North End; she was a little girl again,
and her beloved grandmother was telling her stories of other times and
far-off places.

Frank Joyce, wedged into a corner of the hall, waved at her and
winked, and she waved back. She was with her own, and she knew it.

The Harvard College graduation was blessed with sun: wealthy
sun that streaked down as if from Mount Olympus. Mothers, fathers,
grandparents, relatives, and friends assembled on the crowded playing
field to watch the graduates in flowing burgundy robes march up to
the platform to receive their diplomas.

Kate sat with her back to the curious onlookers who stood three
and four deep on Massachusetts Avenue, gawking and craning their
necks to watch the affluent sons of Harvard in their golden moment.
For most of them it was just a show that could be observed but never
experienced in their own lives.

She fingered the gold lettering on the invitation, and when Peter
Marshal Hazleton's name was called, and he joined the legions of the
select who claimed a Harvard College education, she applauded with
sincerity. She was proud for Peter and for her part in his eduaction.

Only that morning Kate had sat in the private quarters of Estelle
Kent, explaining her fears and doubts about the future. She had just
about decided that she would not attend the ceremony, but Miss Kent
had wisely counseled, "It would be a discourtesy, Kate. It is a special
day for him, and he thought enough of you to send you an invitation."
And so Kate acquiesced, but still she was plagued by a conflict she could
not resolve.

Both Peter and Frank wanted to marry her. She knew Peter loved
her, and daily Frank Joyce sent notes to her, accompanied by a long-
stemmed rose. The notes always asked the same, simple question:
"When will you say yes? All my love, Frank."

The notes not only amused her but gave her a giddy, feathery
feeling around her heart.

Both Peter and Frank were fun to be with. Peter, of course, talked
of foreign ports, his further apprenticeship in the family business, and
the eventual role he would assume as prime stockholder. Frank's vision
was gladiatorial. He would slay all the Brahmin lions on his way to
the mayor's office. "It will take time, Kate, but with a good woman
like you standing beside me, I will make it. You will be Boston's first
lady."

Another name was called, Channing Patch Evans III. Her gaze
followed the crescendo of applause near the front. There, sitting in
patrician elegance, was the leader of the Evans clan, his white hair
covered by a tall silk hat. Beside him was his frail wife, a younger
couple, obviously Patch's parents, and Alicia.

The names of the graduates floated in the air accompanied by polite applause. But Kate's mind was elsewhere. The midnight tryst had only served to confuse her more. She had enjoyed Peter's kisses and had none of those inhibitions she found so often in Irish women. No, it was not the rendezvous. It was something deeper, something she had refused to accept, even though she had known it so clearly sitting in the cool grass at the Rockport band concert. She was not entirely comfortable with these people.

Peter Hazleton's name cut through her thoughts and she watched as he ascended the platform to accept his degree. Then he ambled boyishly off the platform and took his place among the graduates.

She focused her gaze on Channing Evans. Why had he been so inquisitive? At their first meeting on Decoration Night he had been the perfect gentleman, even showing her a slight deference. But it was that deference which unnerved her. She did not understand these people, and it was becoming increasingly clearer to her the longer she lived in Boston. She looked over the assembled crowd. They all were very much alike: tall, mustchioed, well-tailored plutocrats and their bustled, thin, whey-faced wives. There was no color to them, no dash or adventure. They sat straight and rigid, never appearing casual or, for that matter, even comfortable. It was much the way they passed through life— dutifully.

Her mind flashed back to her own graduation day from Prince of Wales University. There had been laughter and joy mixed with the island warmth. Tears, too, had been the order of the day. Her grandparents had behaved as though Kate had succumbed to a fatal disease, and then, when all the emotion was drained, everyone had queued up for a festive celebration. The abundant tables had rivaled the Charlottetown Round Market.

A speaker droned on, alluding to all the great names that had appeared on Harvard degrees, and then, stumbling over his own prepared text, in all his crusty senility he repeated the first five minutes of the speech. No one seemed to notice; no one coughed. No one offered a whispered suggestion. They just sat back, and in true, Puritan fashion they politely and discreetly endured.

The traditional ritual of passing the four-year baton to the marshal of the upcoming class was a signal for the graduates to cheer and shake one another's hands.

Parents joined their graduating sons and, with a formal handshake and tight-lipped congratulations, gradually began an exodus across the yard.

Kate hung back along the iron fence, and when Peter caught her eye, he excused himself from his family and hurried up to her. "Oh, Kate, you came. I am so happy. Come, I want you to meet my family." He took her hand and virtually raced her back to a family group disconcertingly like all the others.

"Father, this is Miss Ahearn. She is my tutor and the friend I told you about."

Mr. Hazleton, stern and straight-backed, bowed icily. It was plain that a Miss Ahearn fitted nowhere in the plans he had for his son. "Yes, yes, Miss Ahearn. I believe Peter has mentioned what a fine instructor you have been. I hope he has paid you promptly for your services."

Kate cocked her head, puzzled at first, and then she shrugged. "Oh, there is no need to worry about that, sir. Peter is very prompt."

Peter turned to his mother, a dour and surprisingly unattractive woman. Kate found herself wondering how such a handsome and gay young man could have two such stern parents.

"Peter tells me you come from Canada, Miss Ahearn. How terribly quaint. I do believe I have never met a Canada person before, I daresay."

"A Canadian person, Mrs. Hazleton." Kate's voice was even and balanced.

"Oh, of course, please forgive me, Miss Ahearn. Is Ahearn a Canada, excuse me, a Canadian name?"

"No, ma'am, it is Irish. My family is Canadian Irish."

Kate knew she was in command. She had learned that from Frank. He had said more than once, "Keep your feelings to yourself. Don't let anyone know what you are thinking. It is good politics, but it is also a good practice in dealing with people."

"Oh, how quaint. Not only are you Canadian, but you are Irish as well. It was very pleasant meeting you, Miss Ahearn. Possibly we will meet again sometime. Peter, we must be off to the Soames's house; they are expecting us for an early dinner."

"Yes, Mother. I wonder if I could join you and Father there. Putney Street? Number thirty-four? I shall be there soon. I just wish to speak with Kate, ah, Miss Ahearn. It won't take long."

Peter's mother turned to her husband with an undisguised air of exasperation, leaving the father to articulate the feelings of both.

"Do not be late for dinner, *Peter*." He said "Peter" with the distinct tone of someone who was dismissing all others in sight who might be bold enough to dare think that they too might be welcome at the Soames's house.

Peter nodded sheepishly as his mother and father moved off stiffly with Charity, torn, it seemed, between parent and teacher.

"Mother has always been somewhat cool to strangers, but she will warm up."

"Oh, how thoughtful of her. I can't wait for the moment." Kate drifted along, her taffeta skirt skimming the grass, her manner haughty.

"Please, Kate, don't be angry. Try to understand."

"Oh, I understand perfectly well. I don't have to be hit over my thick Canadian skull with a club. But don't trouble yourself with their discourtesies, Peter. You, fortunately enough, have not inherited their manner. Now what was it you wished to ask me? You told them you wished to speak with me."

"Well, it's just that I shall be leaving for the Far East next week, and I—I—oh, Kate, I love you. Will you wait for me?"

"Wait for you, Peter? What would I be waiting for if I might be so bold?"

CHAPTER XXXI

THE DOUBLE-DECKER house on Perkins Street was a dazzling display of illumination. Even the centerpiece on the oval dining room table held two large candelabra the pale flames of which were almost artificial-looking in their pear-shaped symmetry.

It was a small but intimate group, and Kate still felt the need to pinch herself to make sure she was not dreaming. There, sitting on the long couch, sipping her tea alongside Margaret Joyce, was her own dear grandmother, Mary McMahon. And to Mary's left, Brendan balanced a cup and saucer and a plate of marble cake while he smiled at his lovely granddaughter.

Christopher Joyce stood in the pantry that separated the dining room from the kitchen, pointing out certain political realities to Frank.

Mary was sharing memories of Kate, much to the delight of Gabriella, Edward, and James Laughlin, who sat perched on the arm of a chair that was occupied by his date for the evening, Alice Sullivan.

"She was always bright and beautiful, eh?" The grandmother's intensely blue eyes sparkled the way they had years before on a green hill in Ireland when Brendan McMahon realized she was the only woman he would ever love. "Wasn't she, now, Brendan, eh? Sure, Mrs. Joyce, he used to hold her on his lap by the fire, and when she would cry, he would give her a dollop or two of fine Canadian whiskey, but I never told her mother and father." Gabriella and Edward, proud of this daughter who was to be married in the morning, chuckled at Mary's storytelling.

Margaret Joyce laughed and clutched her bosom. "Please, dear, we are practically related, call me Margaret, for heaven's sake." Her County Clare brogue was as true as it was the day she, Christopher, and the children had boarded the ship for America.

"Tell me," Laughlin said in obvious consternation as he leaned toward Brendan, "just what is fine Canadian whiskey? Do you buy it some place? That is, do you have stores, ah, merchants who sell such items?"

Brendan placed his cup and saucer on a low table to his left,

"Well, me, of course. We could take our favorite coach rides out to the country the way we have in the past. We could resume our splendid Sundays. Please say you'll wait for my return." Kate studied his boyish and ingenuous face. He was a good person, and there had been pleasure in their relationship; but that club across the skull was not necessary to wake her to the hard realistic facts of life. She and Peter lived in different worlds, and those differences would always be obstacles. At that moment she could not help remembering her chat over a friendly cup of tea with Margaret Joyce. The red-brick barricades and balustrades of Harvard College seemed to dwarf her by their overbearing coldness.

"Peter," she said evenly, "I shall not be seeing you again. You know the reasons as well as I do, but more important, I must tell you something. No one else knows this, but I am going to be married."

His mouth opened in shock. "Married? Married? But who? When? Why? Christ, Kate, when did this happen?"

"Please, Peter, calm down. I am marrying someone who loves me very much, and I love him very much, I might add. He is my own kind, Peter. Surely you can see how important that is. I am very fond of you, but—but—" She did not finish. It was not necessary. She had made her point, and he saw only too clearly that she was right. He nodded slowly, took her gloved hand in his, and lifted it gently to his lips.

"I shall always love you, Kate. Always." Then he relinquished his hold on her hand and walked away across Harvard Yard, soon to be swallowed up in the sea of red-gowned graduates. She watched him until he was gone and then made her way back across the grass to the noise and bustle of Massachusetts Avenue. The working world streamed on past the iron gates. She smiled. Peter was the only one who knew, and that included her future husband, Mr. Francis Michael Joyce, of the Boston City Council.

straightened up, and gestured with his plateful of cake. "Excuse me, young man, but are you serious, eh? Is that really a serious inquiry?" he persisted.

"Why, of course." His voice was brittle and had the tone of one who had been offended. "I am not in the habit of acting the comedian."

"Oh, well then," Brendan answered quite seriously, "you see in Charlottetown we have these things called streets and avenues, and on these streets and avenues there are other things called buildings. Some are wooden, and some are cement, stone, you see. And if you have money, you can walk right into those buildings and buy whiskey or guns, and if you are a stranger, you can buy Indian scalps."

A tomblike silence descended on the room as Brendan took a bite of cake.

Then Margaret began chuckling, as did Frank, Christopher Joyce, and Father James, who was returning from the kitchen with a fresh cup of strong tea.

Laughlin's usually white-parchment face turned red, and he stammered defensively, "Well, there's probably more truth to that statement than your obvious attempt at sarcasm. But tell me this, old man—" He tried to keep his tone level, but the term *old man* stabbed Brendan in the pit of his stomach.

Laughlin studied his white hands, clean as a priest's, and he gestured with them in a theatrical fashion when he spoke. Brendan watched with contempt.

"You live in a wilderness of snow and ice," he continued in the broad, nasal tones of Harvard and Boston. "You are overrun with the downtrodden, the itinerant, and the French, who cannot even speak the language of the American continent. You certainly can't expect us here in Boston to believe that your daily lives are the same as ours. Now really, old man, can you? So why become so defensive when one asks you a logical question?"

Kate had heard it all before from Laughlin, the pedantic dandy whom she tolerated only because he, for some unknown reason, was Frank's best friend.

On one of their first evenings together in Laughlin's company, he had referred to her as both a herring choker and a two-boater. His ignorance of Canada and Canadians sent her into silent fury, but for Frank's sake she managed to bury her antagonism. But now this pedant was attacking her grandfather with his snide sarcasm. She saw Brendan's eyes narrow and turn to flame and his broad back arch and straighten. She looked up at Frank, who wore an embarrassed smile. No one spoke. She knew that her grandfather could break Laughlin's nose with one punch and that he might be tempted to do so. But that would not solve anything. She would have to speak up, as much for her own future happiness as for the dignity of her people. She could no longer submit to ignorant remarks from a weasel like Laughlin.

She stalked to the center of the floor, as if it were a podium. All heads turned to her.

"*Mr.* Laughlin, hear me. And hear me on this subject for the last time. You and your lace-curtained Irish are newcomers to these shores compared to my people, my Irish Canadian people. My grandparents came to these shores in 1830, and they found bogtrotters and shanty Irish living like pigs in Yankee mill towns. They moved north, out of your precious United States, so they could attain some dignity. And in Canada they found dignity. My grandfather is a wealthy man, and he did it all by himself, with no help of a Harvard education. And what are you but a bookkeeper in a Yankee firm on State Street because you went to a school that opened its doors to a few of you *because* you were poor Irish? What gives you the right to be so high and mighty? My grandfather served in the Assembly for more than twenty years, and he knows more about politics than anyone in this room, and that includes Frank Joyce."

Frank's eyebrows arched, but he said nothing.

She stared into the colorless eyes of Laughlin, who at that moment wanted desperately to be anywhere else in the world. Even Canada.

"I'll tell you one thing about Canada, Mr. Laughlin. In Canada we don't have signs in store windows that say, 'No Irish Need Apply.' You think about that for a moment." The chandelier vibrated with her words, and the flickering of the candles in the candelabra could almost be heard.

Brendan smiled, and then he threw back his head and roared as Mary beamed with pride. Then to break the spell of the moment entirely, Frank Joyce applauded. "Say, who is going to give the speeches in this family anyway?"

"Just a moment, Frank, I have something else to say, and then I must prepare for my wedding."

She turned to the stunned Laughlin and spoke almost like a teacher analyzing a sentence for a bewildered student. "You see, Mr. Laughlin, the reason I told you all this was to instruct you before you made any more social blunders. And, oh, yes"—she smiled—"I was afraid my grandfather would break your dainty little jaw. Now, if you will excuse me, I shall serve more tea."

She walked between a smiling Christopher Joyce and his shocked son, who followed her into the kitchen. "She will be a handful, Francis." Christopher chuckled after him.

"Damn, Kate, you were quite hard on him, weren't you? He was only joking. You know Jimmy and how he gets. He doesn't mean any harm."

She looked at him fiercely. "Look, Frank, no one insults my family, and that goes for you, too. I don't like that kind of joking."

Then she smiled, and he kissed her on the cheek. "I'm damn glad I saw you like this. It will teach me to act the proper husband. I would not want you for an enemy, political or otherwise."

Channing Evans sat in the leather darkness of his coach, watching the guests arrive at Holy Cross Cathedral. Indian summer warmed the October morning, and it reminded him of the day so many years before, when he had first met Mary Roark. Now he leaned forward as the wedding party arrived. There in a white gown was Kate Ahearn, looking for all the world like her grandmother. Then several more figures stepped from the coaches, and suddenly—as though all the years had been swept away and Channing Evans were holding the lovely Mary Roark in his arms—she stepped once again into his life. She was still lovely, and there was no mistaking that face with the dimpled high cheekbones and the cocked head. He reached for the handle of the door and then thought better of it. Sitting back into the shadows of the carriage, he reluctantly commanded the driver to move on. "To Miss Kent's school, Dolkins. I think I would like to take Miss Alicia to lunch."

The driver snapped the horse into life and the coach lurched forward. Mary and Brendan turned in the direction of the coach, but all they saw was a white-haired man, staring straight ahead. Then the throaty sound of an organ swelled and summoned them in to the church.

Before them James stood at the altar, waiting to administer the sacrament of marriage, while behind them Kate Ahearn, buoyant and lovely, waited for her father to accompany her down the aisle to the smiling and anxious Francis Michael Joyce.

An ardent devotee of Ireland and the history and literature of the Irish people, JAMES F. MURPHY, JR., lives in Falmouth, Massachusetts, with his wife and six children. He is an Associate Professor of English at The Massachusetts Maritime Academy, Buzzards Bay, Cape Cod, and the author of three other novels including *Quonsett*, *The Mill*, and *Nightwatcher*.